LASER MOOSE AND RABBIT BOY: AS THE DEER FLIES

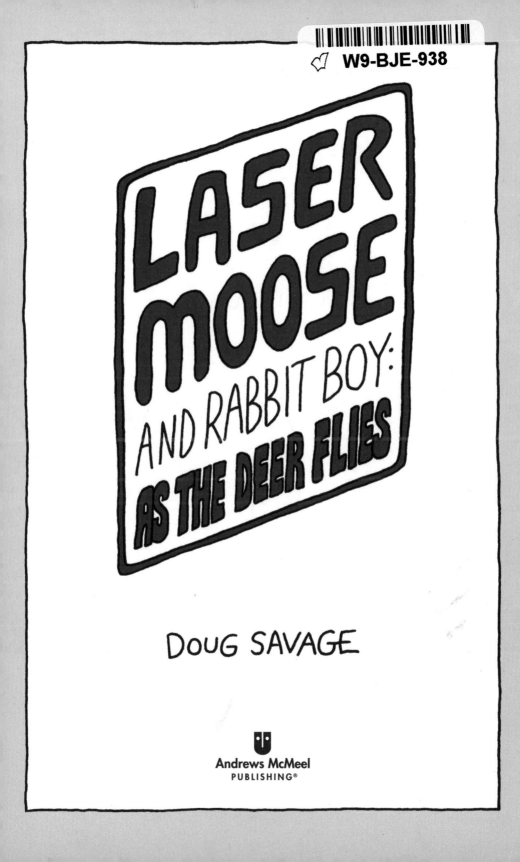

DOUG SAVAGE

Andrews McMeel
PUBLISHING®

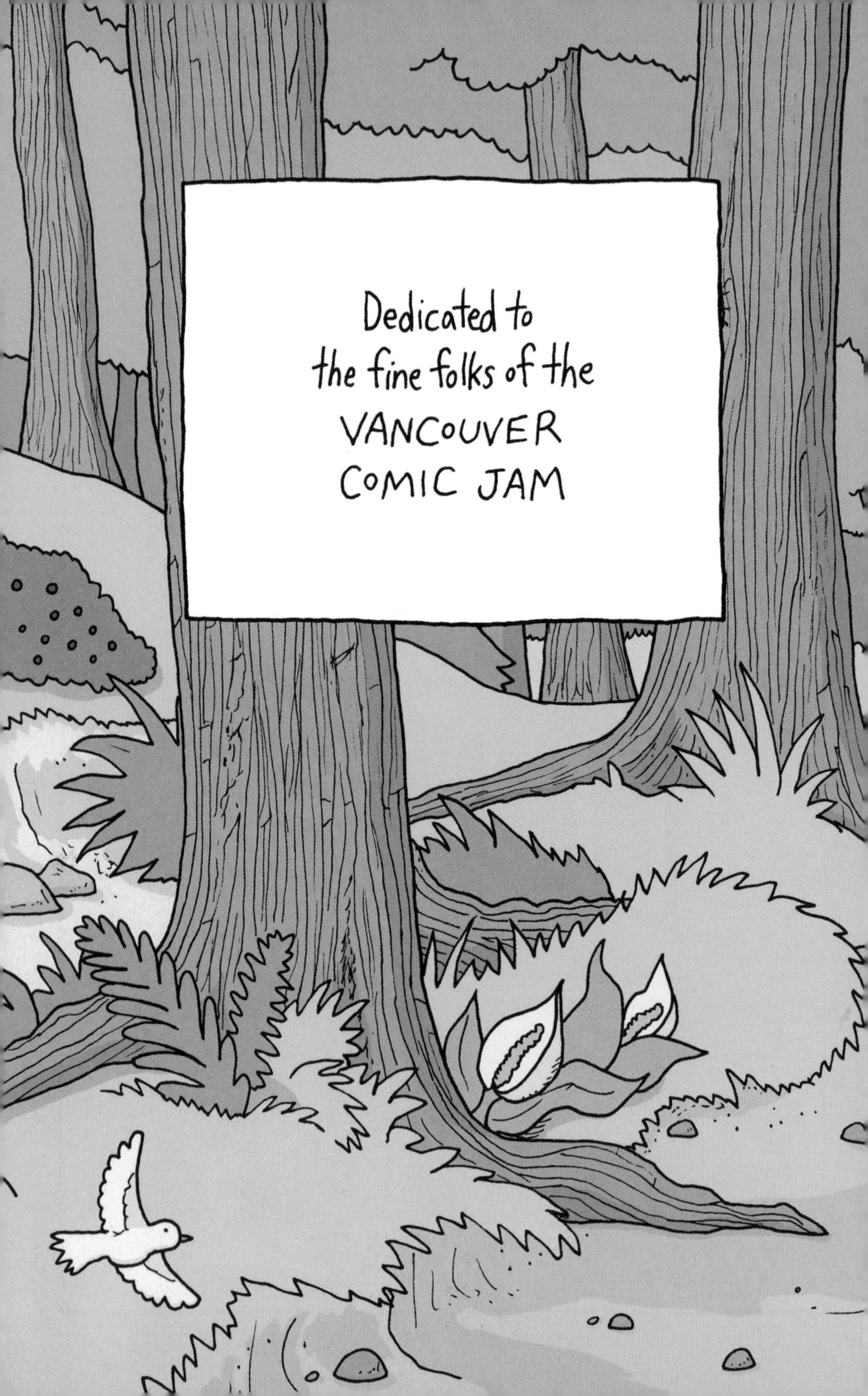
Dedicated to
the fine folks of the
VANCOUVER
COMIC JAM

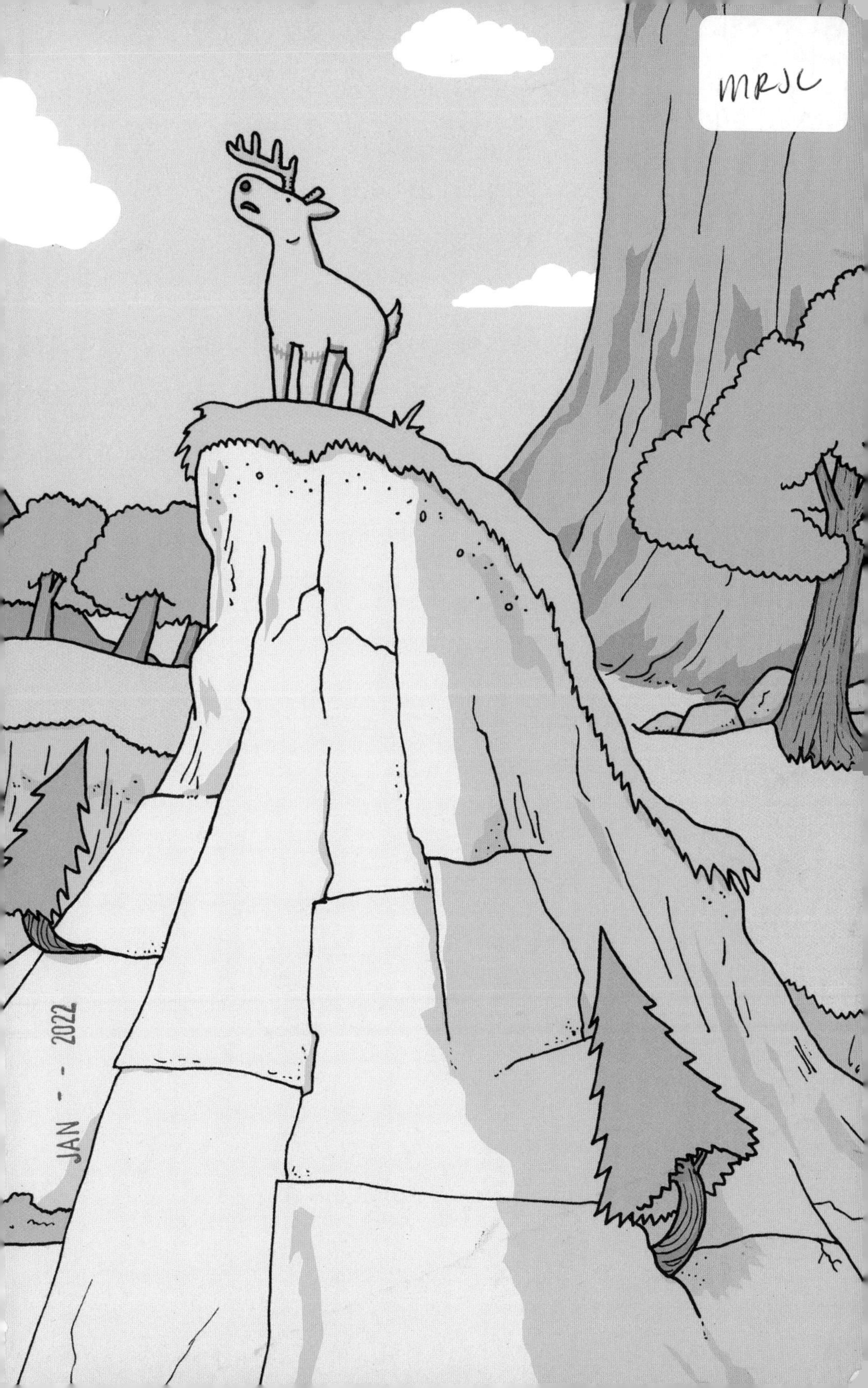

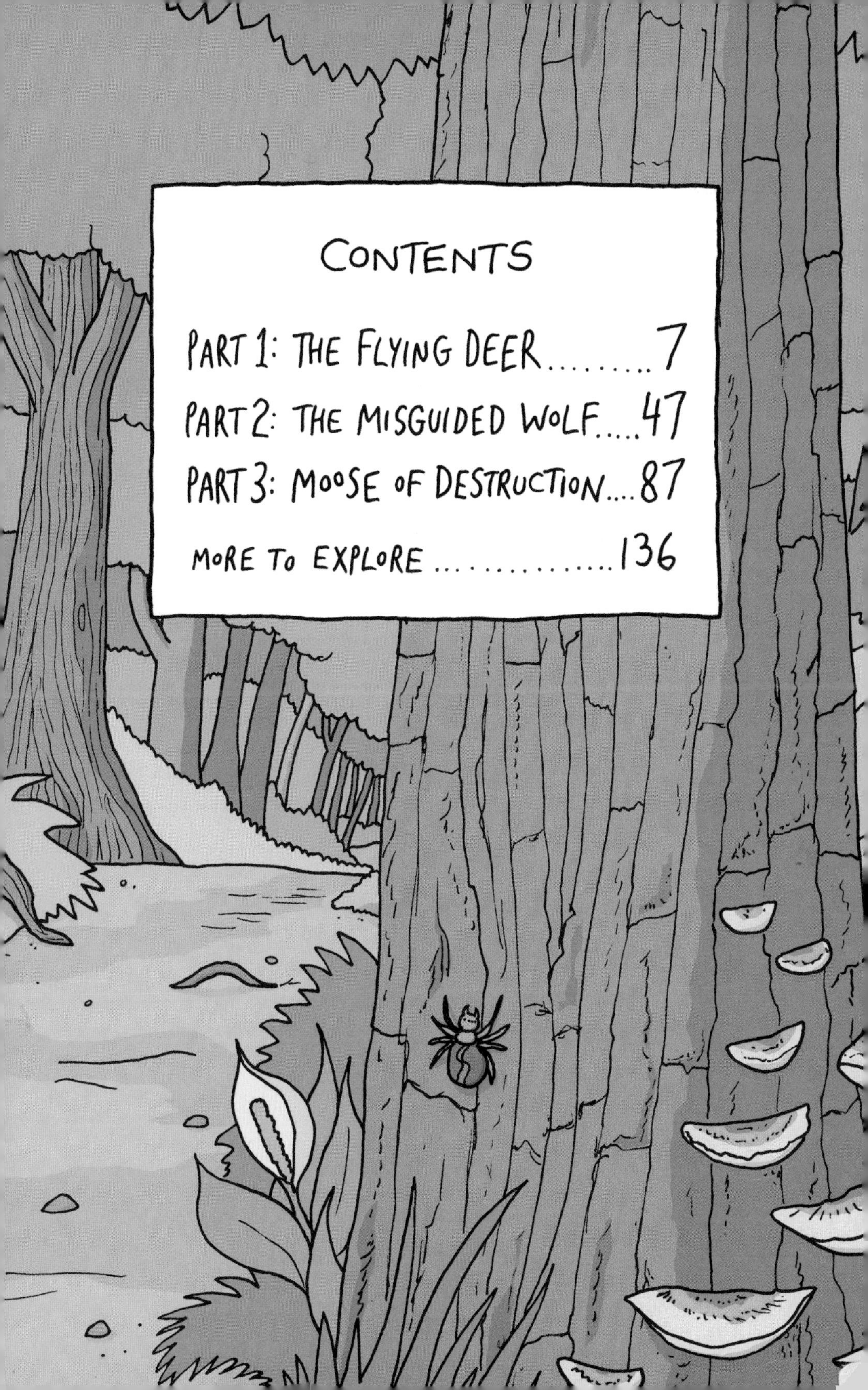

CONTENTS

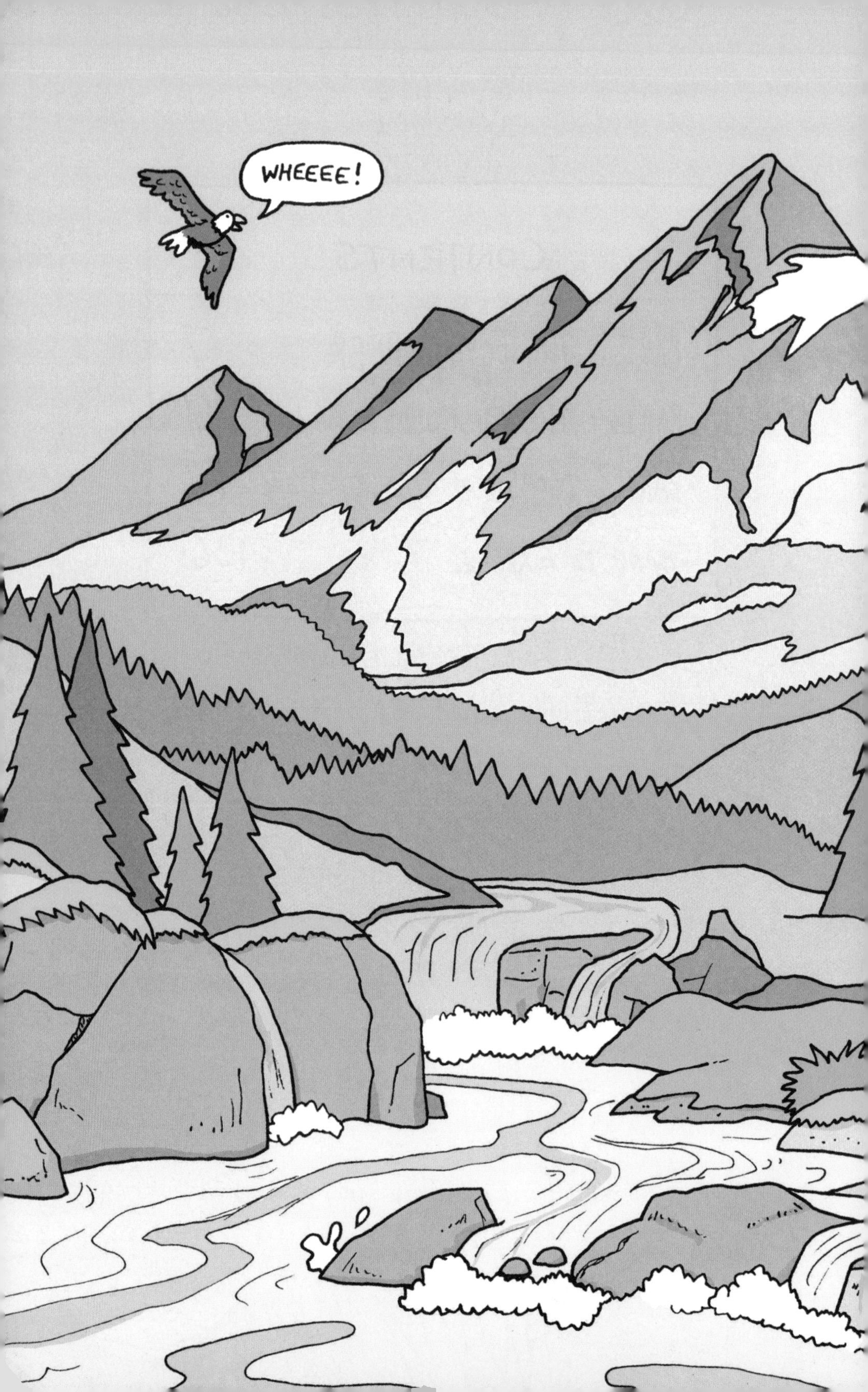
WHEEEE!

PART 1:
THE FLYING DEER

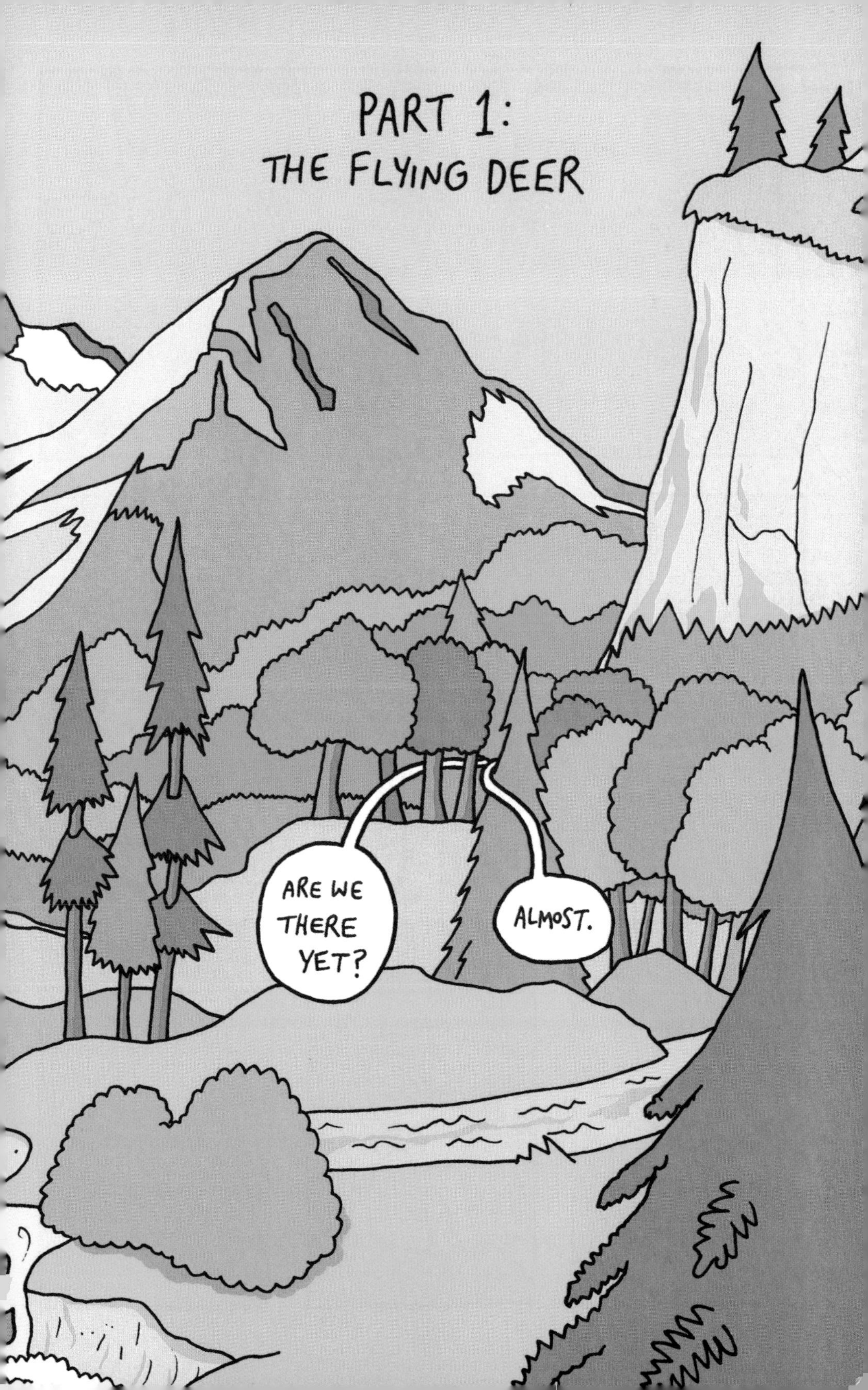

ARE WE THERE YET?
ALMOST.

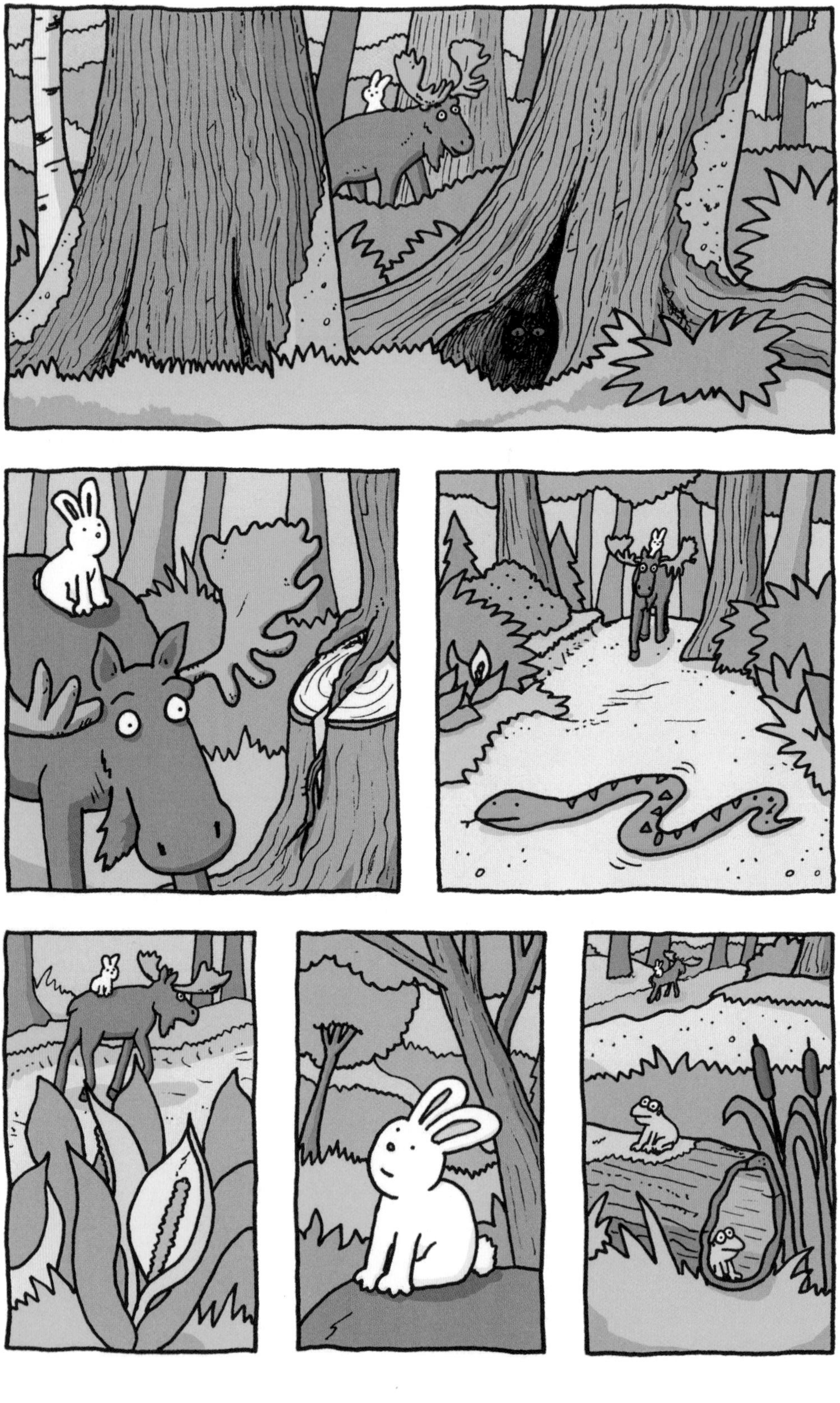

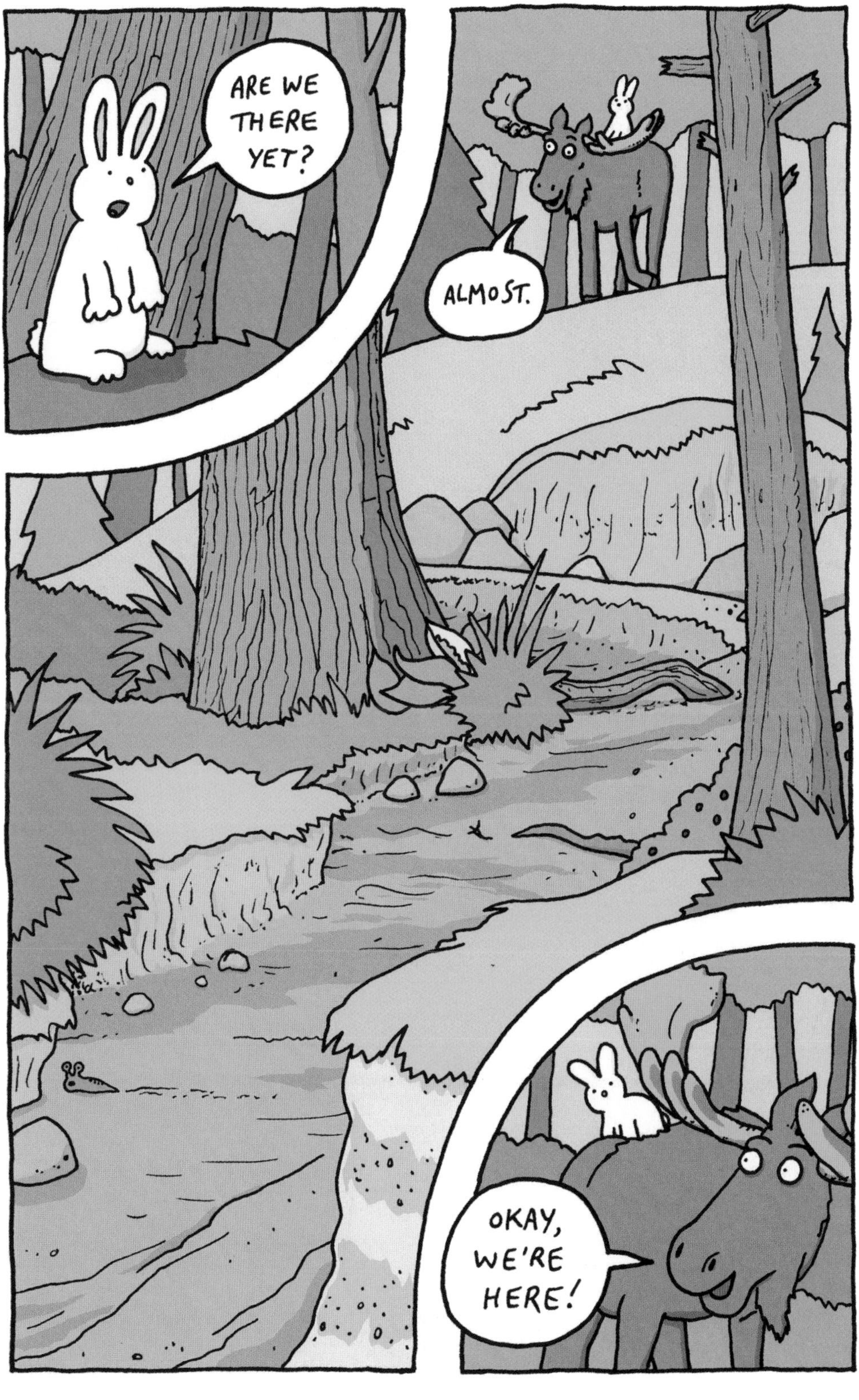
ARE WE THERE YET?
ALMOST.
OKAY, WE'RE HERE!

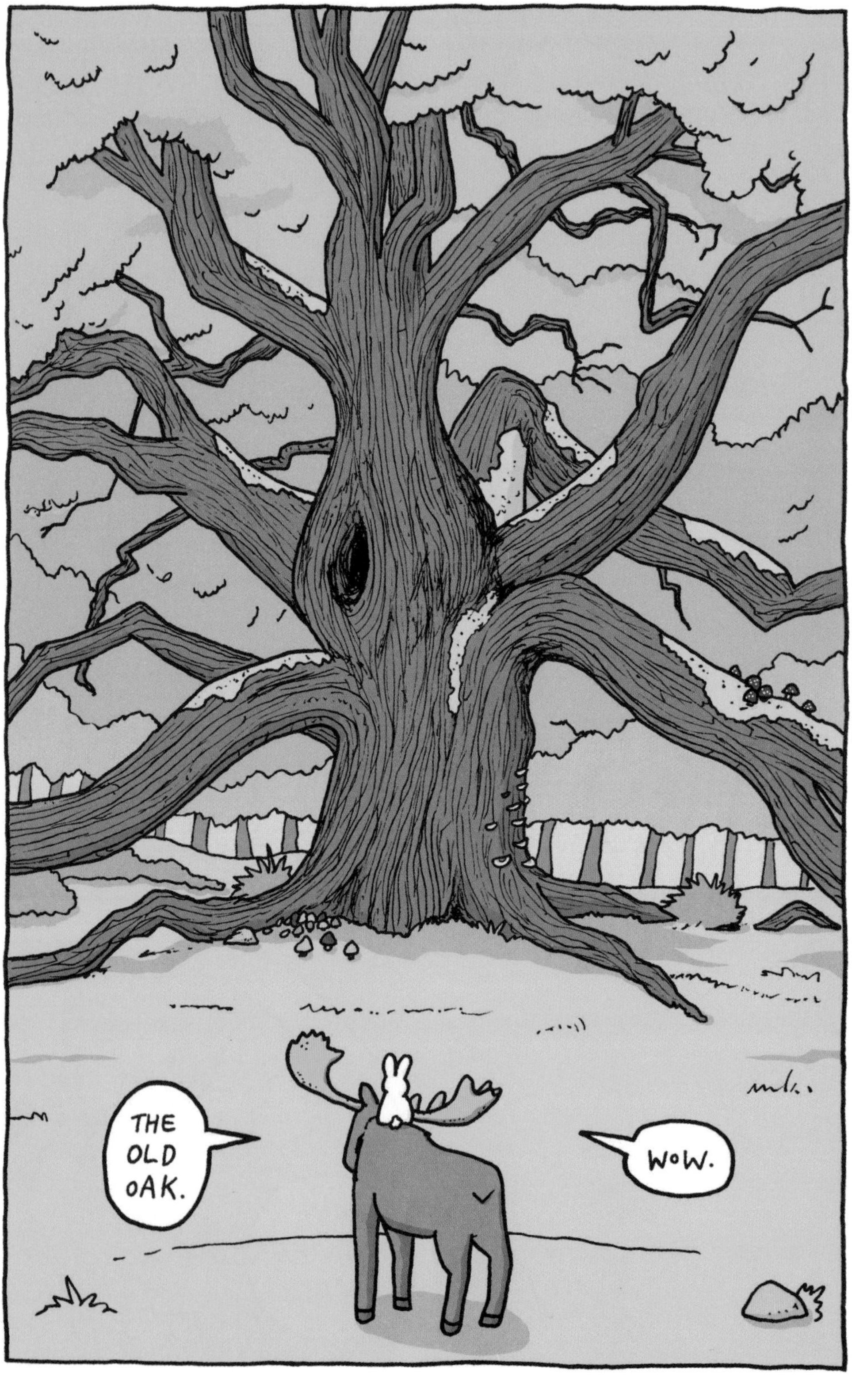
THE OLD OAK.
WOW.

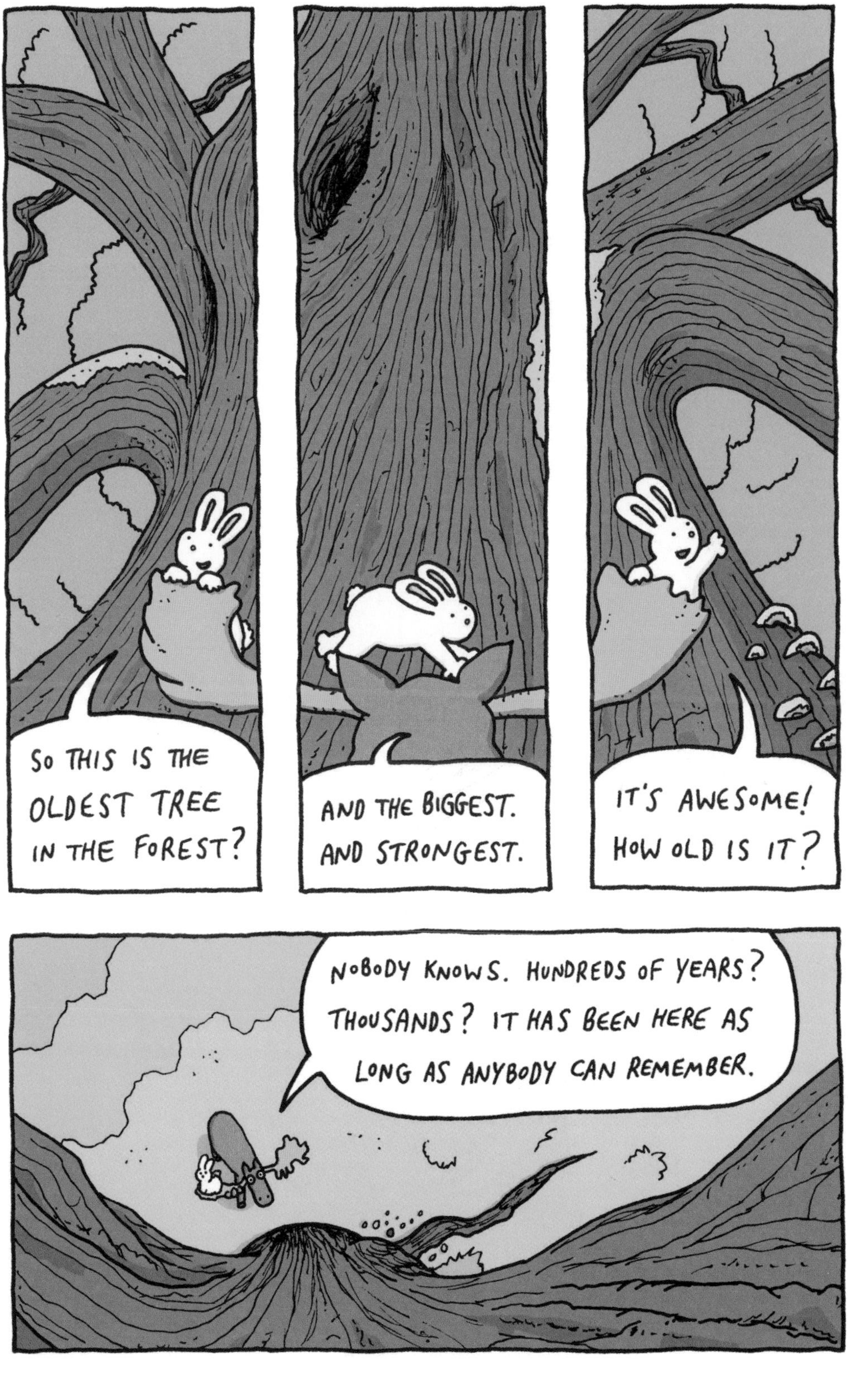
SO THIS IS THE OLDEST TREE IN THE FOREST?
AND THE BIGGEST. AND STRONGEST.
IT'S AWESOME! HOW OLD IS IT?
NOBODY KNOWS. HUNDREDS OF YEARS? THOUSANDS? IT HAS BEEN HERE AS LONG AS ANYBODY CAN REMEMBER.

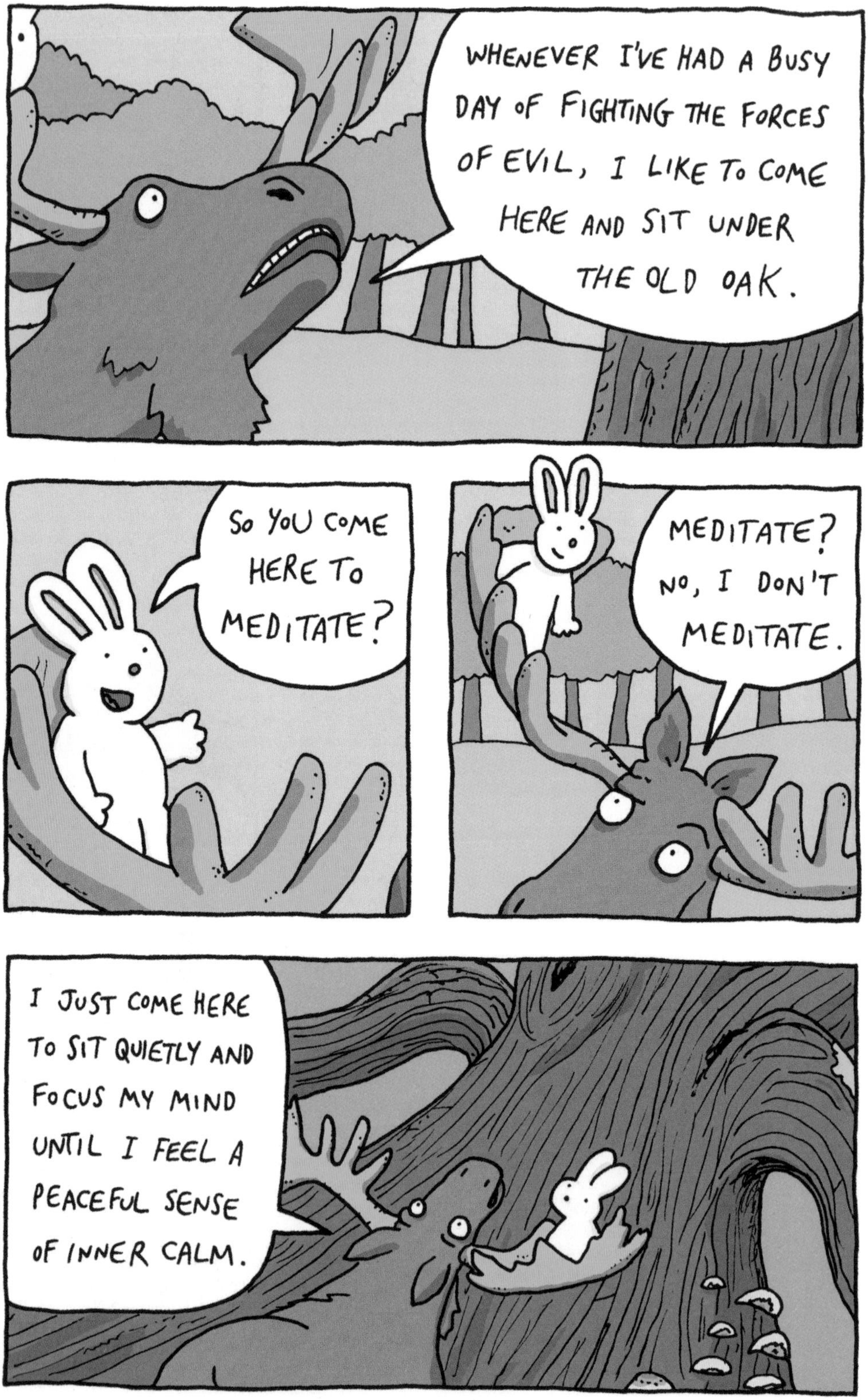
WHENEVER I'VE HAD A BUSY DAY OF FIGHTING THE FORCES OF EVIL, I LIKE TO COME HERE AND SIT UNDER THE OLD OAK.
SO YOU COME HERE TO MEDITATE?
MEDITATE? NO, I DON'T MEDITATE.
I JUST COME HERE TO SIT QUIETLY AND FOCUS MY MIND UNTIL I FEEL A PEACEFUL SENSE OF INNER CALM.

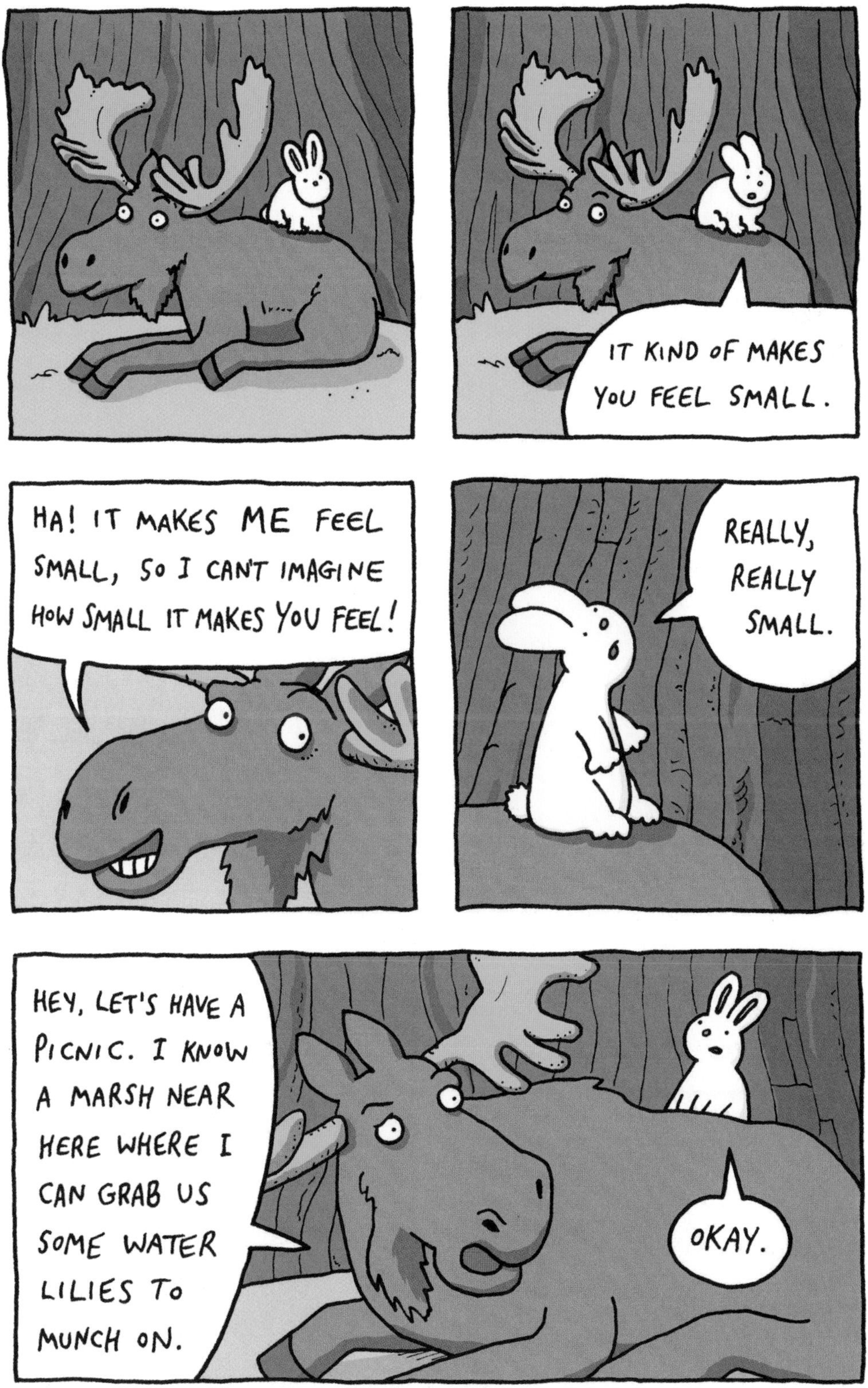
IT KIND OF MAKES YOU FEEL SMALL.
HA! IT MAKES ME FEEL SMALL, SO I CAN'T IMAGINE HOW SMALL IT MAKES YOU FEEL!
REALLY, REALLY SMALL.
HEY, LET'S HAVE A PICNIC. I KNOW A MARSH NEAR HERE WHERE I CAN GRAB US SOME WATER LILIES TO MUNCH ON.
OKAY.

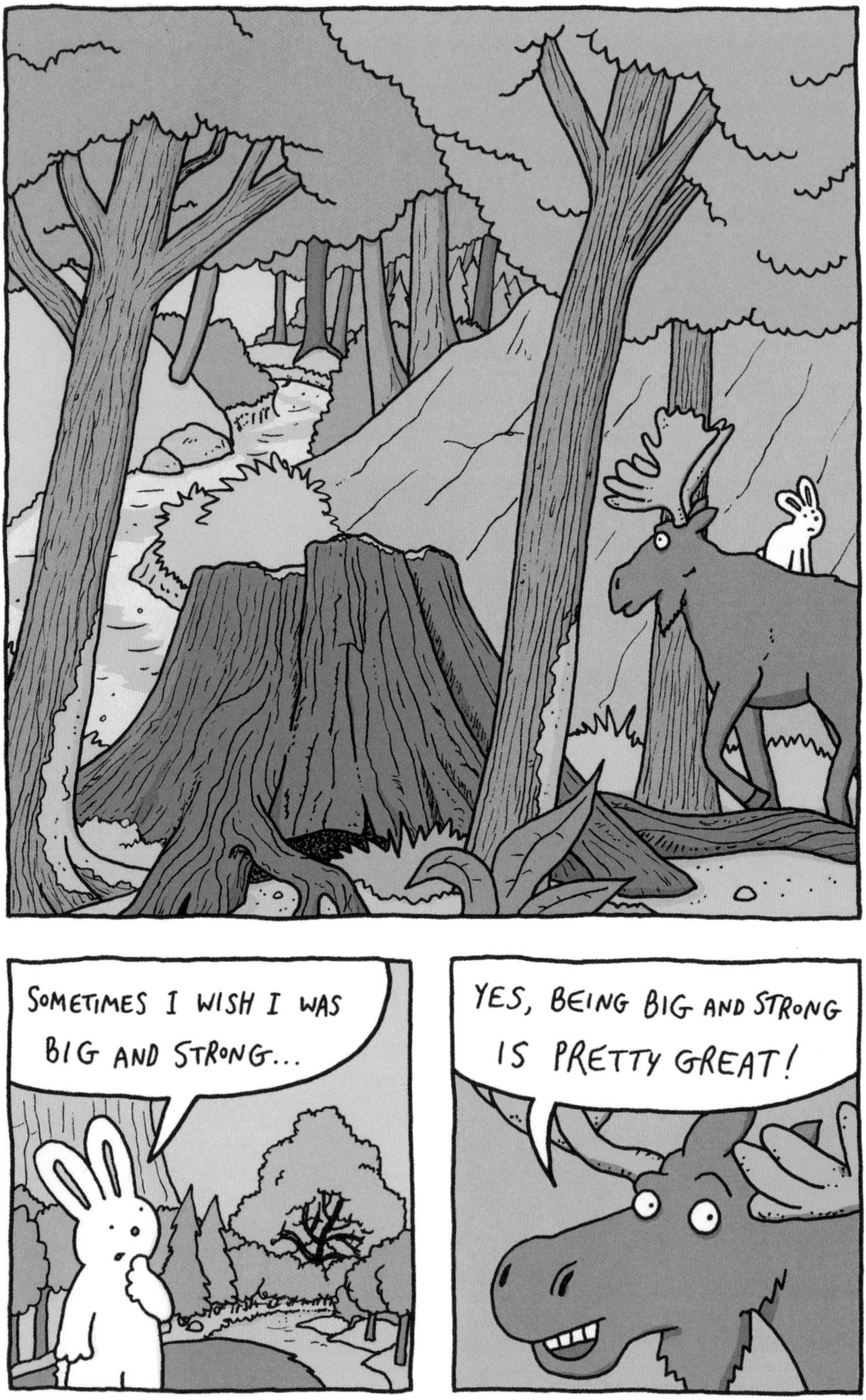
SOMETIMES I WISH I WAS BIG AND STRONG...
YES, BEING BIG AND STRONG IS PRETTY GREAT!

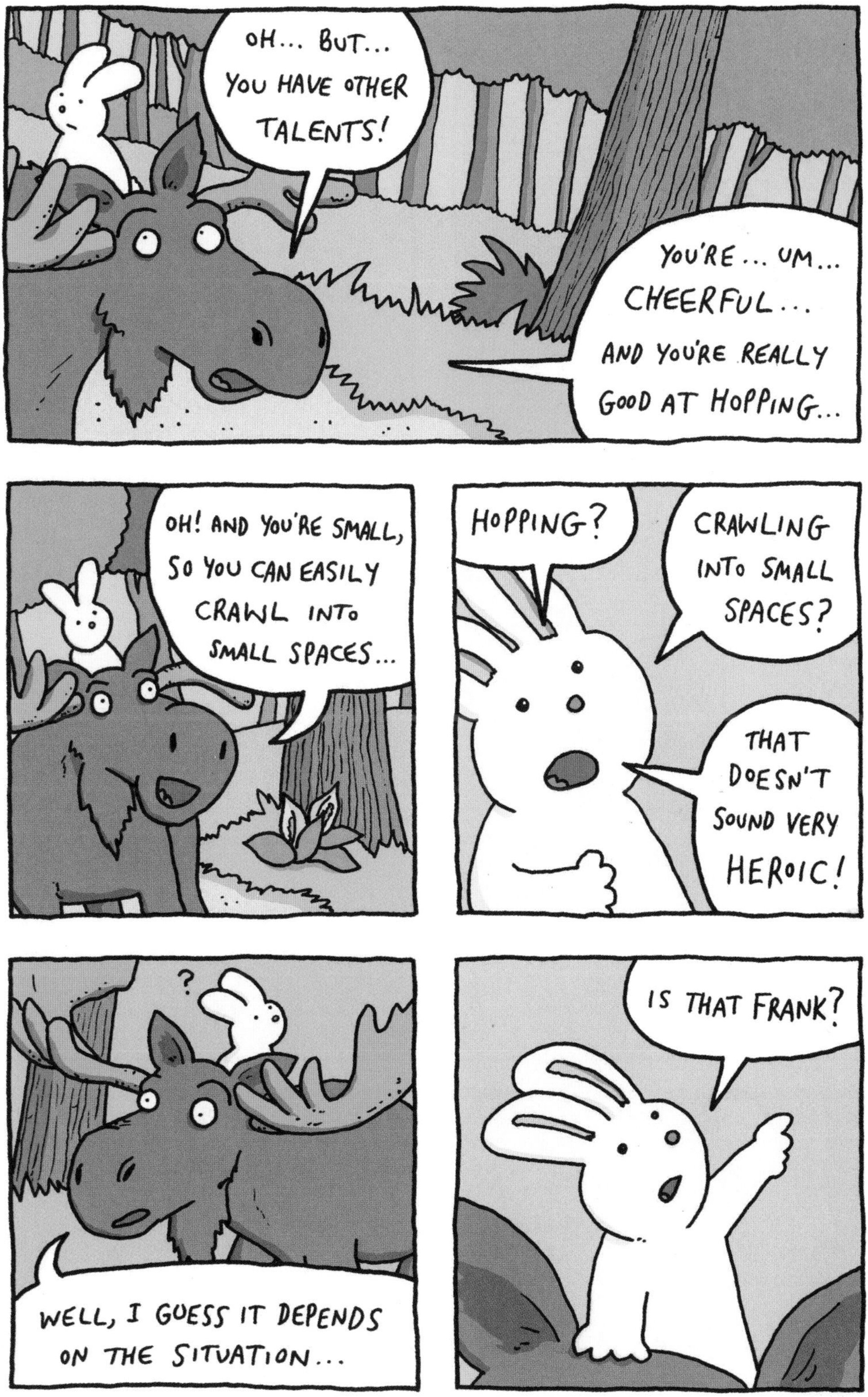
OH... BUT... YOU HAVE OTHER TALENTS!
YOU'RE... UM... CHEERFUL... AND YOU'RE REALLY GOOD AT HOPPING...
OH! AND YOU'RE SMALL, SO YOU CAN EASILY CRAWL INTO SMALL SPACES...
HOPPING?
CRAWLING INTO SMALL SPACES?
THAT DOESN'T SOUND VERY HEROIC!
WELL, I GUESS IT DEPENDS ON THE SITUATION...
IS THAT FRANK?

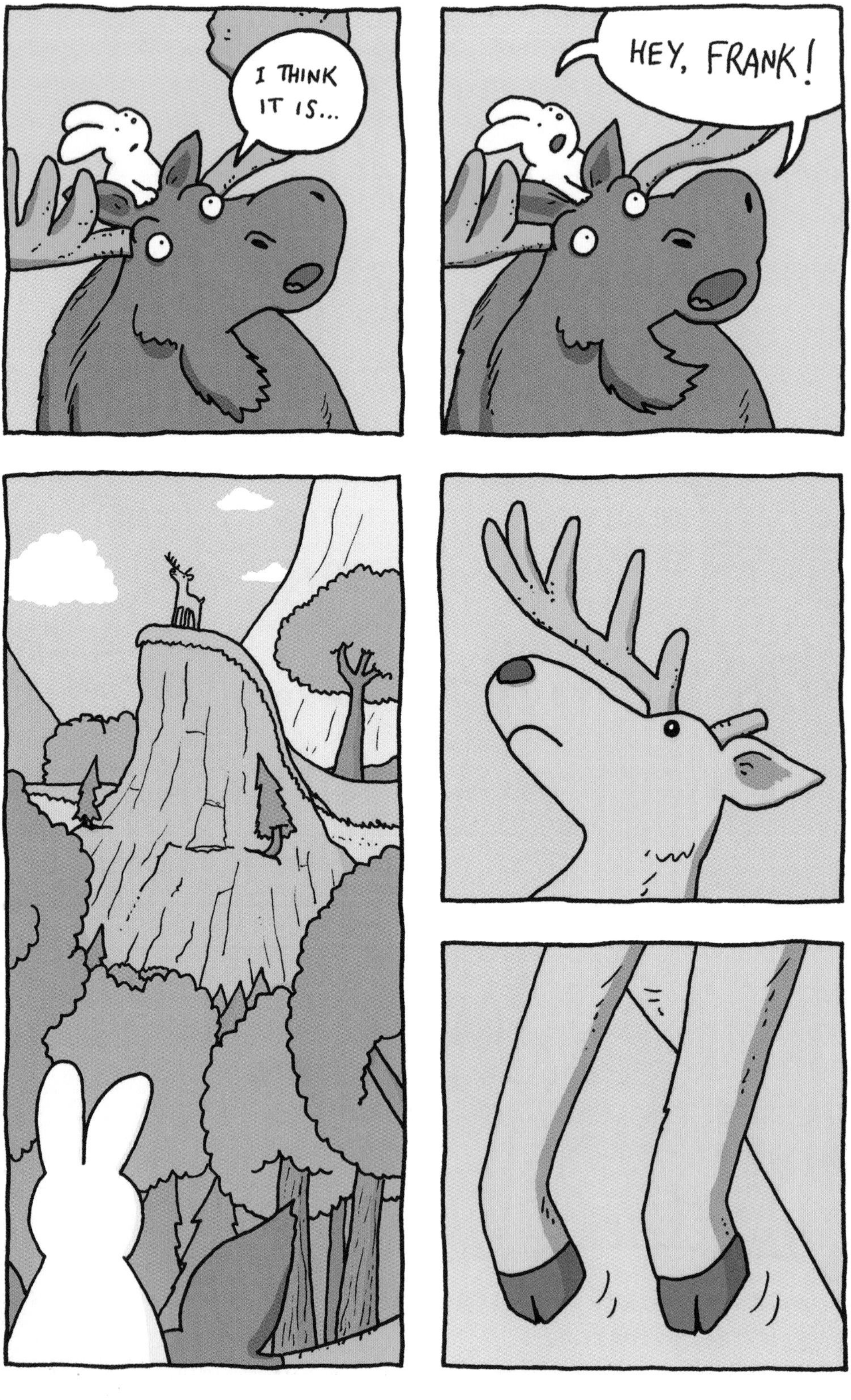
I THINK IT IS...
HEY, FRANK!

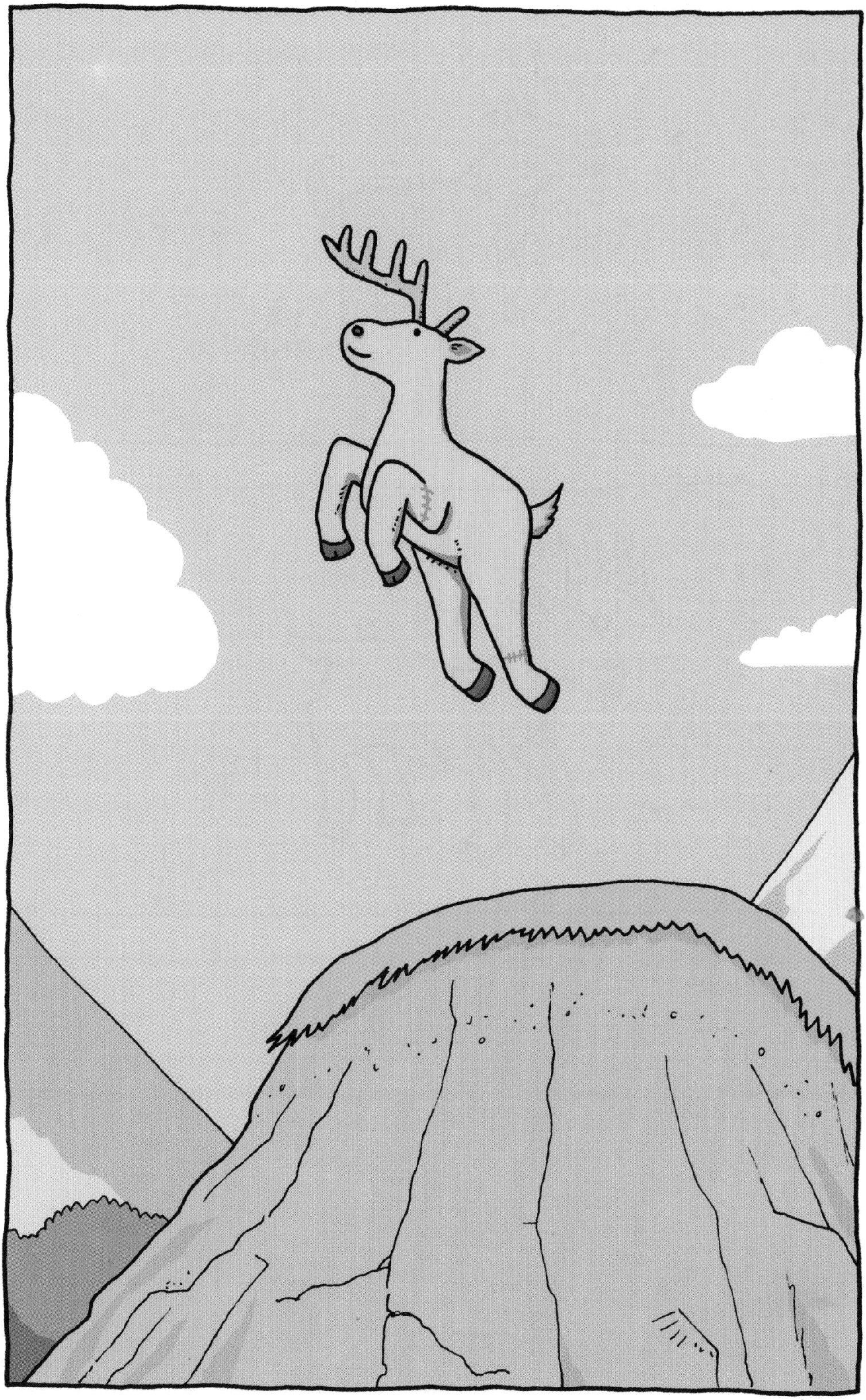

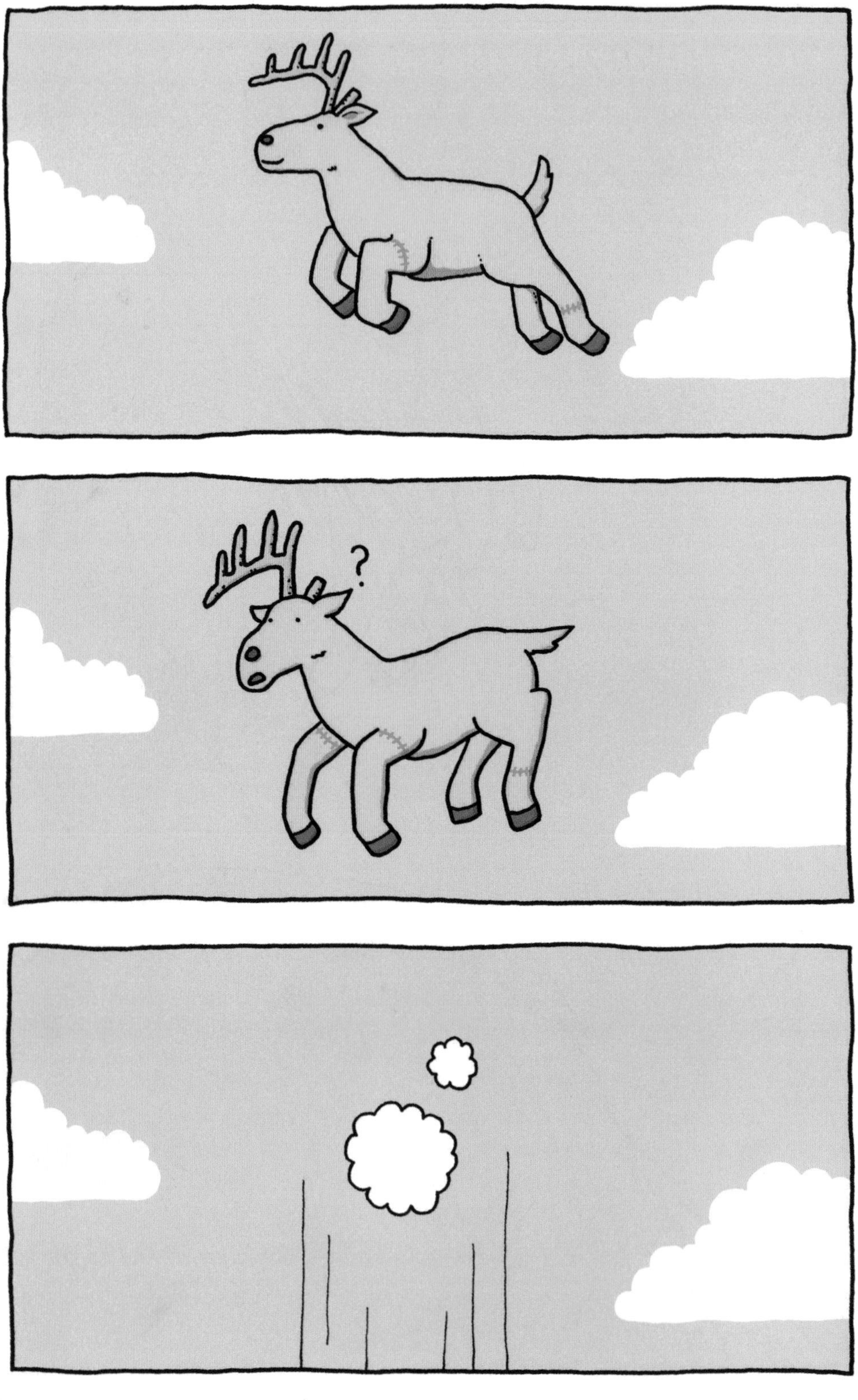
?

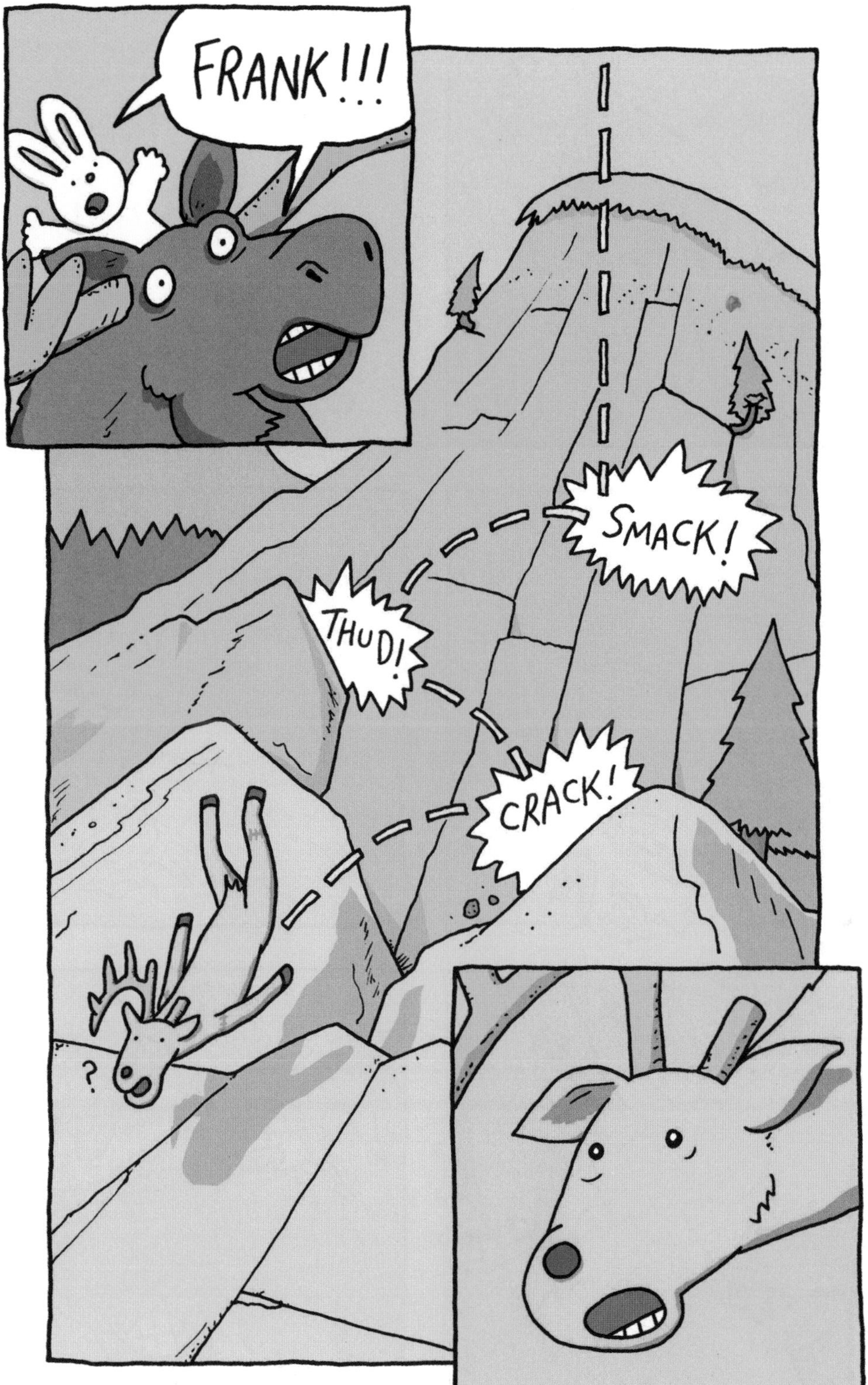
FRANK!!!
SMACK!
THUD!
CRACK!
?

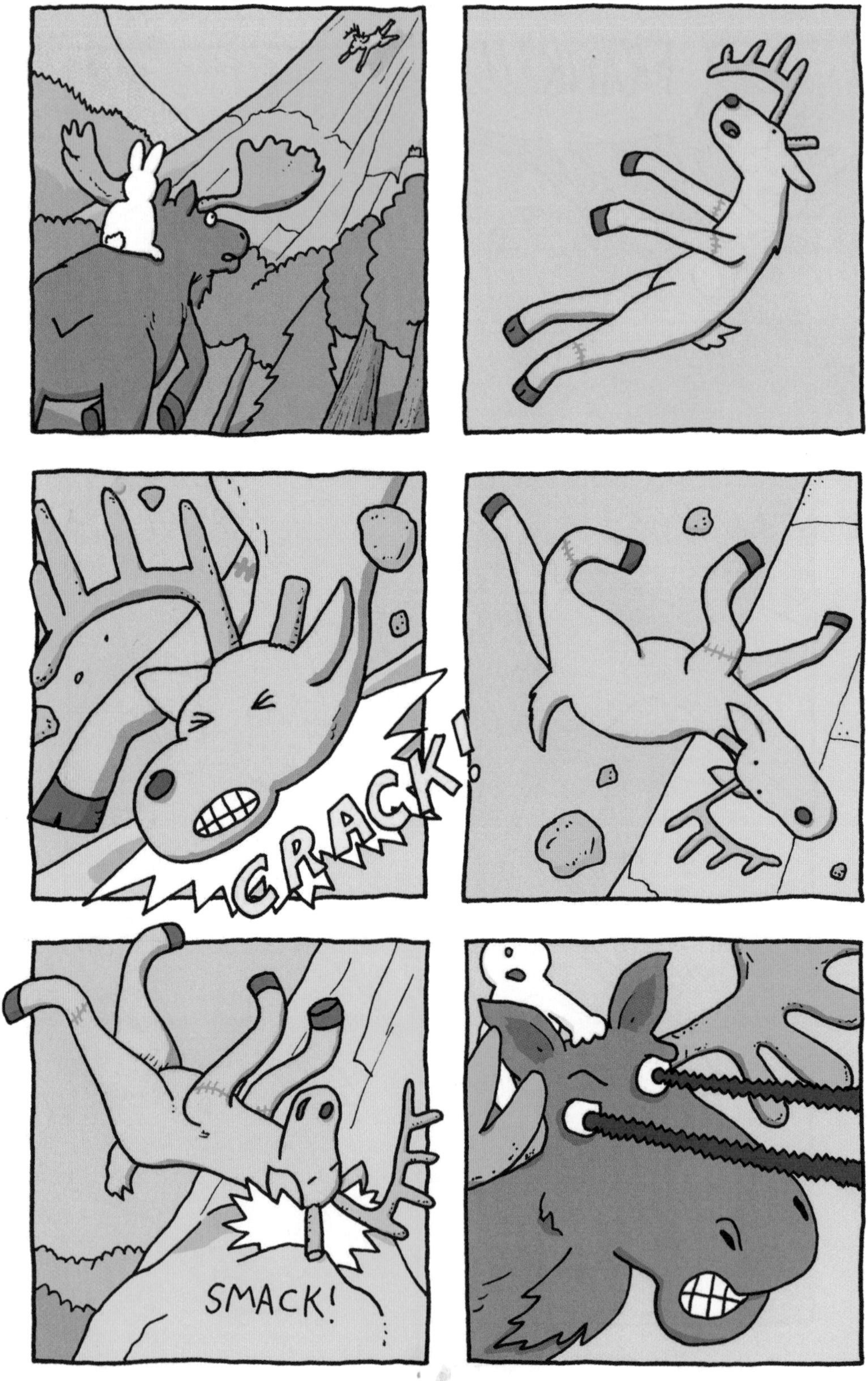
CRACK!
SMACK!

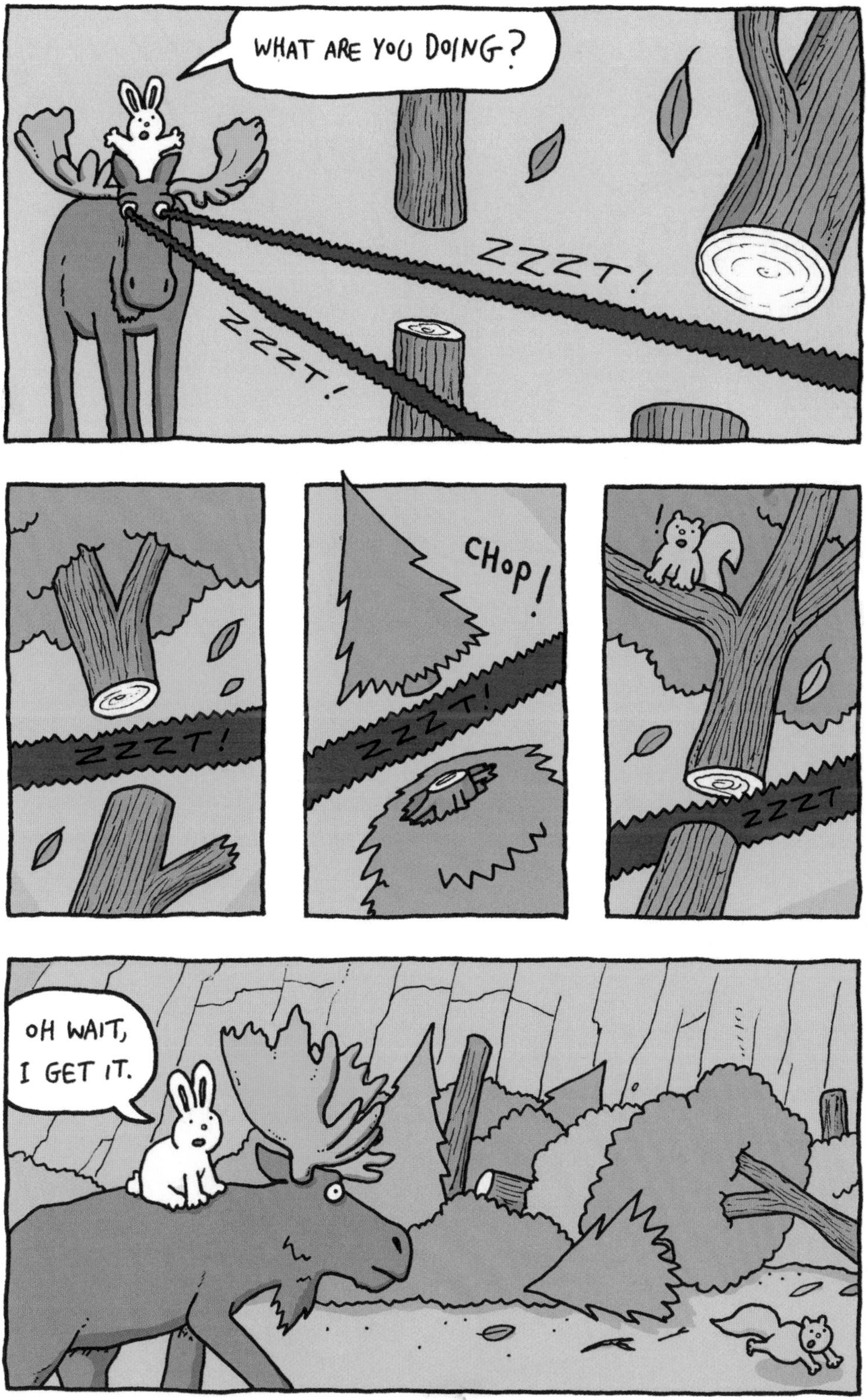
WHAT ARE YOU DOING?
ZZZT!
ZZZT!
ZZZT!
CHOP!
ZZZT!
!
ZZZT
OH WAIT, I GET IT.

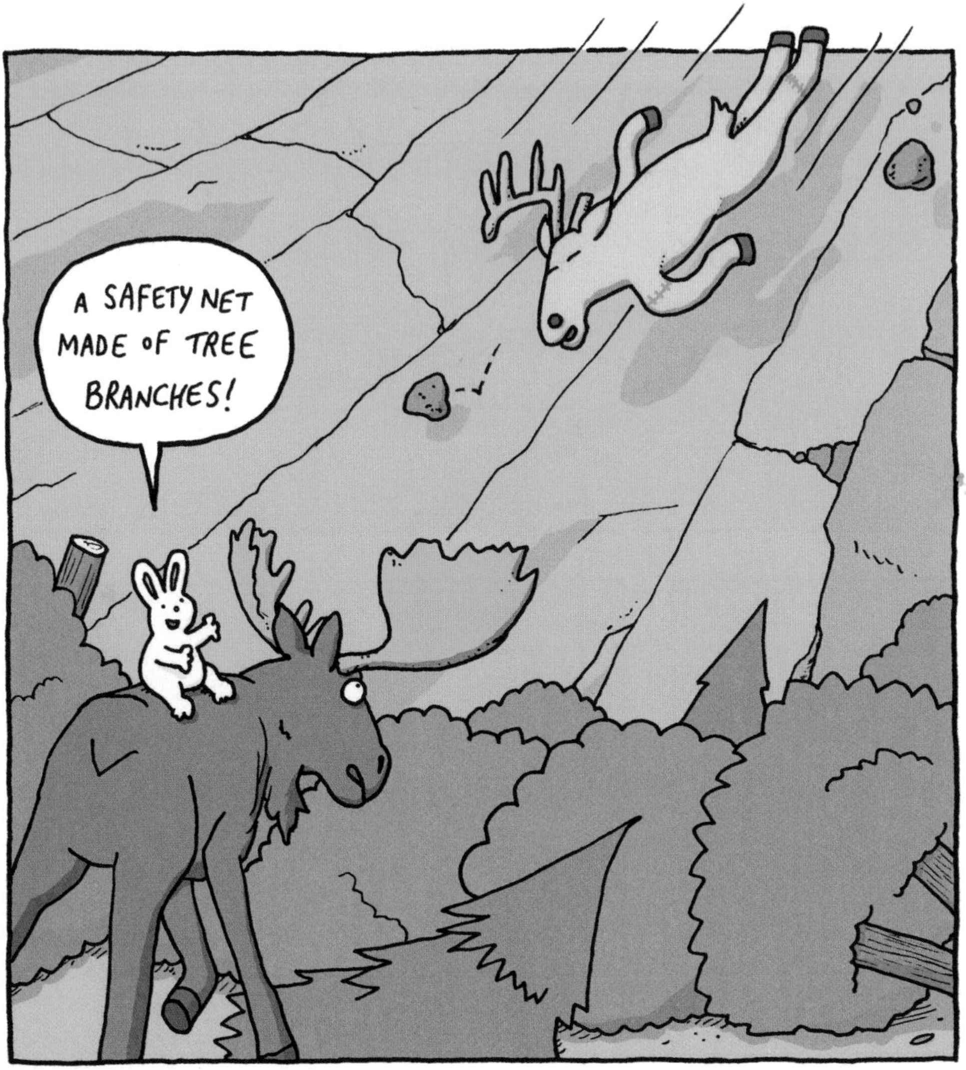
A SAFETY NET MADE OF TREE BRANCHES!

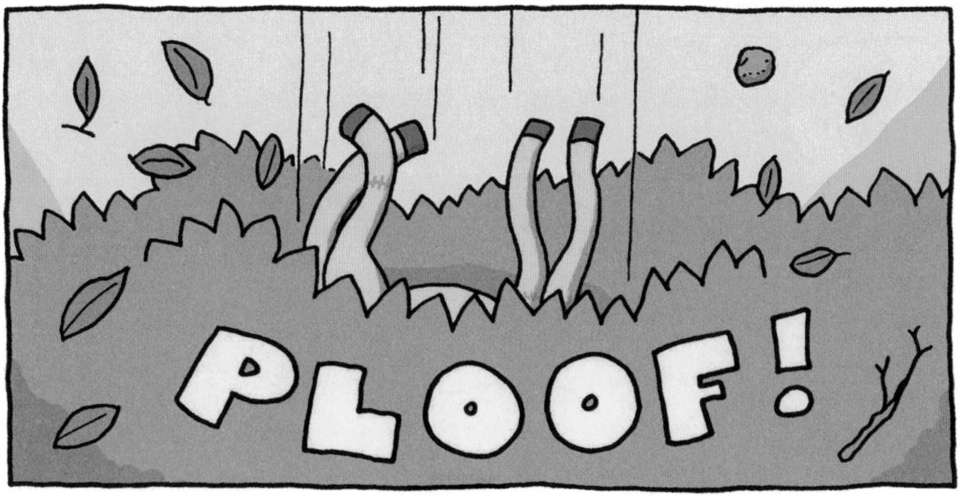
PLOOF!

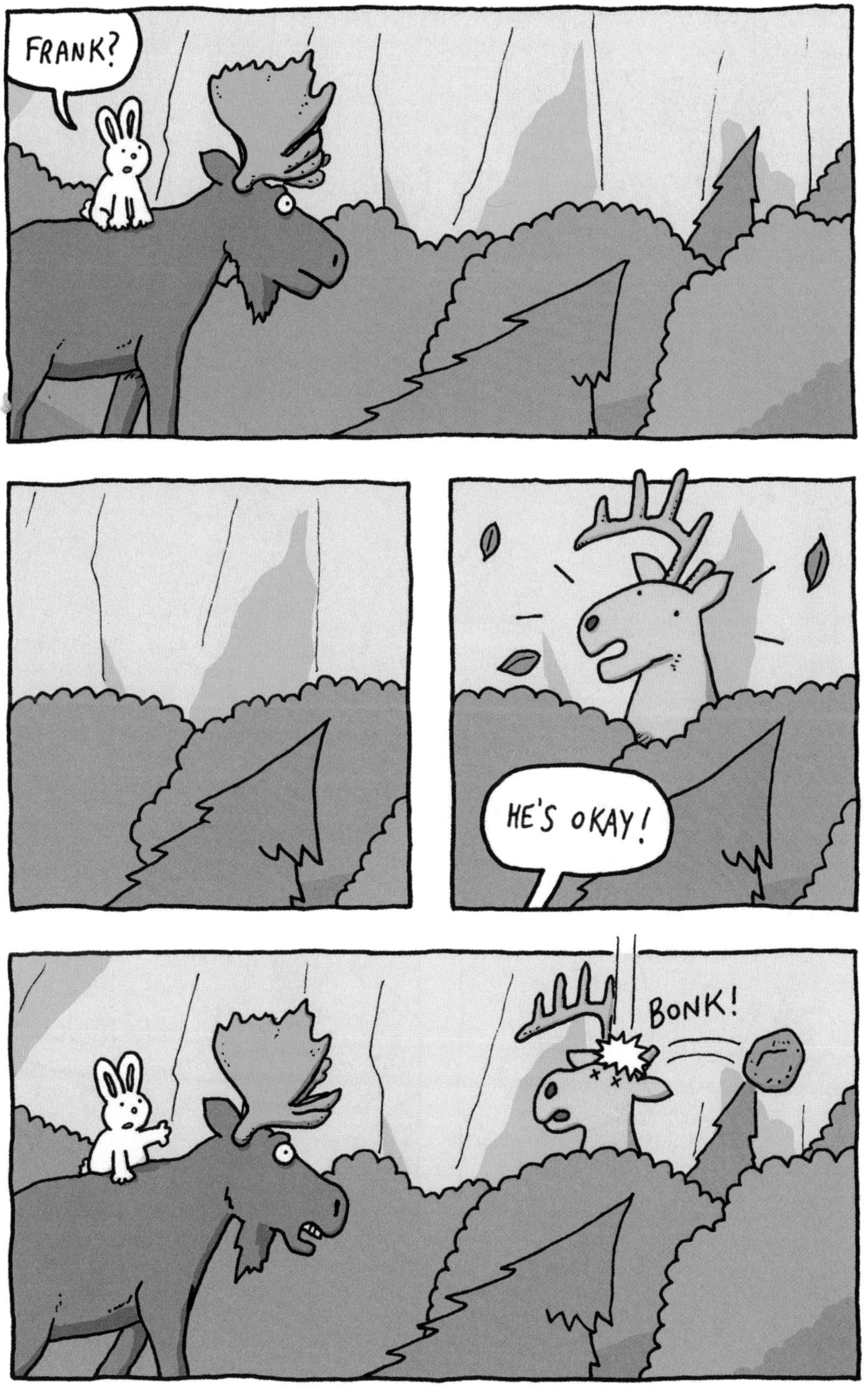
FRANK?
HE'S OKAY!
BONK!

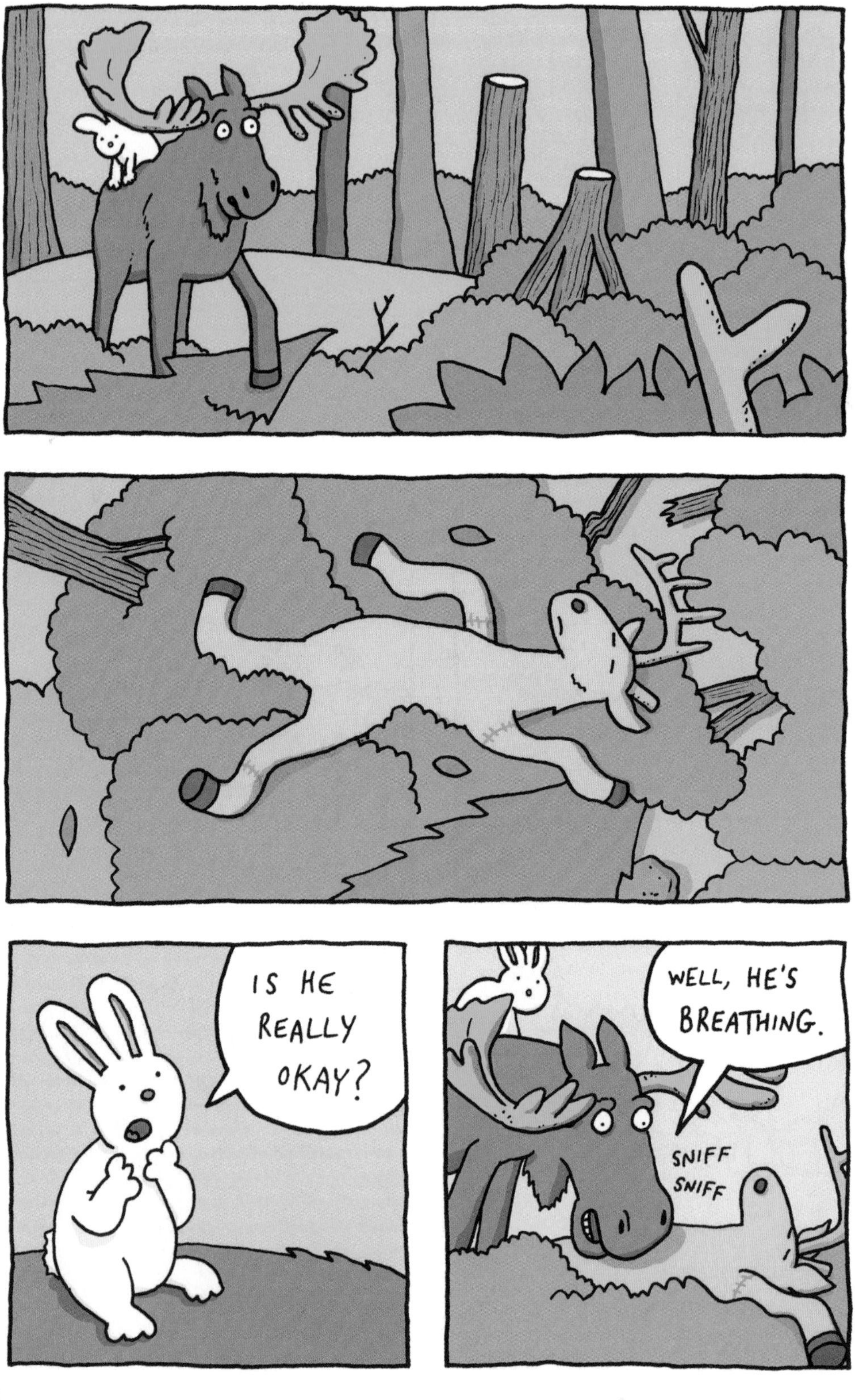
IS HE REALLY OKAY?
WELL, HE'S BREATHING.
SNIFF SNIFF

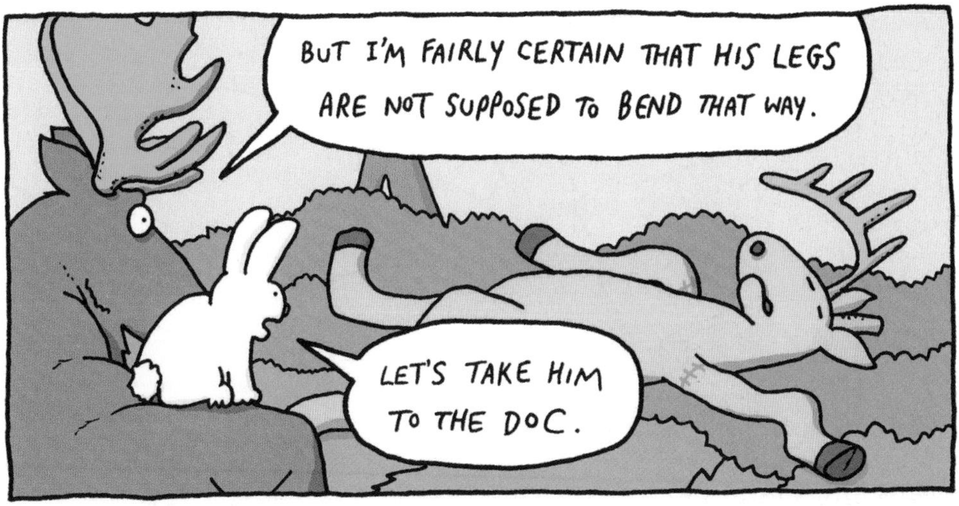
BUT I'M FAIRLY CERTAIN THAT HIS LEGS ARE NOT SUPPOSED TO BEND THAT WAY.
LET'S TAKE HIM TO THE DOC.

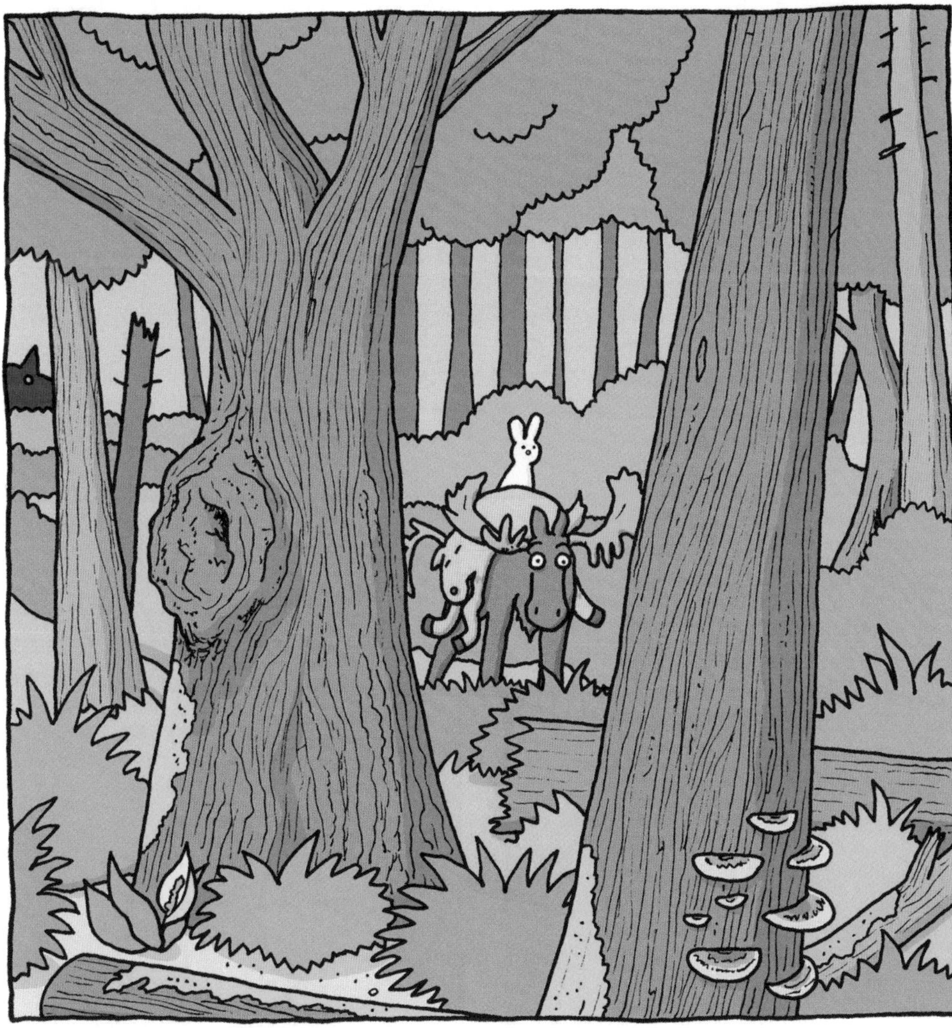

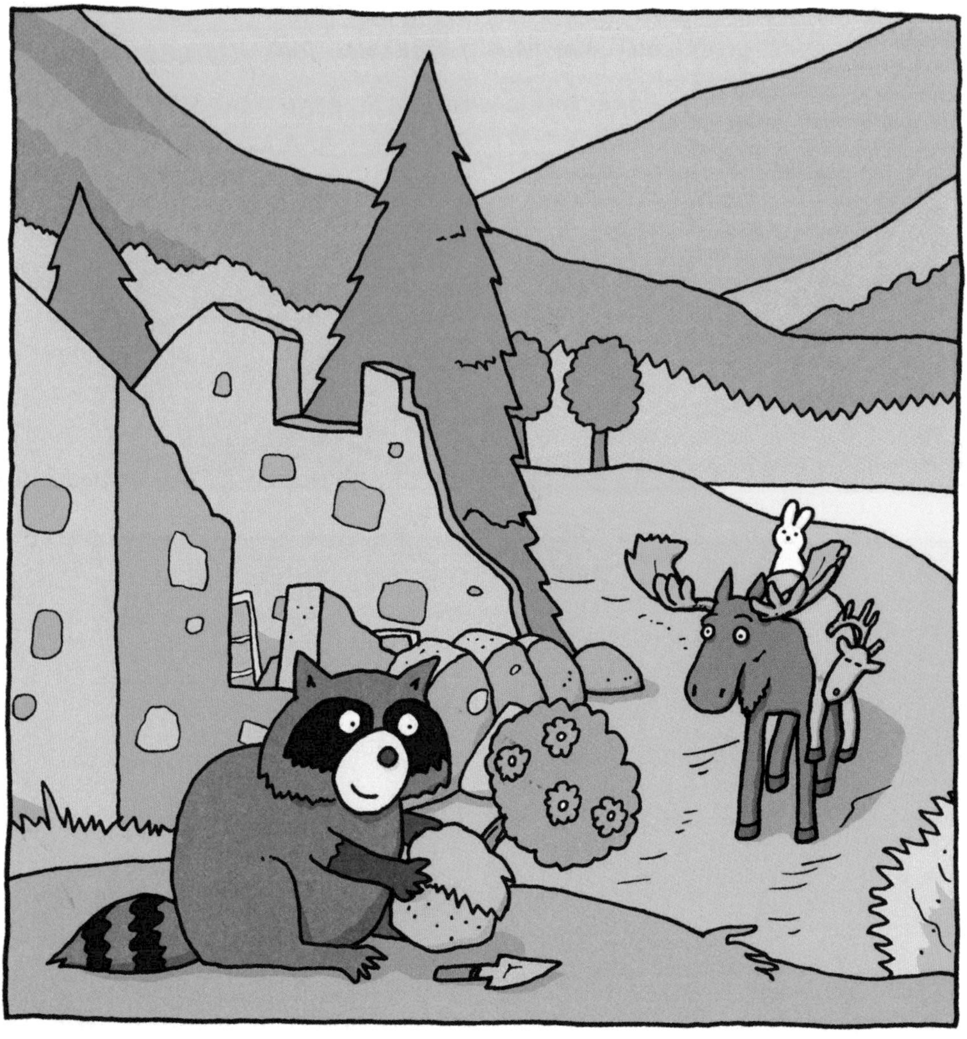

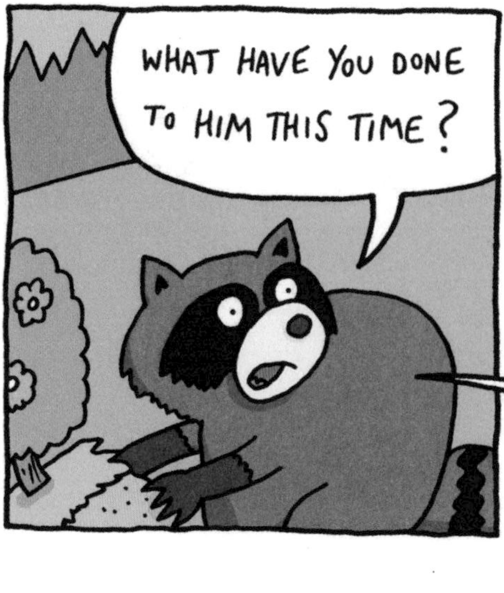
WHAT HAVE YOU DONE TO HIM THIS TIME?

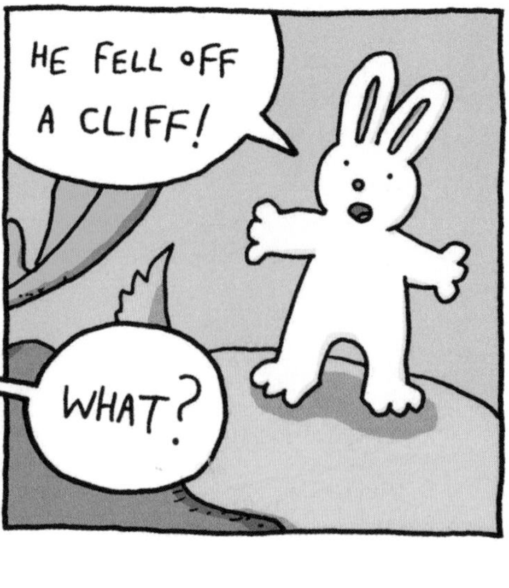
HE FELL OFF A CLIFF!
WHAT?

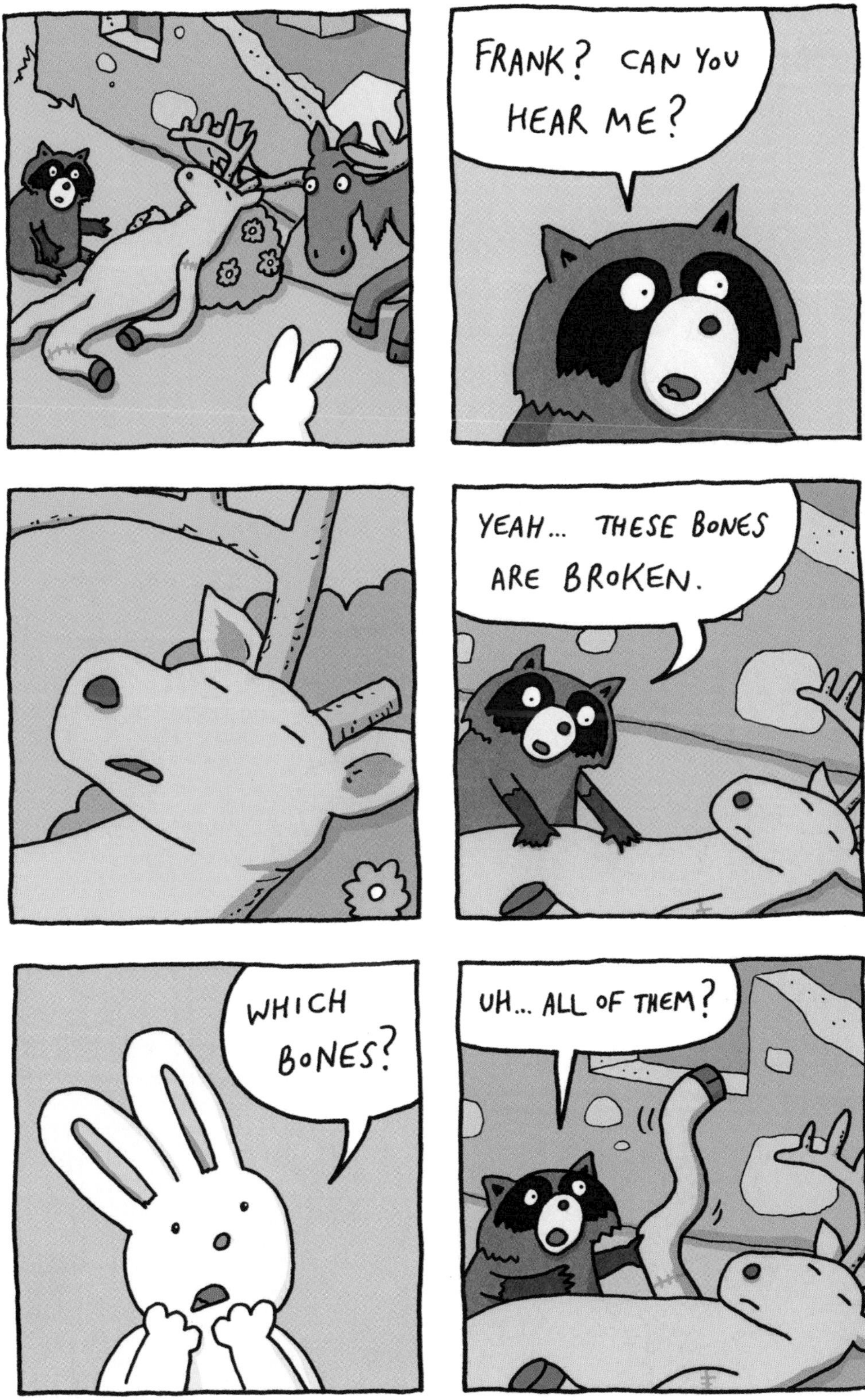
FRANK? CAN YOU HEAR ME?
YEAH... THESE BONES ARE BROKEN.
WHICH BONES?
UH... ALL OF THEM?

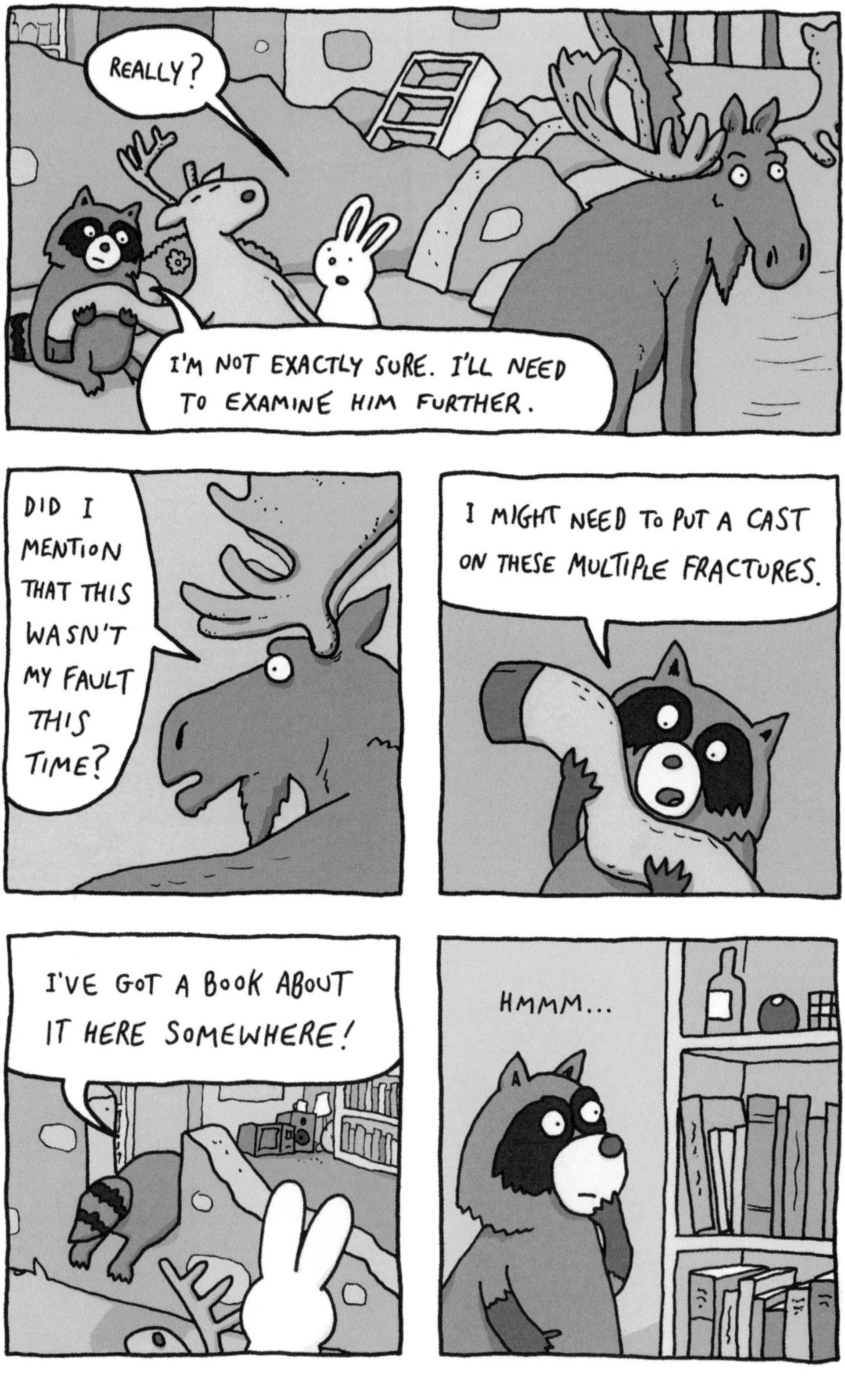
REALLY?
I'M NOT EXACTLY SURE. I'LL NEED TO EXAMINE HIM FURTHER.
DID I MENTION THAT THIS WASN'T MY FAULT THIS TIME?
I MIGHT NEED TO PUT A CAST ON THESE MULTIPLE FRACTURES.
I'VE GOT A BOOK ABOUT IT HERE SOMEWHERE!
HMMM...

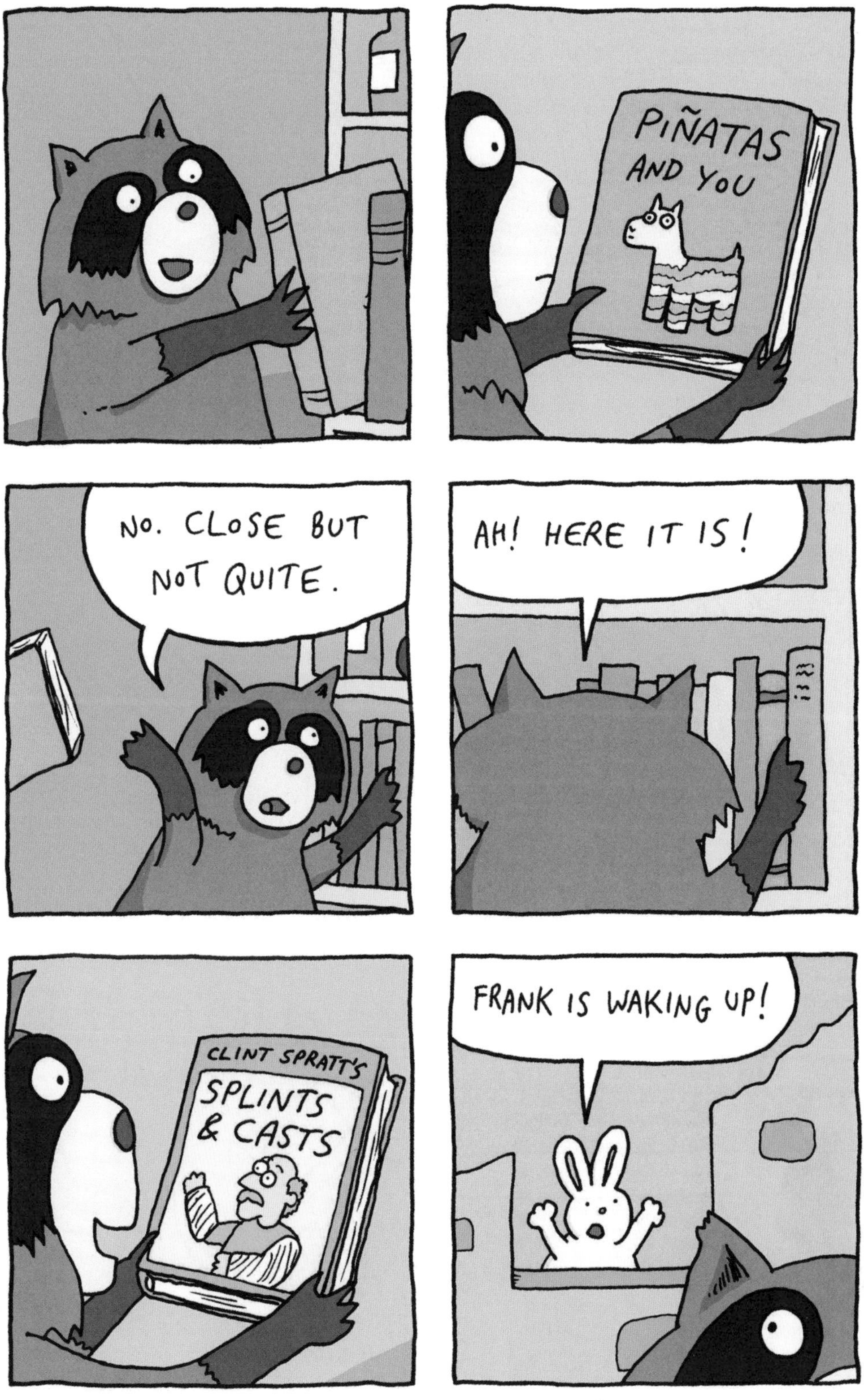
PIÑATAS AND YOU
NO. CLOSE BUT NOT QUITE.
AH! HERE IT IS!
CLINT SPRATT'S
SPLINTS & CASTS
FRANK IS WAKING UP!

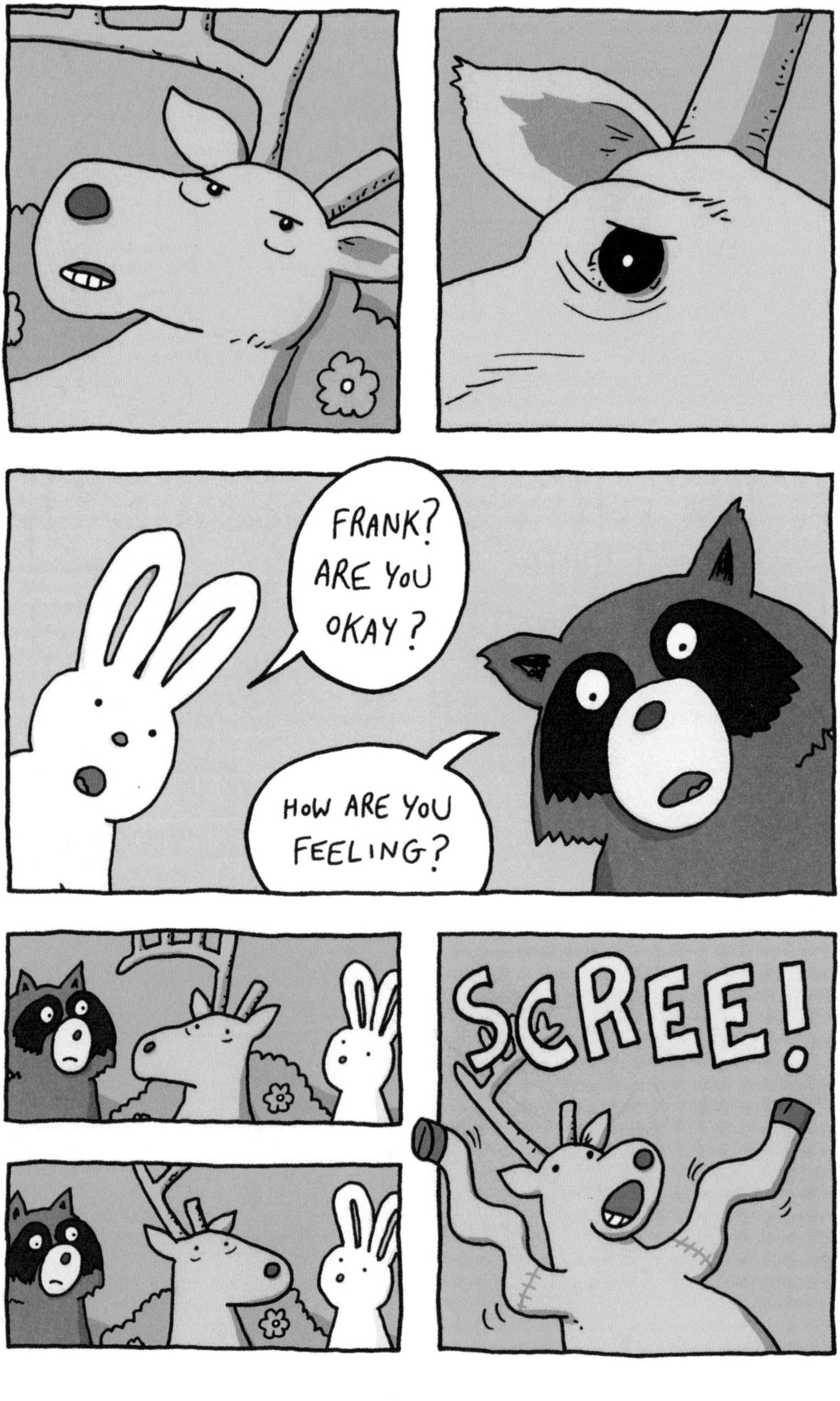
FRANK? ARE YOU OKAY?
HOW ARE YOU FEELING?
SCREE!

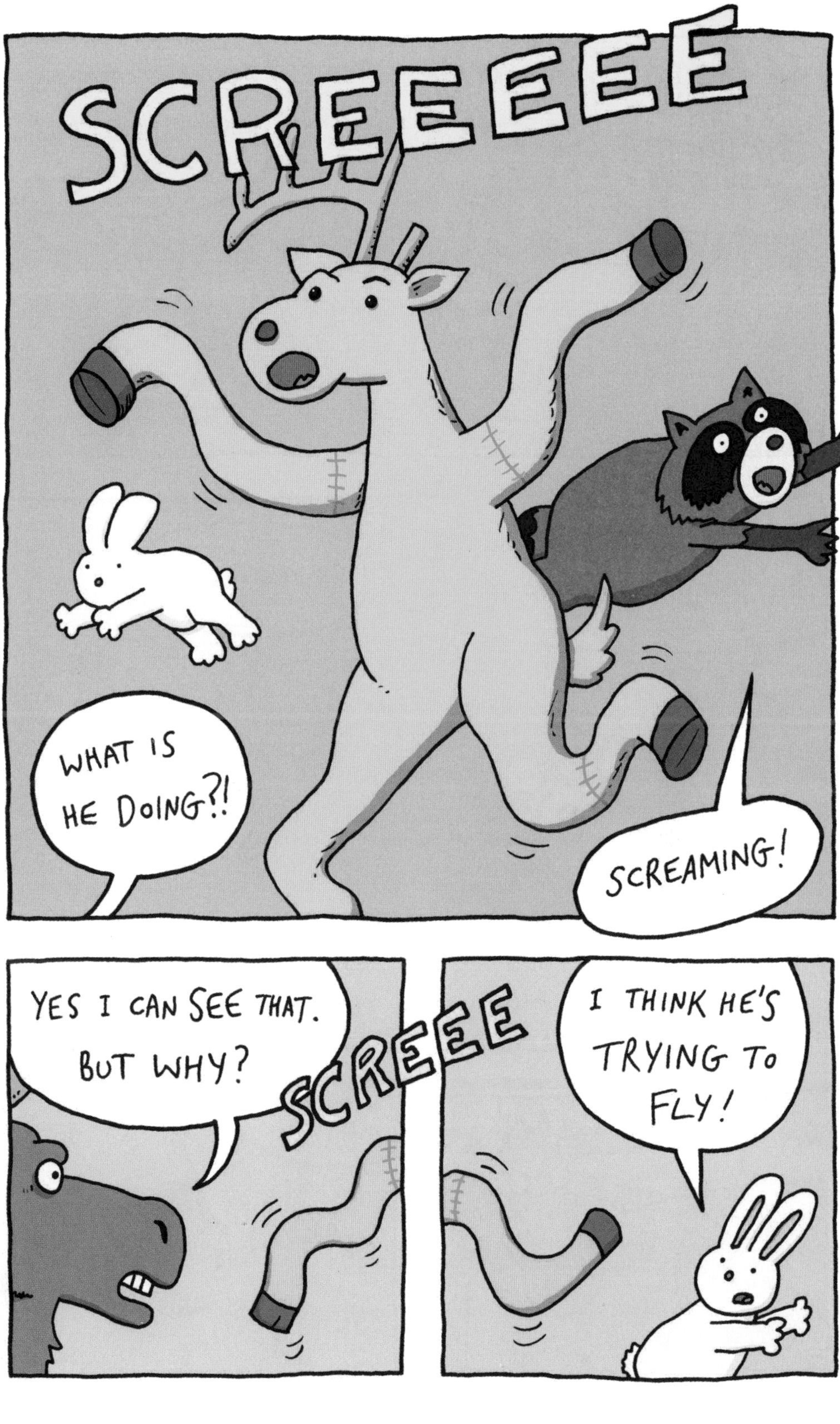
SCREEEEEE
WHAT IS HE DOING?!
SCREAMING!
YES I CAN SEE THAT. BUT WHY?
SCREEE
I THINK HE'S TRYING TO FLY!

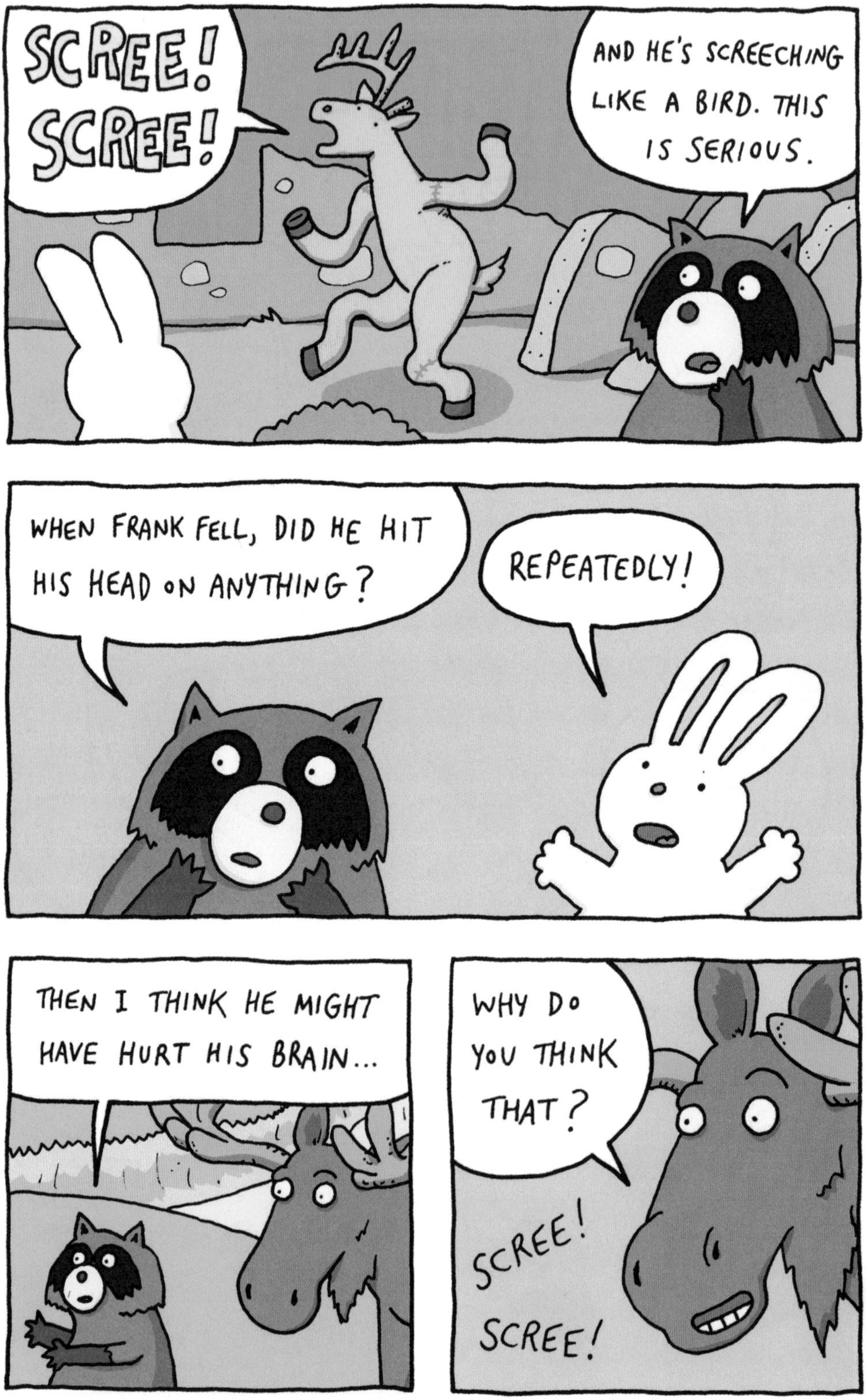
SCREE! SCREE!
AND HE'S SCREECHING LIKE A BIRD. THIS IS SERIOUS.
WHEN FRANK FELL, DID HE HIT HIS HEAD ON ANYTHING?
REPEATEDLY!
THEN I THINK HE MIGHT HAVE HURT HIS BRAIN...
WHY DO YOU THINK THAT?
SCREE!
SCREE!

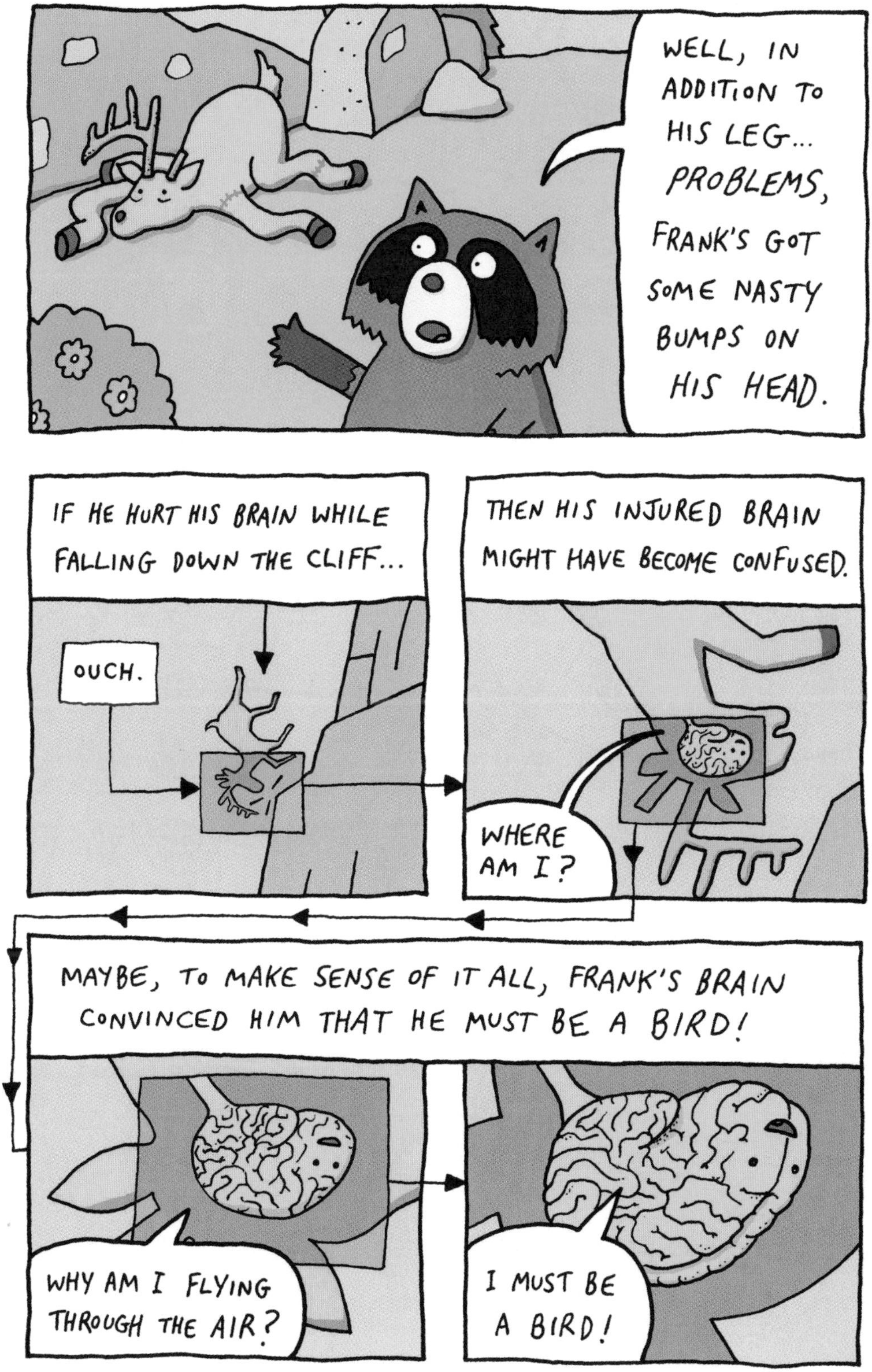
WELL, IN ADDITION TO HIS LEG... PROBLEMS, FRANK'S GOT SOME NASTY BUMPS ON HIS HEAD.
IF HE HURT HIS BRAIN WHILE FALLING DOWN THE CLIFF...
OUCH.
THEN HIS INJURED BRAIN MIGHT HAVE BECOME CONFUSED.
WHERE AM I?
MAYBE, TO MAKE SENSE OF IT ALL, FRANK'S BRAIN CONVINCED HIM THAT HE MUST BE A BIRD!
WHY AM I FLYING THROUGH THE AIR?
I MUST BE A BIRD!

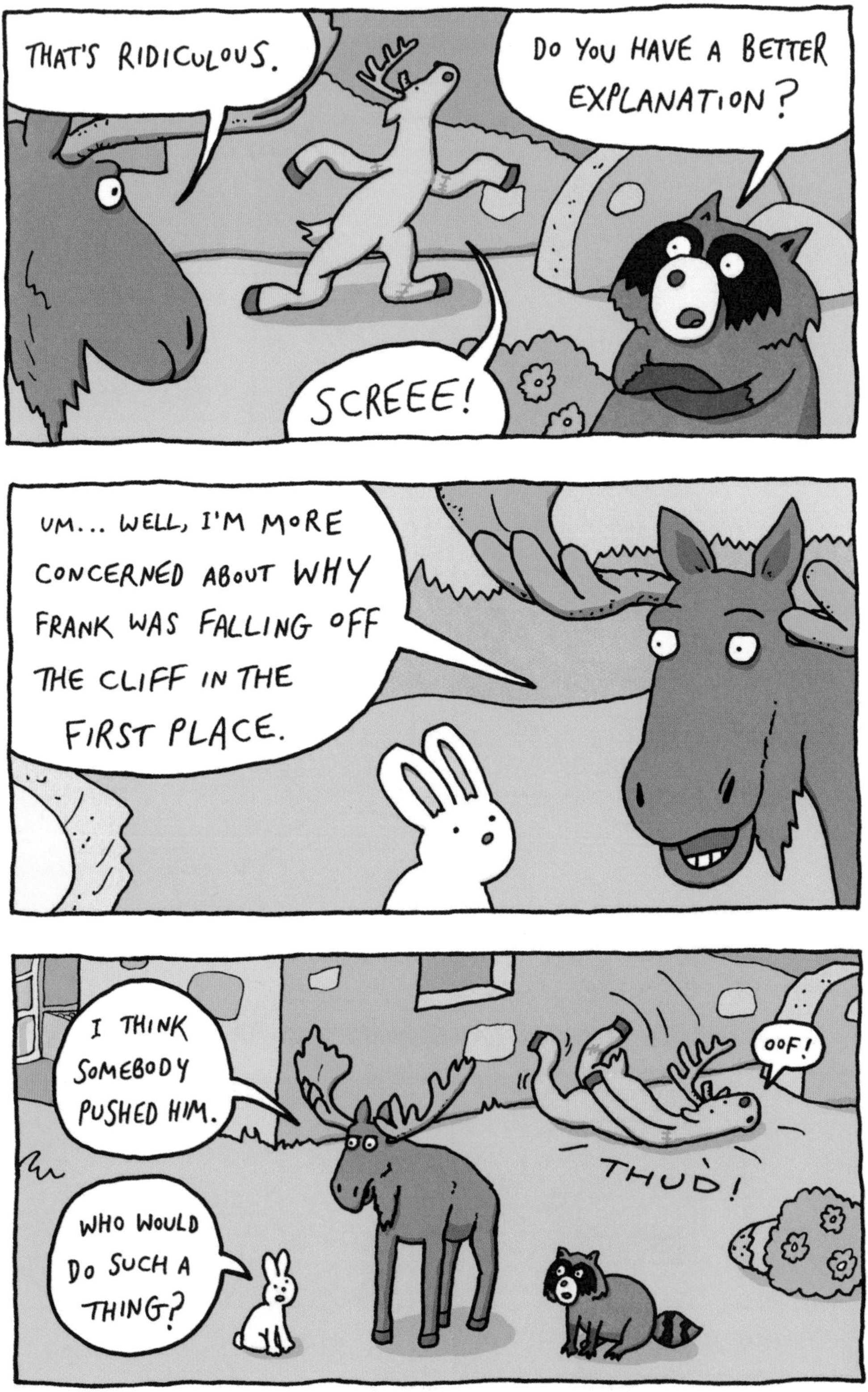
THAT'S RIDICULOUS.
DO YOU HAVE A BETTER EXPLANATION?
SCREEE!
UM... WELL, I'M MORE CONCERNED ABOUT WHY FRANK WAS FALLING OFF THE CLIFF IN THE FIRST PLACE.
I THINK SOMEBODY PUSHED HIM.
OOF!
THUD!
WHO WOULD DO SUCH A THING?

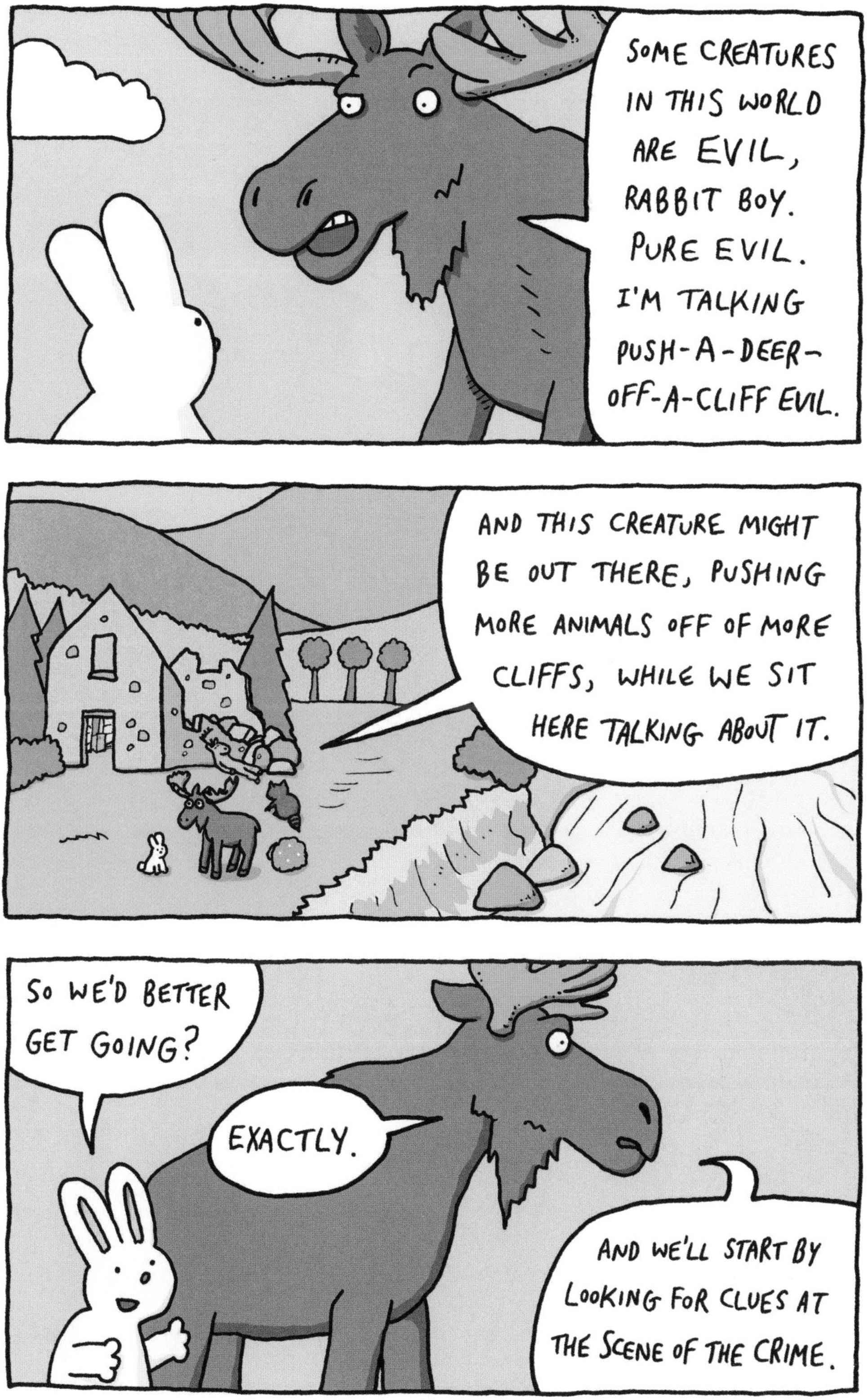

SOME CREATURES IN THIS WORLD ARE EVIL, RABBIT BOY. PURE EVIL. I'M TALKING PUSH-A-DEER-OFF-A-CLIFF EVIL.
AND THIS CREATURE MIGHT BE OUT THERE, PUSHING MORE ANIMALS OFF OF MORE CLIFFS, WHILE WE SIT HERE TALKING ABOUT IT.
SO WE'D BETTER GET GOING?
EXACTLY.
AND WE'LL START BY LOOKING FOR CLUES AT THE SCENE OF THE CRIME.

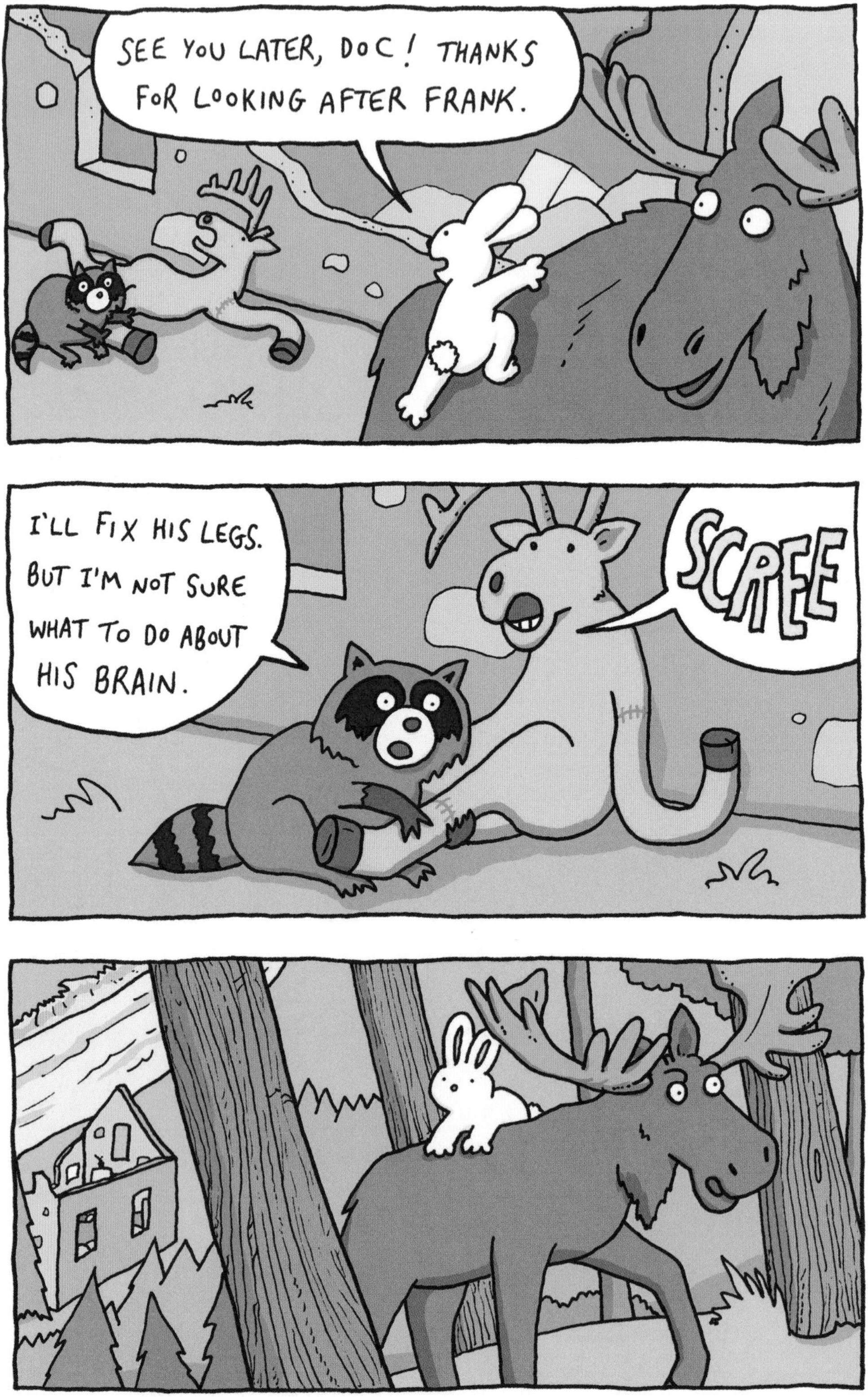
SEE YOU LATER, DOC! THANKS FOR LOOKING AFTER FRANK.
I'LL FIX HIS LEGS. BUT I'M NOT SURE WHAT TO DO ABOUT HIS BRAIN.
SCREE

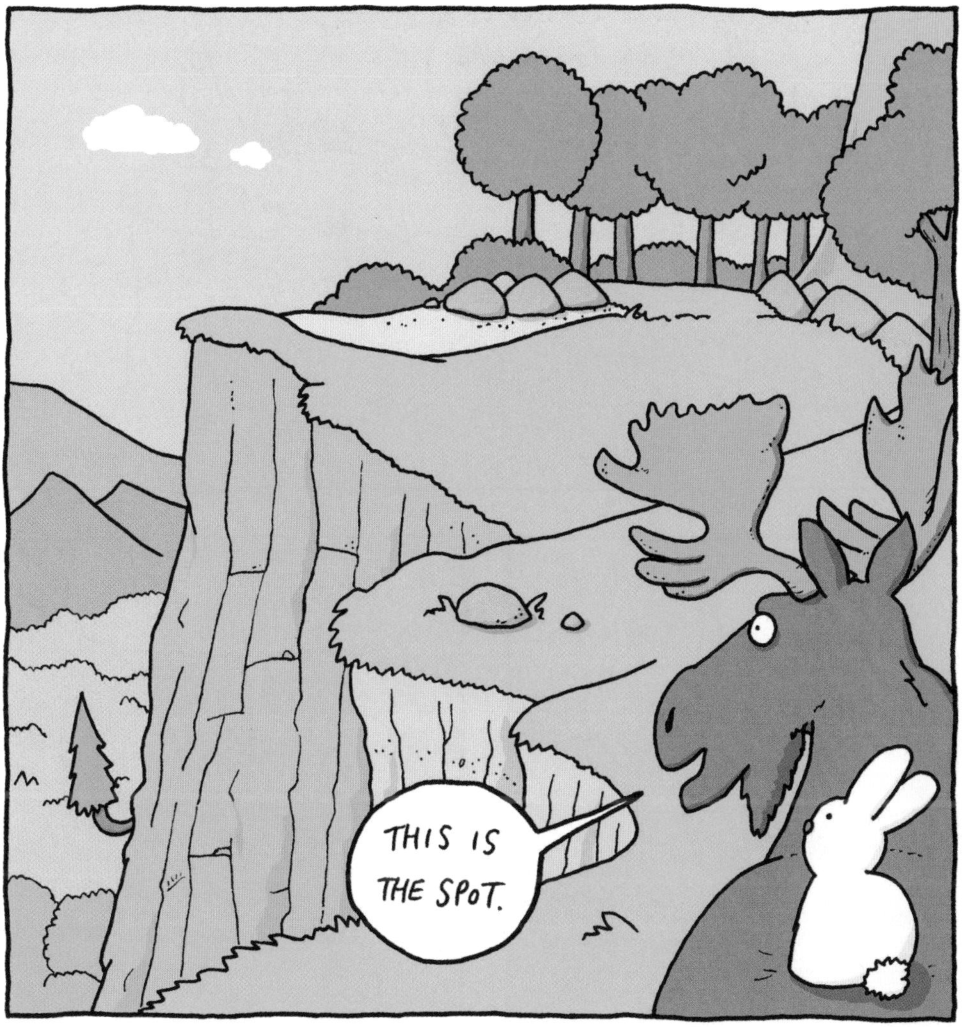
THIS IS THE SPOT.

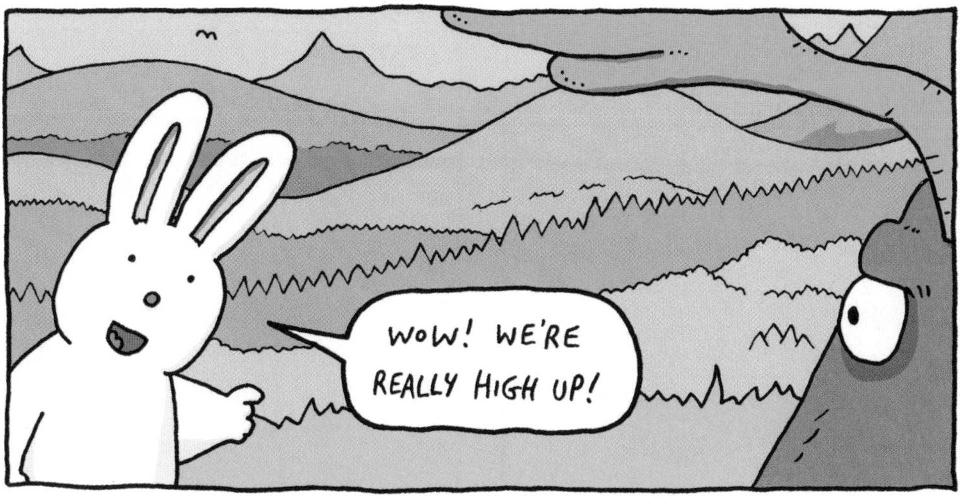
WOW! WE'RE REALLY HIGH UP!

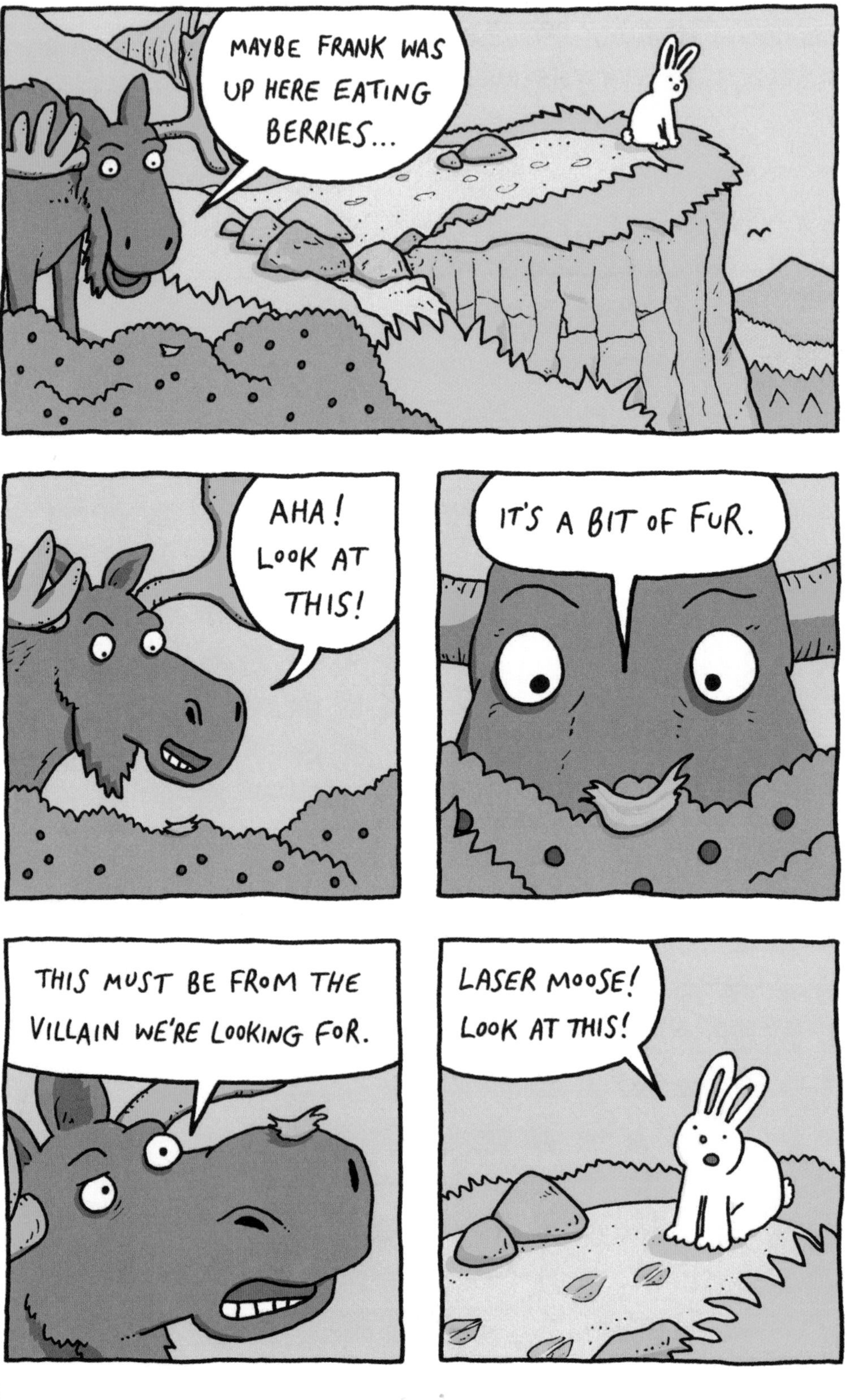
MAYBE FRANK WAS UP HERE EATING BERRIES...
AHA! LOOK AT THIS!
IT'S A BIT OF FUR.
THIS MUST BE FROM THE VILLAIN WE'RE LOOKING FOR.
LASER MOOSE! LOOK AT THIS!

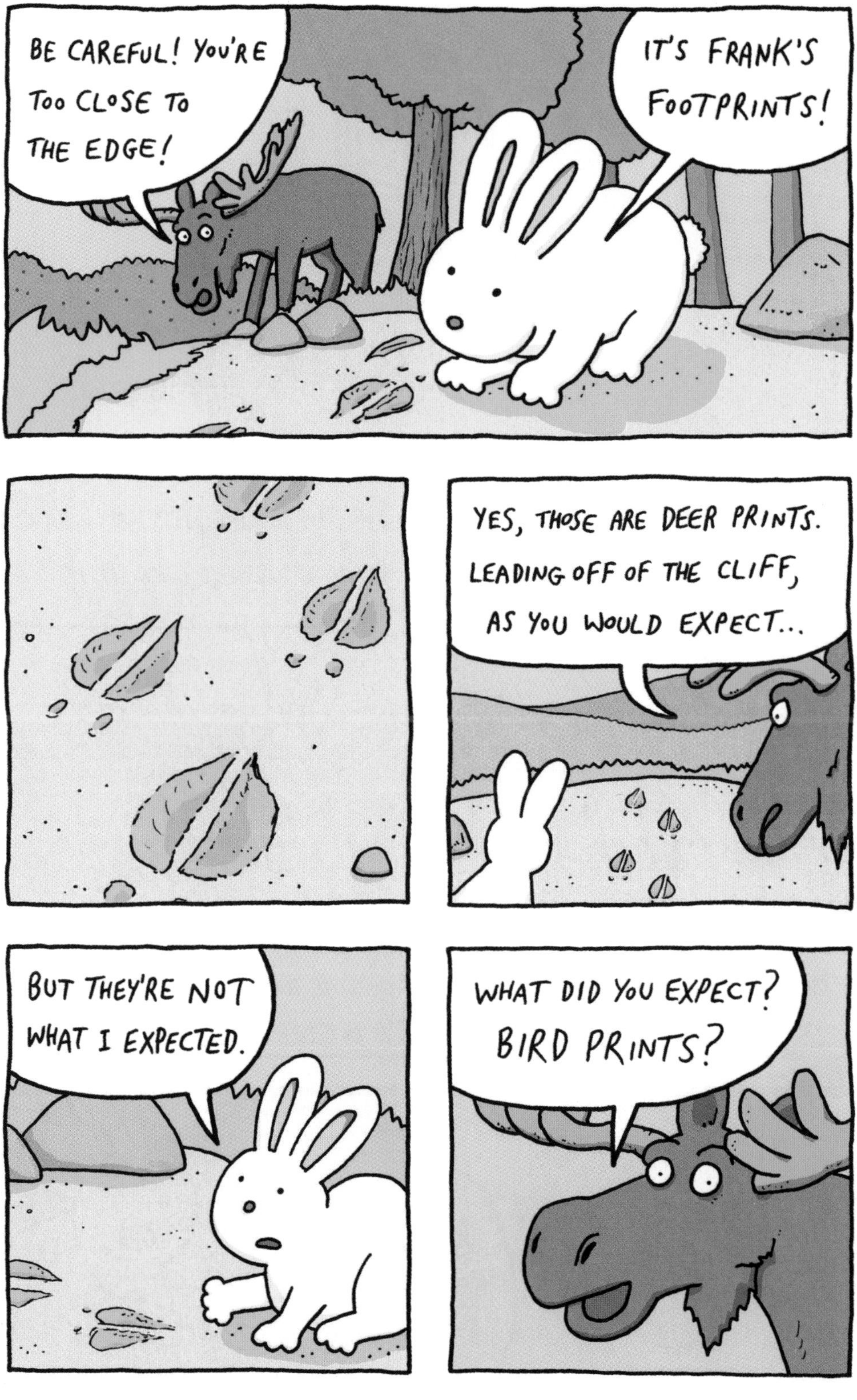
BE CAREFUL! YOU'RE TOO CLOSE TO THE EDGE!
IT'S FRANK'S FOOTPRINTS!
YES, THOSE ARE DEER PRINTS. LEADING OFF OF THE CLIFF, AS YOU WOULD EXPECT...
BUT THEY'RE NOT WHAT I EXPECTED.
WHAT DID YOU EXPECT? BIRD PRINTS?

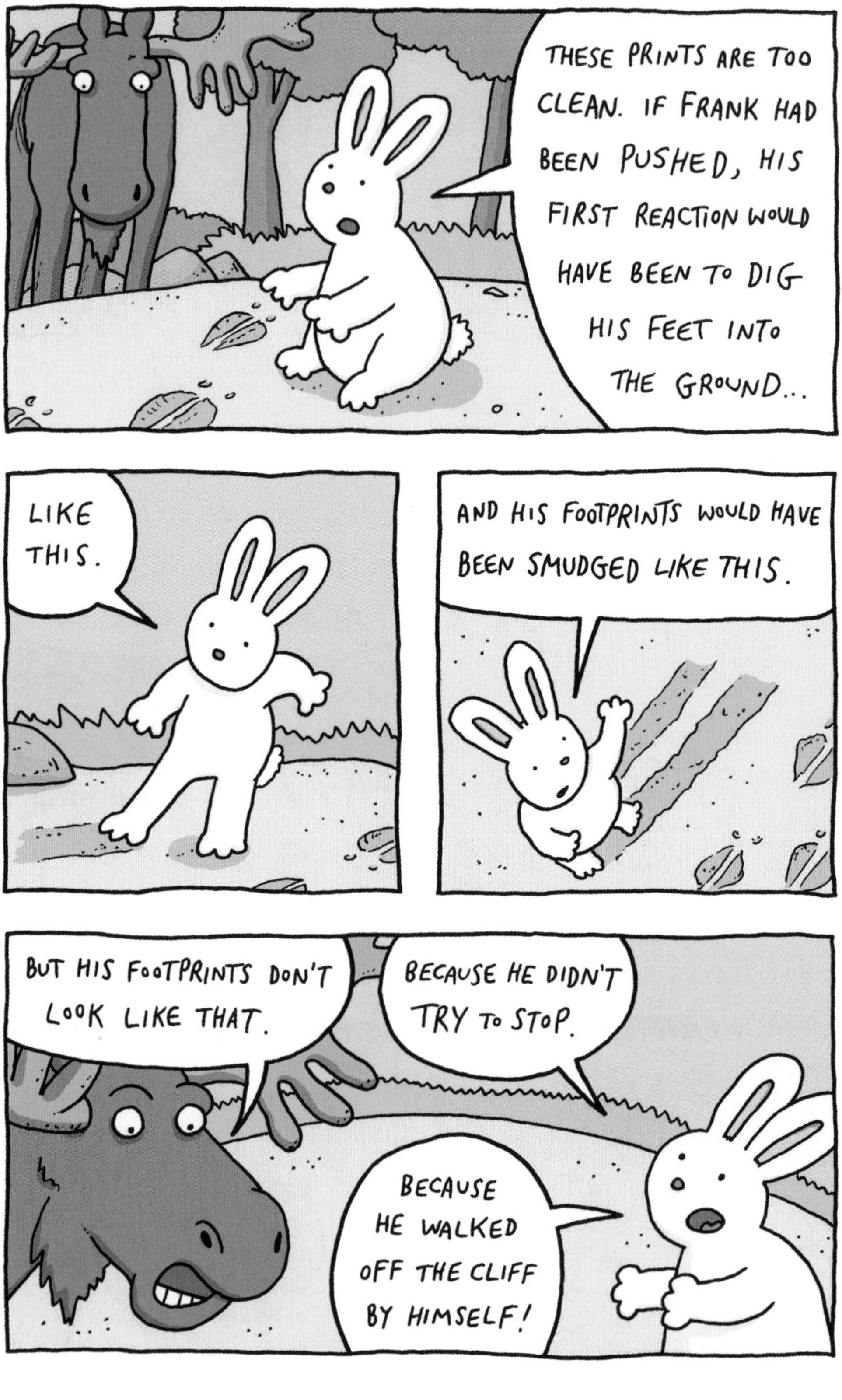
THESE PRINTS ARE TOO CLEAN. IF FRANK HAD BEEN PUSHED, HIS FIRST REACTION WOULD HAVE BEEN TO DIG HIS FEET INTO THE GROUND...
LIKE THIS.
AND HIS FOOTPRINTS WOULD HAVE BEEN SMUDGED LIKE THIS.
BUT HIS FOOTPRINTS DON'T LOOK LIKE THAT.
BECAUSE HE DIDN'T TRY TO STOP.
BECAUSE HE WALKED OFF THE CLIFF BY HIMSELF!

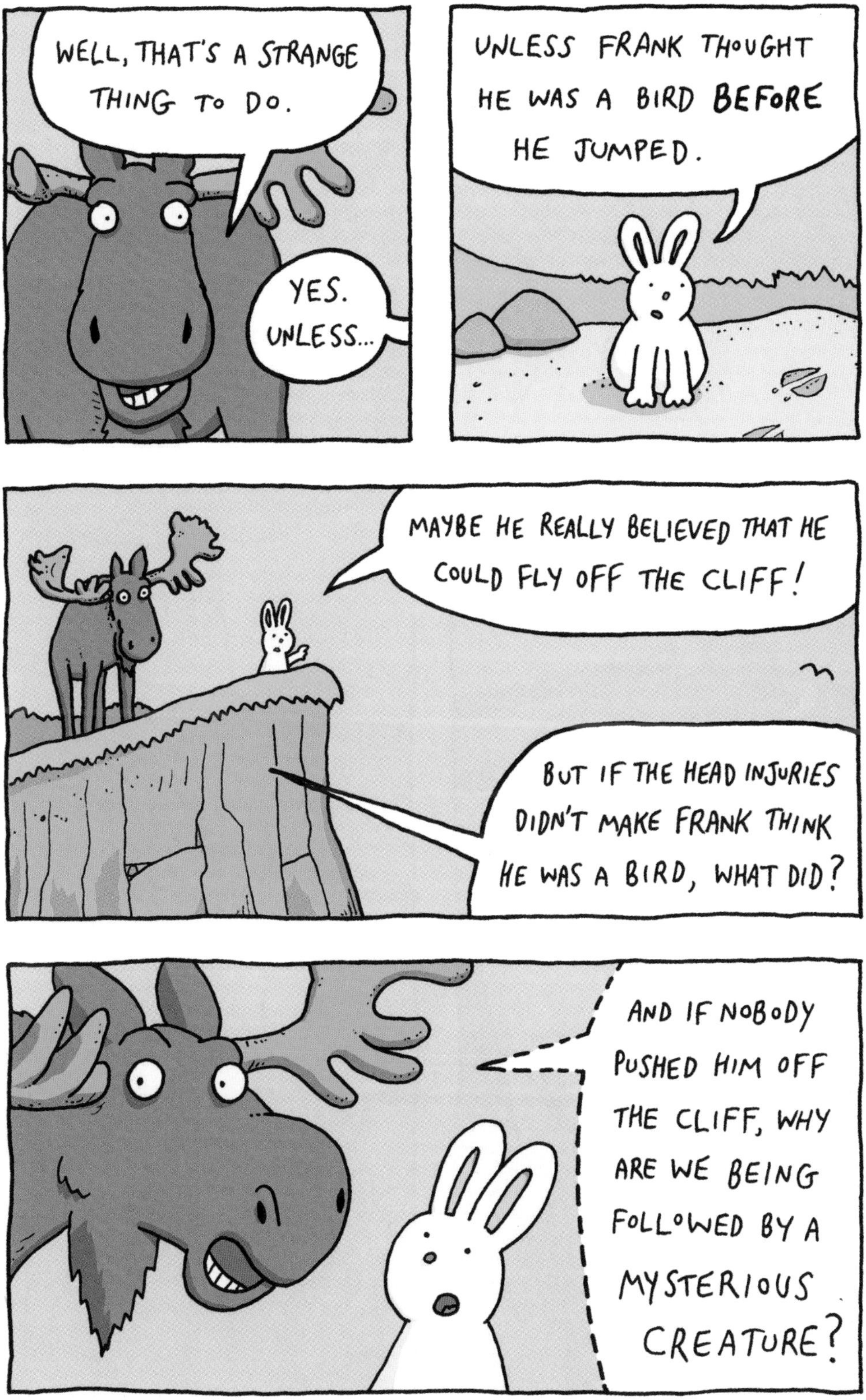
WELL, THAT'S A STRANGE THING TO DO.
YES. UNLESS...
UNLESS FRANK THOUGHT HE WAS A BIRD BEFORE HE JUMPED.
MAYBE HE REALLY BELIEVED THAT HE COULD FLY OFF THE CLIFF!
BUT IF THE HEAD INJURIES DIDN'T MAKE FRANK THINK HE WAS A BIRD, WHAT DID?
AND IF NOBODY PUSHED HIM OFF THE CLIFF, WHY ARE WE BEING FOLLOWED BY A MYSTERIOUS CREATURE?

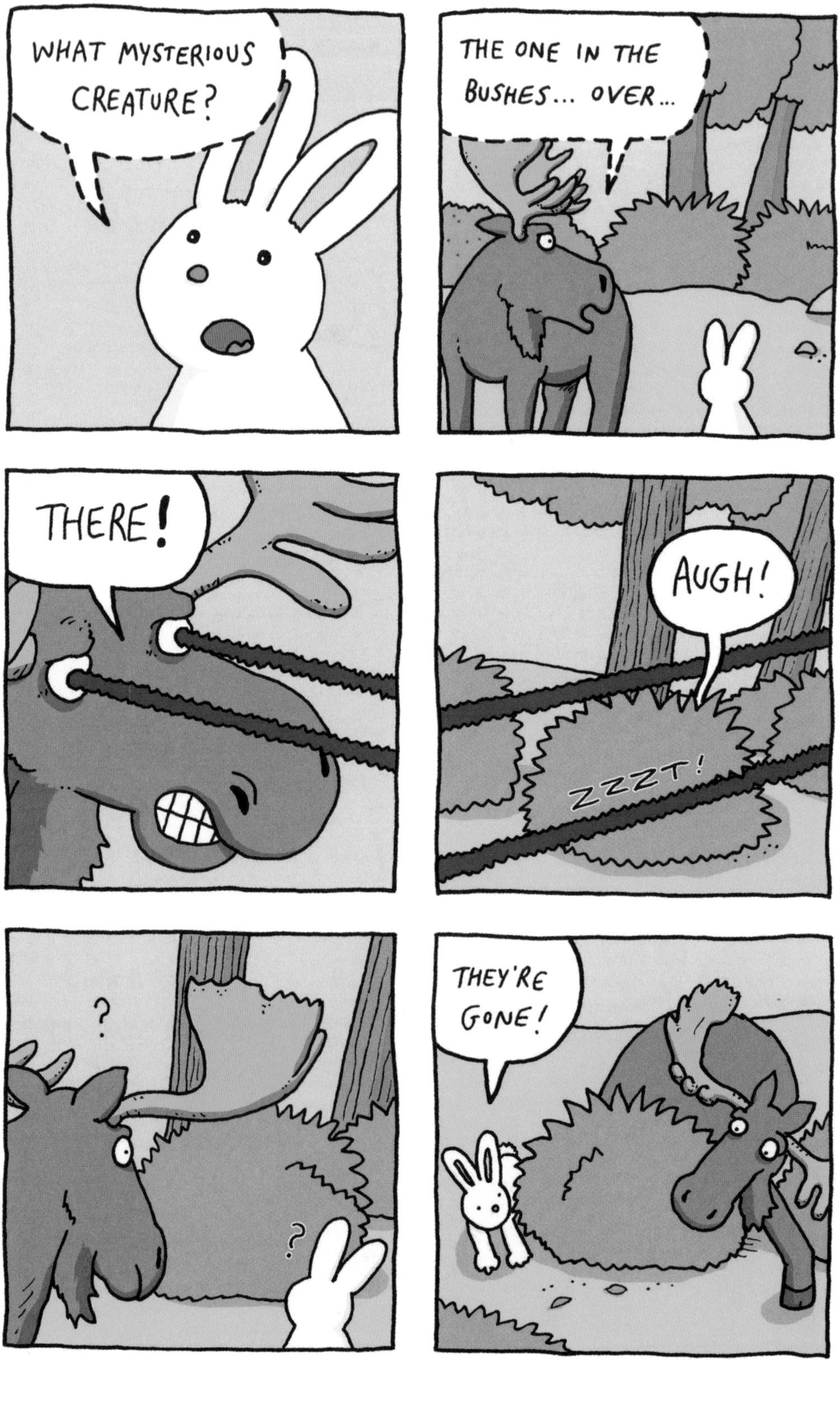
WHAT MYSTERIOUS CREATURE?
THE ONE IN THE BUSHES... OVER...
THERE!
AUGH!
ZZZT!
?
?
THEY'RE GONE!

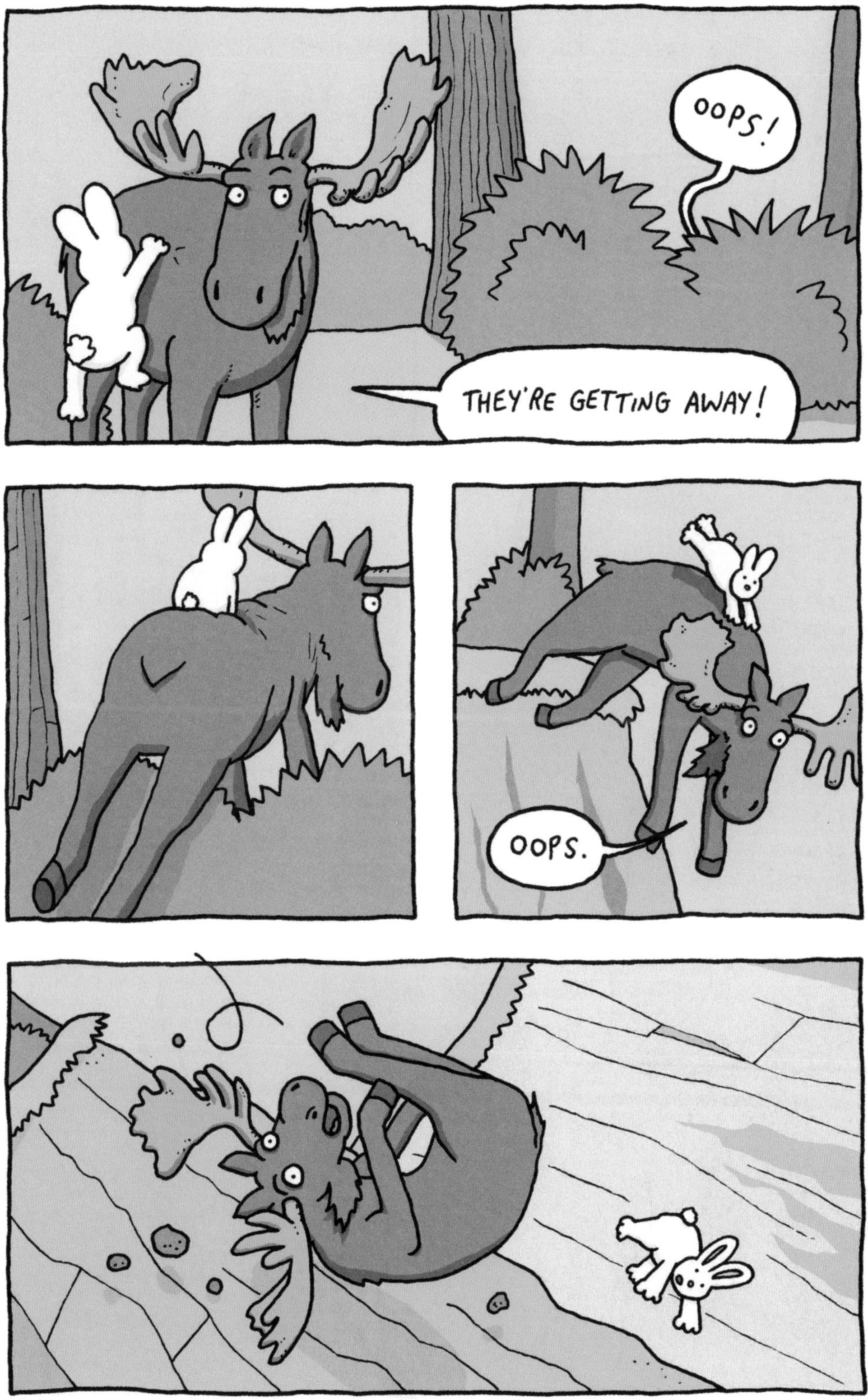
OOPS!
THEY'RE GETTING AWAY!
OOPS.

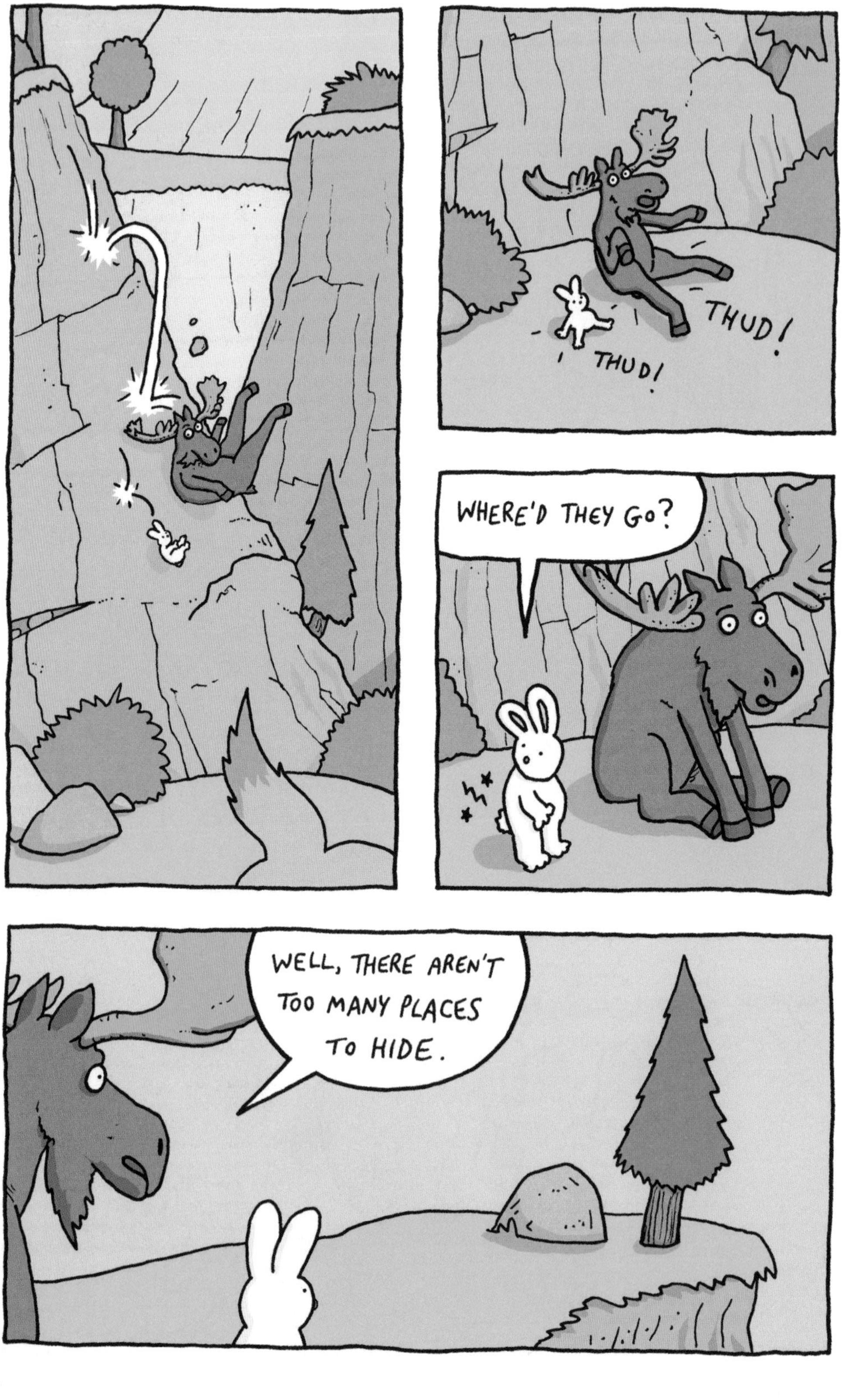
THUD!
THUD!
WHERE'D THEY GO?
WELL, THERE AREN'T TOO MANY PLACES TO HIDE.

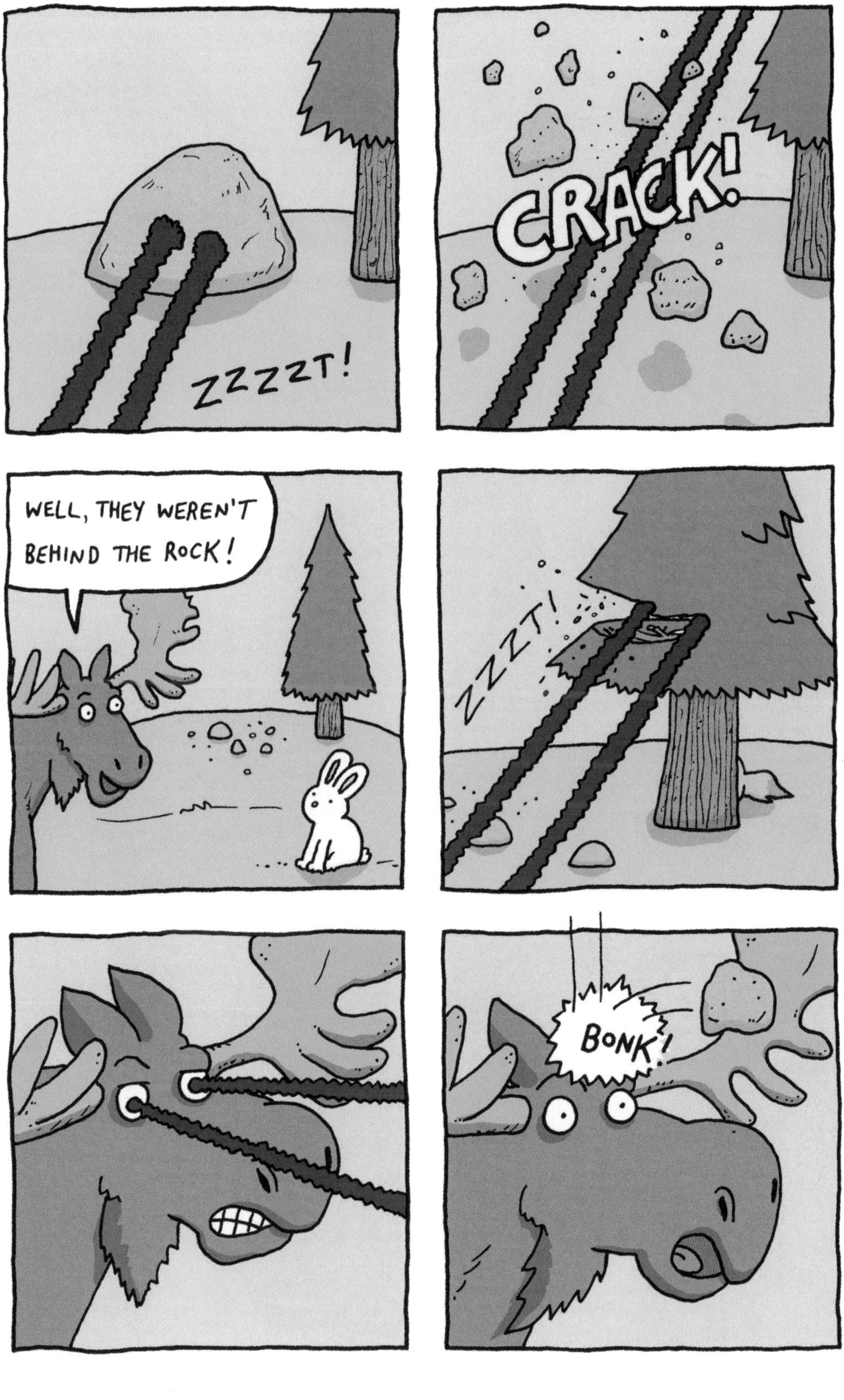
ZZZZZT!
CRACK!
WELL, THEY WEREN'T BEHIND THE ROCK!
ZZZZT!
BONK!

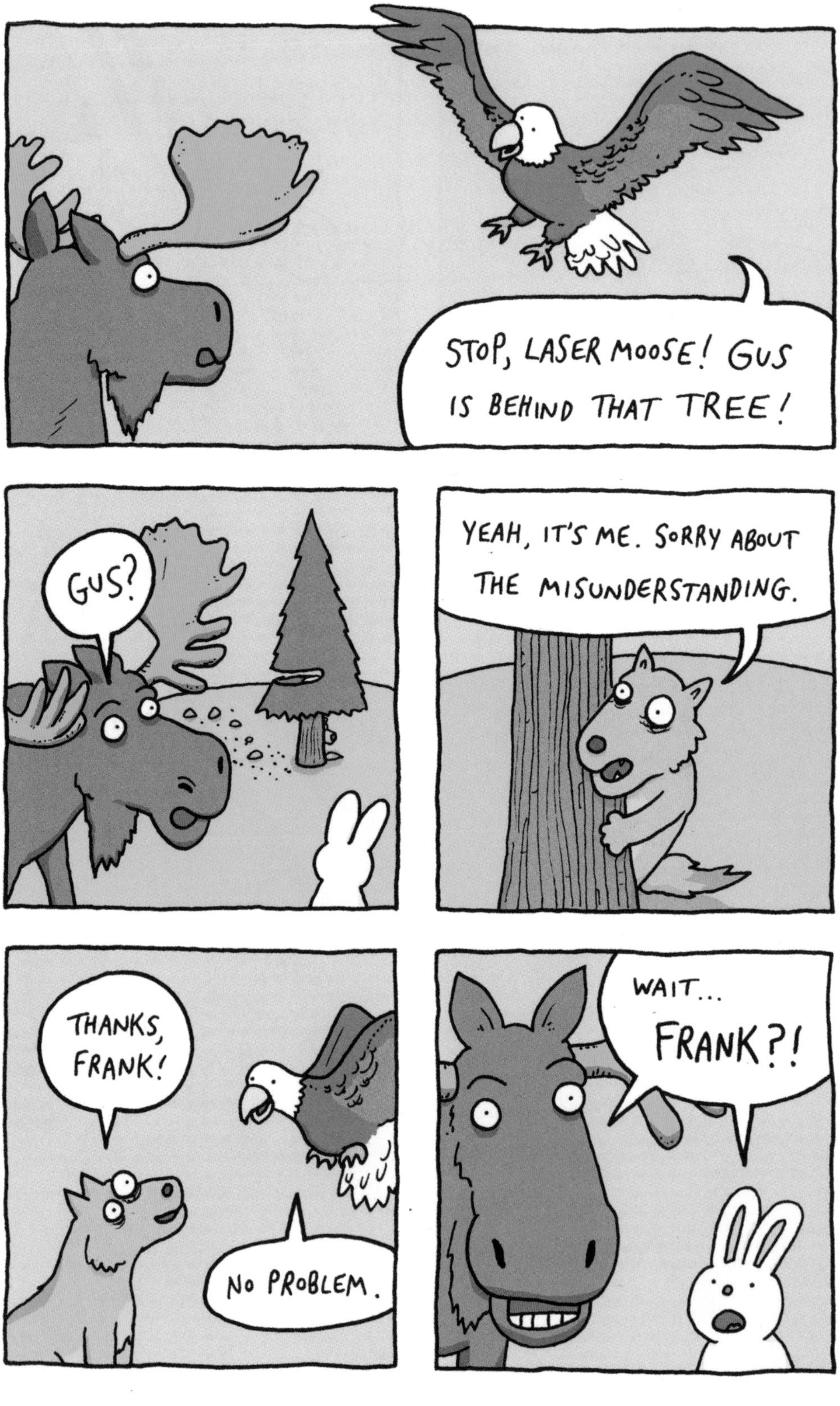
STOP, LASER MOOSE! GUS IS BEHIND THAT TREE!
GUS?
YEAH, IT'S ME. SORRY ABOUT THE MISUNDERSTANDING.
THANKS, FRANK!
NO PROBLEM.
WAIT...
FRANK?!

PART 2:
THE MISGUIDED WOLF

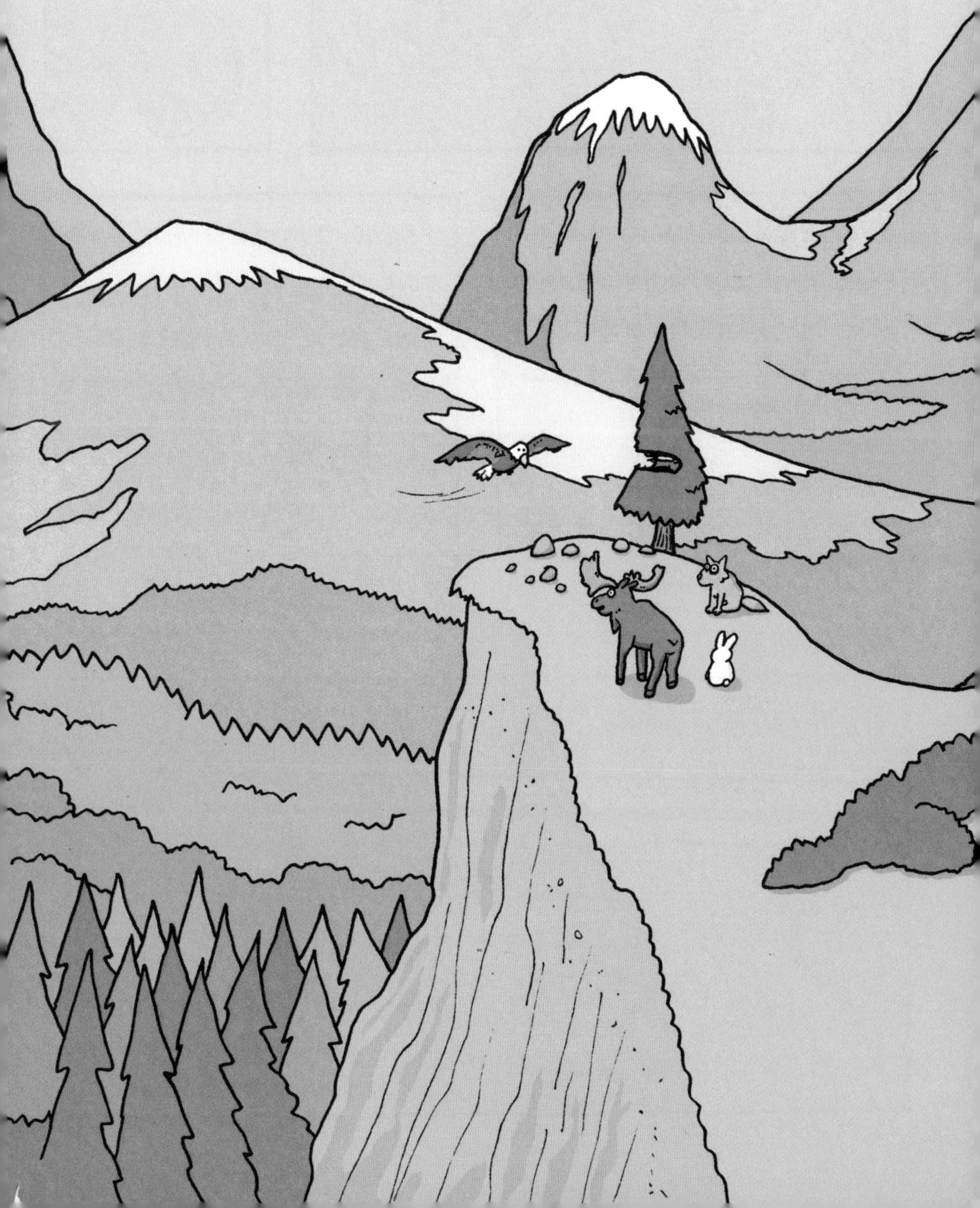

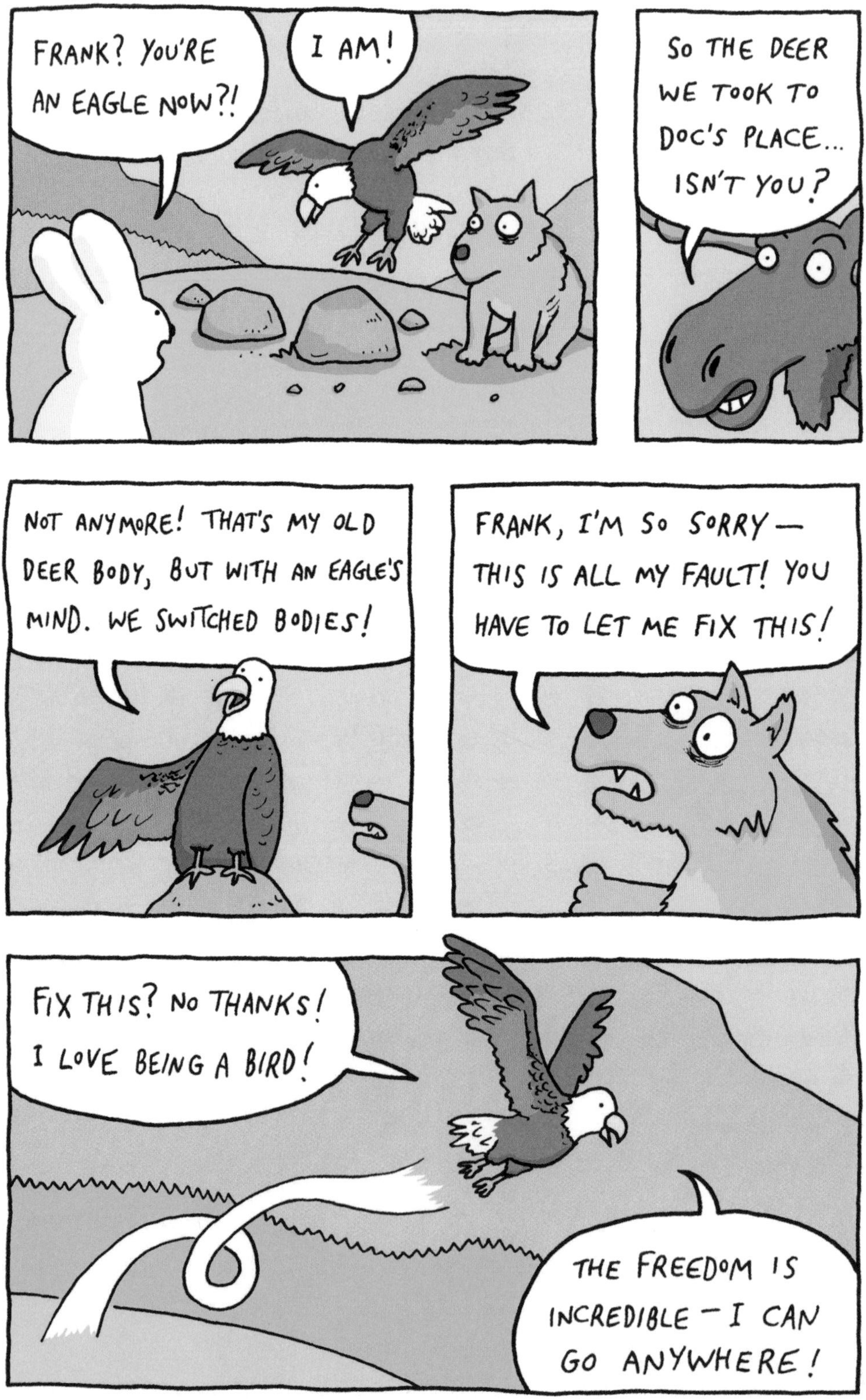
FRANK? YOU'RE AN EAGLE NOW?!
I AM!
SO THE DEER WE TOOK TO DOC'S PLACE... ISN'T YOU?
NOT ANYMORE! THAT'S MY OLD DEER BODY, BUT WITH AN EAGLE'S MIND. WE SWITCHED BODIES!
FRANK, I'M SO SORRY— THIS IS ALL MY FAULT! YOU HAVE TO LET ME FIX THIS!
FIX THIS? NO THANKS! I LOVE BEING A BIRD!
THE FREEDOM IS INCREDIBLE—I CAN GO ANYWHERE!

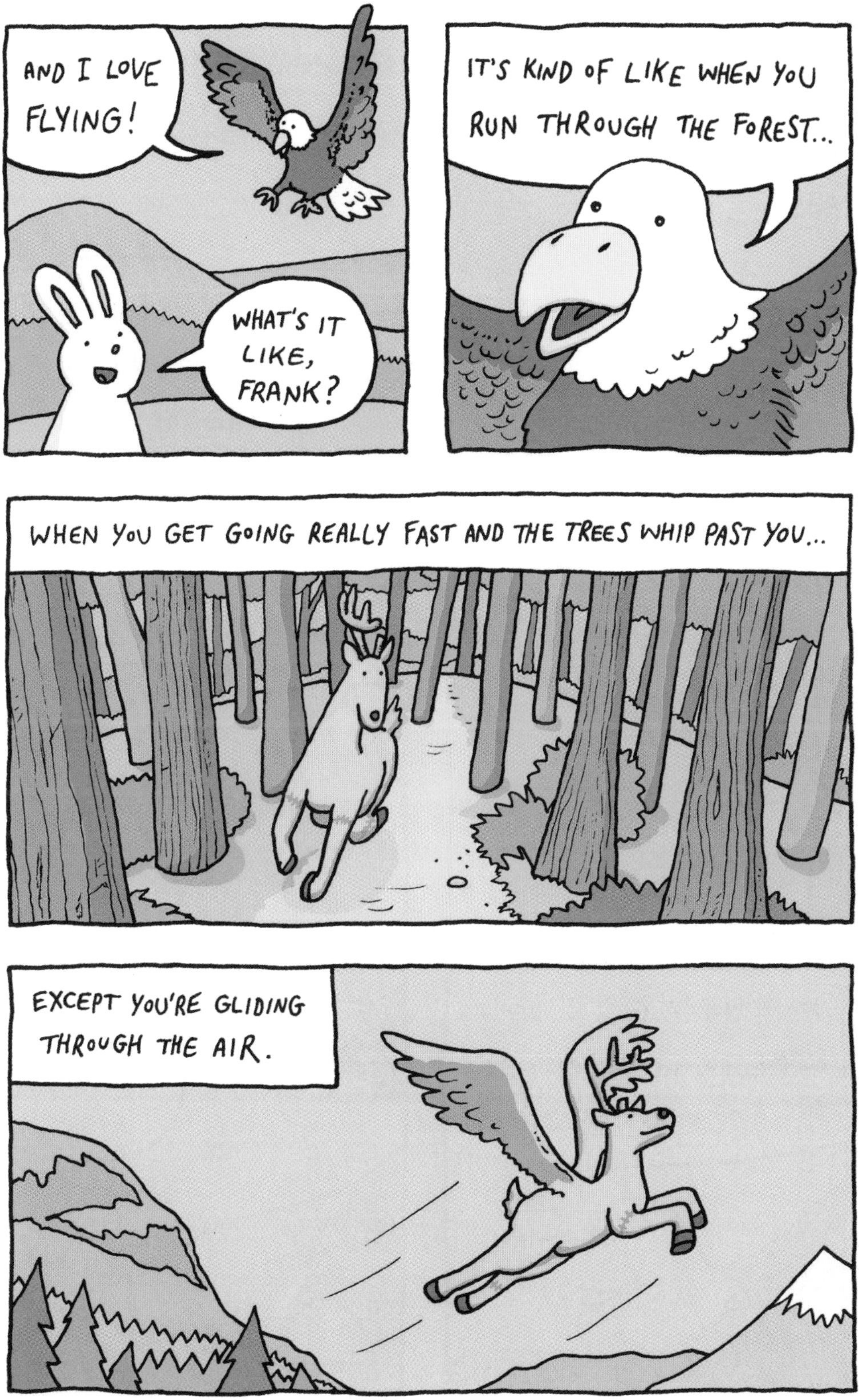
AND I LOVE FLYING!
WHAT'S IT LIKE, FRANK?
IT'S KIND OF LIKE WHEN YOU RUN THROUGH THE FOREST...
WHEN YOU GET GOING REALLY FAST AND THE TREES WHIP PAST YOU...
EXCEPT YOU'RE GLIDING THROUGH THE AIR.

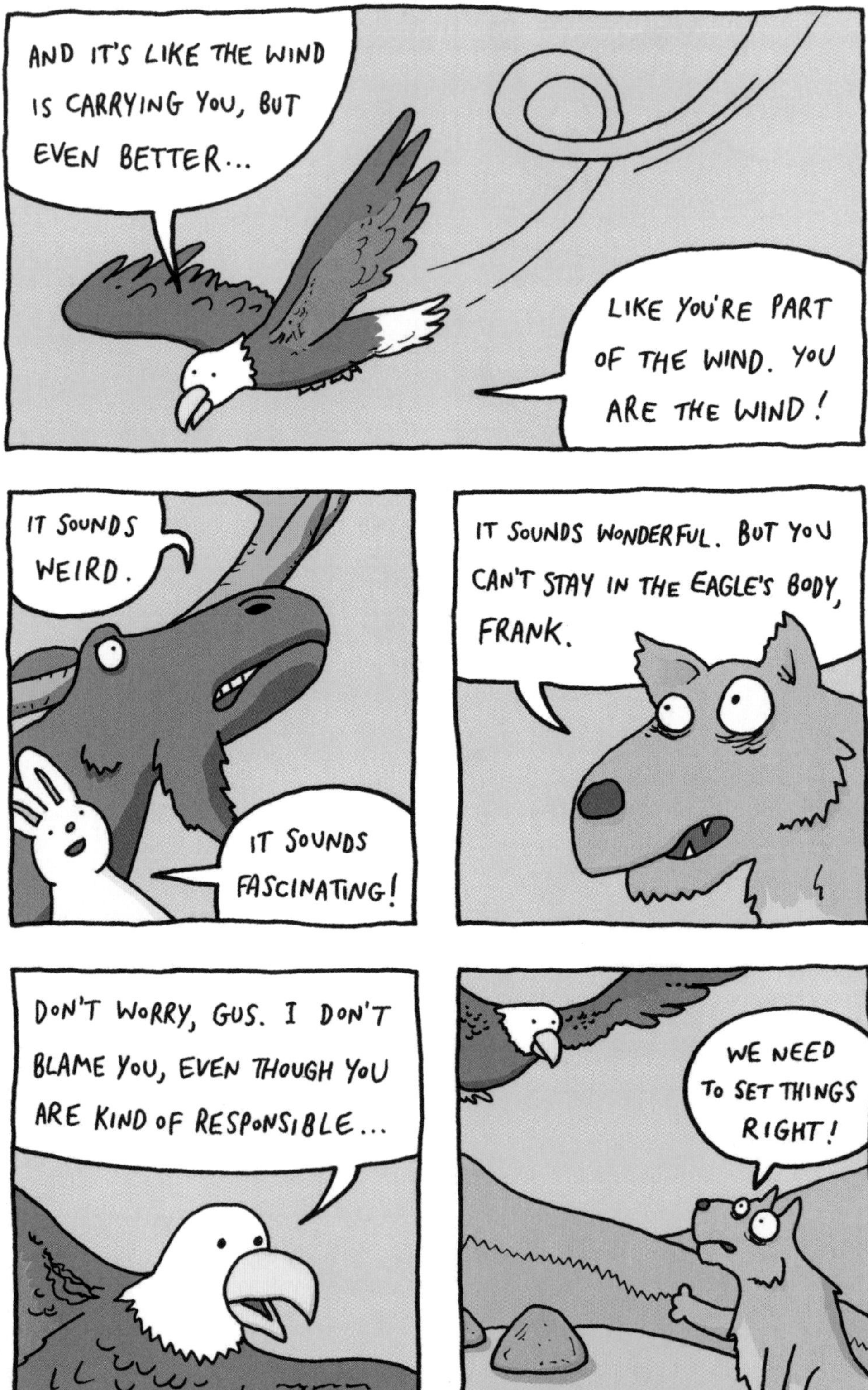
AND IT'S LIKE THE WIND IS CARRYING YOU, BUT EVEN BETTER...
LIKE YOU'RE PART OF THE WIND. YOU ARE THE WIND!
IT SOUNDS WEIRD.
IT SOUNDS FASCINATING!
IT SOUNDS WONDERFUL. BUT YOU CAN'T STAY IN THE EAGLE'S BODY, FRANK.
DON'T WORRY, GUS. I DON'T BLAME YOU, EVEN THOUGH YOU ARE KIND OF RESPONSIBLE...
WE NEED TO SET THINGS RIGHT!

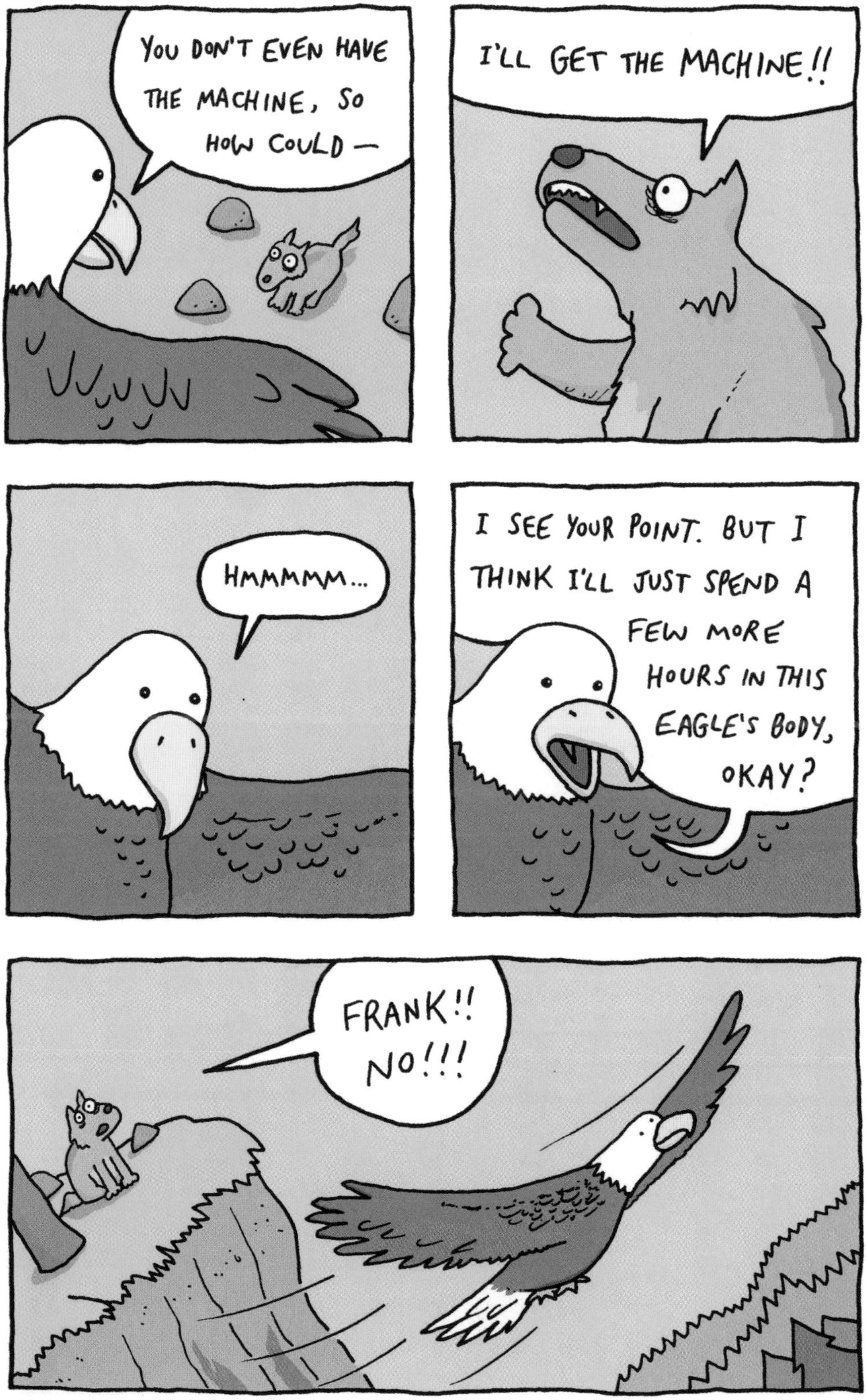
YOU DON'T EVEN HAVE THE MACHINE, SO HOW COULD—
I'LL GET THE MACHINE!!
HMMMMM...
I SEE YOUR POINT. BUT I THINK I'LL JUST SPEND A FEW MORE HOURS IN THIS EAGLE'S BODY, OKAY?
FRANK!! NO!!!

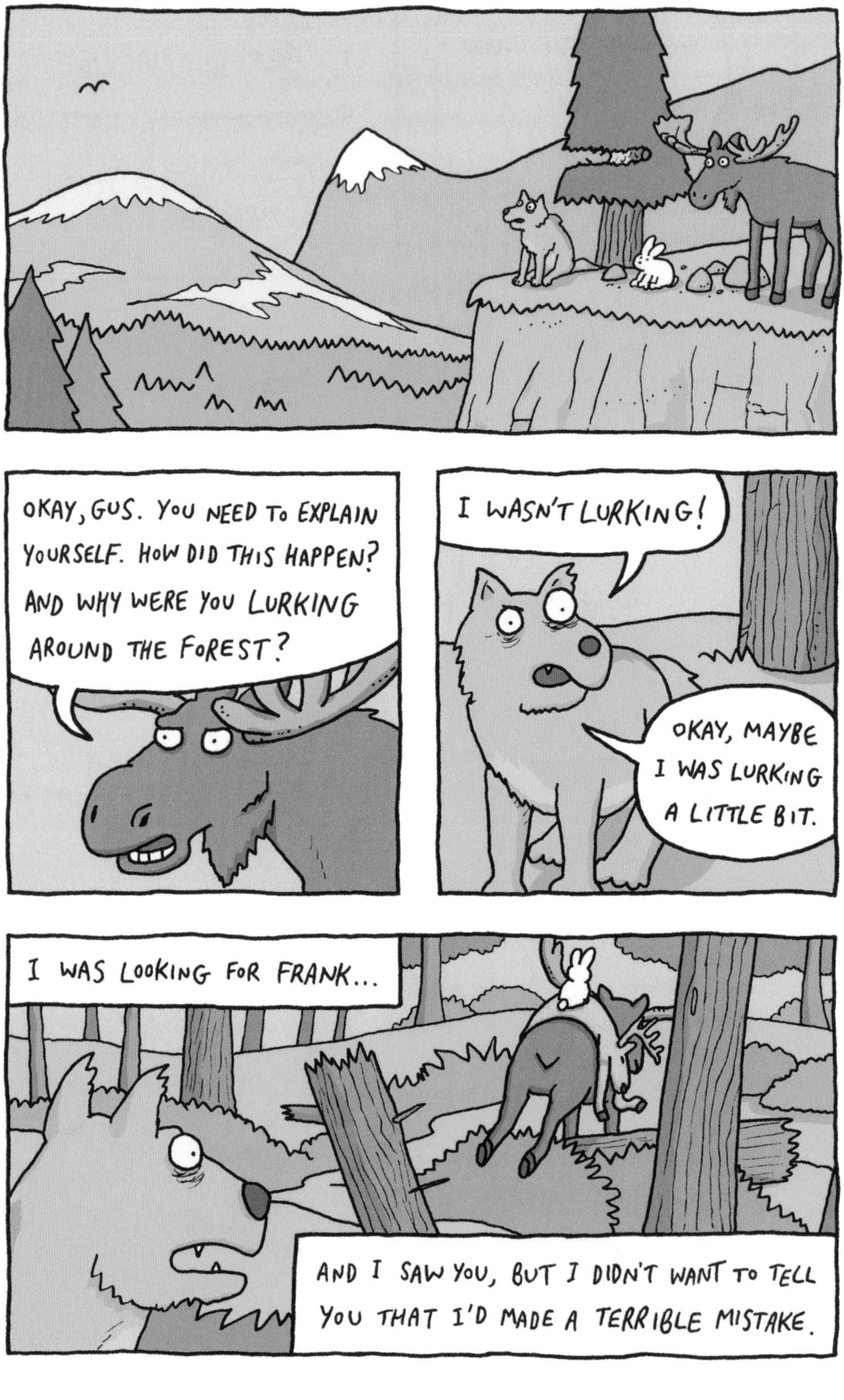

OKAY, GUS. YOU NEED TO EXPLAIN YOURSELF. HOW DID THIS HAPPEN? AND WHY WERE YOU LURKING AROUND THE FOREST?
I WASN'T LURKING!
OKAY, MAYBE I WAS LURKING A LITTLE BIT.
I WAS LOOKING FOR FRANK...
AND I SAW YOU, BUT I DIDN'T WANT TO TELL YOU THAT I'D MADE A TERRIBLE MISTAKE.

I WAS HOPING TO FIX MY MISTAKE FIRST AND THEN TELL YOU ABOUT IT WHEN EVERYTHING WAS COOL AND BACK TO NORMAL AGAIN. BUT I SHOULD HAVE ASKED FOR HELP.

WHAT MISTAKE, GUS?

WHAT DID YOU DO?

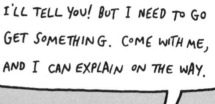

I'LL TELL YOU! BUT I NEED TO GO GET SOMETHING. COME WITH ME, AND I CAN EXPLAIN ON THE WAY.

HOW DID YOU MAKE FRANK AND THE EAGLE SWITCH BODIES?

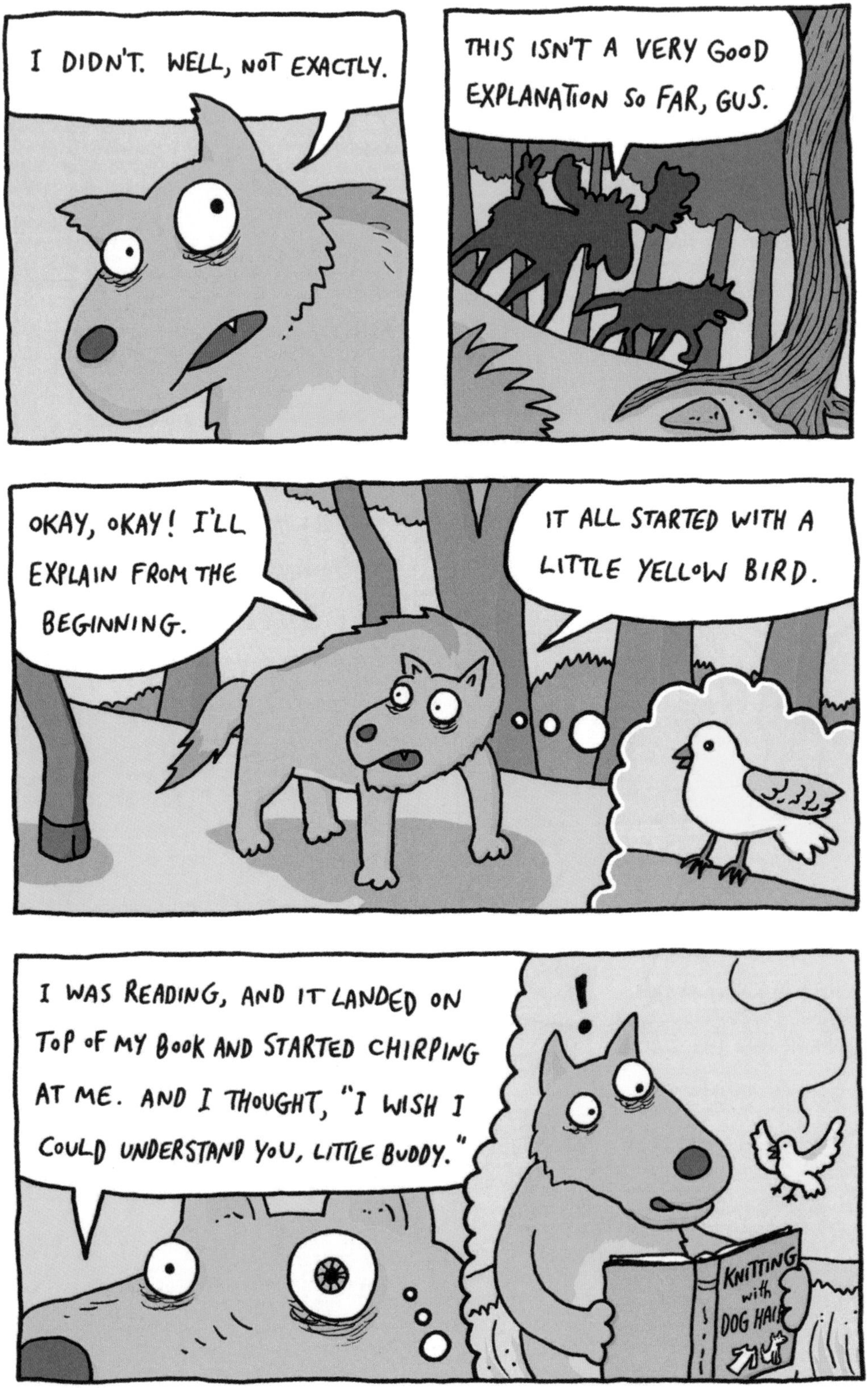
I DIDN'T. WELL, NOT EXACTLY.
THIS ISN'T A VERY GOOD EXPLANATION SO FAR, GUS.
OKAY, OKAY! I'LL EXPLAIN FROM THE BEGINNING.
IT ALL STARTED WITH A LITTLE YELLOW BIRD.
I WAS READING, AND IT LANDED ON TOP OF MY BOOK AND STARTED CHIRPING AT ME. AND I THOUGHT, "I WISH I COULD UNDERSTAND YOU, LITTLE BUDDY."
!
KNITTING with DOG HAIR

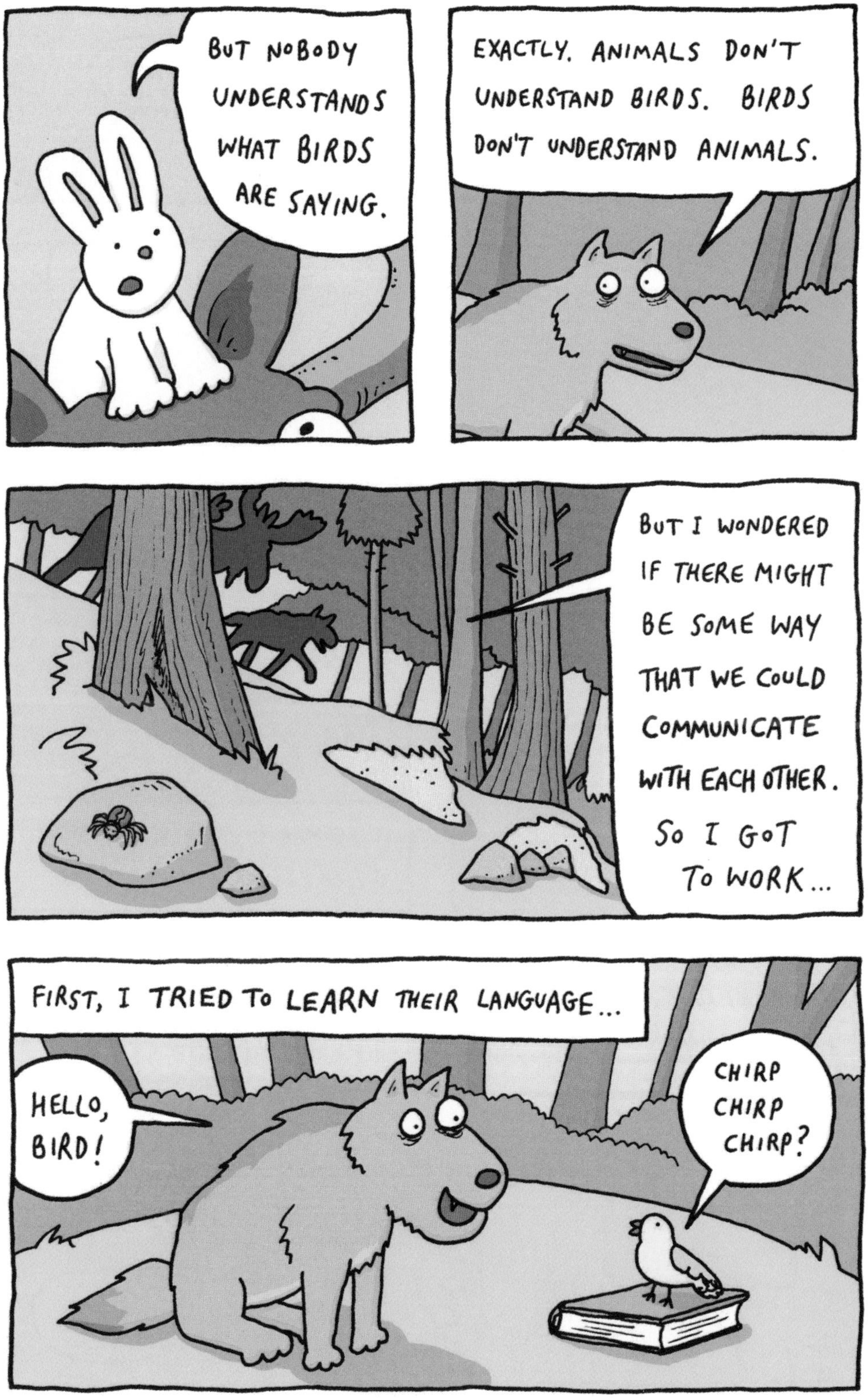
BUT NOBODY UNDERSTANDS WHAT BIRDS ARE SAYING.
EXACTLY. ANIMALS DON'T UNDERSTAND BIRDS. BIRDS DON'T UNDERSTAND ANIMALS.
BUT I WONDERED IF THERE MIGHT BE SOME WAY THAT WE COULD COMMUNICATE WITH EACH OTHER.
SO I GOT TO WORK...
FIRST, I TRIED TO LEARN THEIR LANGUAGE...
HELLO, BIRD!
CHIRP CHIRP CHIRP?

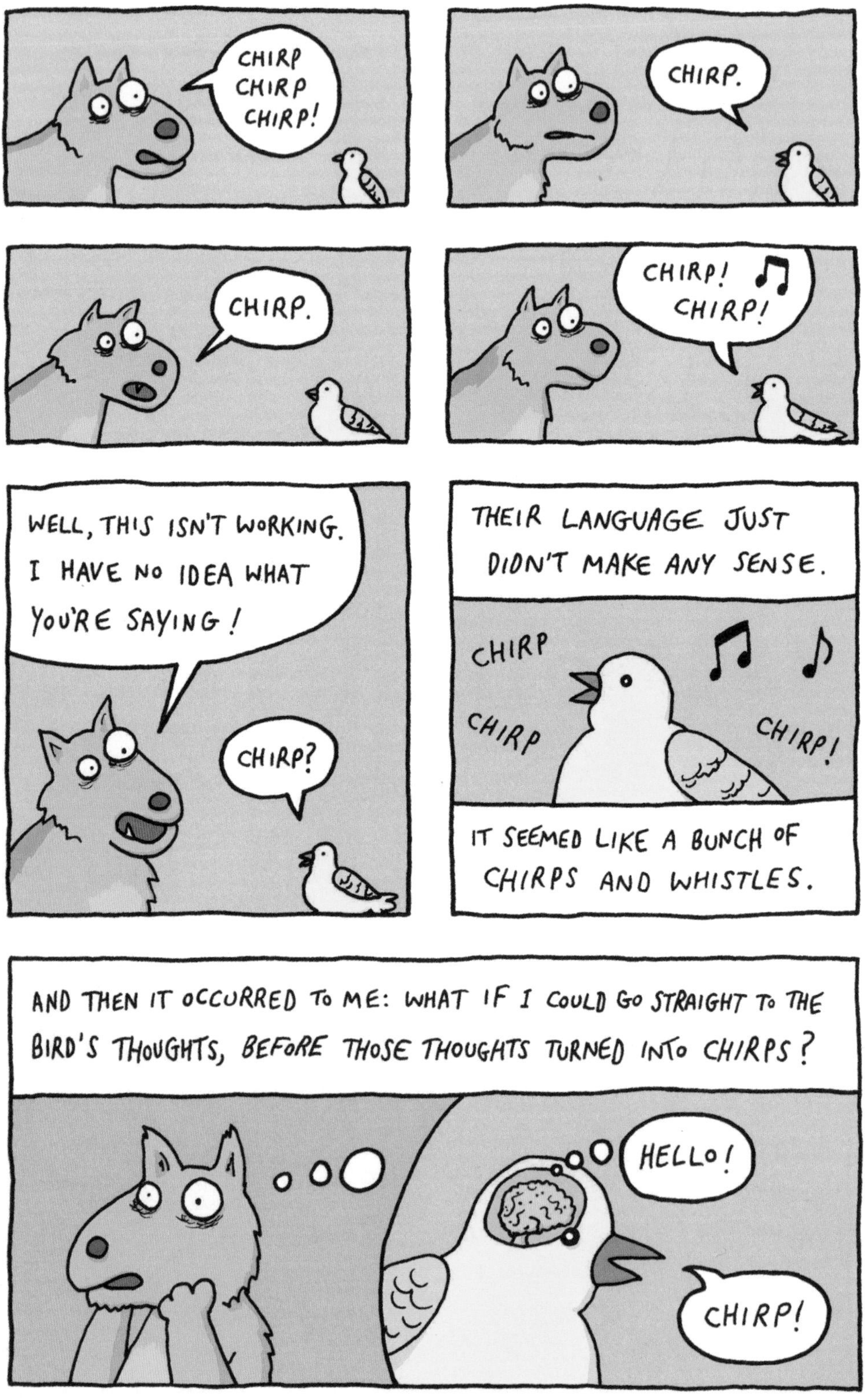
CHIRP CHIRP CHIRP!
CHIRP.
CHIRP.
CHIRP! CHIRP!
WELL, THIS ISN'T WORKING. I HAVE NO IDEA WHAT YOU'RE SAYING!
CHIRP?
THEIR LANGUAGE JUST DIDN'T MAKE ANY SENSE.
CHIRP
CHIRP
CHIRP!
IT SEEMED LIKE A BUNCH OF CHIRPS AND WHISTLES.
AND THEN IT OCCURRED TO ME: WHAT IF I COULD GO STRAIGHT TO THE BIRD'S THOUGHTS, *BEFORE* THOSE THOUGHTS TURNED INTO CHIRPS?
HELLO!
CHIRP!

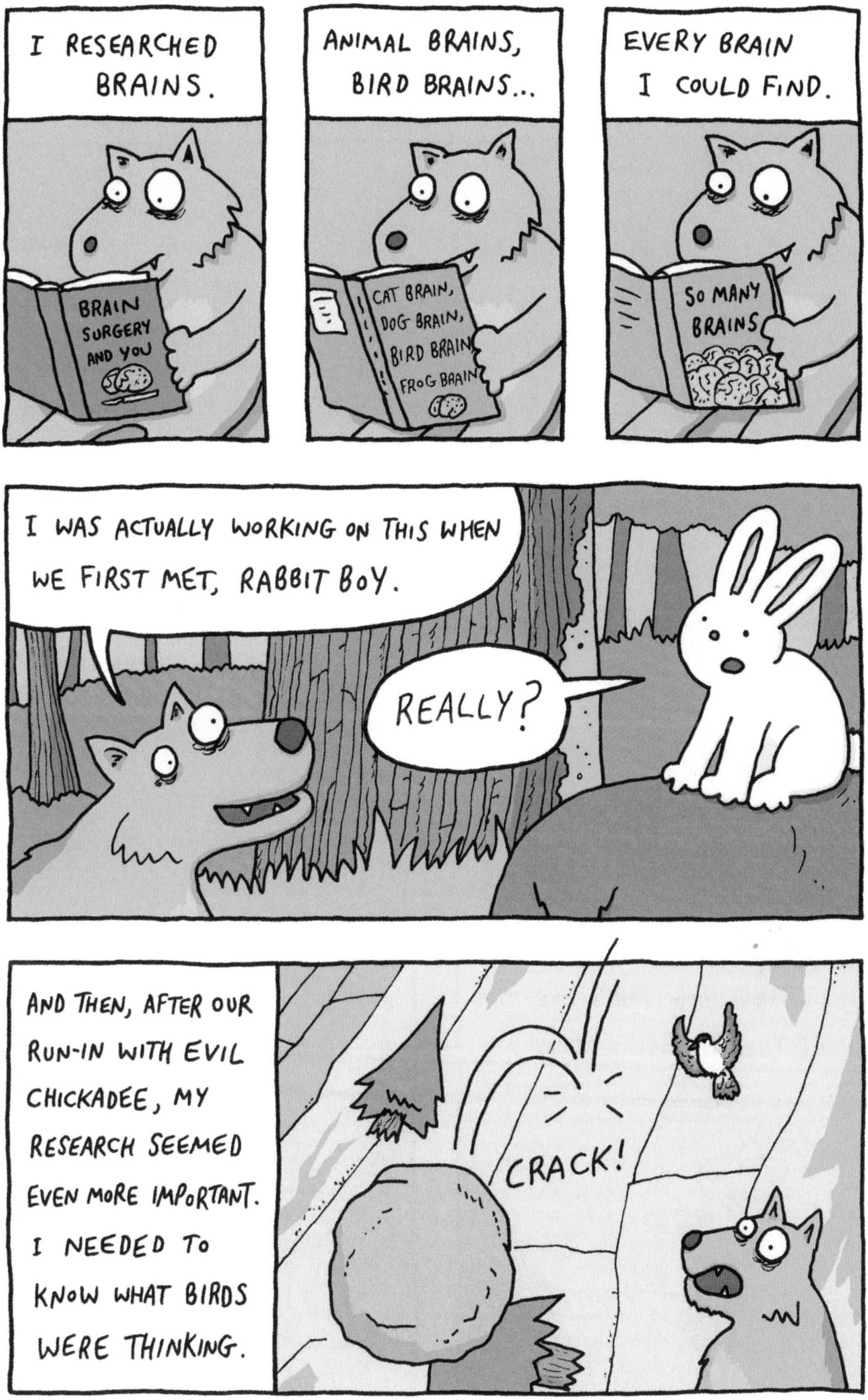
I RESEARCHED BRAINS.
BRAIN SURGERY AND YOU
ANIMAL BRAINS, BIRD BRAINS...
CAT BRAIN, DOG BRAIN, BIRD BRAIN FROG BRAIN
EVERY BRAIN I COULD FIND.
SO MANY BRAINS
I WAS ACTUALLY WORKING ON THIS WHEN WE FIRST MET, RABBIT BOY.
REALLY?
AND THEN, AFTER OUR RUN-IN WITH EVIL CHICKADEE, MY RESEARCH SEEMED EVEN MORE IMPORTANT. I NEEDED TO KNOW WHAT BIRDS WERE THINKING.
CRACK!

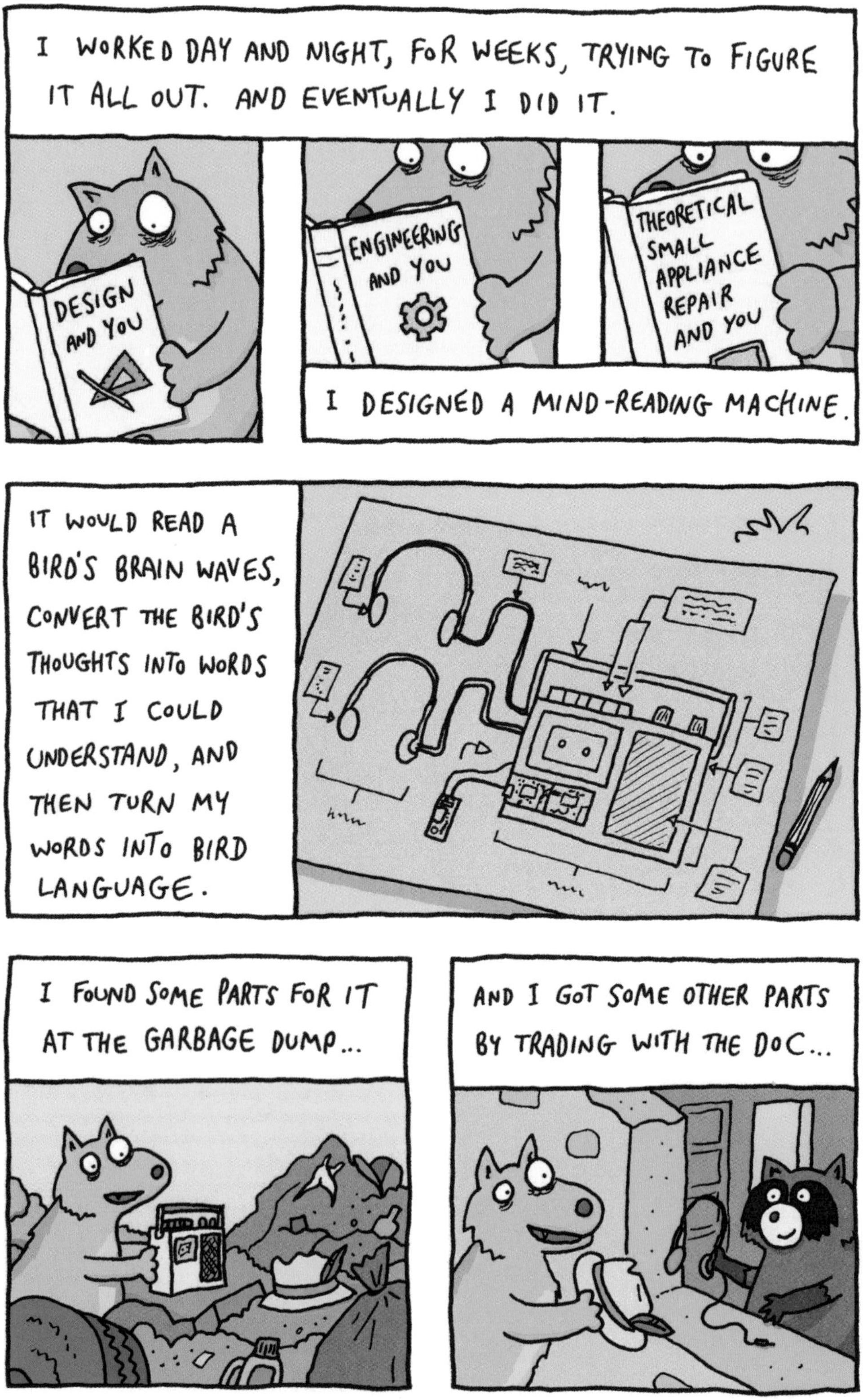
I WORKED DAY AND NIGHT, FOR WEEKS, TRYING TO FIGURE IT ALL OUT. AND EVENTUALLY I DID IT.
DESIGN AND YOU
ENGINEERING AND YOU
THEORETICAL SMALL APPLIANCE REPAIR AND YOU
I DESIGNED A MIND-READING MACHINE.
IT WOULD READ A BIRD'S BRAIN WAVES, CONVERT THE BIRD'S THOUGHTS INTO WORDS THAT I COULD UNDERSTAND, AND THEN TURN MY WORDS INTO BIRD LANGUAGE.
I FOUND SOME PARTS FOR IT AT THE GARBAGE DUMP...
AND I GOT SOME OTHER PARTS BY TRADING WITH THE DOC...

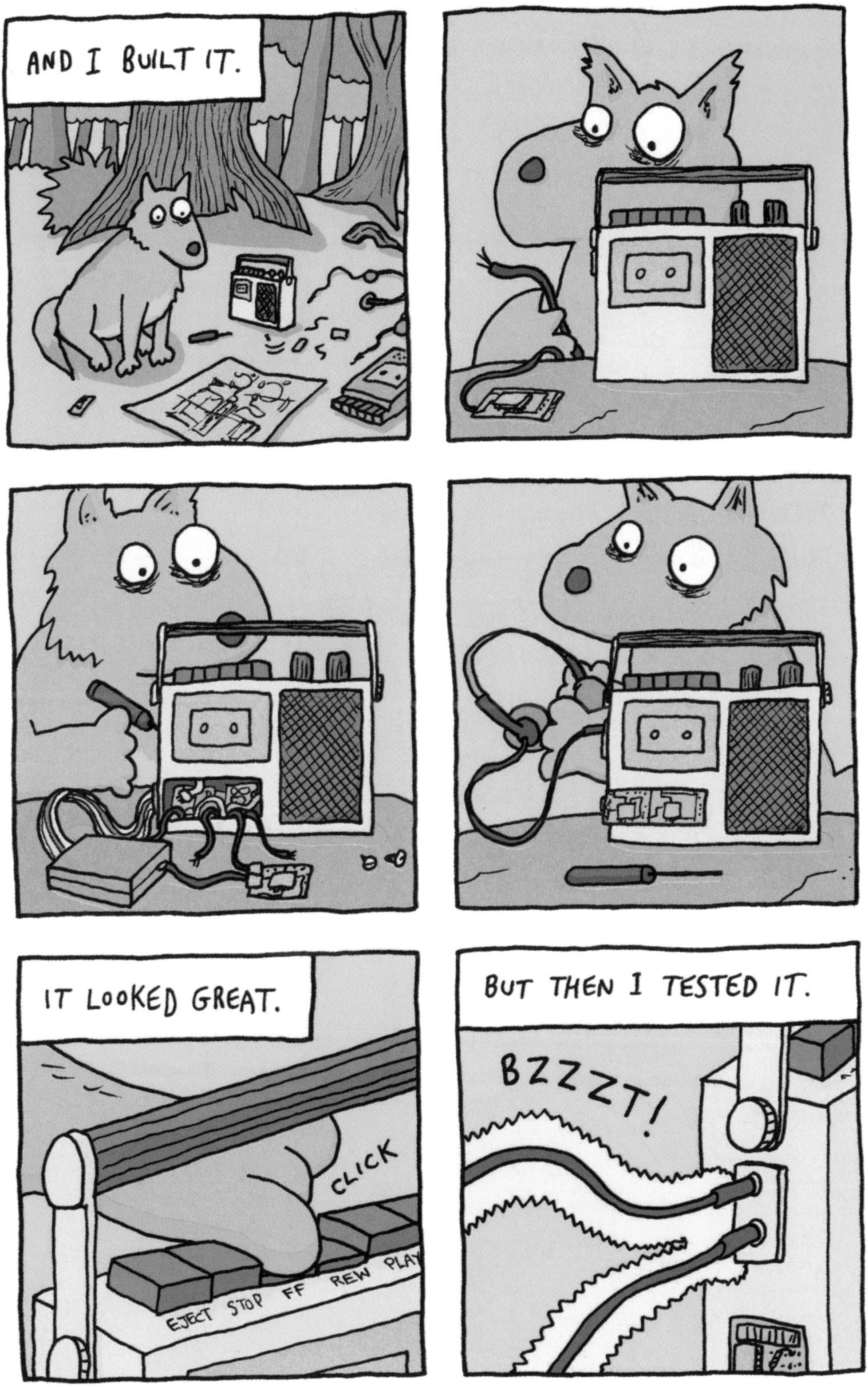
AND I BUILT IT.
IT LOOKED GREAT.
CLICK
EJECT STOP FF REW PLAY
BUT THEN I TESTED IT.
BZZZT!

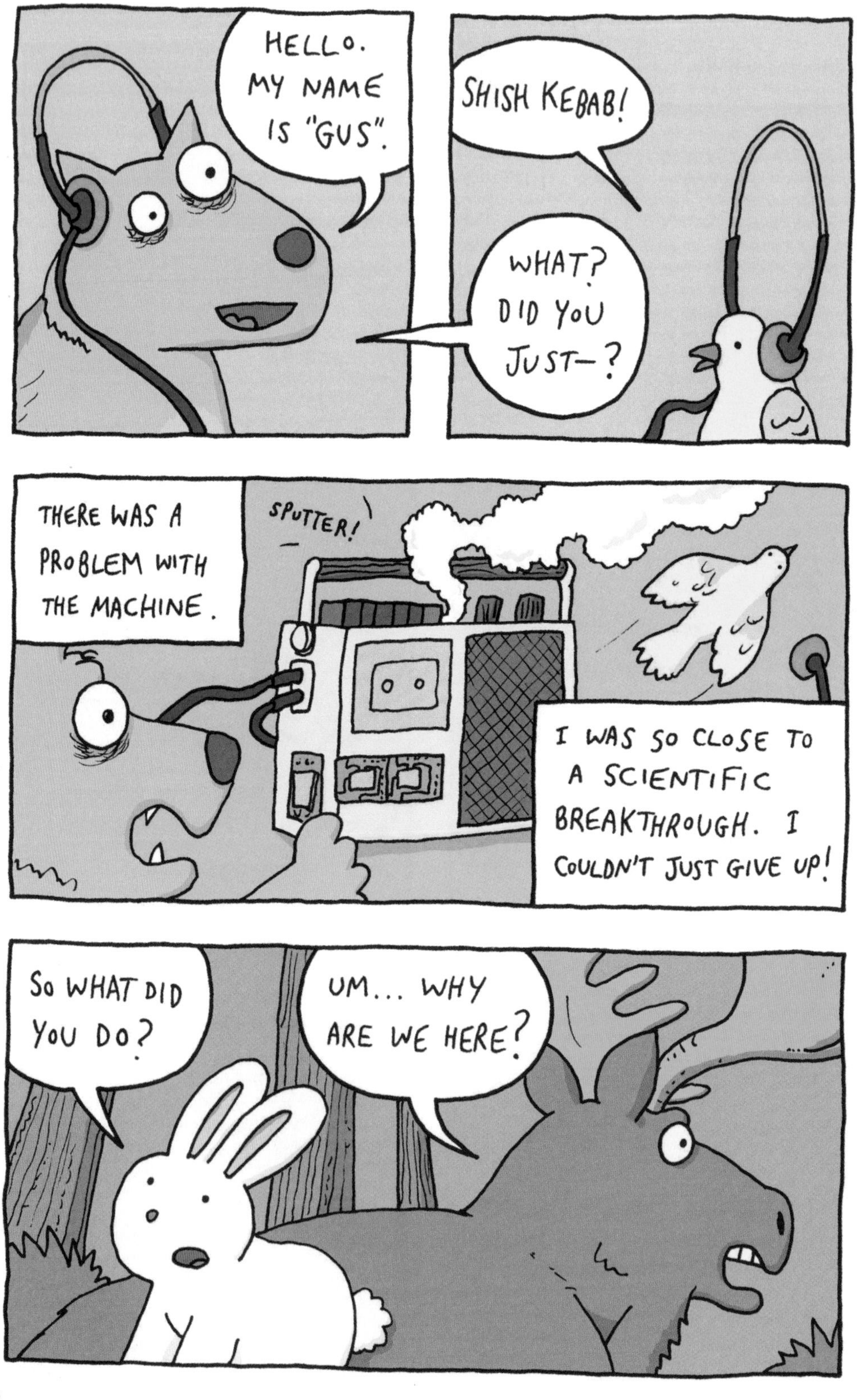
HELLO. MY NAME IS "GUS".
SHISH KEBAB!
WHAT? DID YOU JUST—?
THERE WAS A PROBLEM WITH THE MACHINE.
SPUTTER!
I WAS SO CLOSE TO A SCIENTIFIC BREAKTHROUGH. I COULDN'T JUST GIVE UP!
SO WHAT DID YOU DO?
UM... WHY ARE WE HERE?

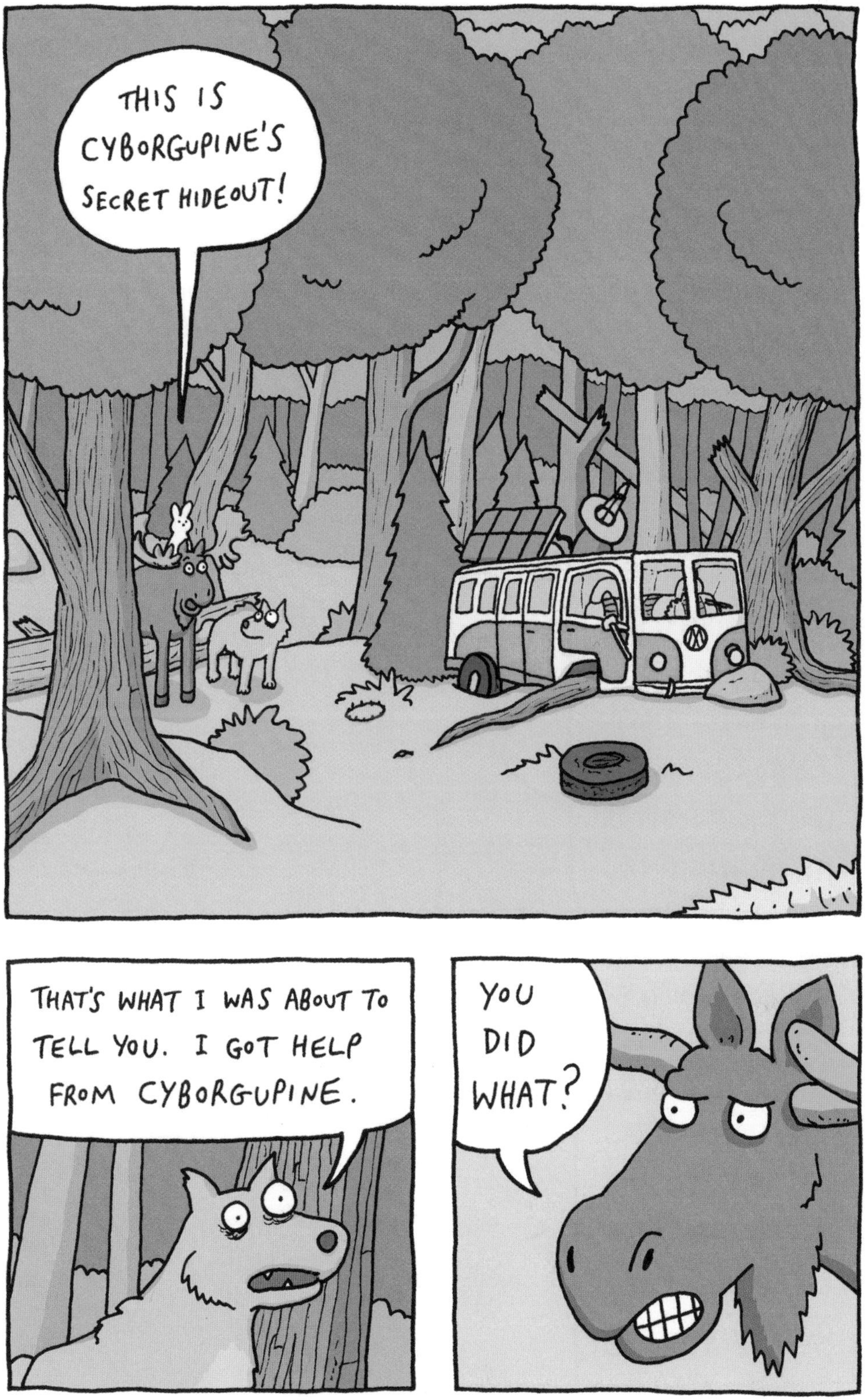
THIS IS CYBORGUPINE'S SECRET HIDEOUT!
THAT'S WHAT I WAS ABOUT TO TELL YOU. I GOT HELP FROM CYBORGUPINE.
YOU DID WHAT?

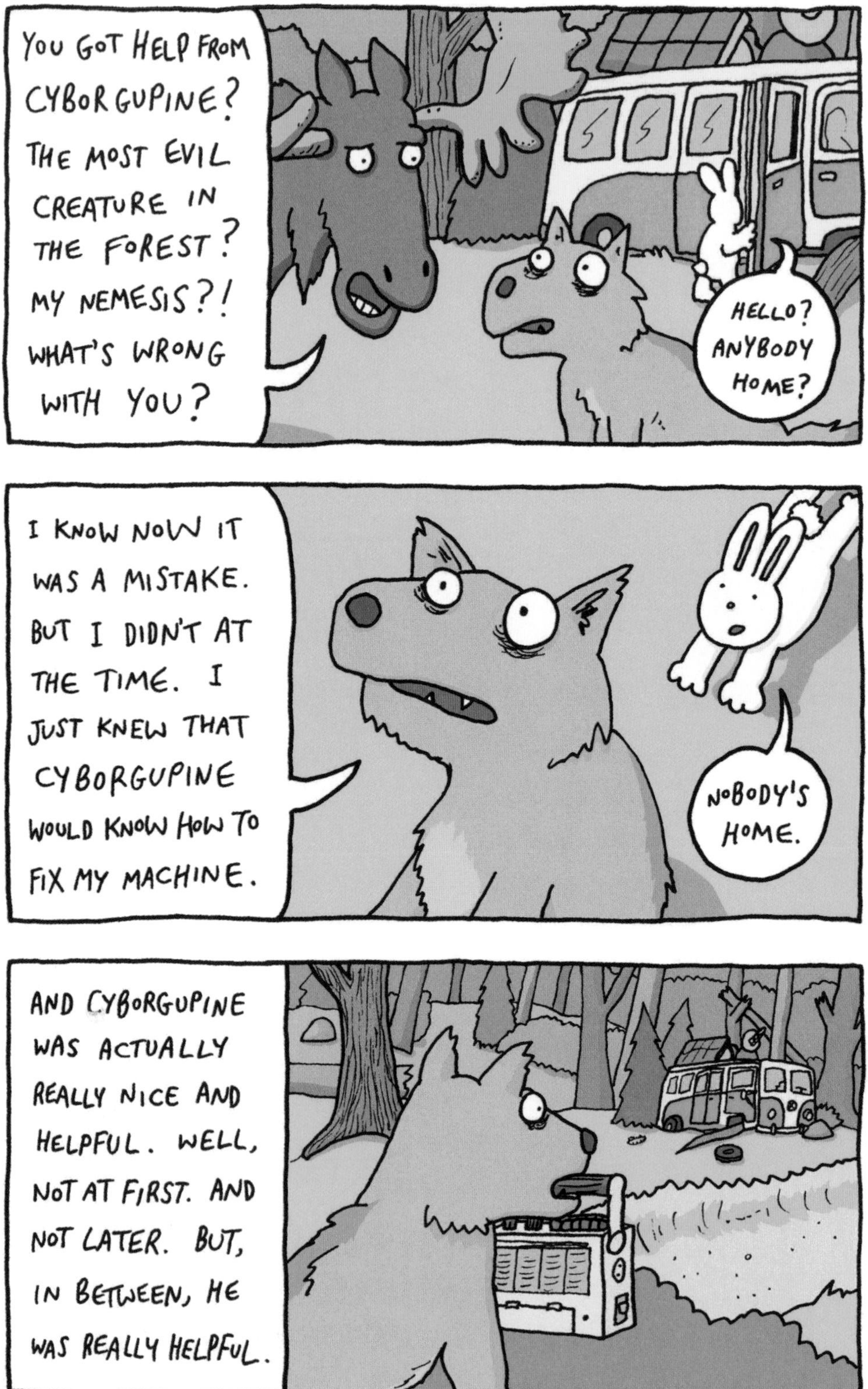

YOU GOT HELP FROM CYBORGUPINE? THE MOST EVIL CREATURE IN THE FOREST? MY NEMESIS?! WHAT'S WRONG WITH YOU?
HELLO? ANYBODY HOME?
I KNOW NOW IT WAS A MISTAKE. BUT I DIDN'T AT THE TIME. I JUST KNEW THAT CYBORGUPINE WOULD KNOW HOW TO FIX MY MACHINE.
NOBODY'S HOME.
AND CYBORGUPINE WAS ACTUALLY REALLY NICE AND HELPFUL. WELL, NOT AT FIRST. AND NOT LATER. BUT, IN BETWEEN, HE WAS REALLY HELPFUL.

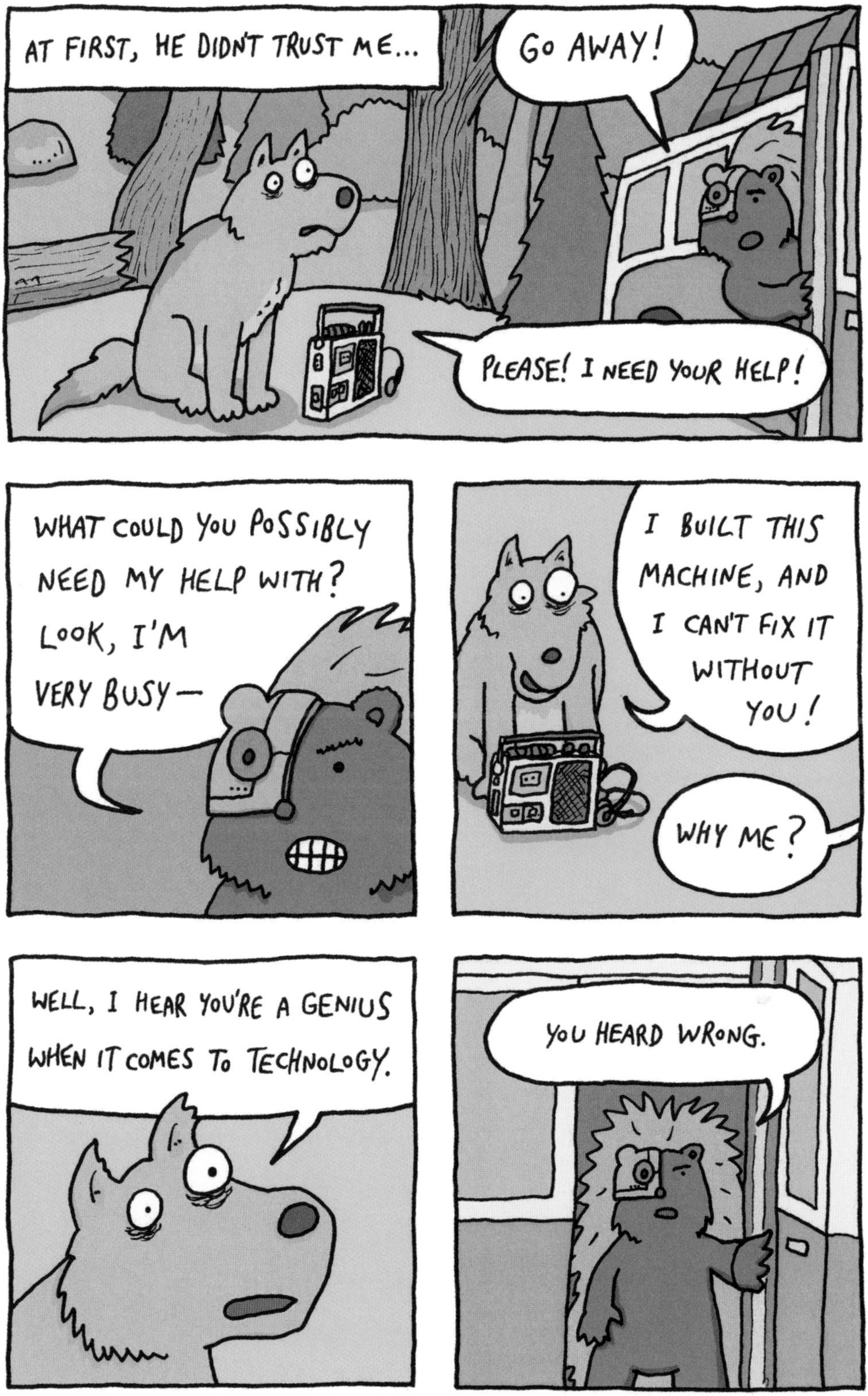
AT FIRST, HE DIDN'T TRUST ME...
GO AWAY!
PLEASE! I NEED YOUR HELP!
WHAT COULD YOU POSSIBLY NEED MY HELP WITH? LOOK, I'M VERY BUSY—
I BUILT THIS MACHINE, AND I CAN'T FIX IT WITHOUT YOU!
WHY ME?
WELL, I HEAR YOU'RE A GENIUS WHEN IT COMES TO TECHNOLOGY.
YOU HEARD WRONG.

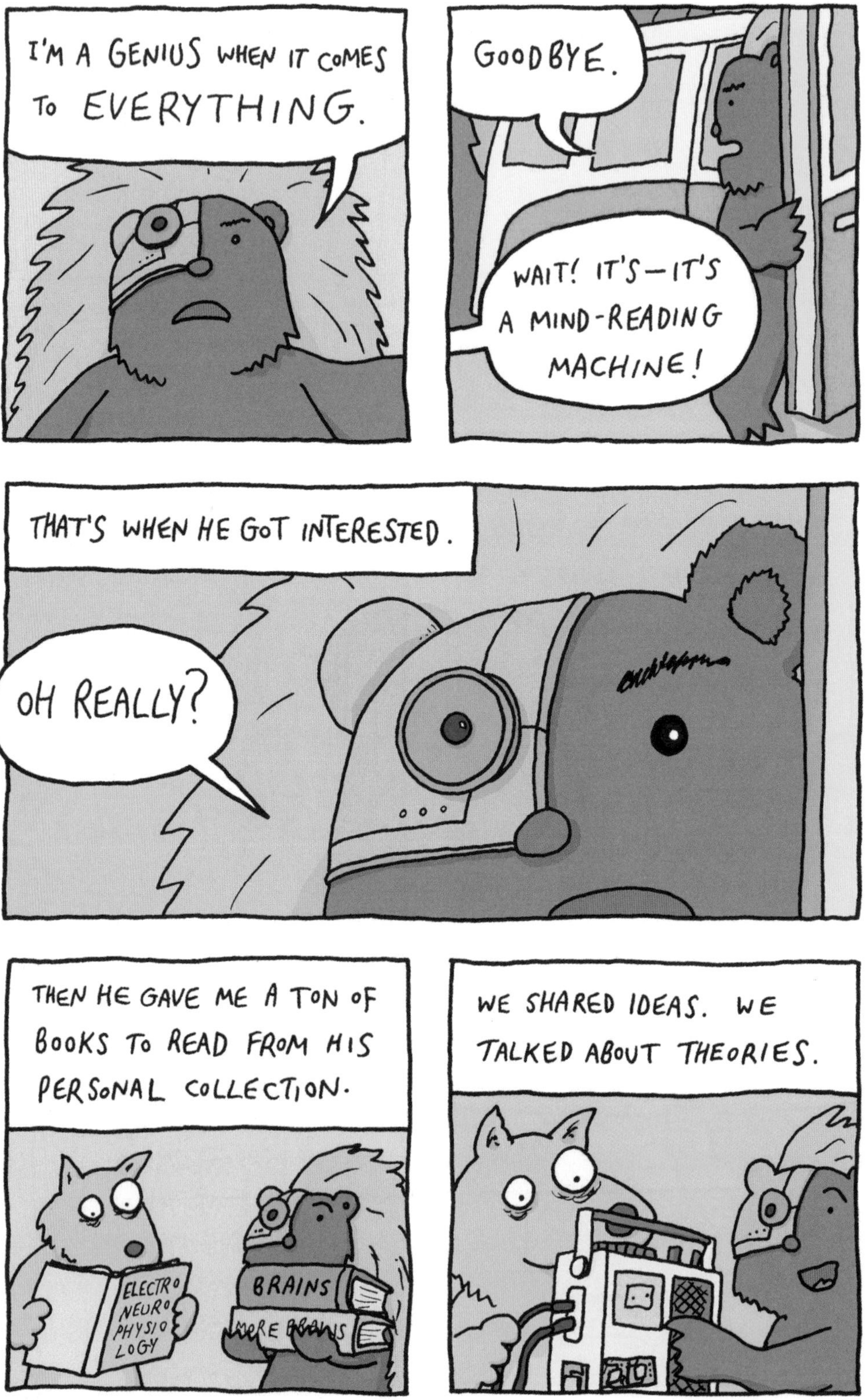
I'M A GENIUS WHEN IT COMES TO EVERYTHING.
GOODBYE.
WAIT! IT'S—IT'S A MIND-READING MACHINE!
THAT'S WHEN HE GOT INTERESTED.
OH REALLY?
THEN HE GAVE ME A TON OF BOOKS TO READ FROM HIS PERSONAL COLLECTION.
ELECTRO NEURO PHYSIO LOGY
BRAINS
MORE BRAINS
WE SHARED IDEAS. WE TALKED ABOUT THEORIES.

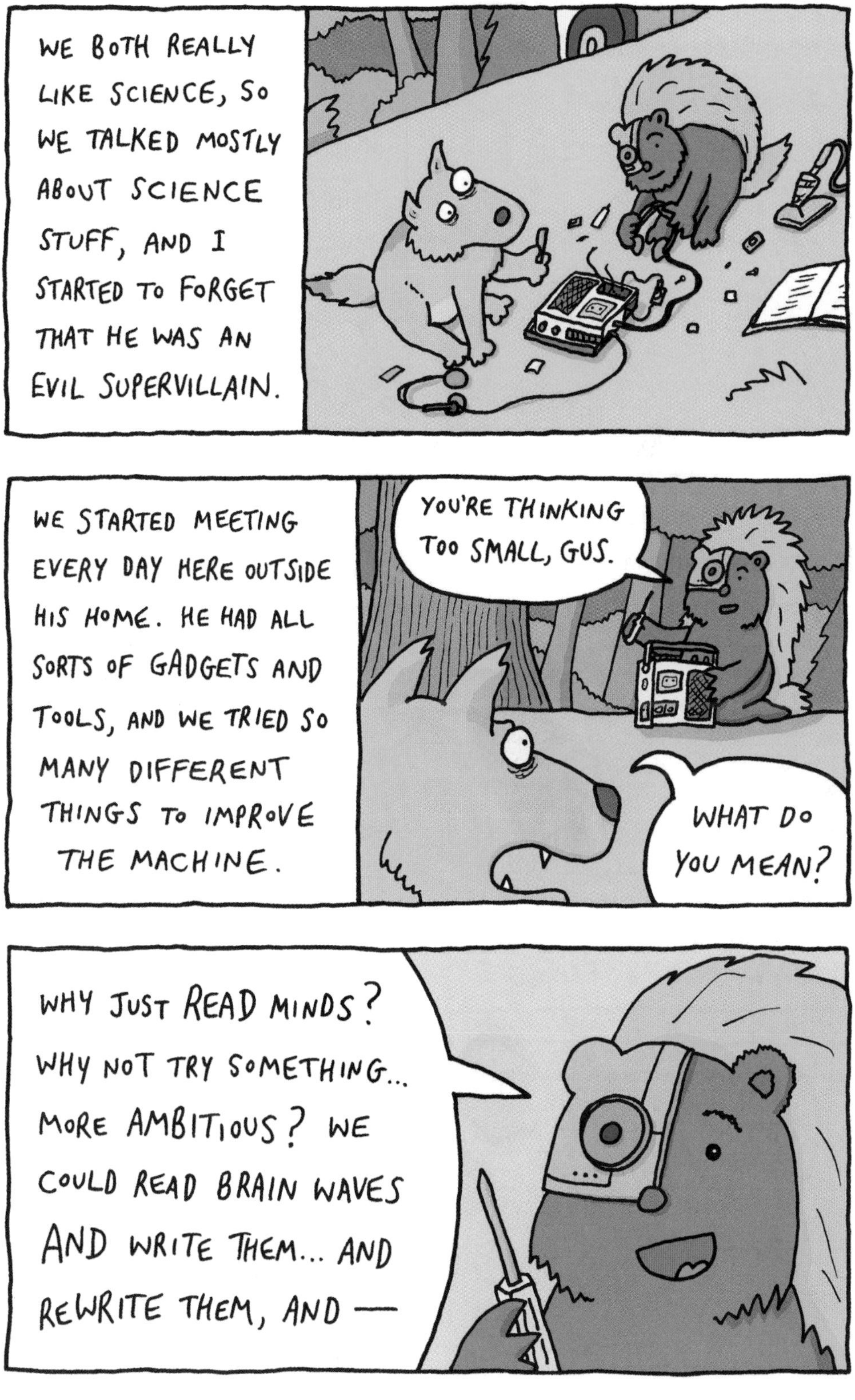
WE BOTH REALLY LIKE SCIENCE, SO WE TALKED MOSTLY ABOUT SCIENCE STUFF, AND I STARTED TO FORGET THAT HE WAS AN EVIL SUPERVILLAIN.
WE STARTED MEETING EVERY DAY HERE OUTSIDE HIS HOME. HE HAD ALL SORTS OF GADGETS AND TOOLS, AND WE TRIED SO MANY DIFFERENT THINGS TO IMPROVE THE MACHINE.
YOU'RE THINKING TOO SMALL, GUS.
WHAT DO YOU MEAN?
WHY JUST READ MINDS? WHY NOT TRY SOMETHING... MORE AMBITIOUS? WE COULD READ BRAIN WAVES AND WRITE THEM... AND REWRITE THEM, AND —

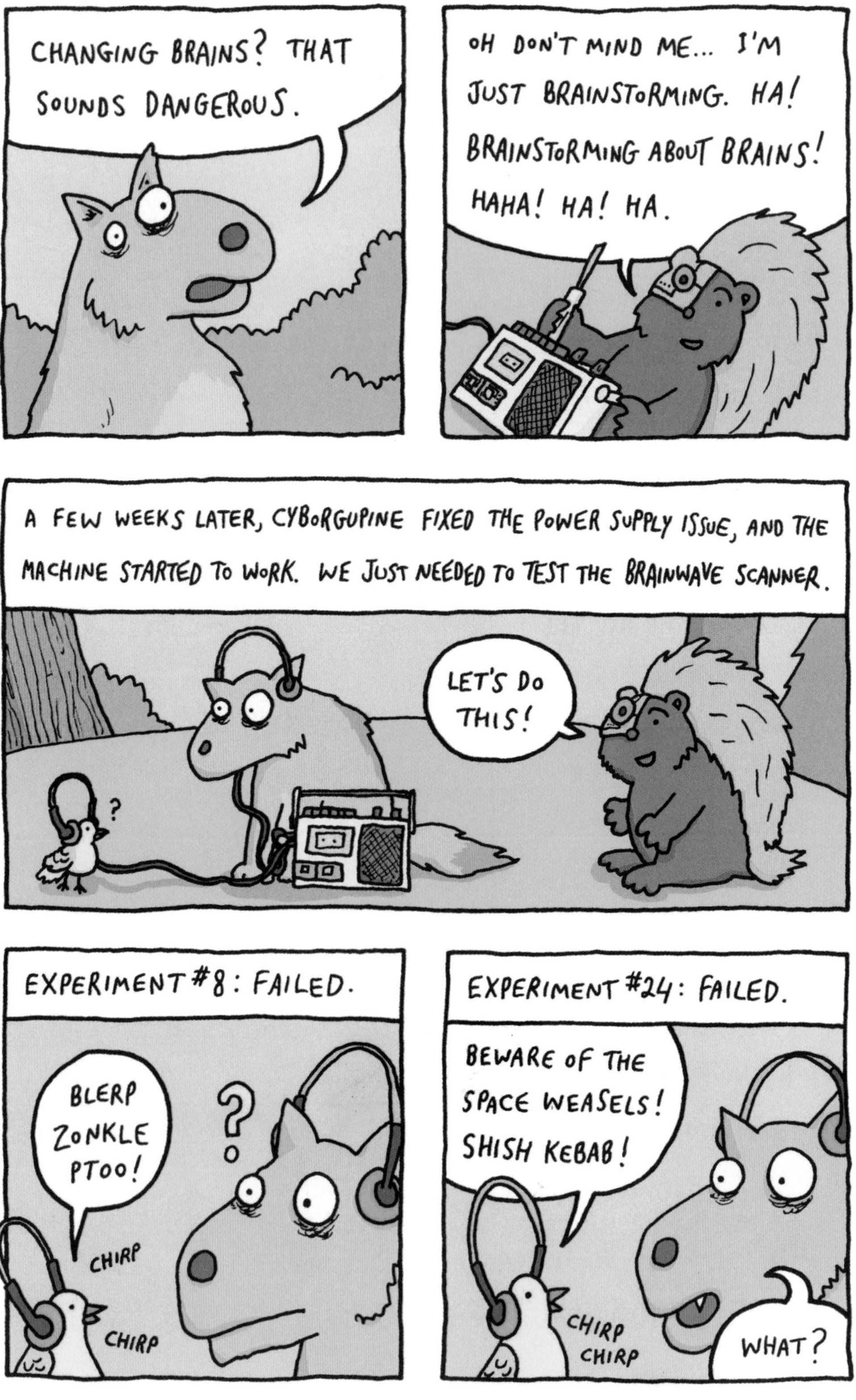
CHANGING BRAINS? THAT SOUNDS DANGEROUS.
OH DON'T MIND ME... I'M JUST BRAINSTORMING. HA! BRAINSTORMING ABOUT BRAINS! HAHA! HA! HA.
A FEW WEEKS LATER, CYBORGUPINE FIXED THE POWER SUPPLY ISSUE, AND THE MACHINE STARTED TO WORK. WE JUST NEEDED TO TEST THE BRAINWAVE SCANNER.
?
LET'S DO THIS!
EXPERIMENT #8: FAILED.
BLERP ZONKLE PTOO!
?
CHIRP
CHIRP
EXPERIMENT #24: FAILED.
BEWARE OF THE SPACE WEASELS! SHISH KEBAB!
CHIRP CHIRP
WHAT?

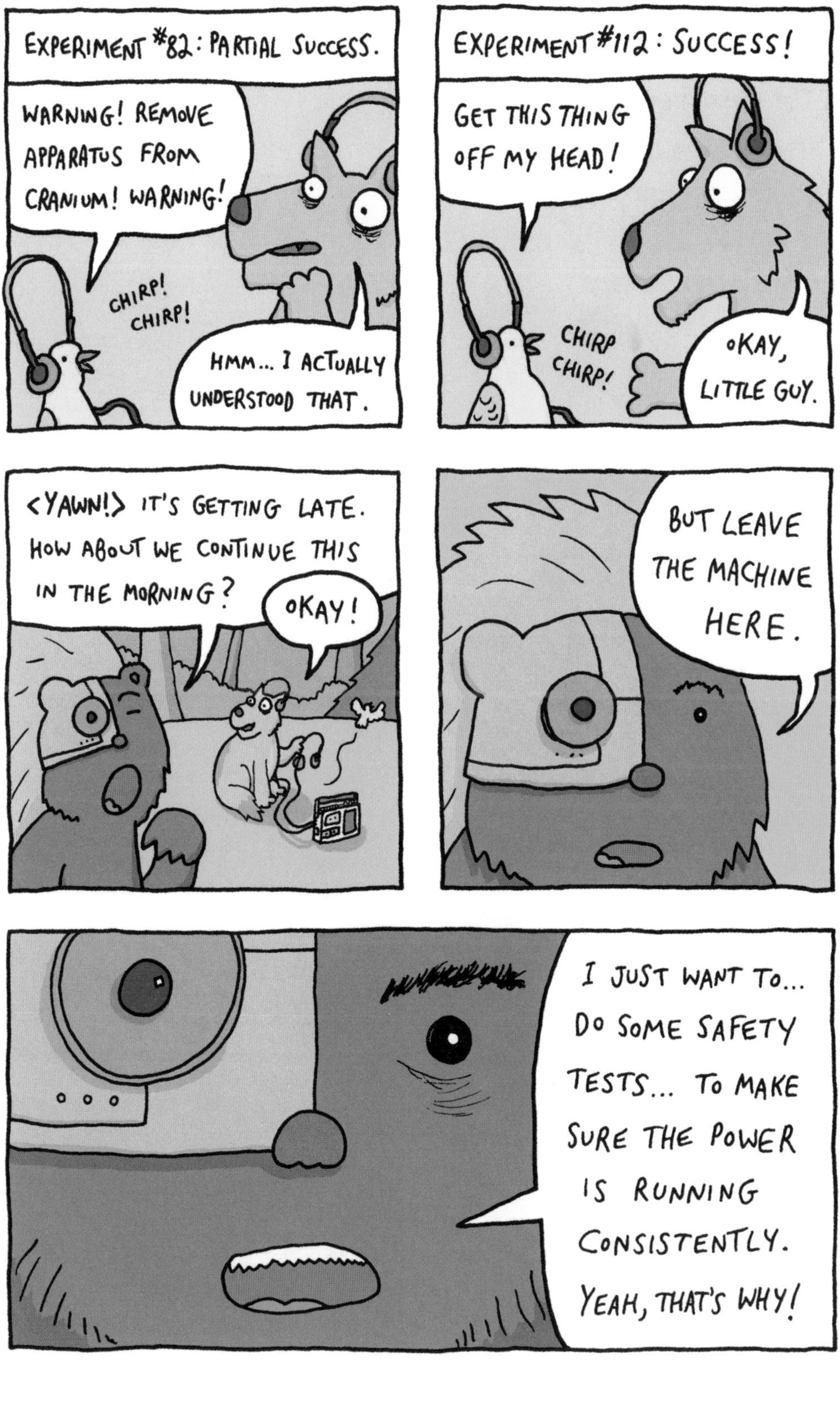
EXPERIMENT #82: PARTIAL SUCCESS.
WARNING! REMOVE APPARATUS FROM CRANIUM! WARNING!
CHIRP! CHIRP!
HMM... I ACTUALLY UNDERSTOOD THAT.
EXPERIMENT #112: SUCCESS!
GET THIS THING OFF MY HEAD!
CHIRP CHIRP!
OKAY, LITTLE GUY.
<YAWN!> IT'S GETTING LATE. HOW ABOUT WE CONTINUE THIS IN THE MORNING?
OKAY!
BUT LEAVE THE MACHINE HERE.
I JUST WANT TO... DO SOME SAFETY TESTS... TO MAKE SURE THE POWER IS RUNNING CONSISTENTLY. YEAH, THAT'S WHY!

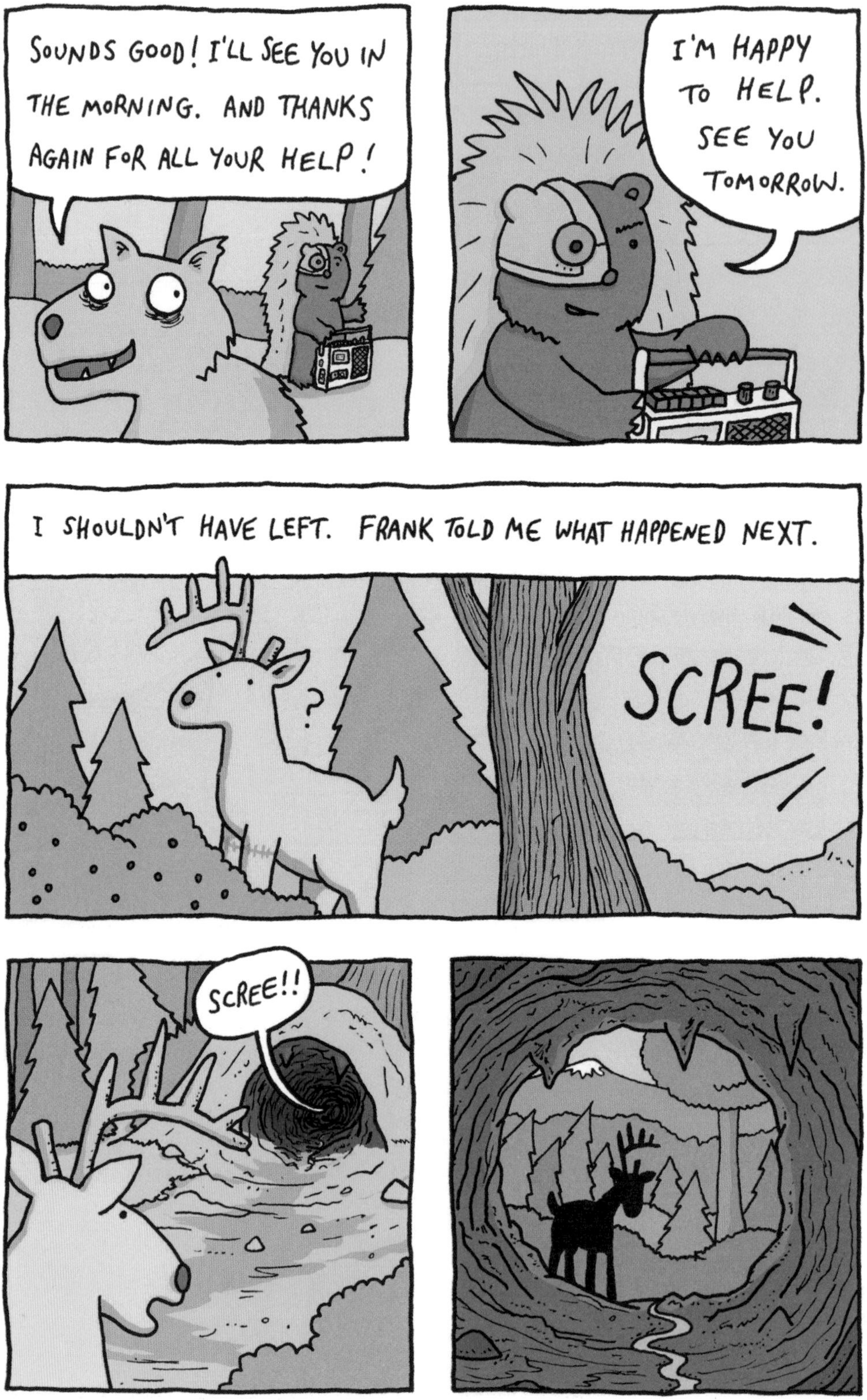
SOUNDS GOOD! I'LL SEE YOU IN THE MORNING. AND THANKS AGAIN FOR ALL YOUR HELP!
I'M HAPPY TO HELP. SEE YOU TOMORROW.
I SHOULDN'T HAVE LEFT. FRANK TOLD ME WHAT HAPPENED NEXT.
?
SCREE!
SCREE!!

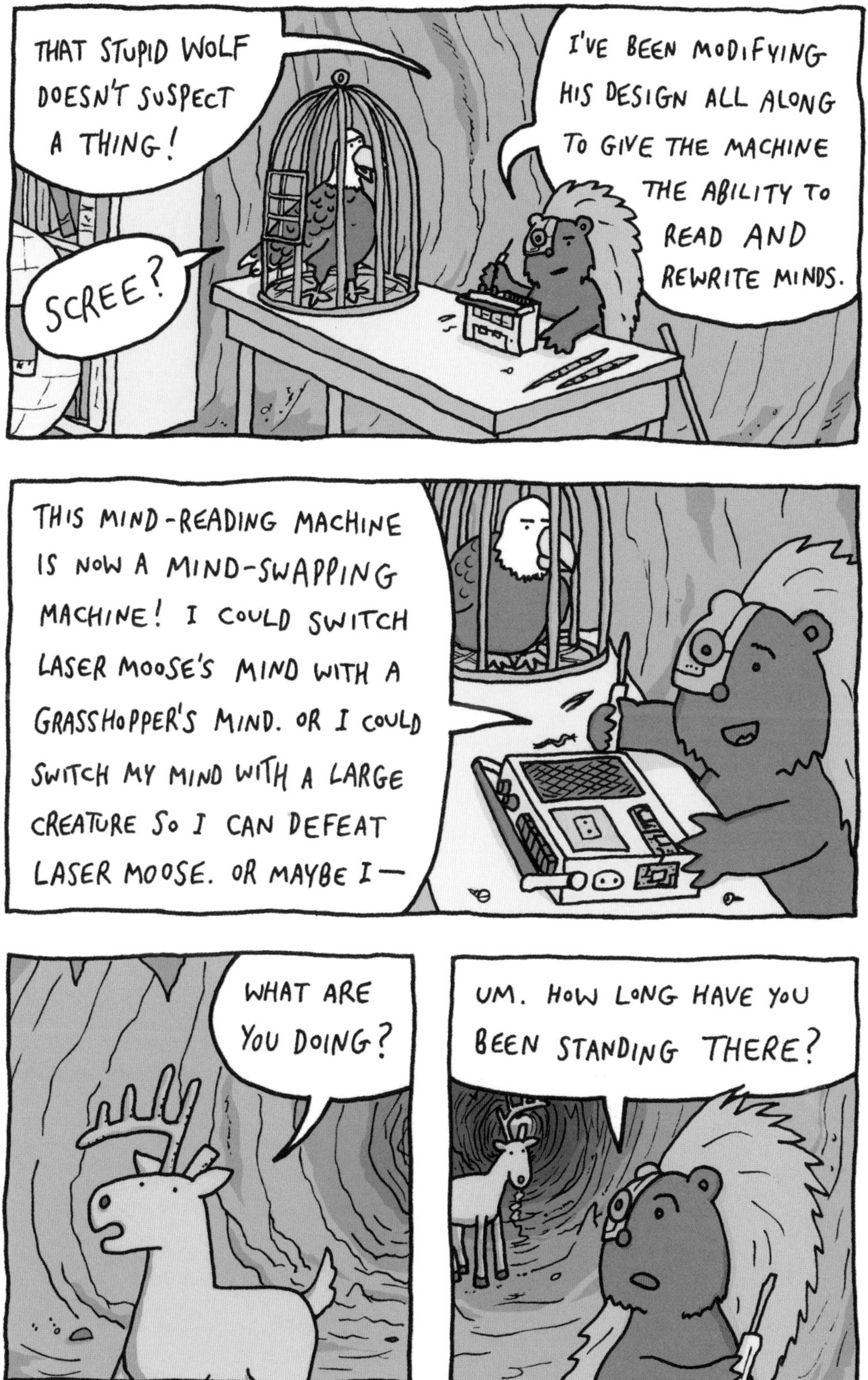
THAT STUPID WOLF DOESN'T SUSPECT A THING!
I'VE BEEN MODIFYING HIS DESIGN ALL ALONG TO GIVE THE MACHINE THE ABILITY TO READ AND REWRITE MINDS.
SCREE?
THIS MIND-READING MACHINE IS NOW A MIND-SWAPPING MACHINE! I COULD SWITCH LASER MOOSE'S MIND WITH A GRASSHOPPER'S MIND. OR I COULD SWITCH MY MIND WITH A LARGE CREATURE SO I CAN DEFEAT LASER MOOSE. OR MAYBE I—
WHAT ARE YOU DOING?
UM. HOW LONG HAVE YOU BEEN STANDING THERE?

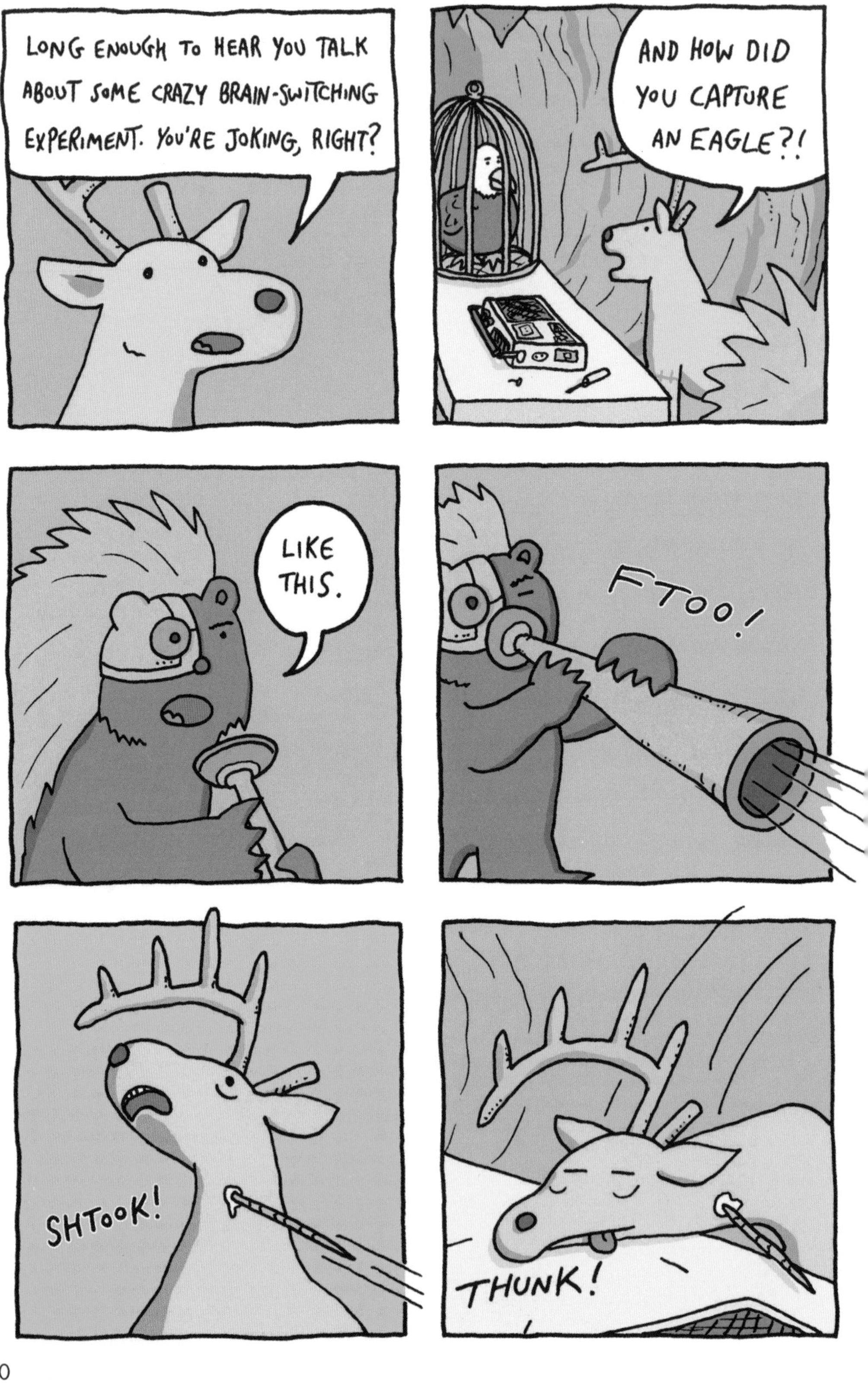
LONG ENOUGH TO HEAR YOU TALK ABOUT SOME CRAZY BRAIN-SWITCHING EXPERIMENT. YOU'RE JOKING, RIGHT?
AND HOW DID YOU CAPTURE AN EAGLE?!
LIKE THIS.
FTOO!
SHTOOK!
THUNK!

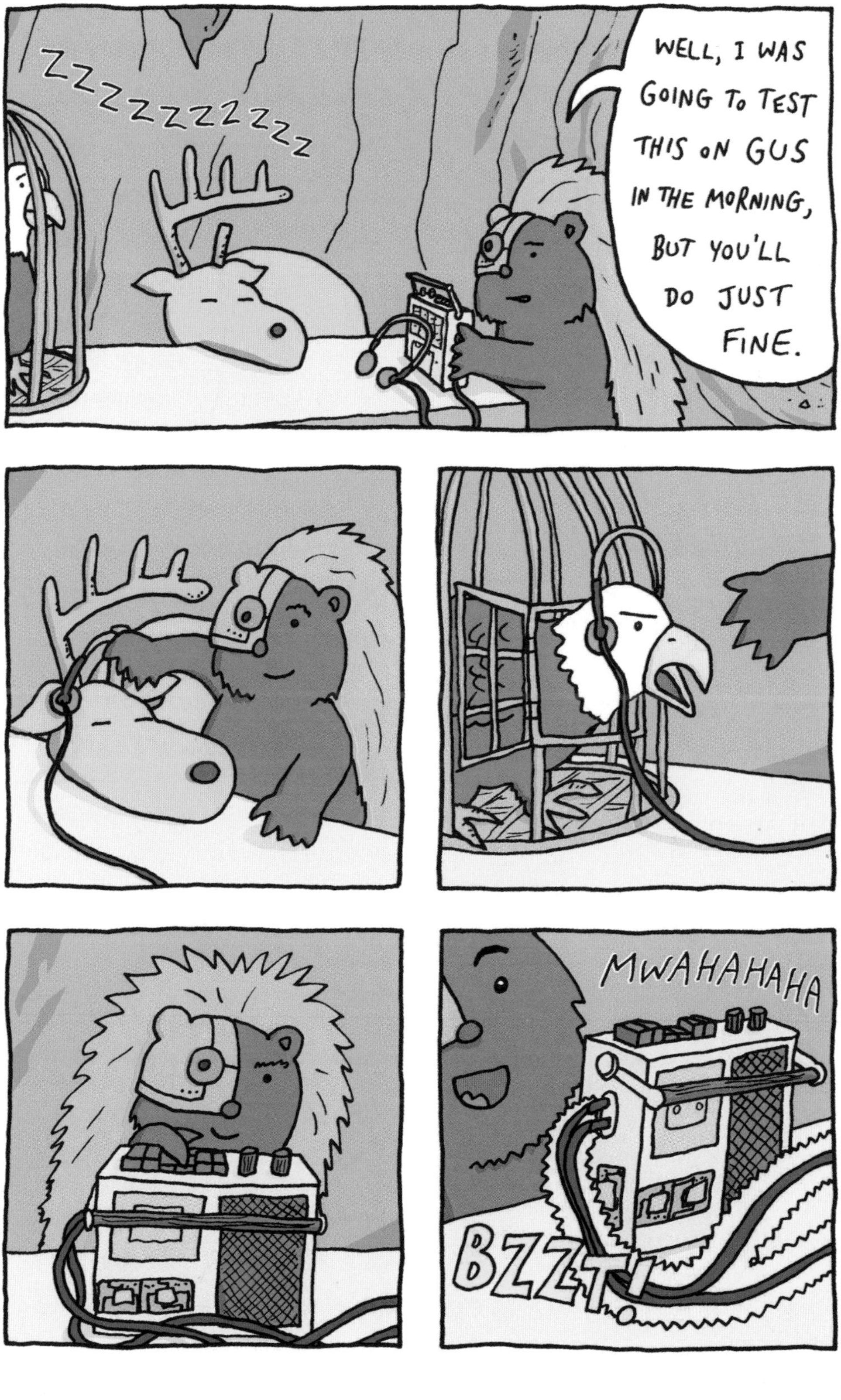
ZZZZZZZZZZZZ
WELL, I WAS GOING TO TEST THIS ON GUS IN THE MORNING, BUT YOU'LL DO JUST FINE.
MWAHAHAHAHA
BZZT!

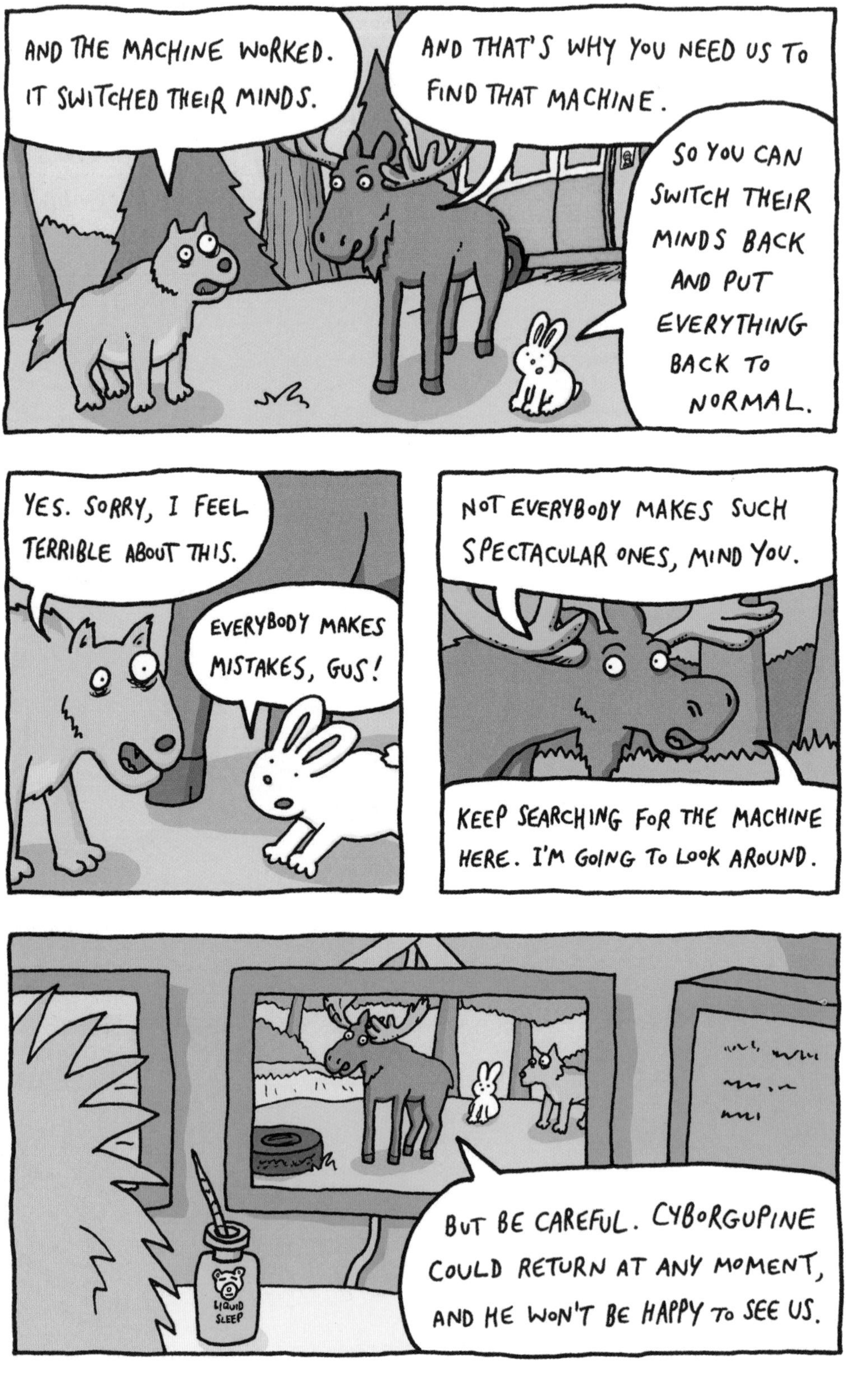
AND THE MACHINE WORKED. IT SWITCHED THEIR MINDS.
AND THAT'S WHY YOU NEED US TO FIND THAT MACHINE.
SO YOU CAN SWITCH THEIR MINDS BACK AND PUT EVERYTHING BACK TO NORMAL.
YES. SORRY, I FEEL TERRIBLE ABOUT THIS.
EVERYBODY MAKES MISTAKES, GUS!
NOT EVERYBODY MAKES SUCH SPECTACULAR ONES, MIND YOU.
KEEP SEARCHING FOR THE MACHINE HERE. I'M GOING TO LOOK AROUND.
LIQUID SLEEP
BUT BE CAREFUL. CYBORGUPINE COULD RETURN AT ANY MOMENT, AND HE WON'T BE HAPPY TO SEE US.

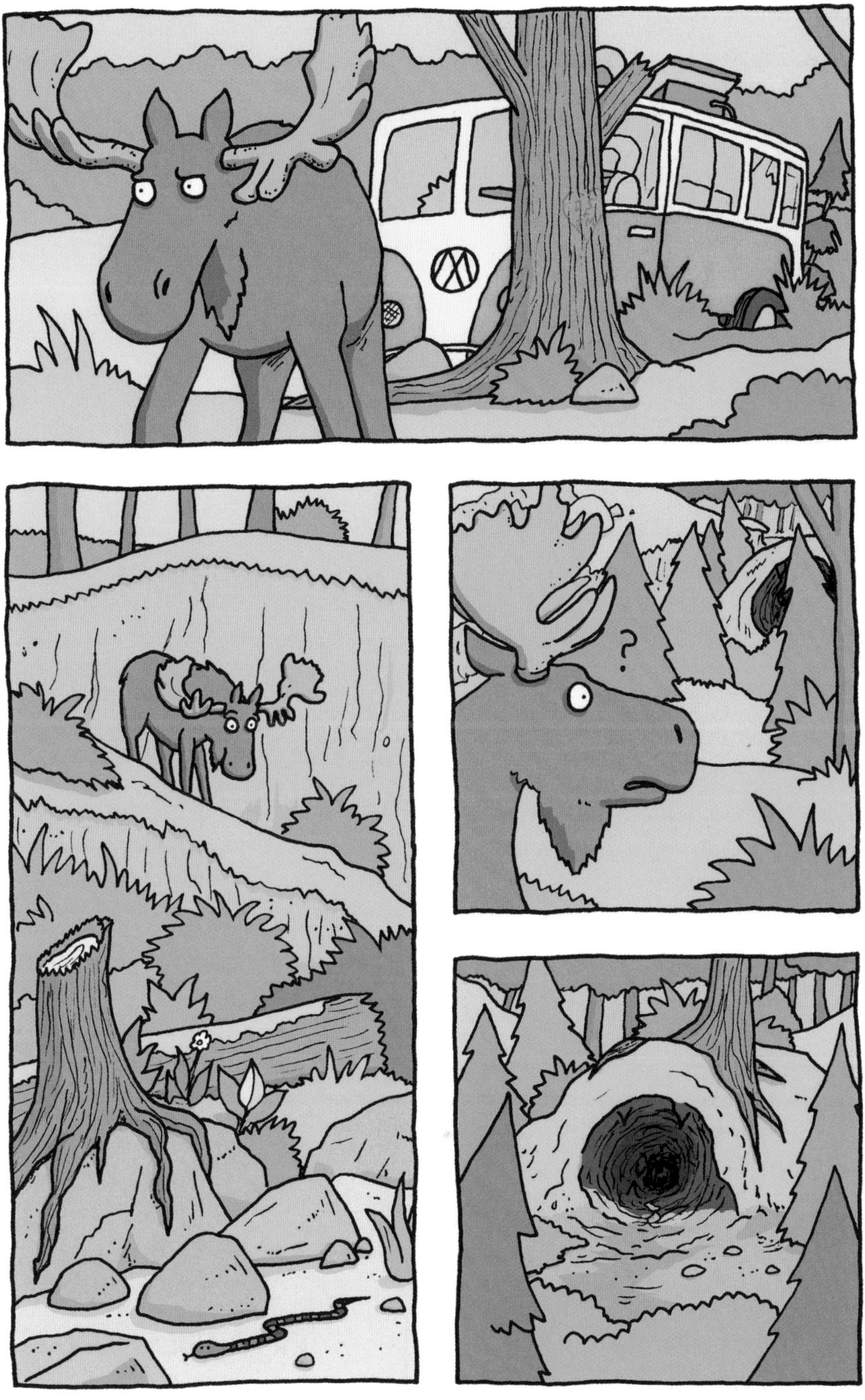
?

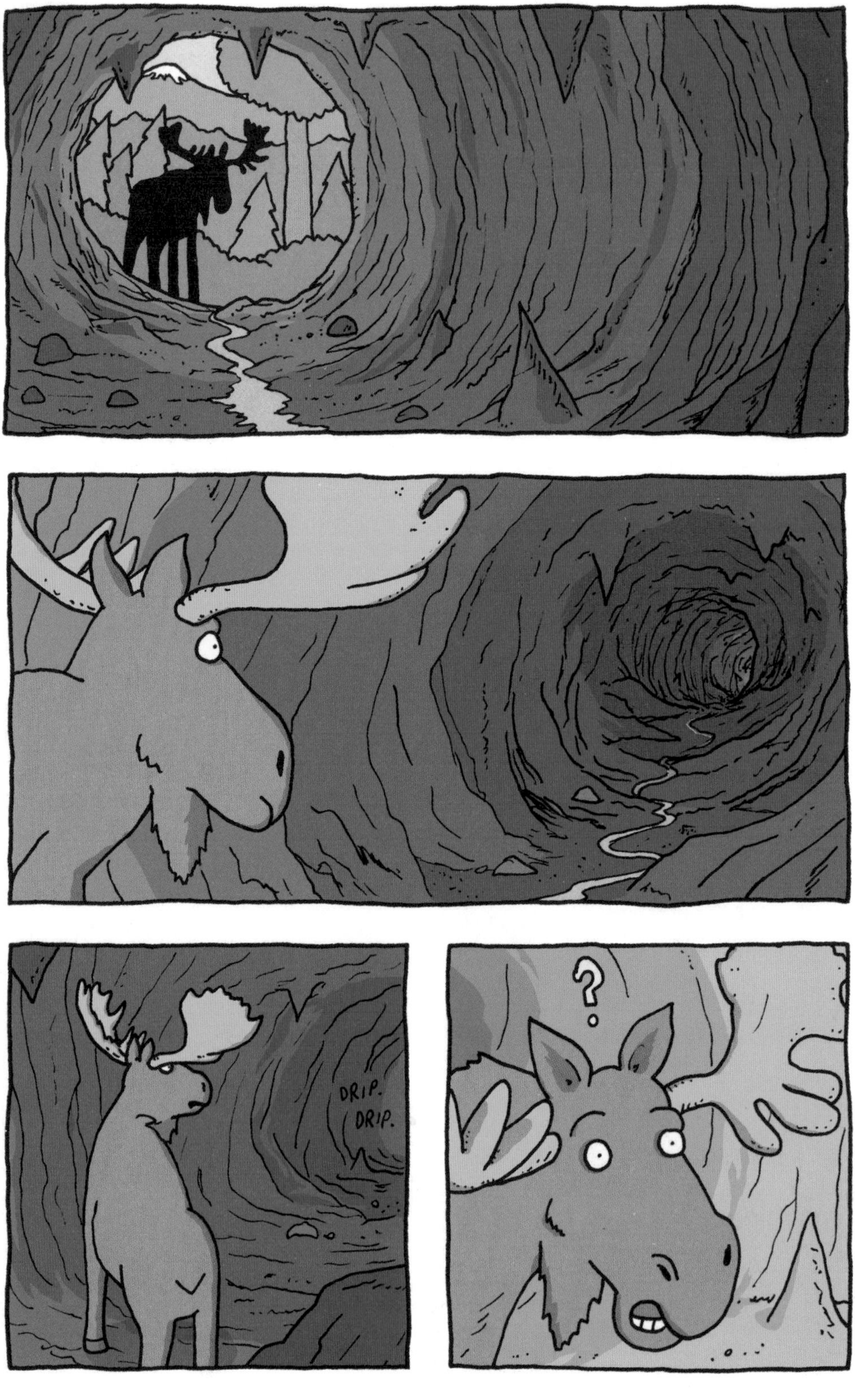
DRIP.
DRIP.
?

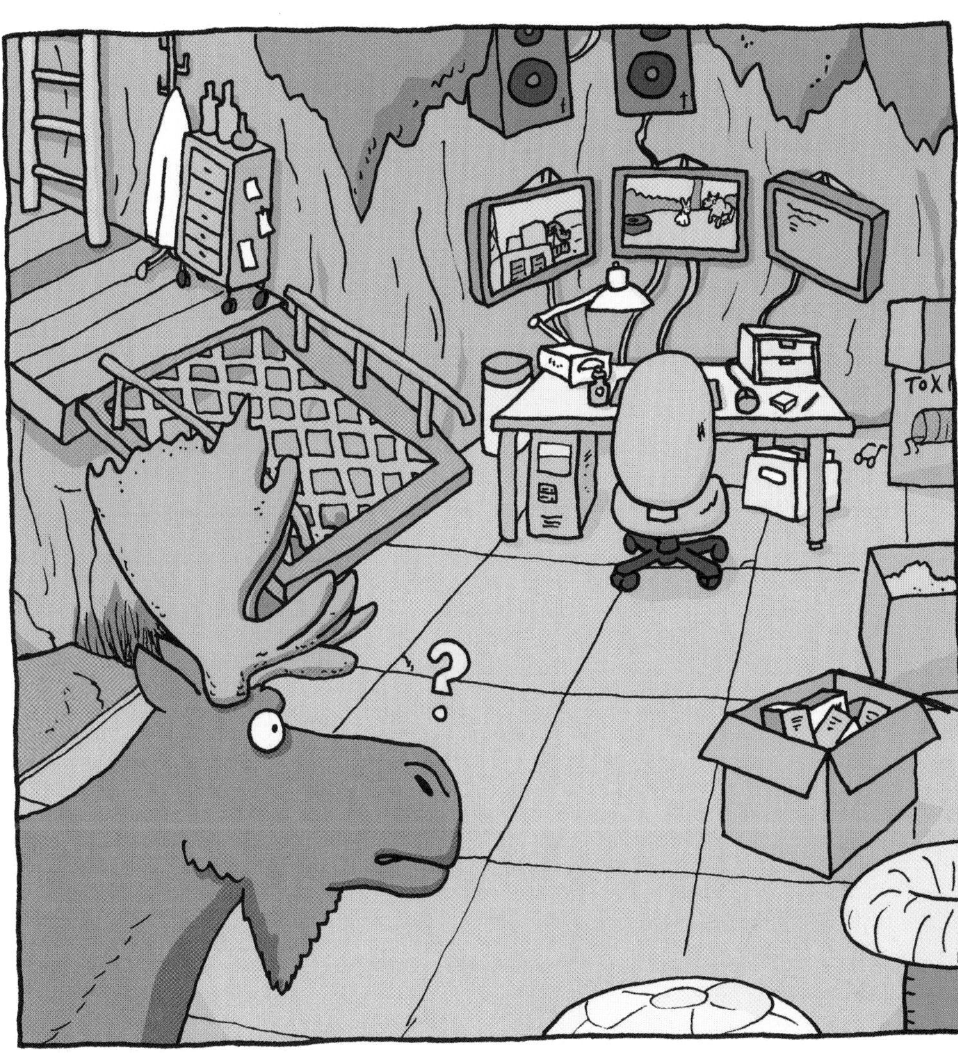
TOX

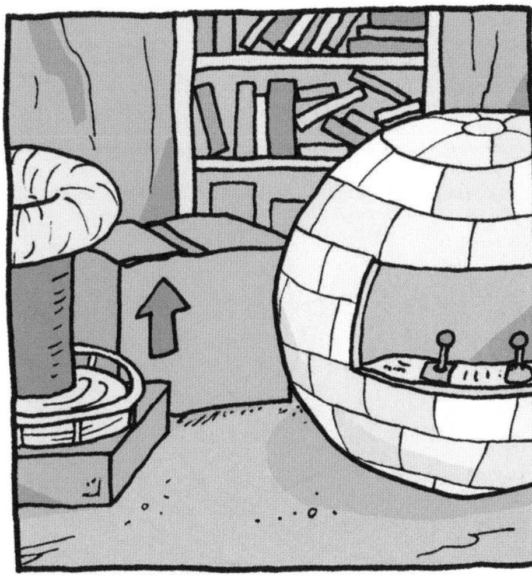

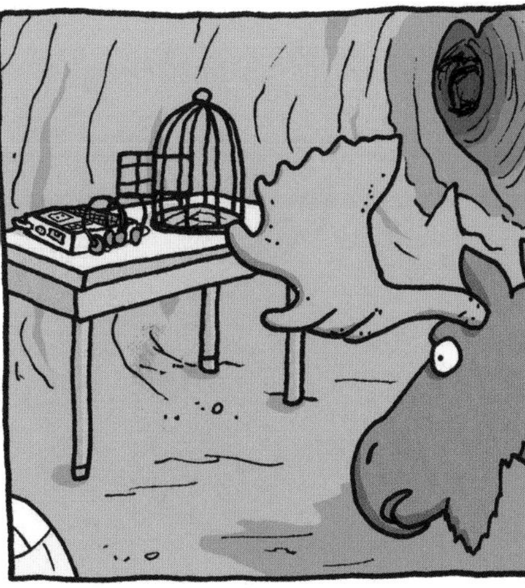

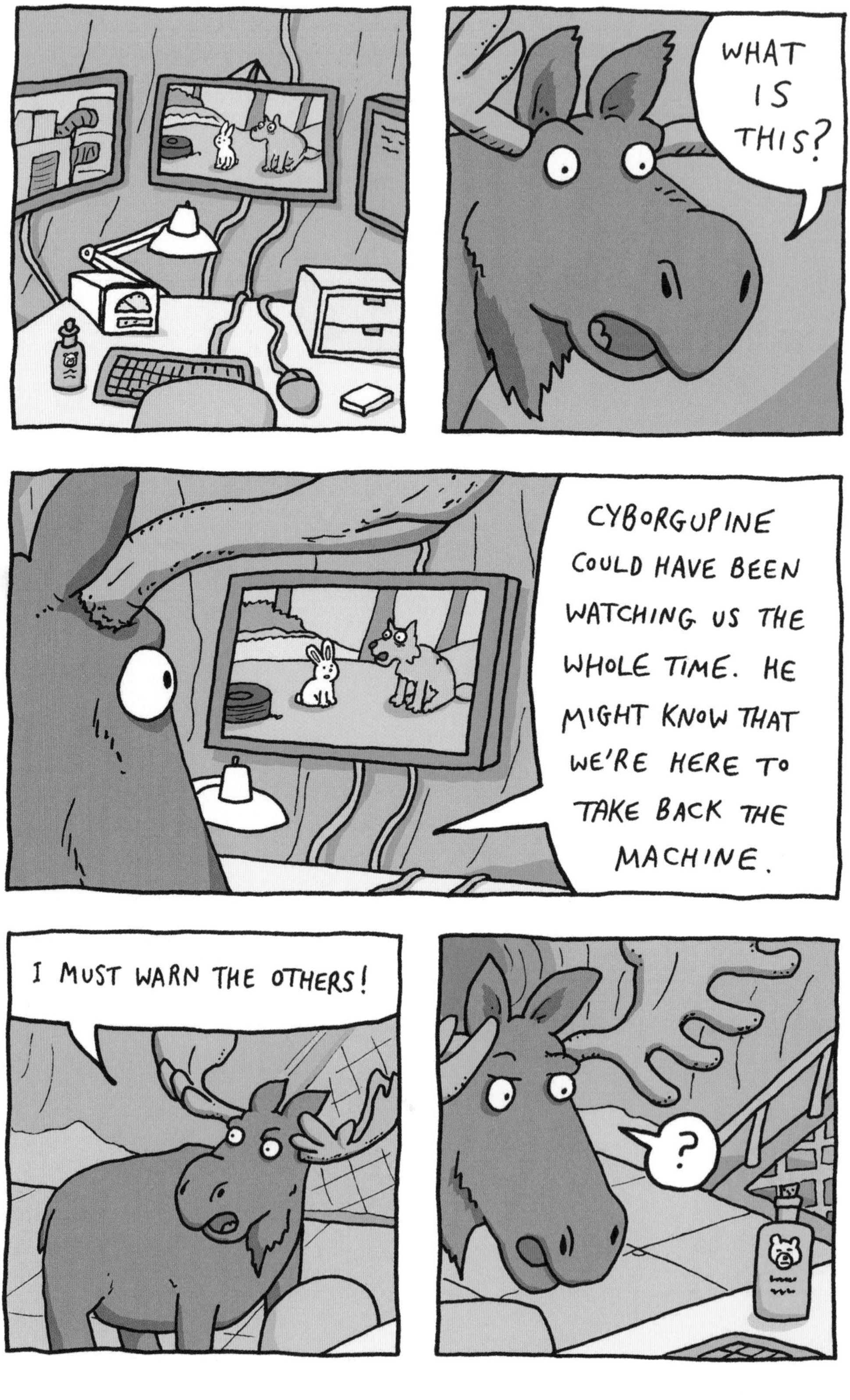
WHAT IS THIS?
CYBORGUPINE COULD HAVE BEEN WATCHING US THE WHOLE TIME. HE MIGHT KNOW THAT WE'RE HERE TO TAKE BACK THE MACHINE.
I MUST WARN THE OTHERS!
?

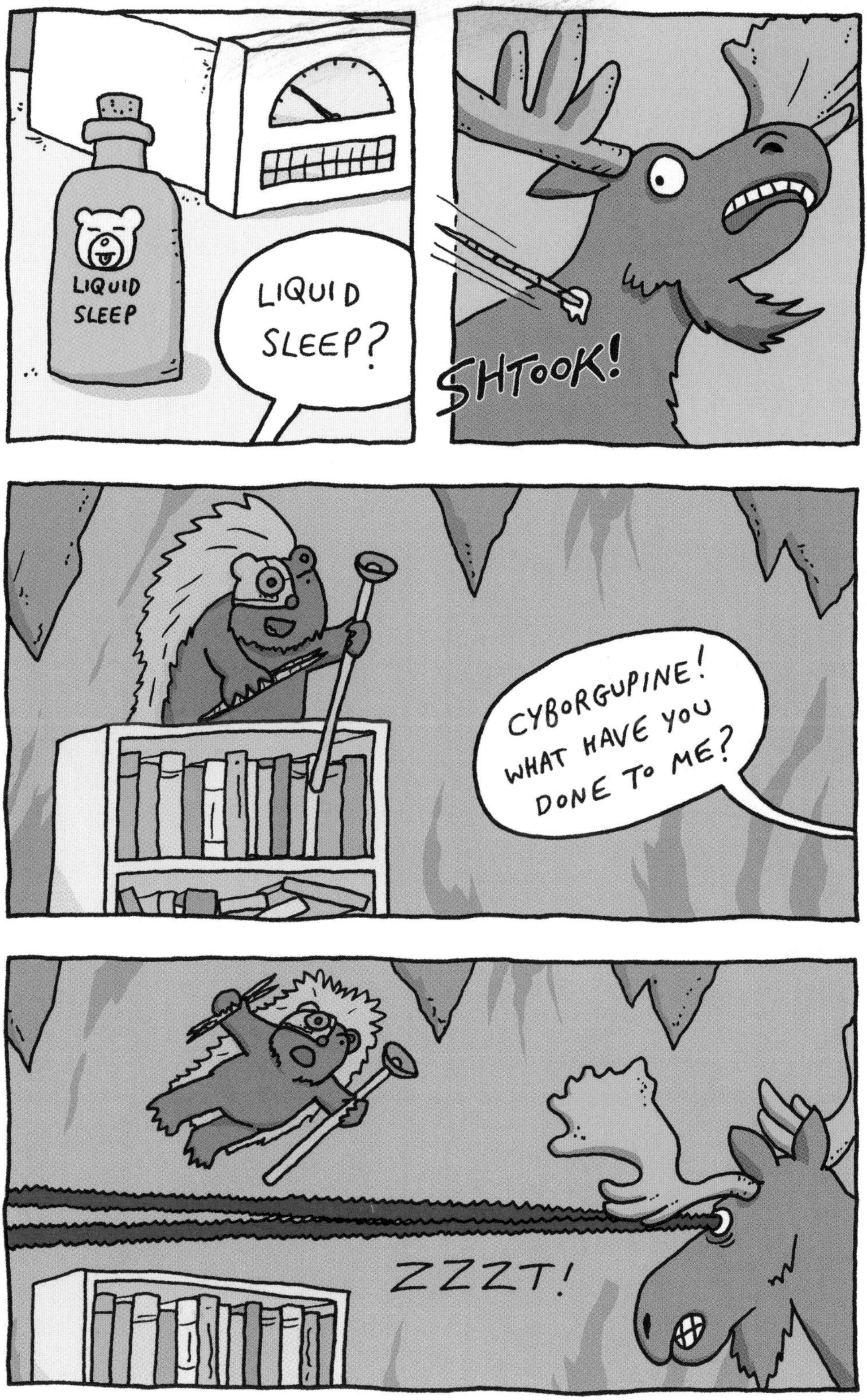
LIQUID SLEEP
LIQUID SLEEP?
SHTOOK!
CYBORGUPINE! WHAT HAVE YOU DONE TO ME?
ZZZT!

ZZZT!
ZZZT!
ZZZT!
SHUK!
SHUK!

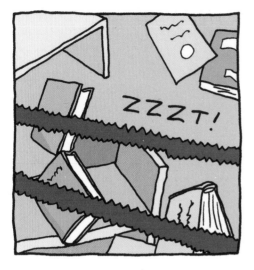

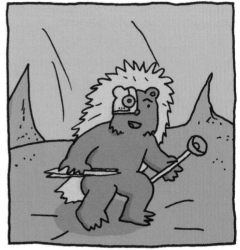

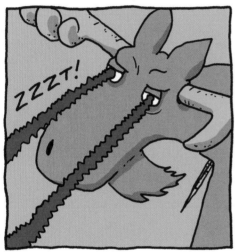

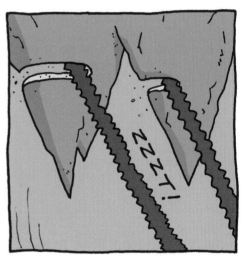

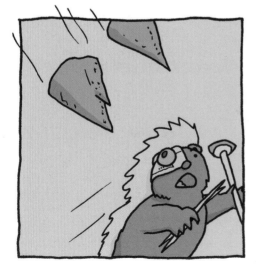

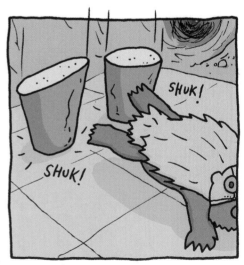

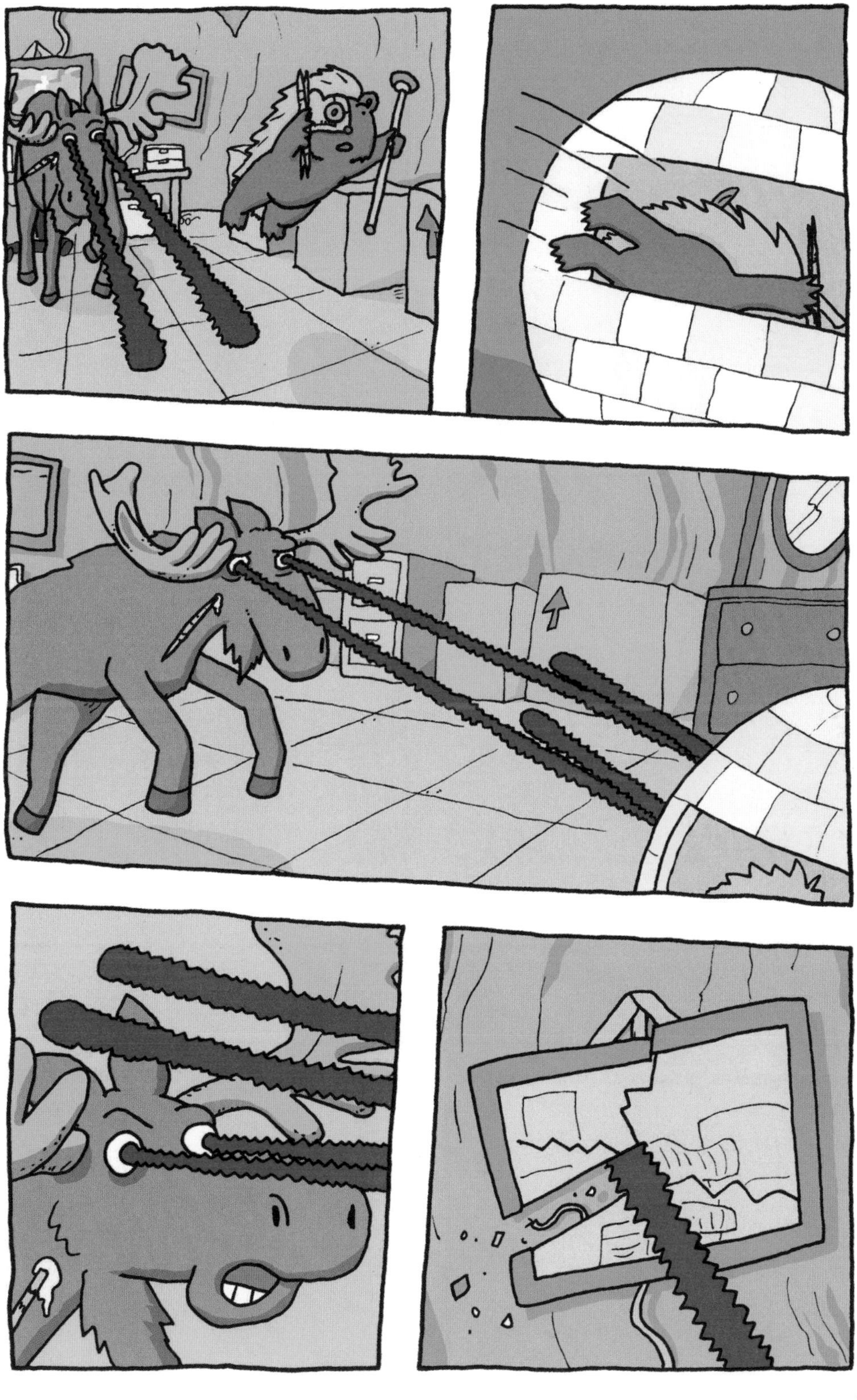

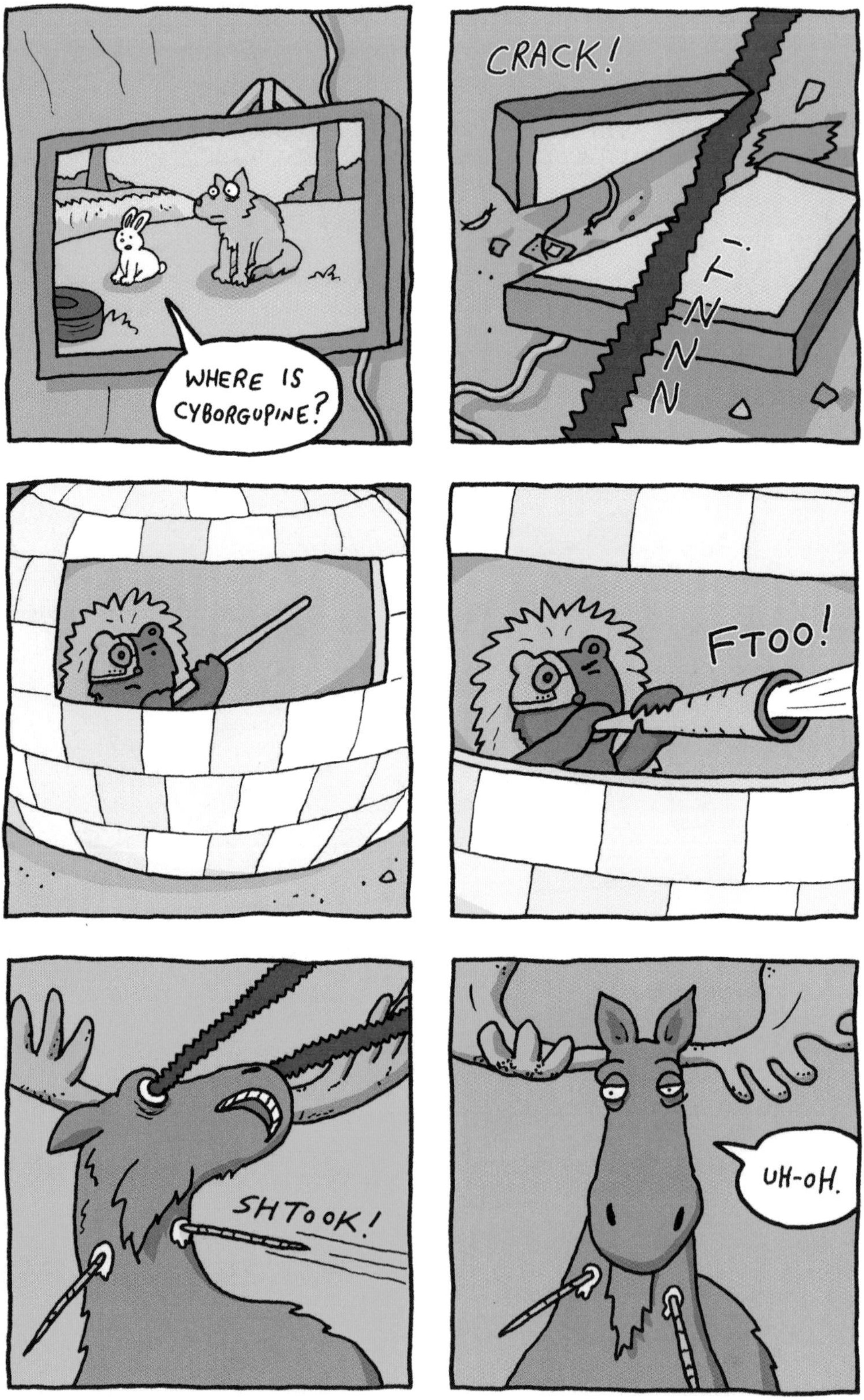
WHERE IS CYBORGUPINE?
CRACK!
NNNT!
FTOO!
SHTOOK!
UH-OH.

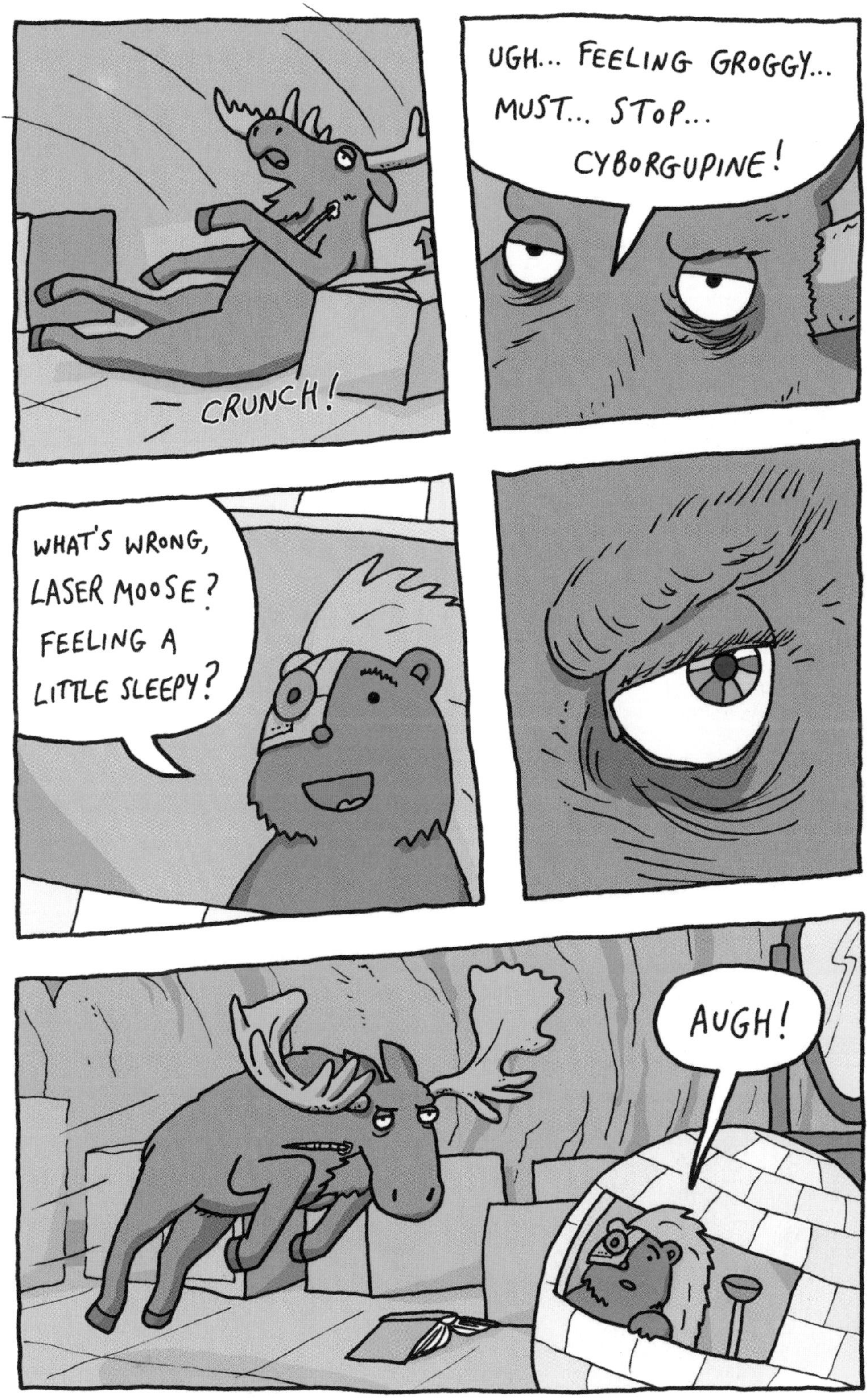
CRUNCH!
UGH... FEELING GROGGY... MUST... STOP... CYBORGUPINE!
WHAT'S WRONG, LASER MOOSE? FEELING A LITTLE SLEEPY?
AUGH!

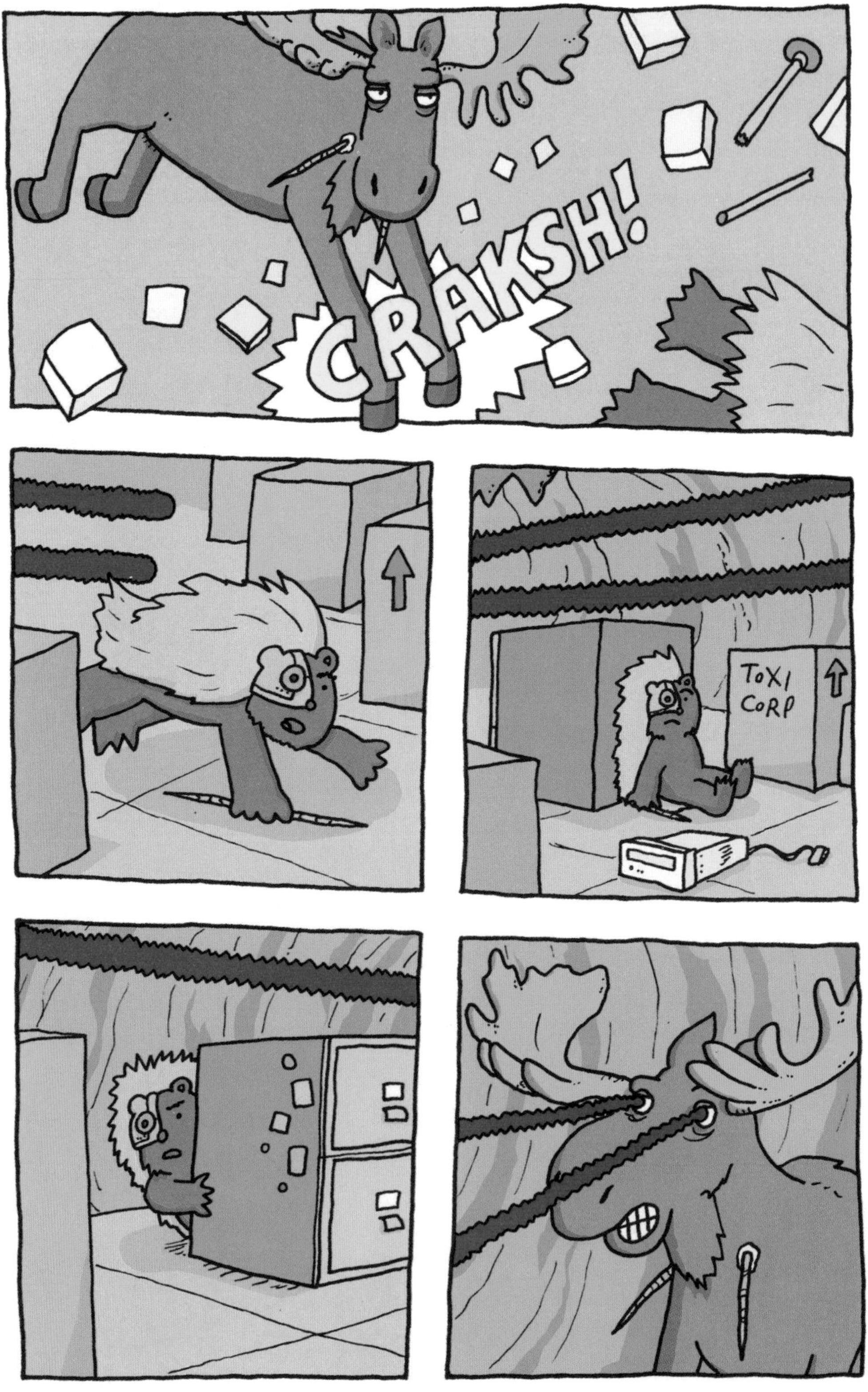
CRAKSH!
TOXI CORP

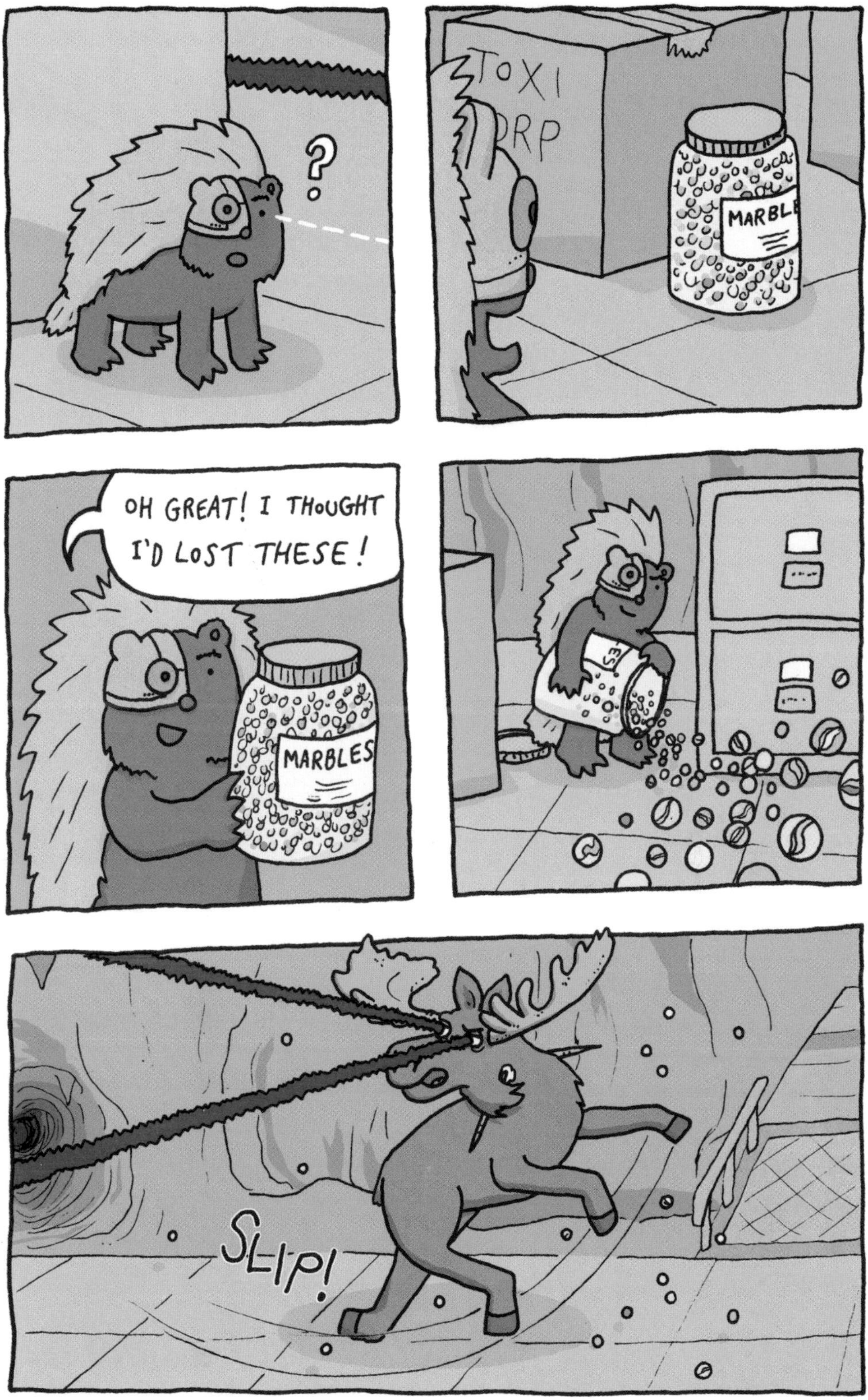
?
TOXI
ORP
MARBLE
OH GREAT! I THOUGHT I'D LOST THESE!
MARBLES
SLIP!

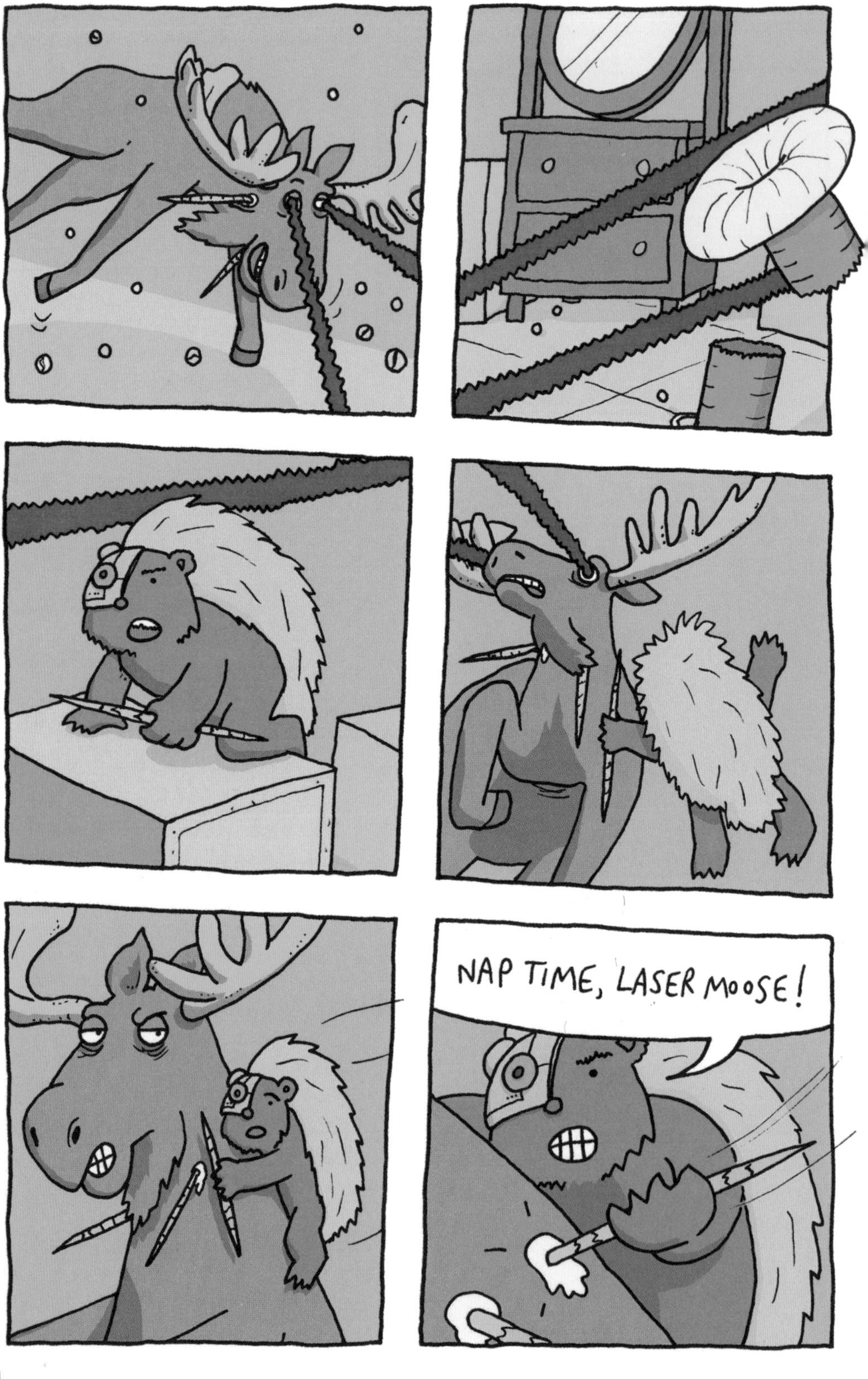
NAP TIME, LASER MOOSE!

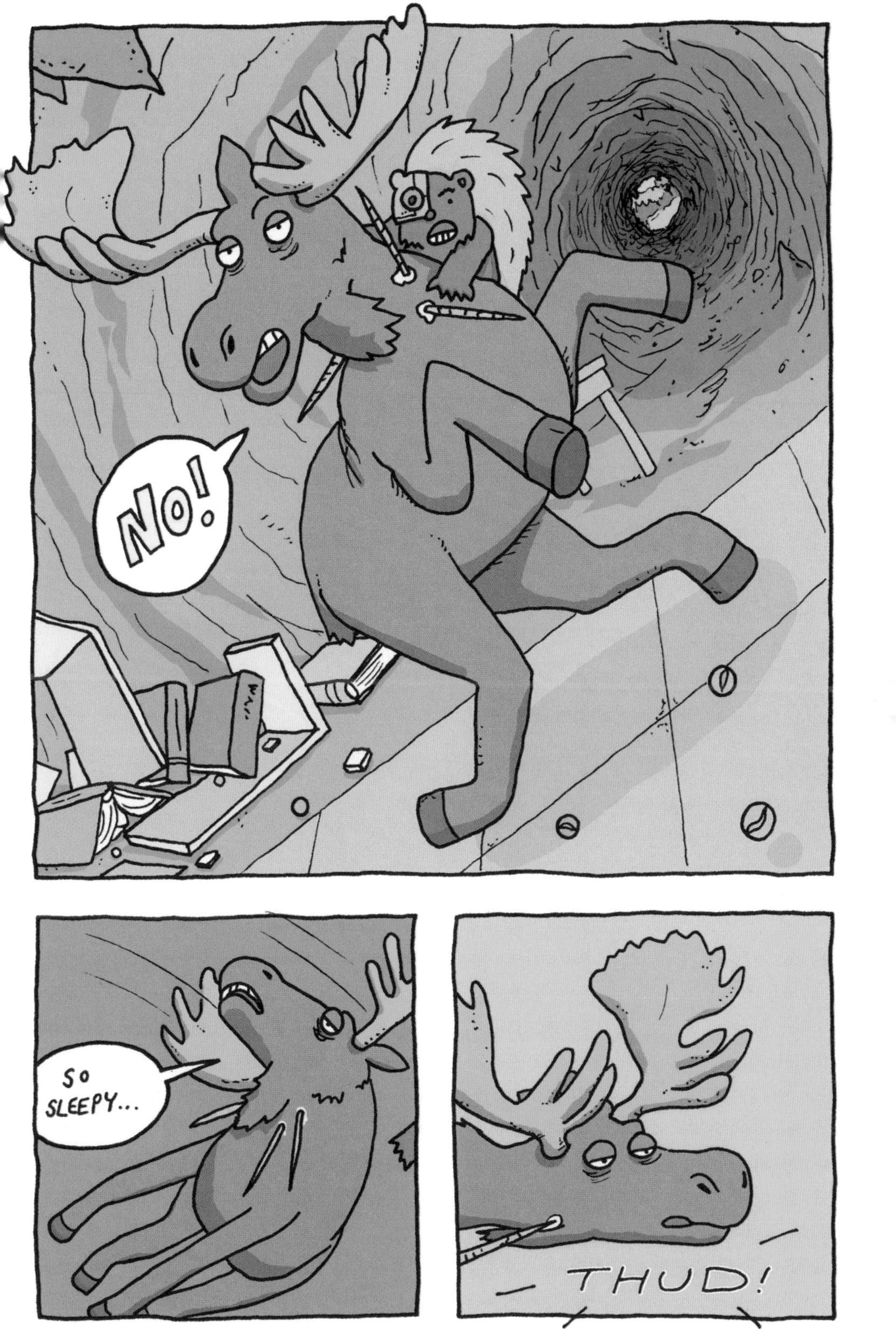
NO!
SO SLEEPY...
THUD!

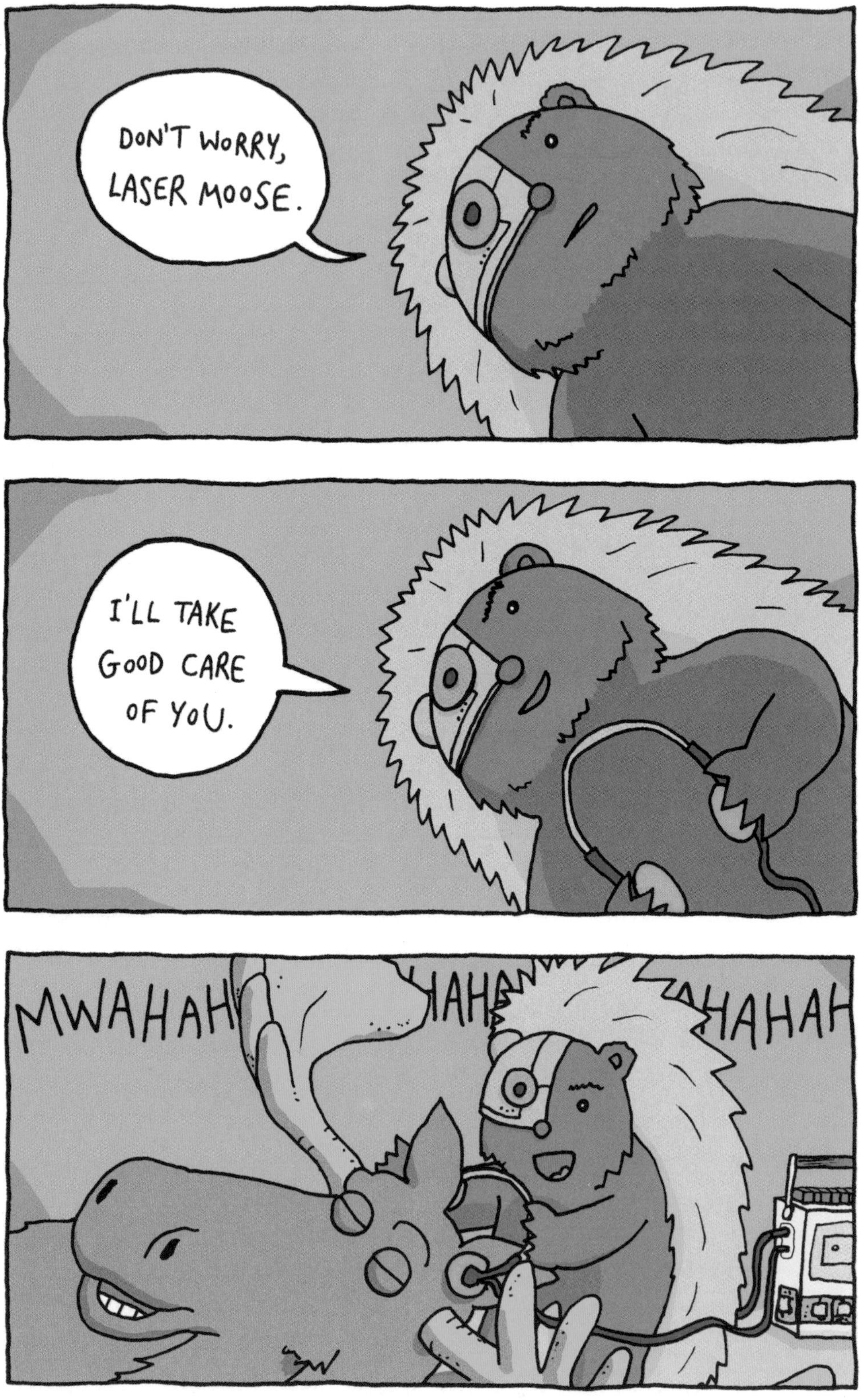
DON'T WORRY, LASER MOOSE.
I'LL TAKE GOOD CARE OF YOU.
MWAHAHAHAHAHAHAHAH

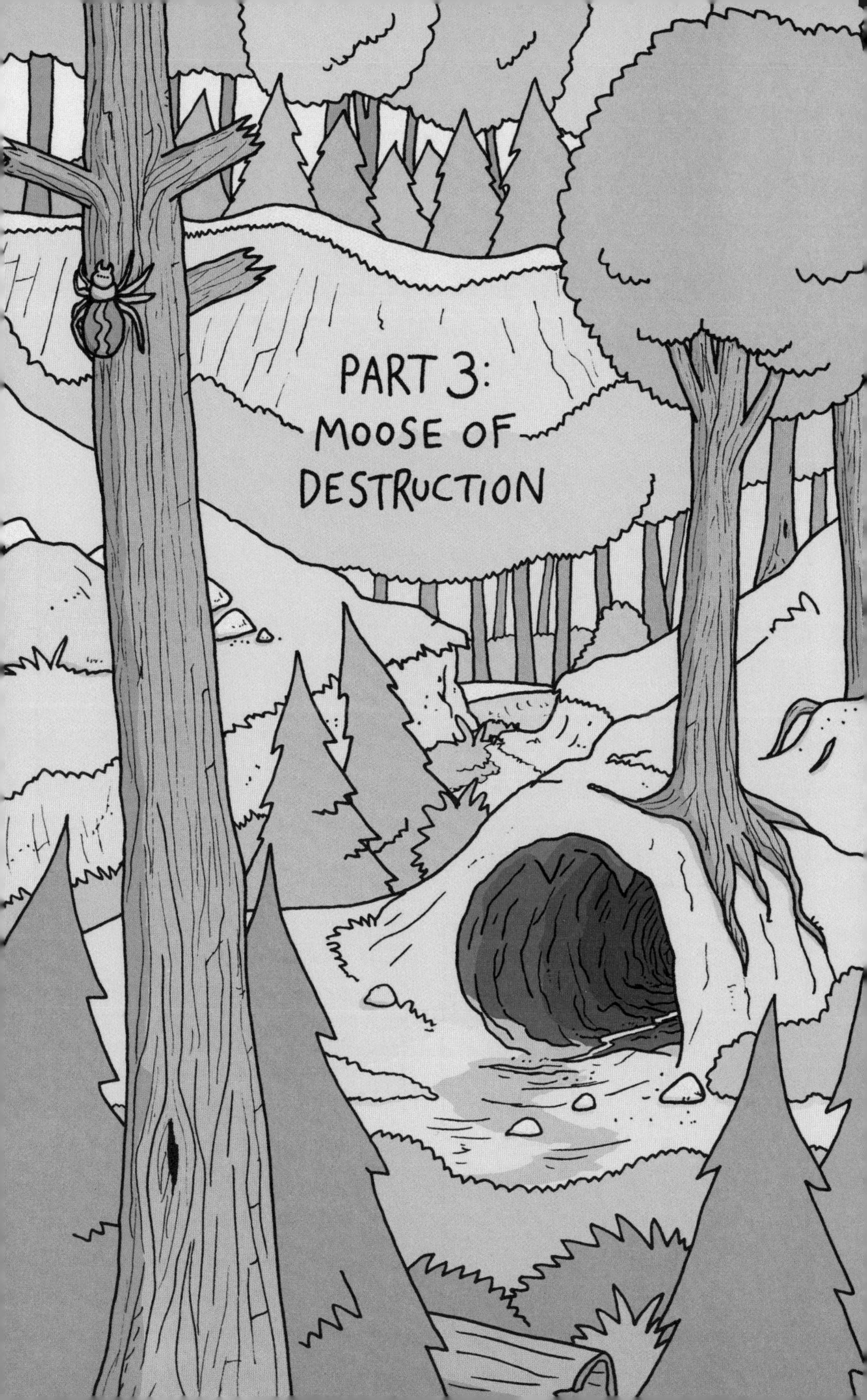
PART 3:
MOOSE OF
DESTRUCTION

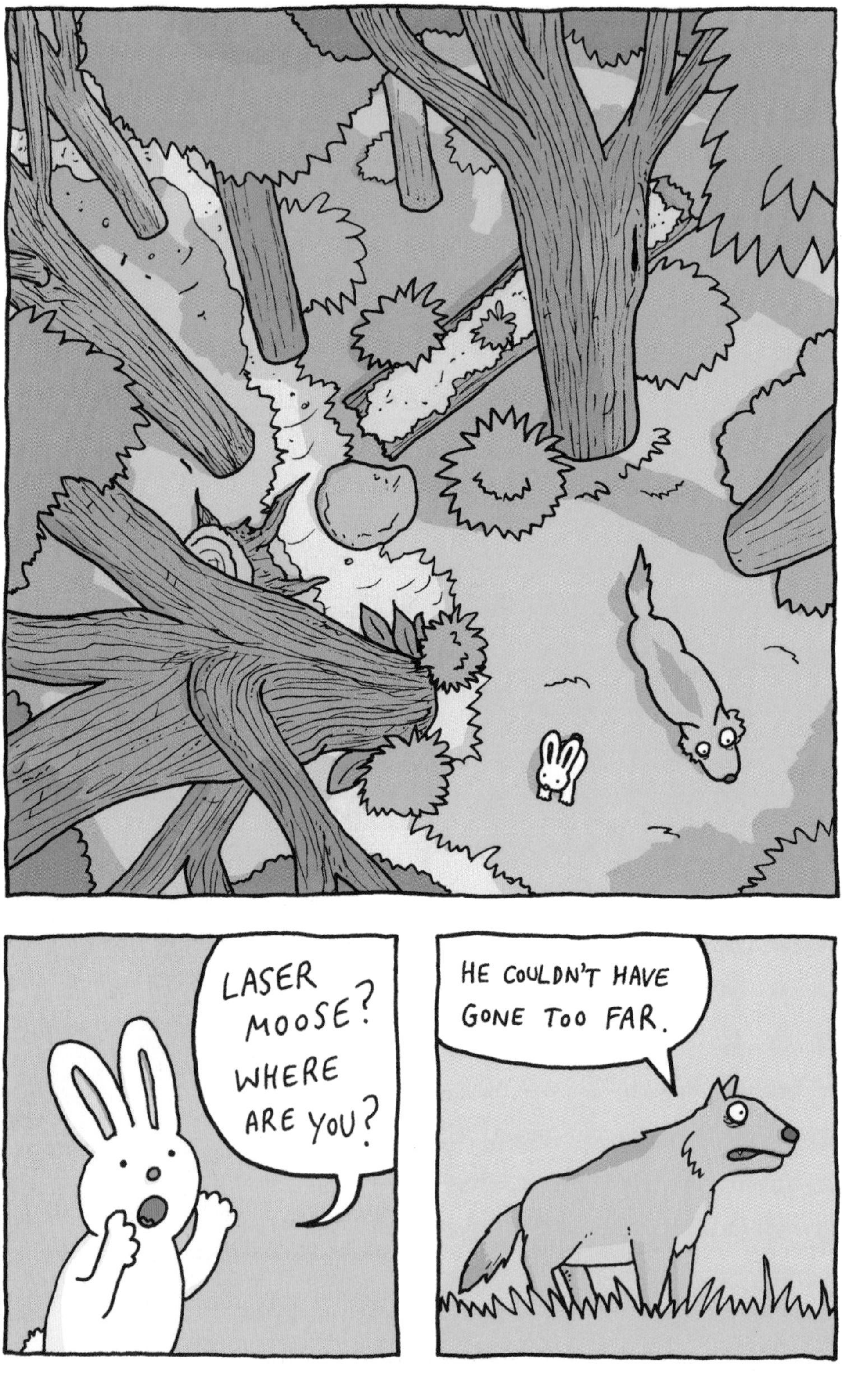
LASER MOOSE? WHERE ARE YOU?
HE COULDN'T HAVE GONE TOO FAR.

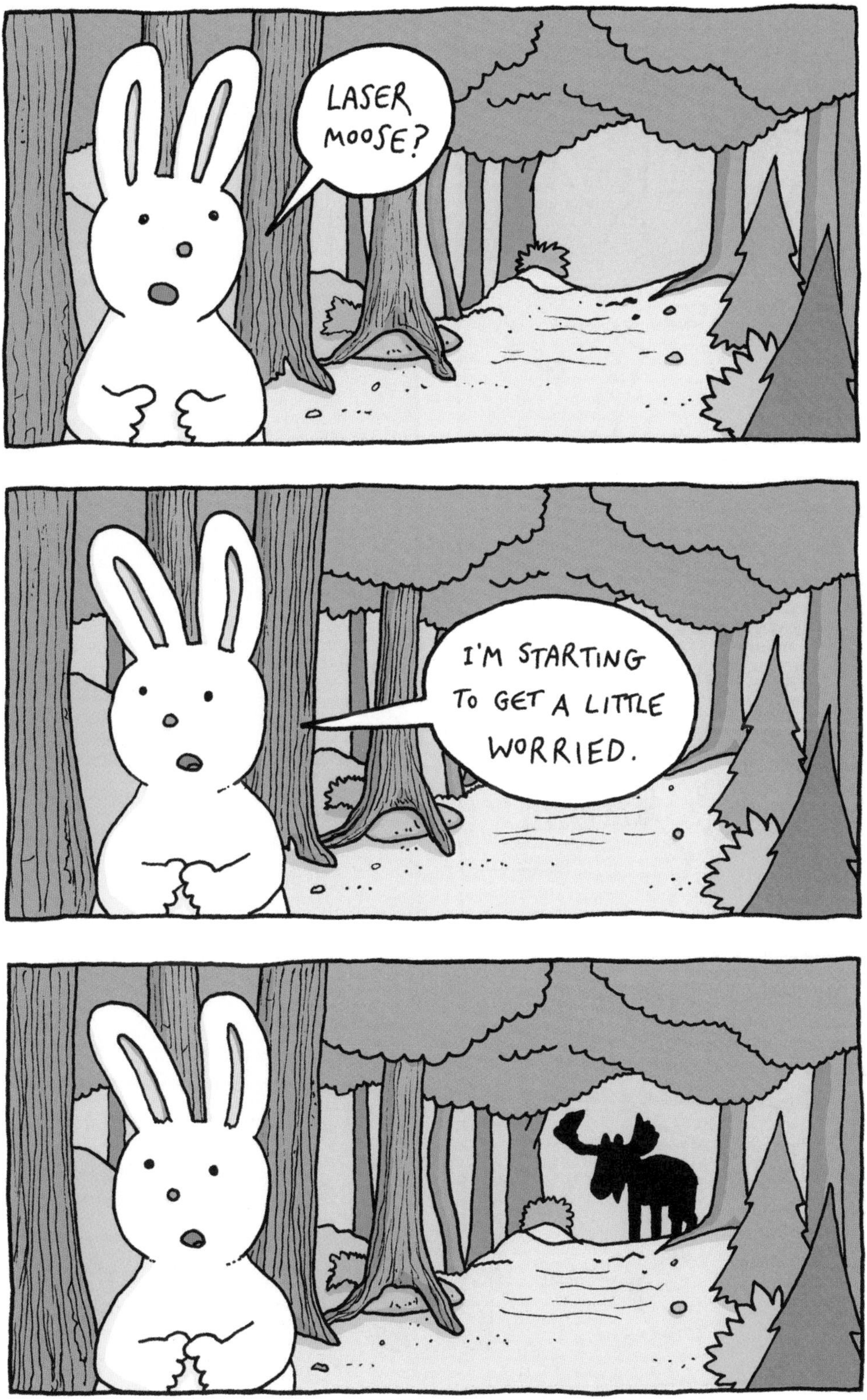
LASER MOOSE?
I'M STARTING TO GET A LITTLE WORRIED.

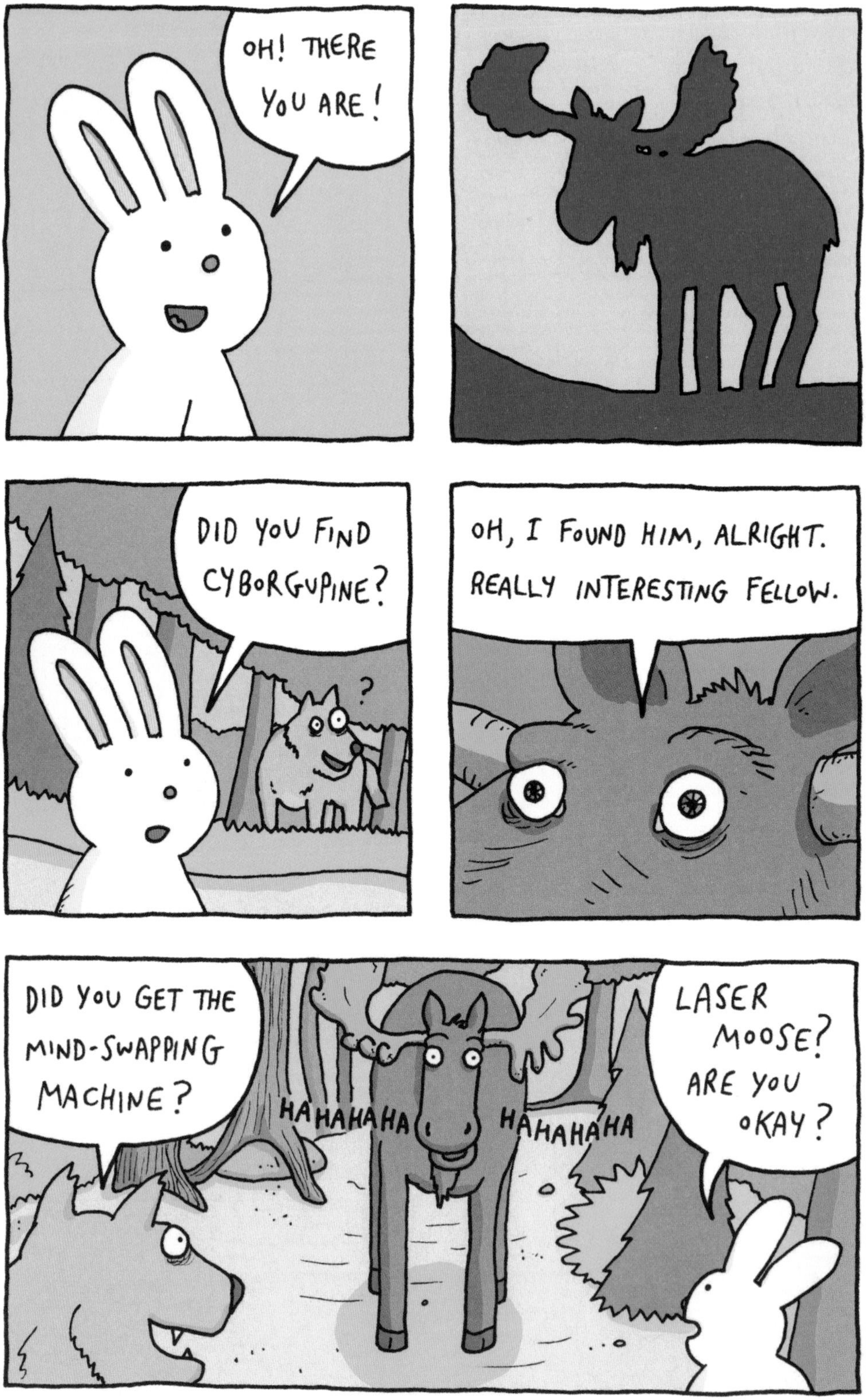
OH! THERE YOU ARE!
DID YOU FIND CYBORGUPINE?
?
OH, I FOUND HIM, ALRIGHT. REALLY INTERESTING FELLOW.
DID YOU GET THE MIND-SWAPPING MACHINE?
HAHAHAHA
HAHAHAHA
LASER MOOSE? ARE YOU OKAY?

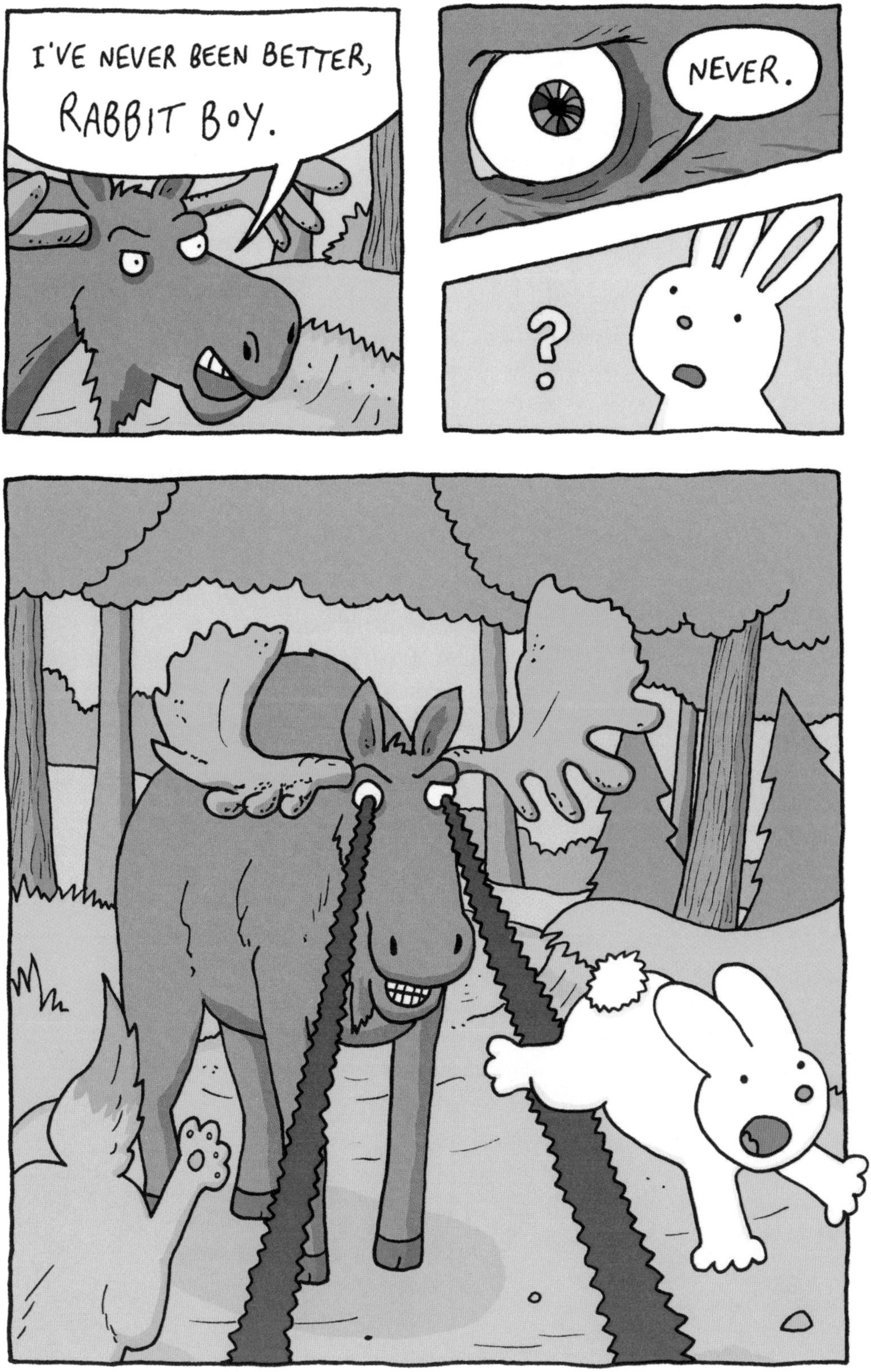
I'VE NEVER BEEN BETTER, RABBIT BOY.
NEVER.
?

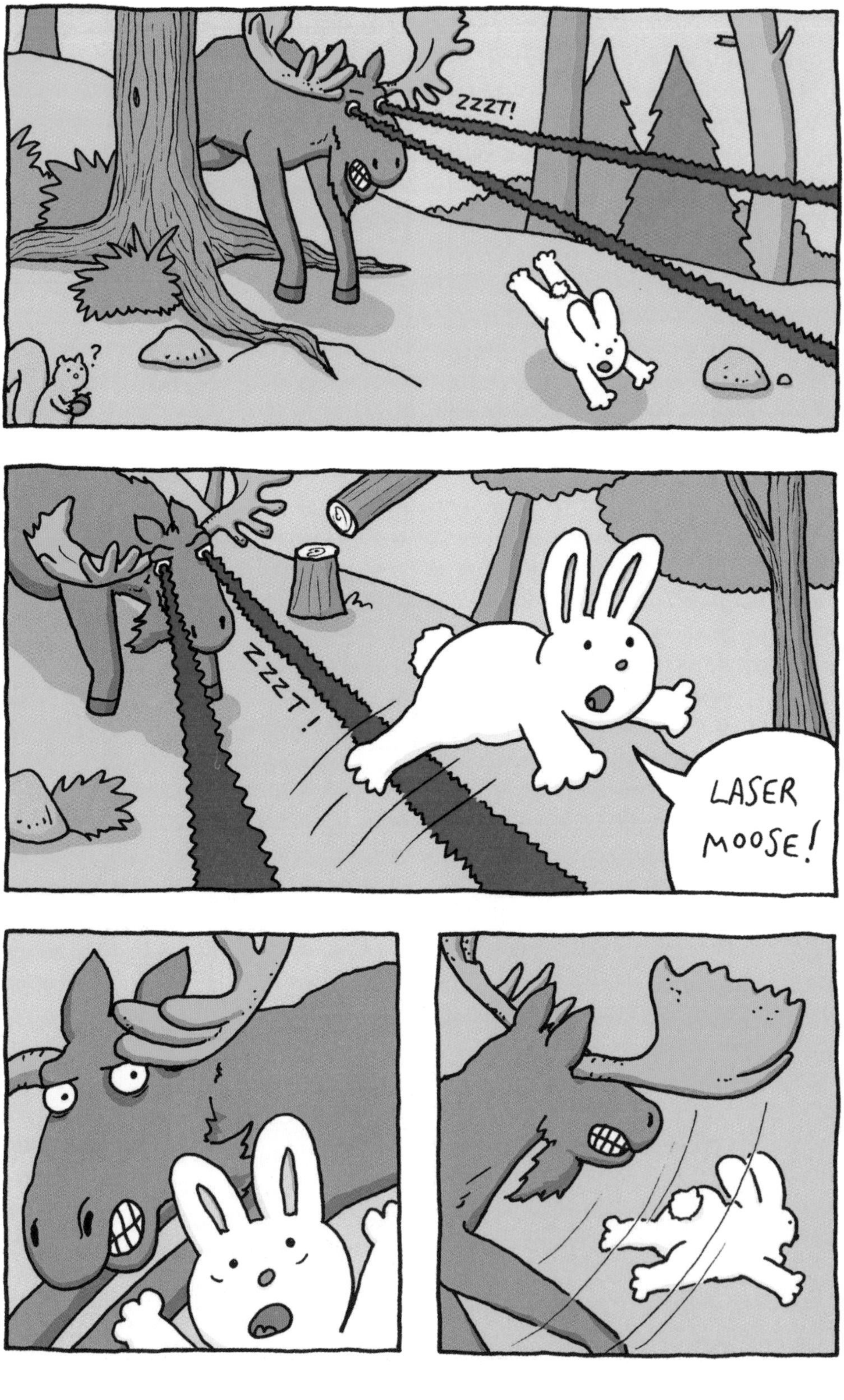
ZZZT!
?
ZZZT!
LASER MOOSE!

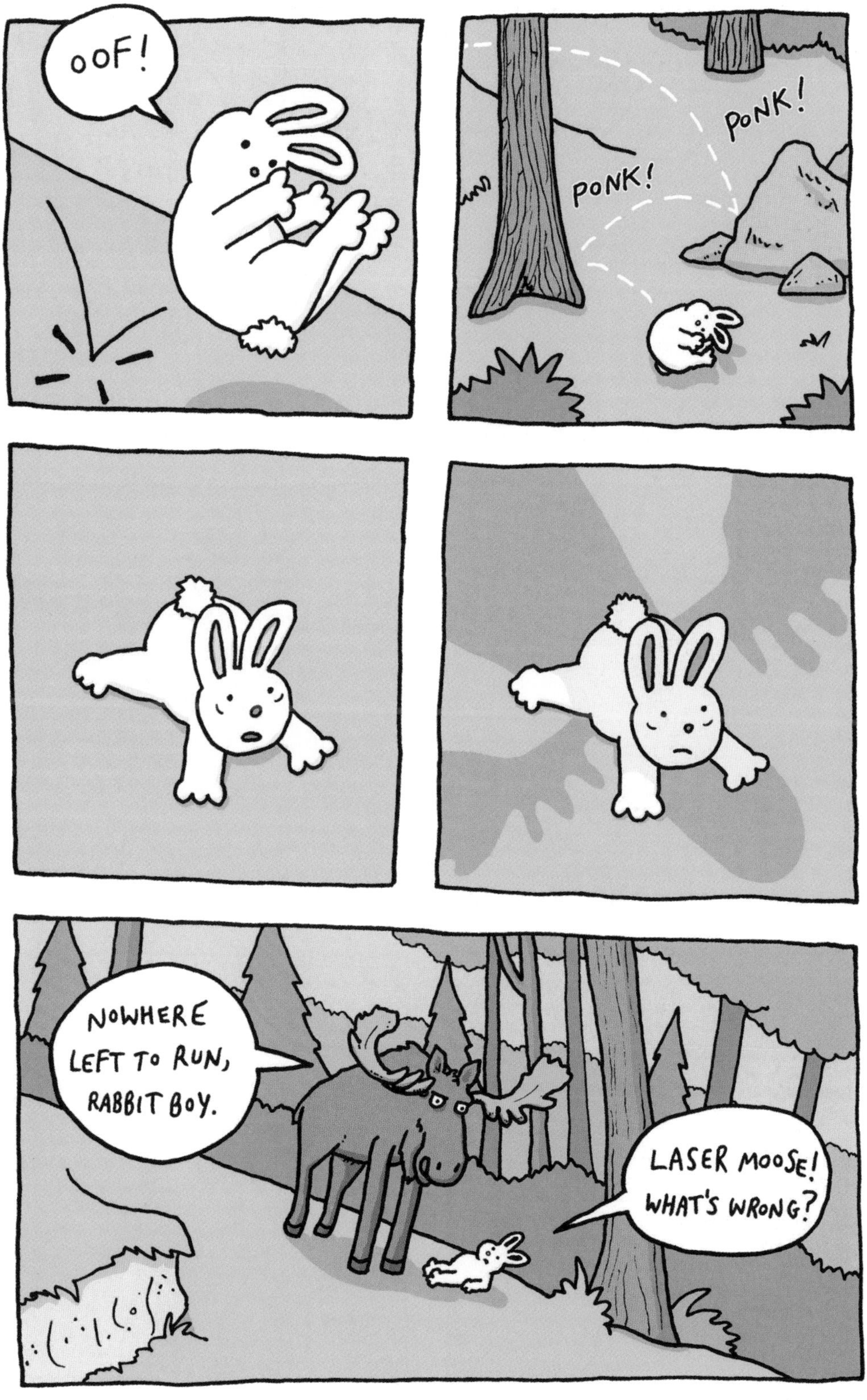
OOF!
PONK!
PONK!
NOWHERE LEFT TO RUN, RABBIT BOY.
LASER MOOSE! WHAT'S WRONG?

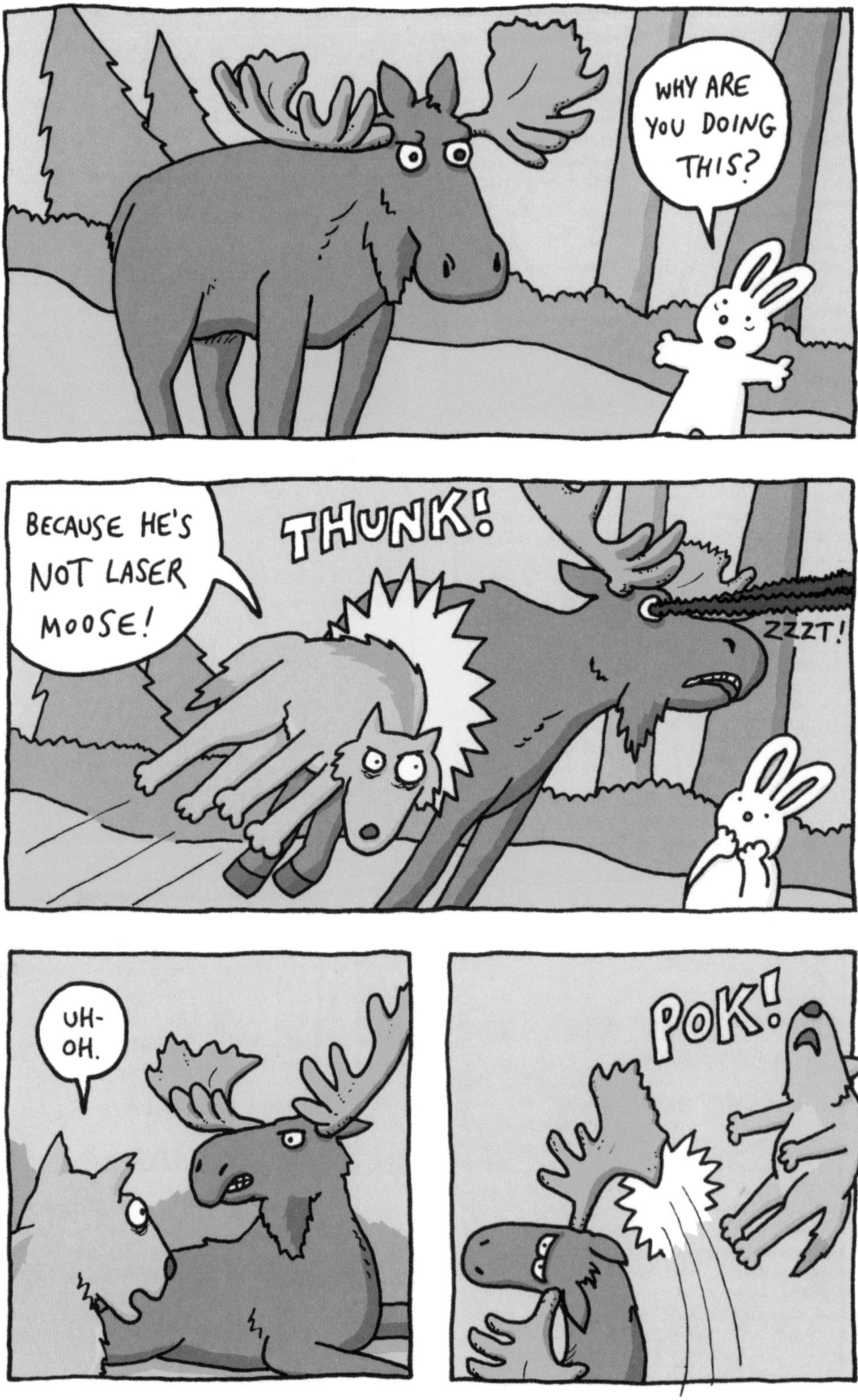
WHY ARE YOU DOING THIS?
BECAUSE HE'S NOT LASER MOOSE!
THUNK!
ZZZT!
UH-OH.
POK!

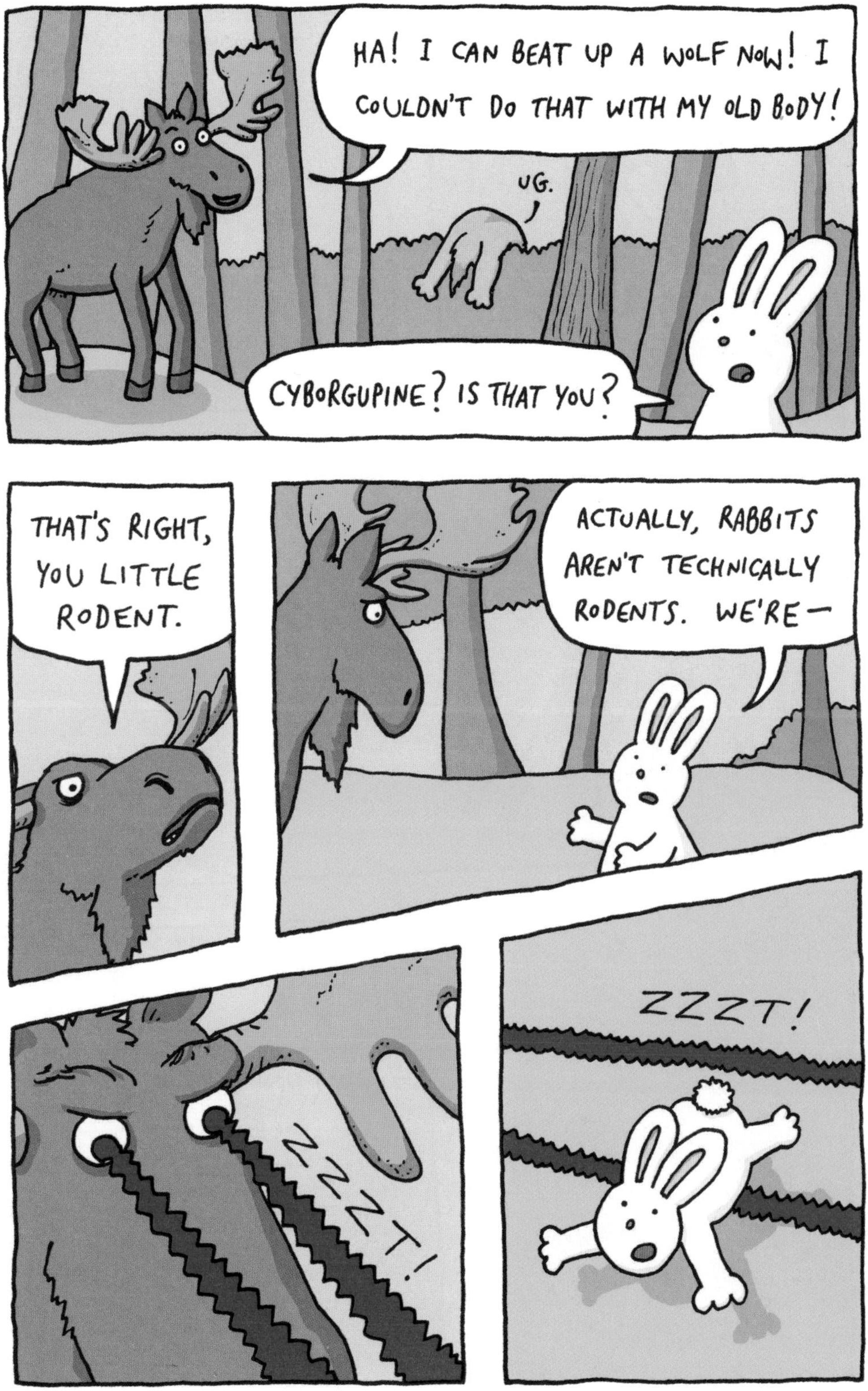
HA! I CAN BEAT UP A WOLF NOW! I COULDN'T DO THAT WITH MY OLD BODY!
UG.
CYBORGUPINE? IS THAT YOU?
THAT'S RIGHT, YOU LITTLE RODENT.
ACTUALLY, RABBITS AREN'T TECHNICALLY RODENTS. WE'RE—
ZZZT!
ZZZT!

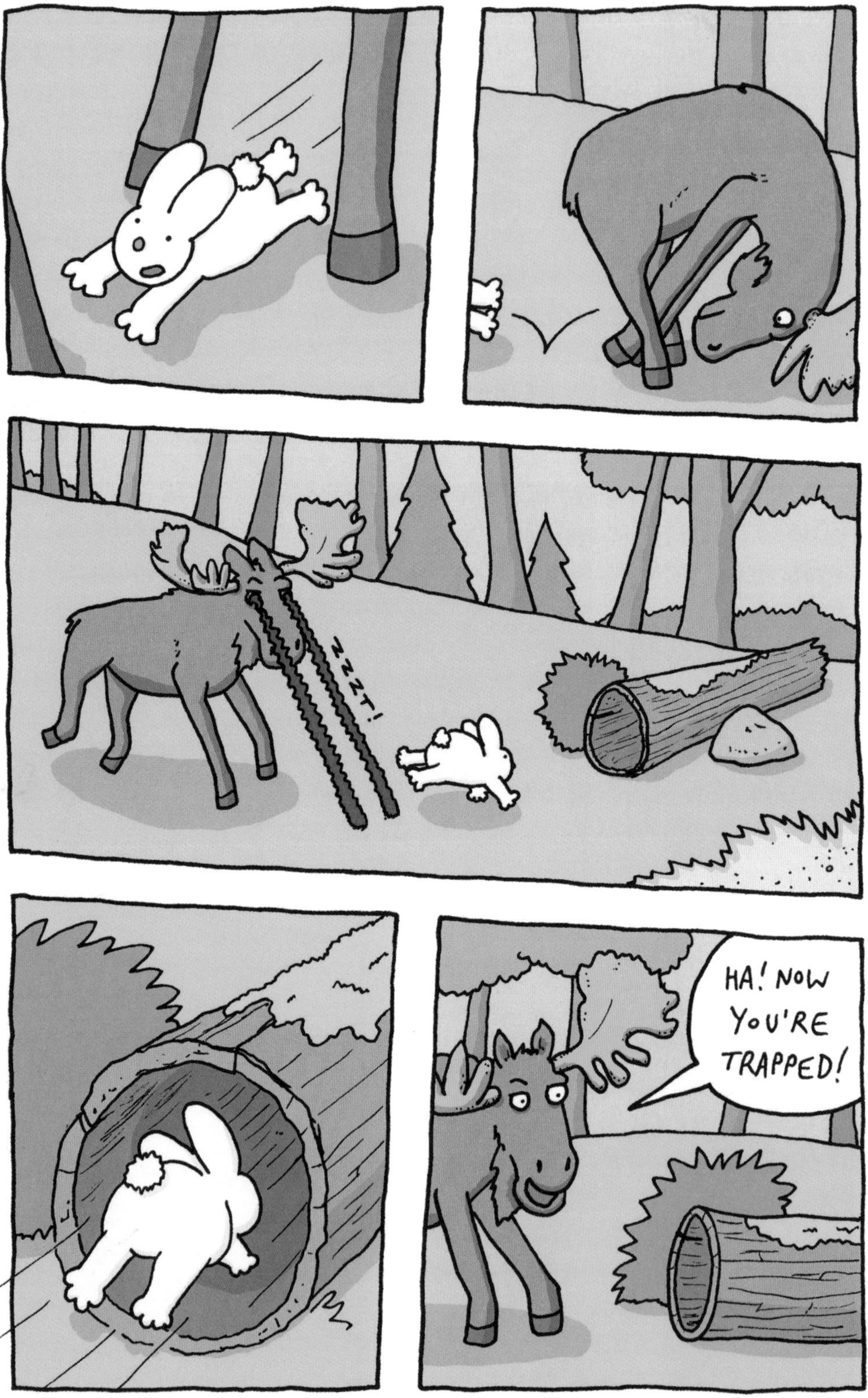
ZZZZT!
HA! NOW YOU'RE TRAPPED!

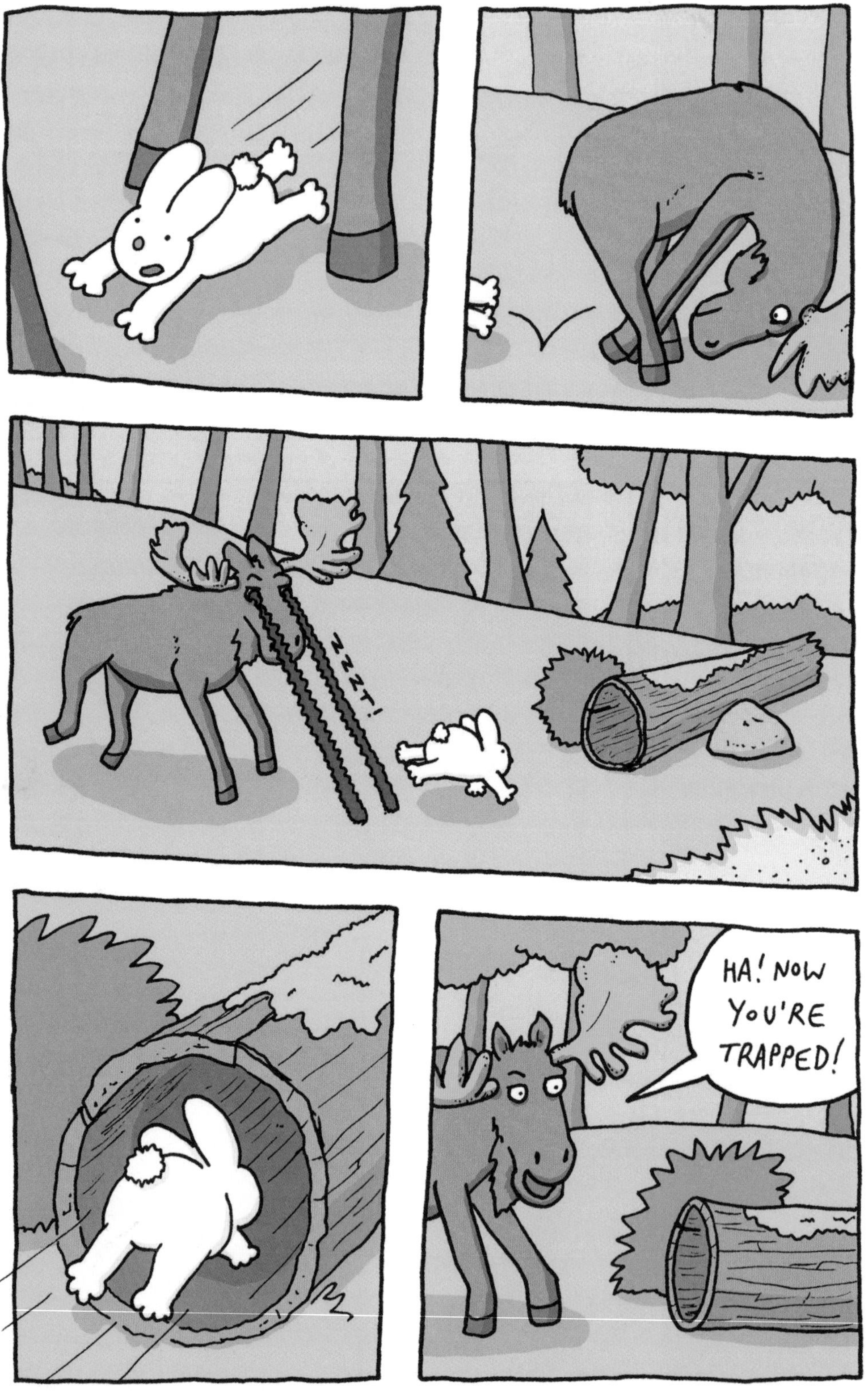
ZZZZT!
HA! NOW YOU'RE TRAPPED!

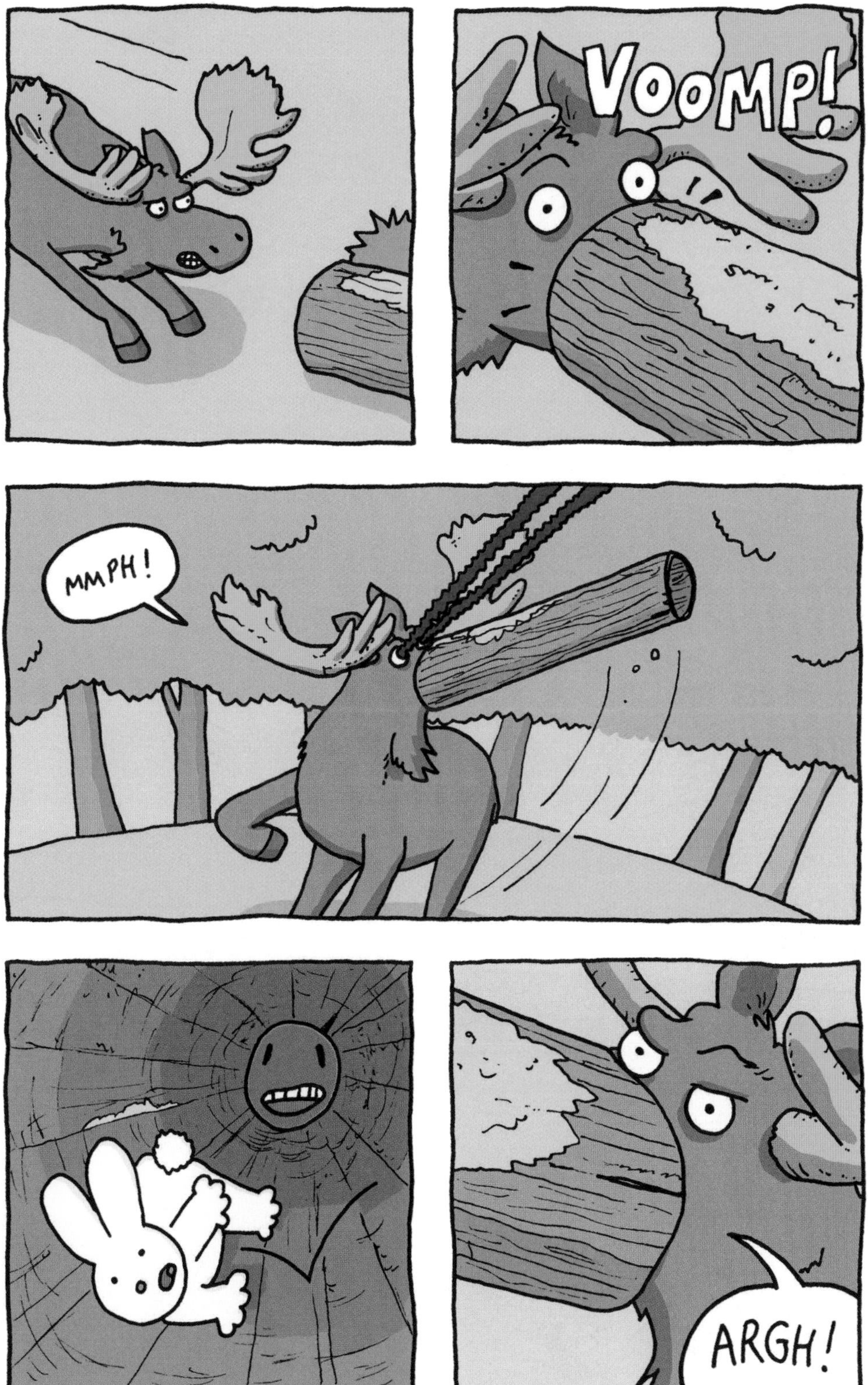
VOOMP!
MMPH!
ARGH!

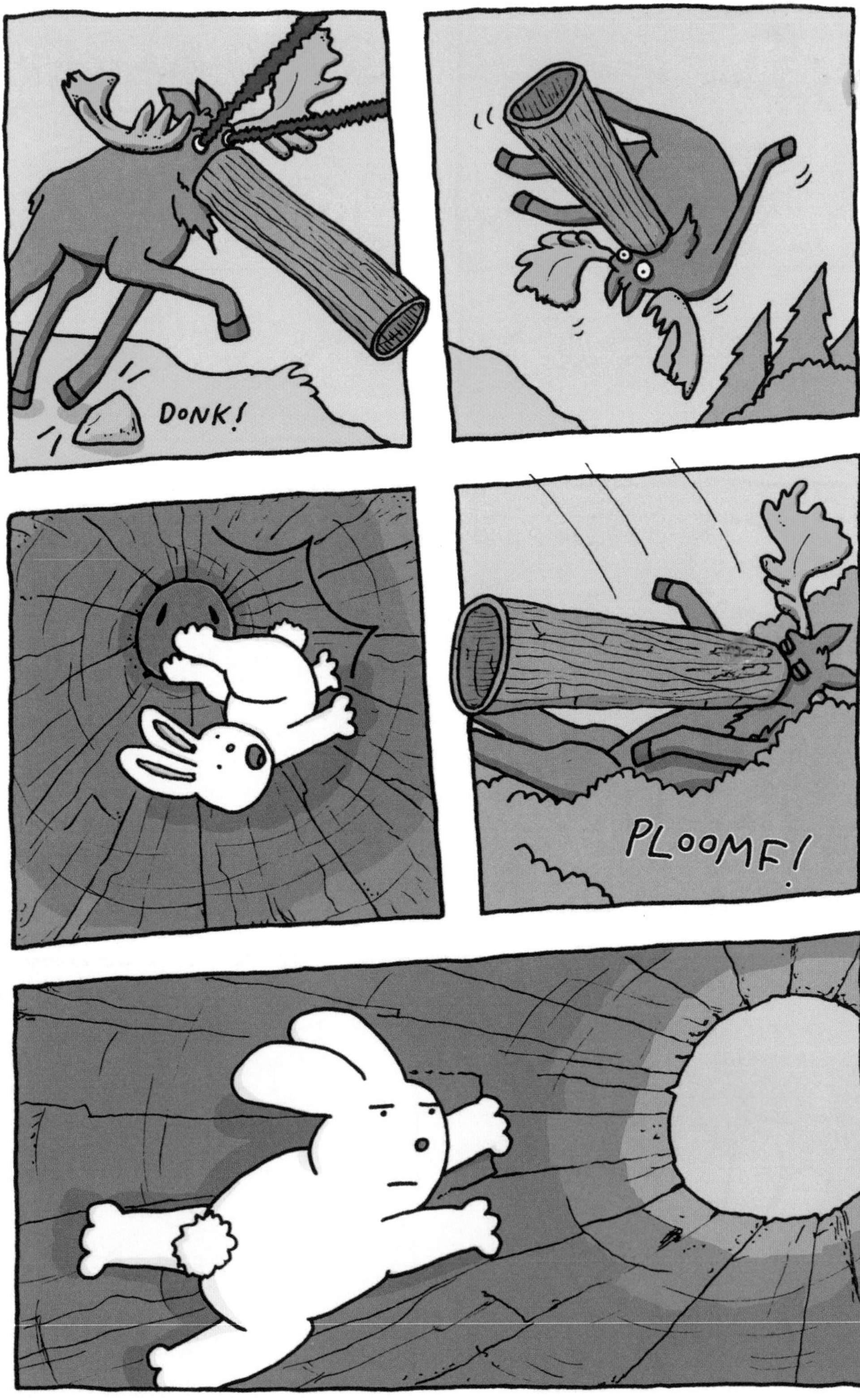
DONK!
PLOOMF!

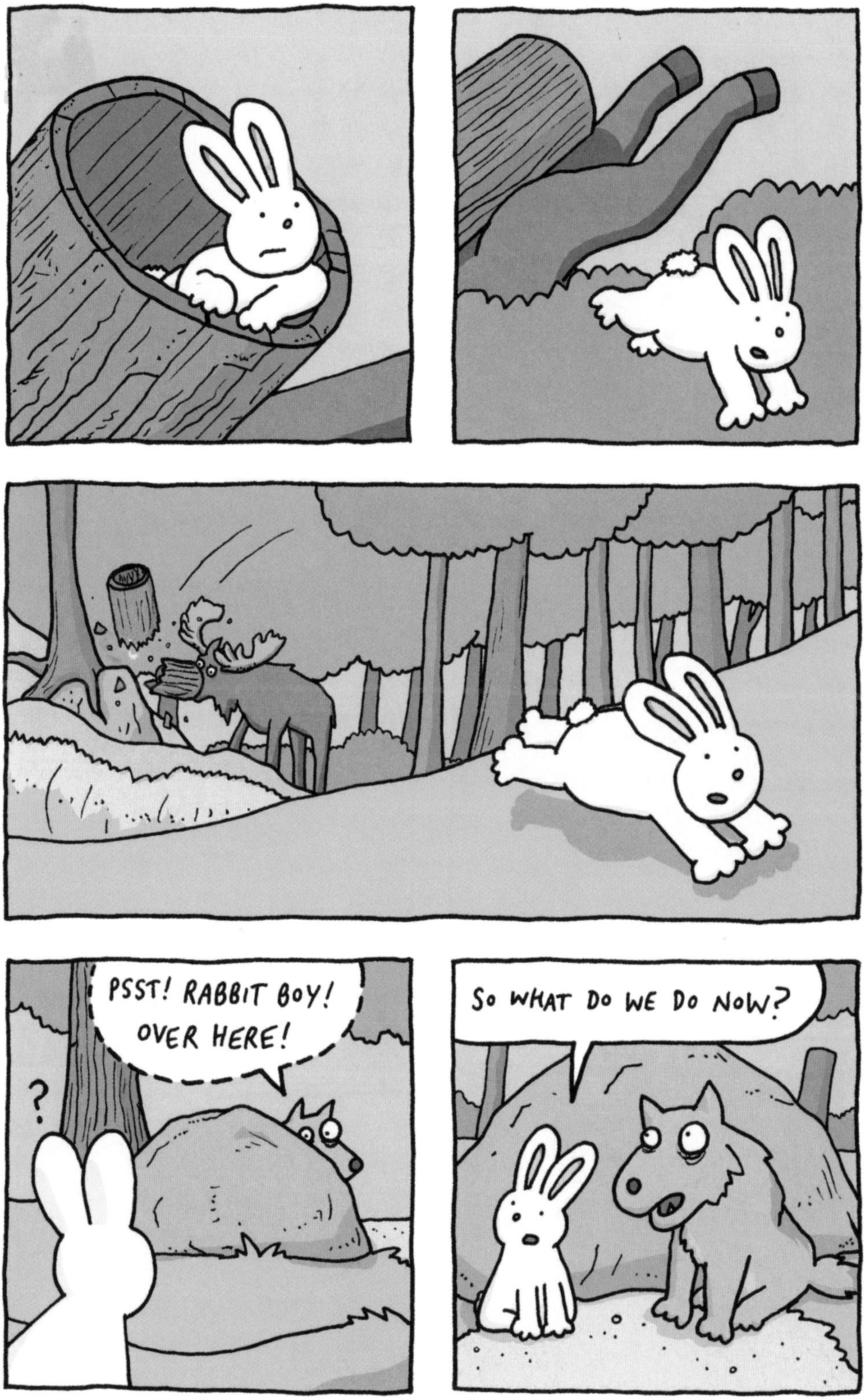
PSST! RABBIT BOY! OVER HERE!
?
SO WHAT DO WE DO NOW?

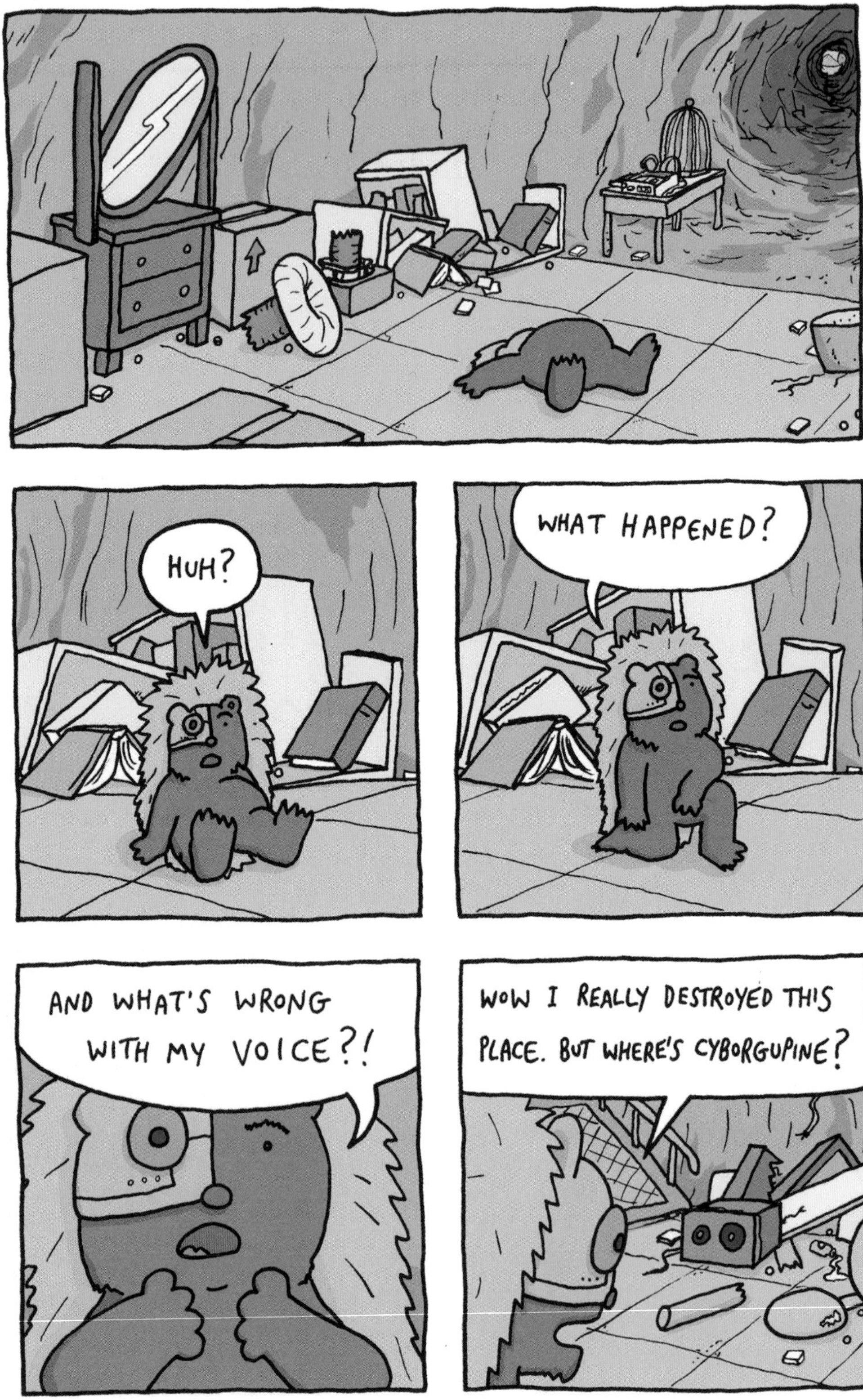
HUH?
WHAT HAPPENED?
AND WHAT'S WRONG WITH MY VOICE?!
WOW I REALLY DESTROYED THIS PLACE. BUT WHERE'S CYBORGUPINE?

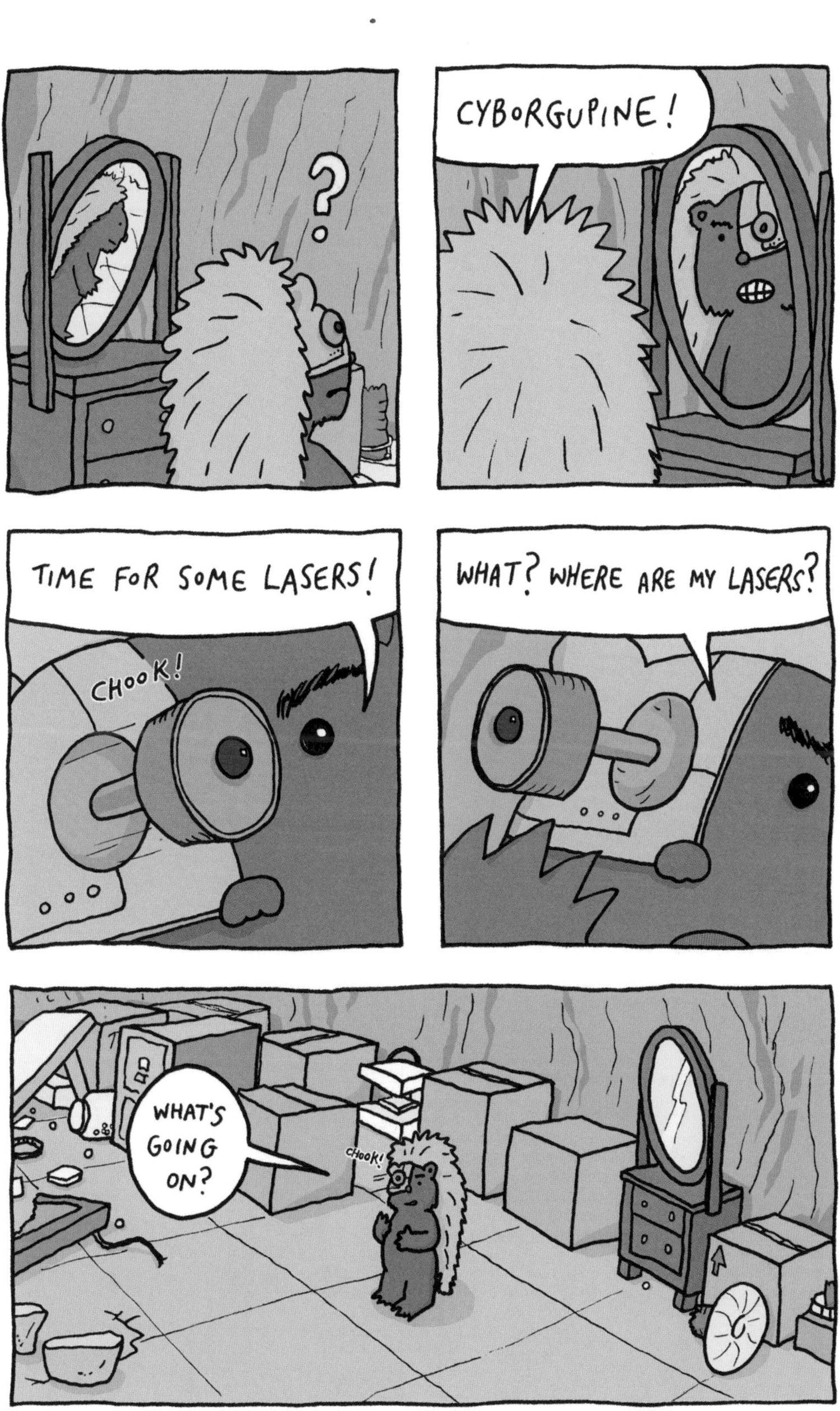
?
CYBORGUPINE!
TIME FOR SOME LASERS!
CHOOK!
WHAT? WHERE ARE MY LASERS?
WHAT'S GOING ON?
CHOOK!

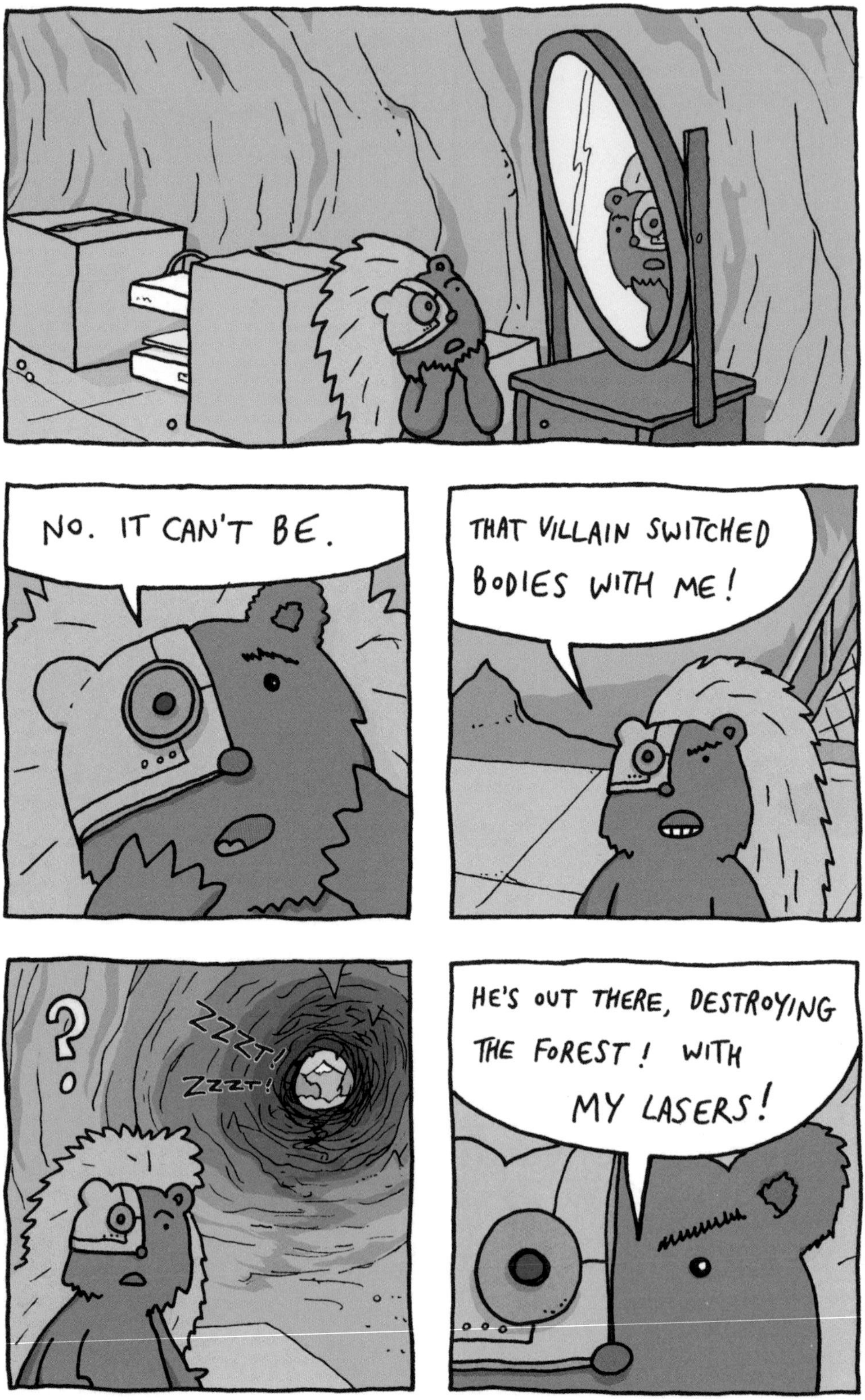
NO. IT CAN'T BE.
THAT VILLAIN SWITCHED BODIES WITH ME!
ZZZT!
ZZZT!
HE'S OUT THERE, DESTROYING THE FOREST! WITH MY LASERS!

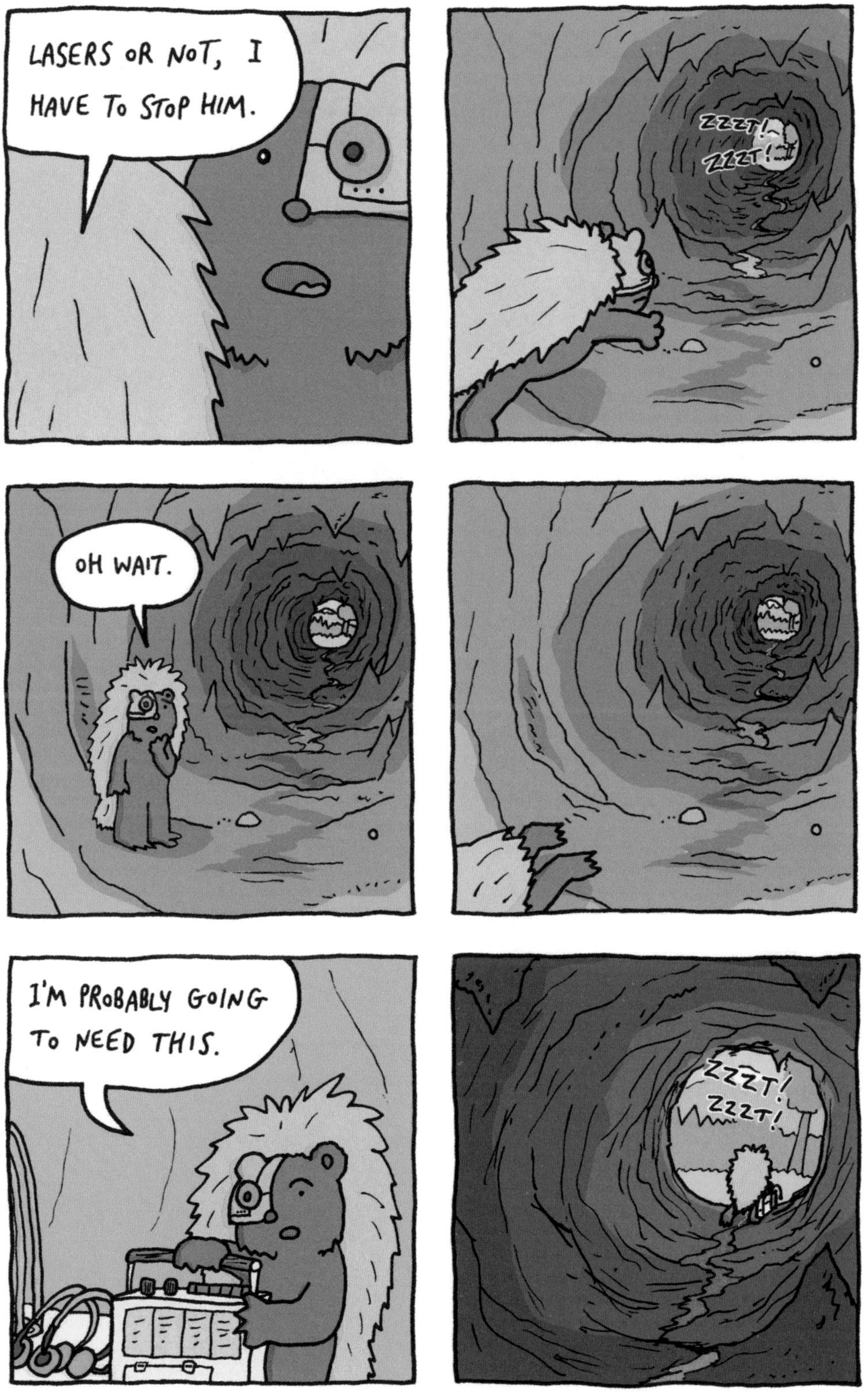
LASERS OR NOT, I HAVE TO STOP HIM.
ZZZT! ZZZT!
OH WAIT.
I'M PROBABLY GOING TO NEED THIS.
ZZZT! ZZZT!

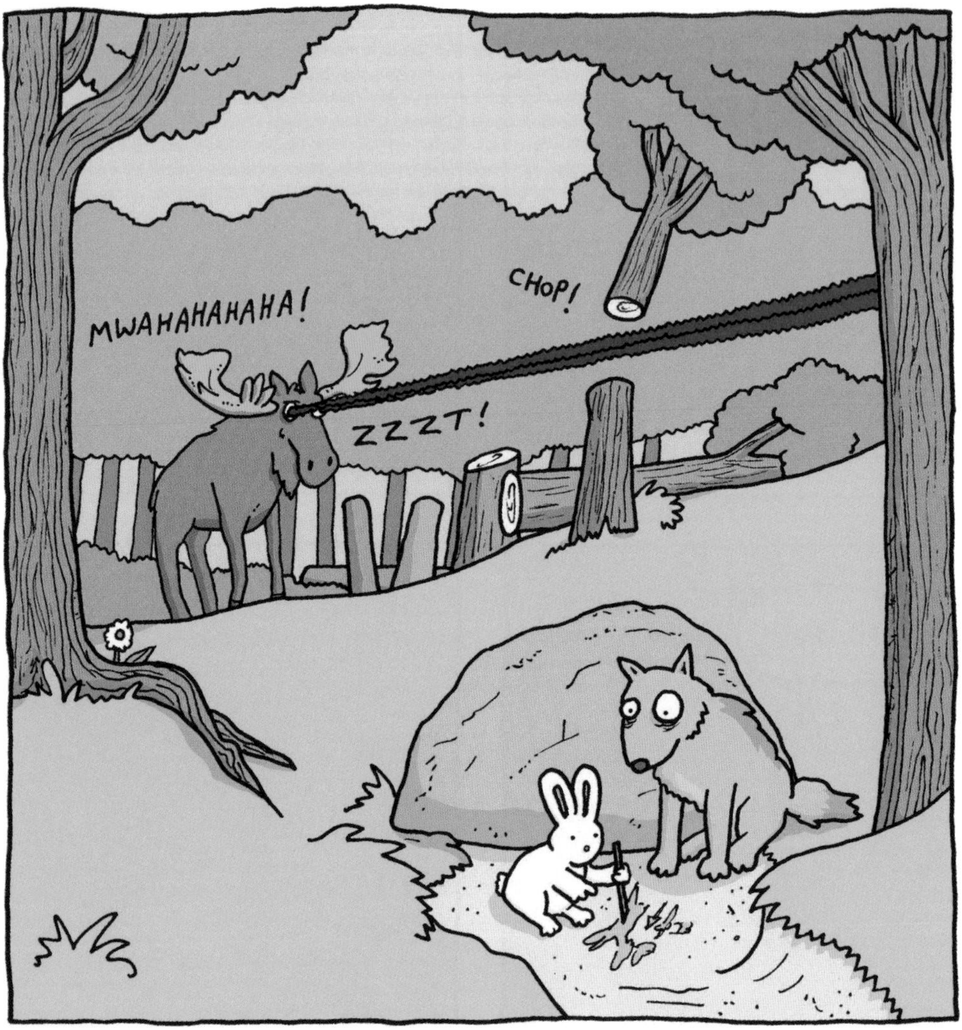
MWAHAHAHAHA!
CHOP!
ZZZT!

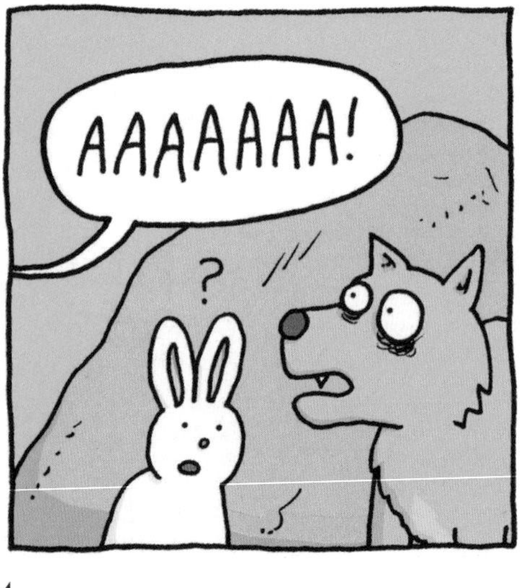
AAAAAAA!
?

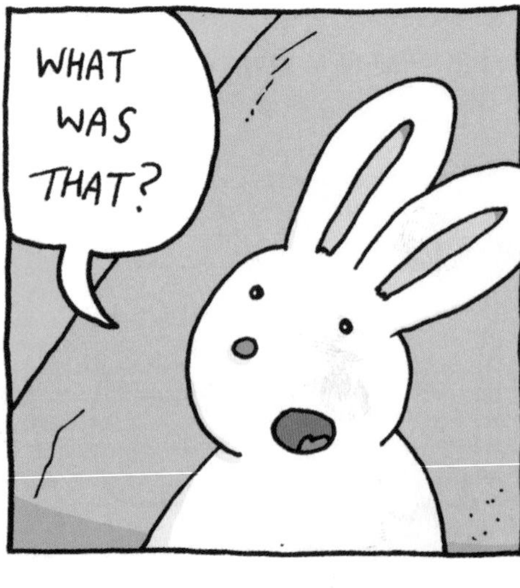
WHAT WAS THAT?

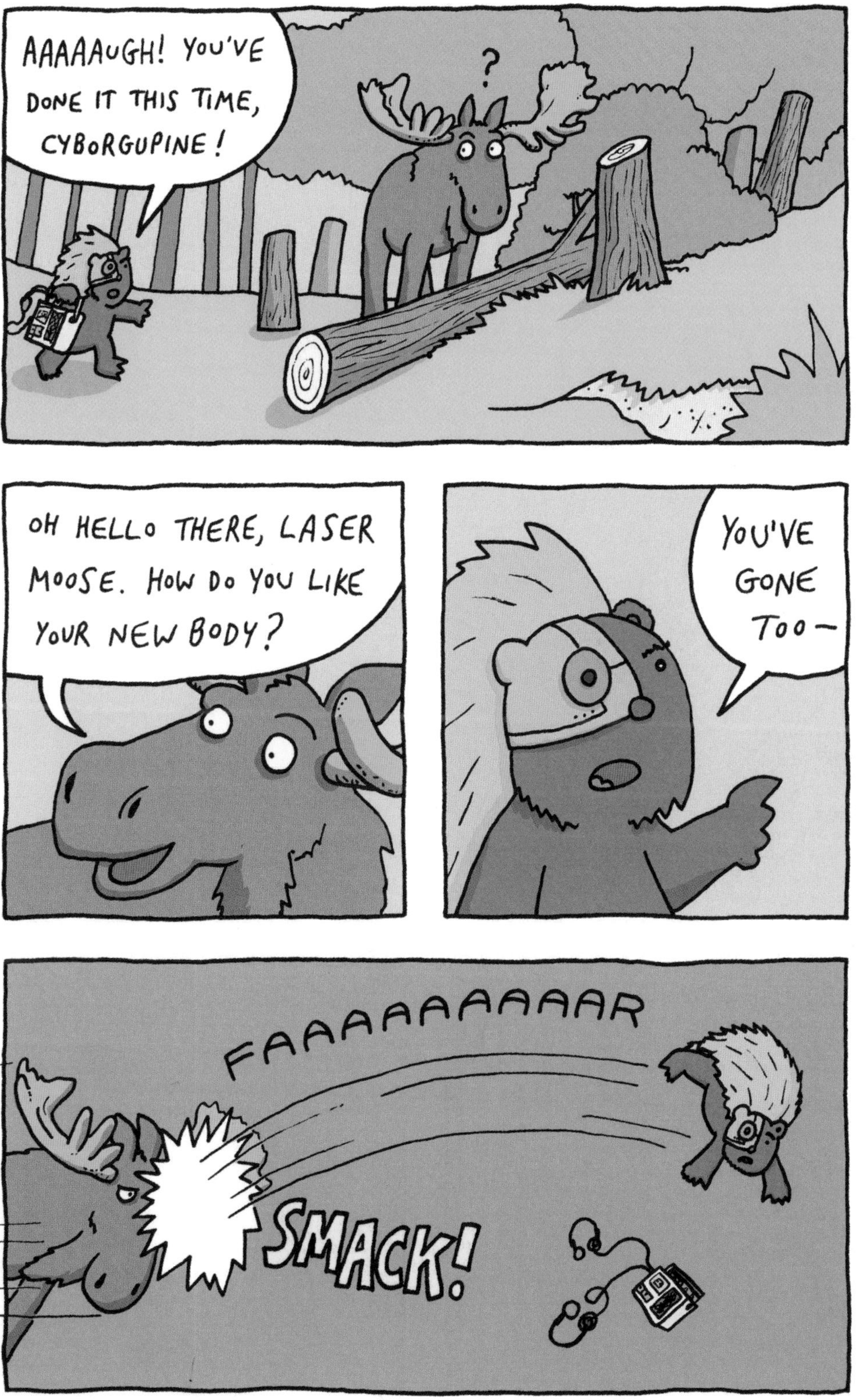
AAAAAUGH! YOU'VE DONE IT THIS TIME, CYBORGUPINE!
?
OH HELLO THERE, LASER MOOSE. HOW DO YOU LIKE YOUR NEW BODY?
YOU'VE GONE TOO—
FAAAAAAAAAR
SMACK!

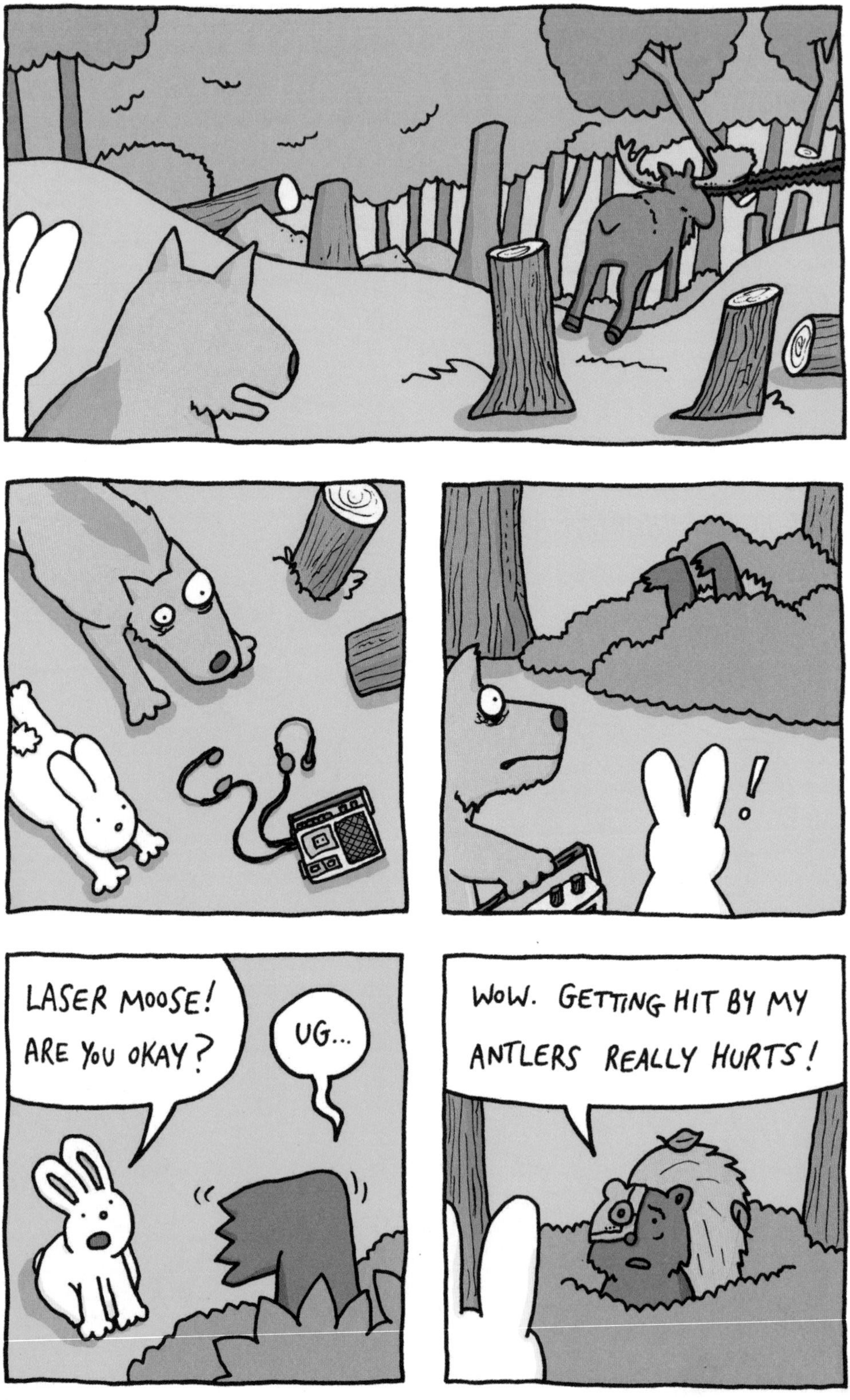
!
LASER MOOSE! ARE YOU OKAY?
UG...
WOW. GETTING HIT BY MY ANTLERS REALLY HURTS!

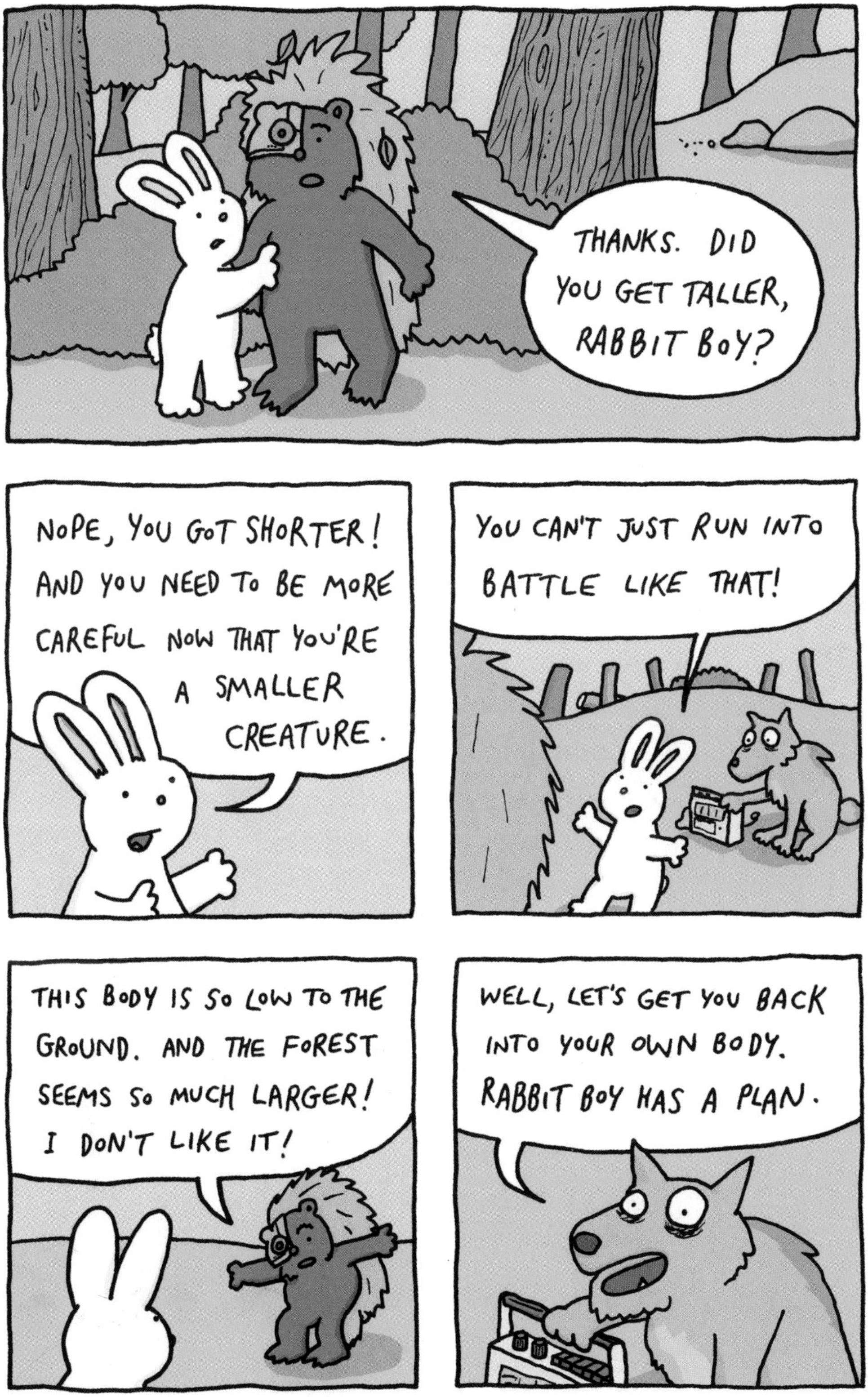
THANKS. DID YOU GET TALLER, RABBIT BOY?
NOPE, YOU GOT SHORTER! AND YOU NEED TO BE MORE CAREFUL NOW THAT YOU'RE A SMALLER CREATURE.
YOU CAN'T JUST RUN INTO BATTLE LIKE THAT!
THIS BODY IS SO LOW TO THE GROUND. AND THE FOREST SEEMS SO MUCH LARGER! I DON'T LIKE IT!
WELL, LET'S GET YOU BACK INTO YOUR OWN BODY. RABBIT BOY HAS A PLAN.

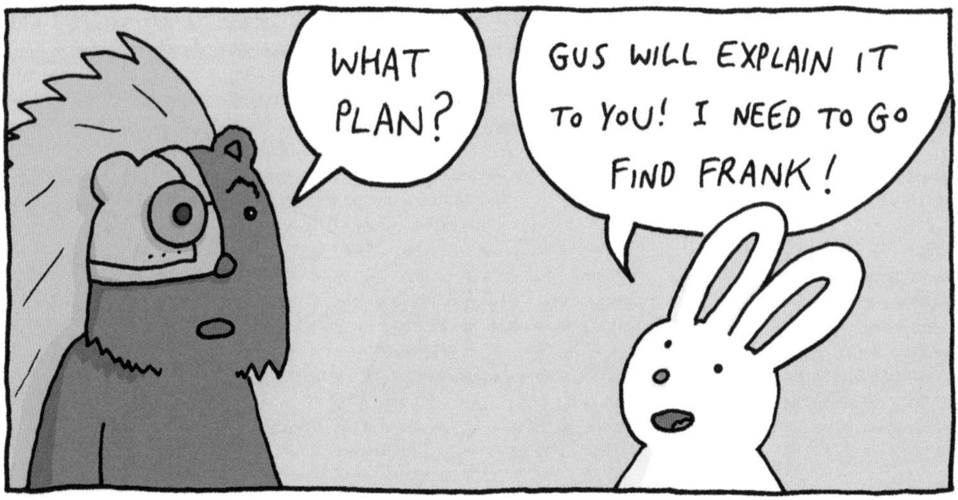
WHAT PLAN?
GUS WILL EXPLAIN IT TO YOU! I NEED TO GO FIND FRANK!

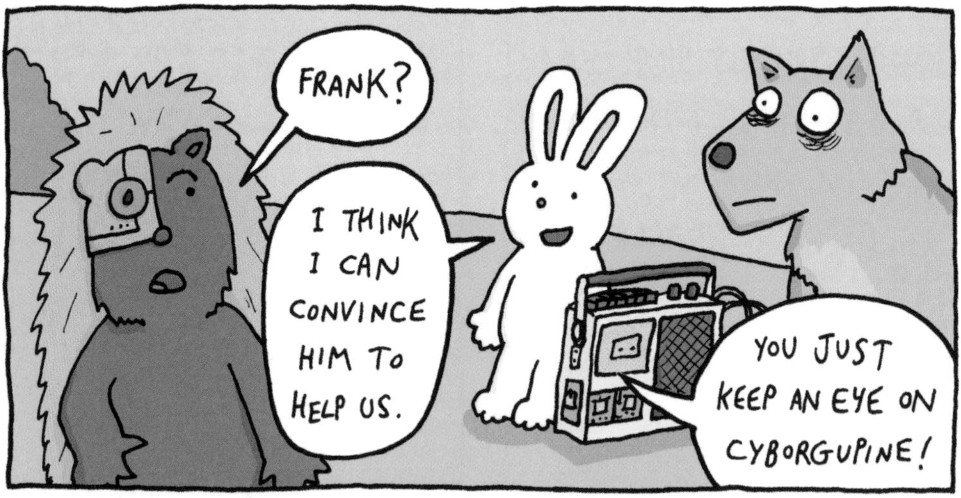
FRANK?
I THINK I CAN CONVINCE HIM TO HELP US.
YOU JUST KEEP AN EYE ON CYBORGUPINE!

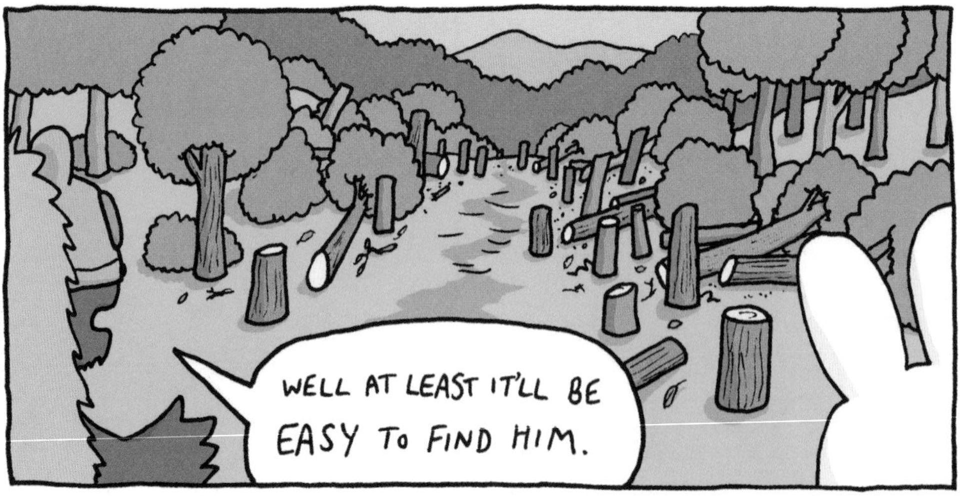
WELL AT LEAST IT'LL BE EASY TO FIND HIM.

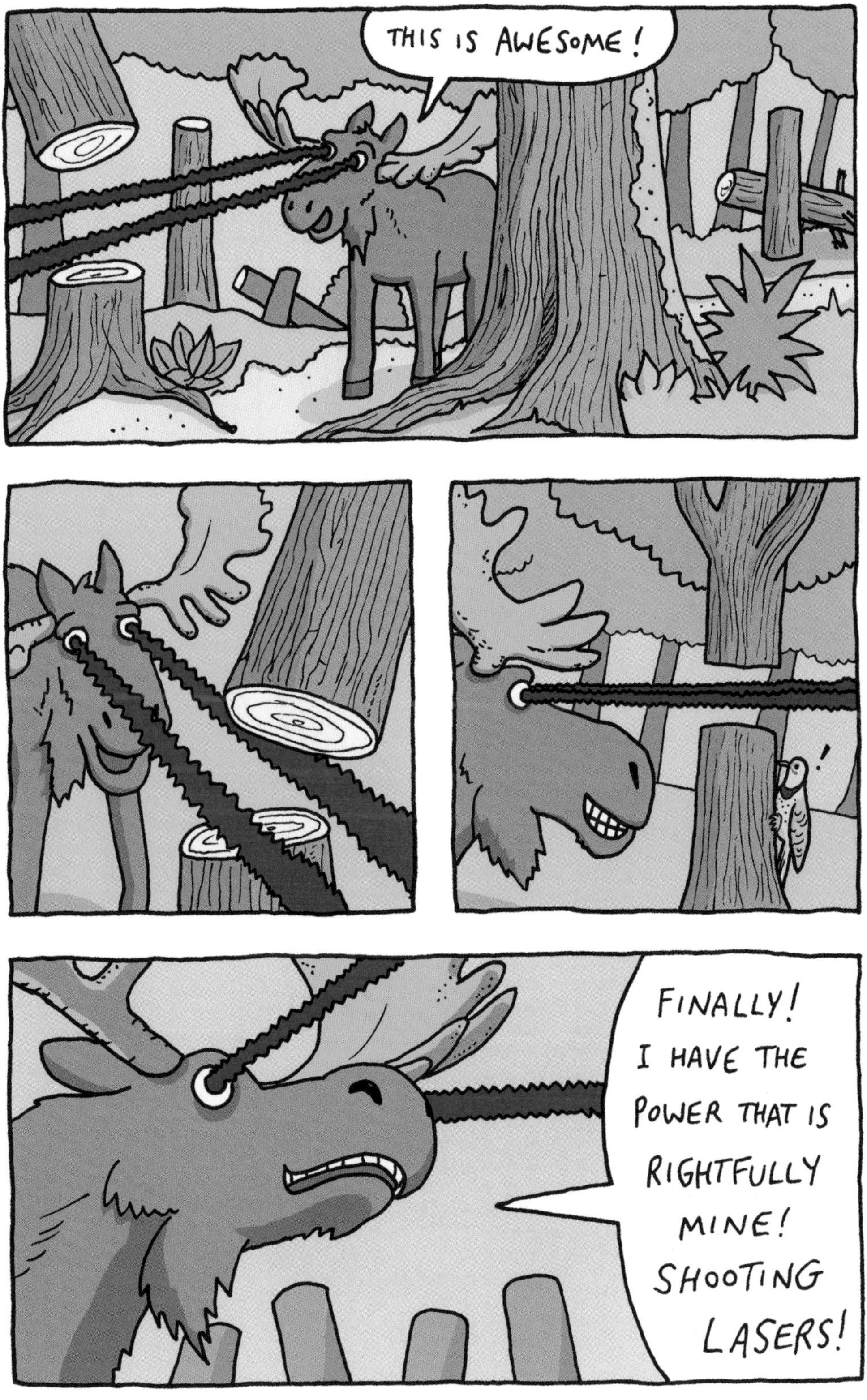
THIS IS AWESOME!
FINALLY! I HAVE THE POWER THAT IS RIGHTFULLY MINE! SHOOTING LASERS!

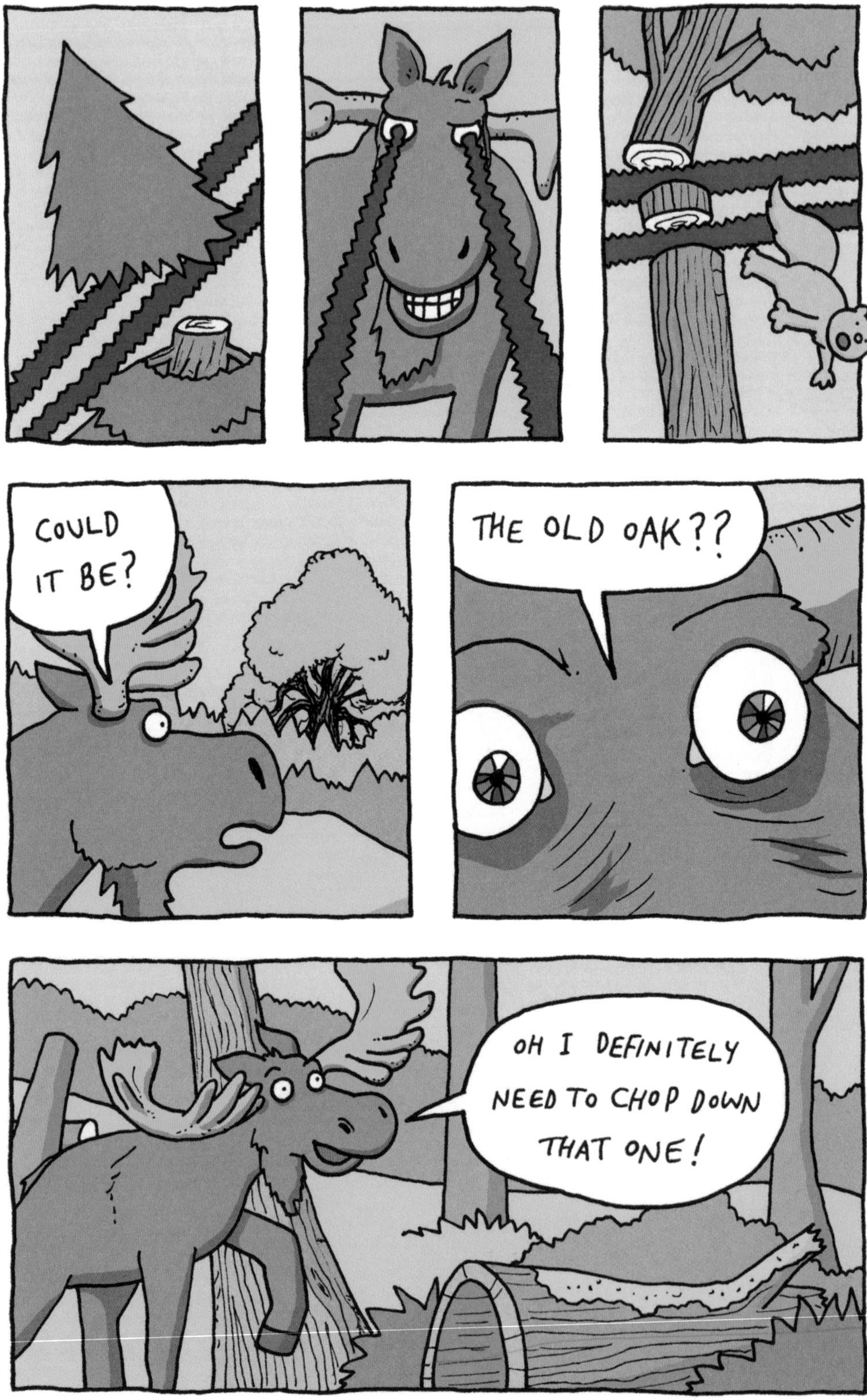
COULD IT BE?
THE OLD OAK??
OH I DEFINITELY NEED TO CHOP DOWN THAT ONE!

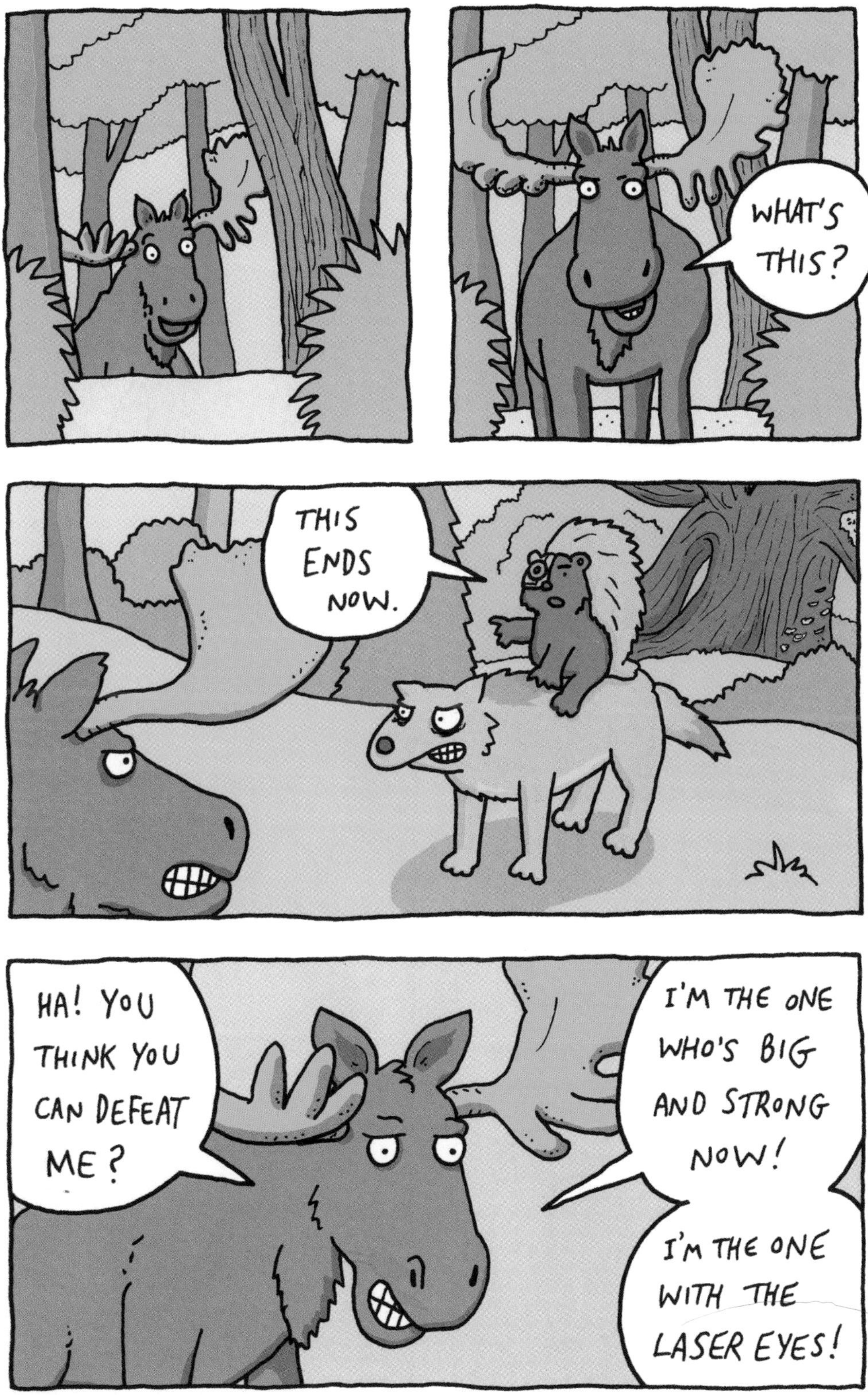
WHAT'S THIS?
THIS ENDS NOW.
HA! YOU THINK YOU CAN DEFEAT ME?
I'M THE ONE WHO'S BIG AND STRONG NOW!
I'M THE ONE WITH THE LASER EYES!

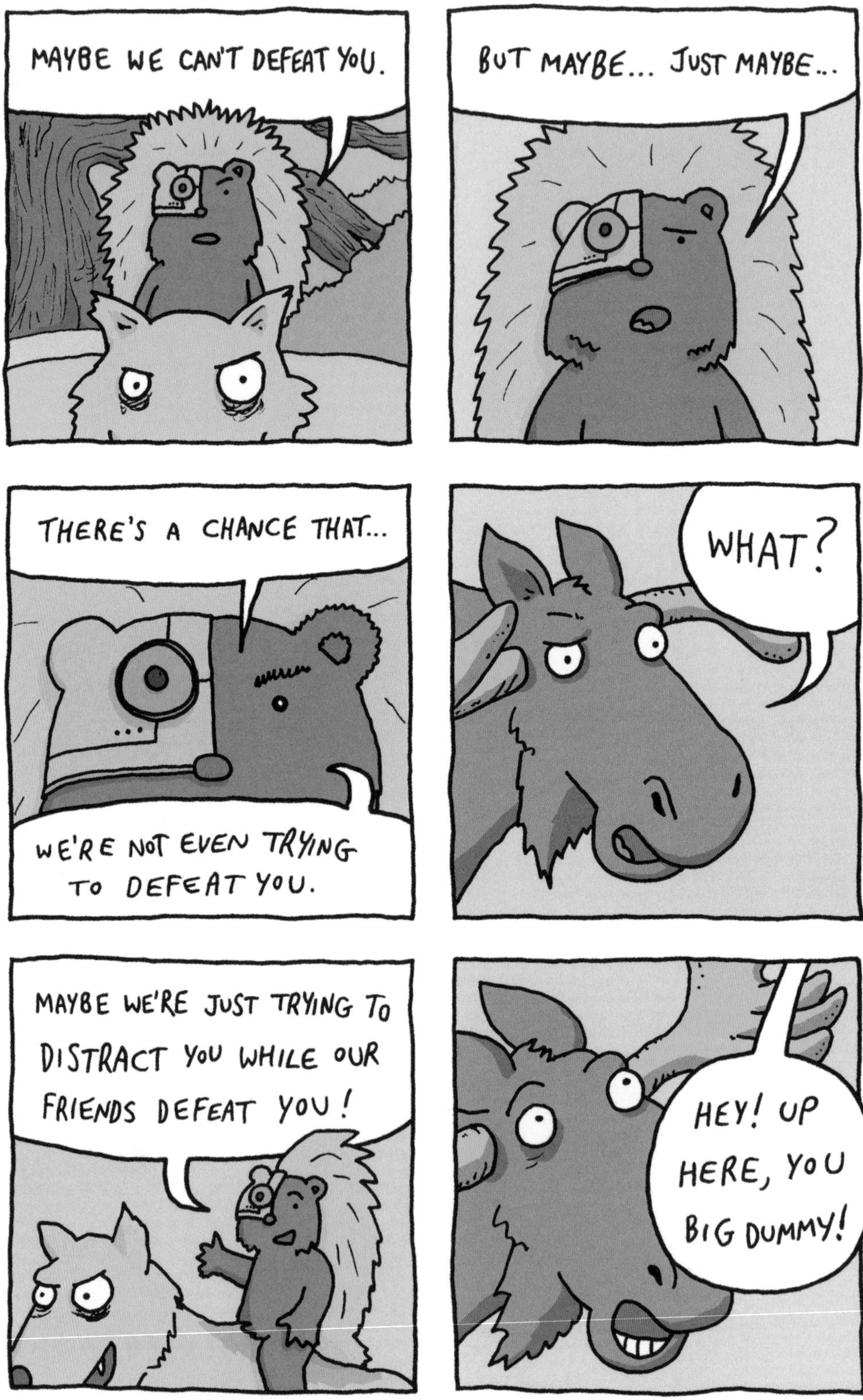
MAYBE WE CAN'T DEFEAT YOU.
BUT MAYBE... JUST MAYBE...
THERE'S A CHANCE THAT...
WE'RE NOT EVEN TRYING TO DEFEAT YOU.
WHAT?
MAYBE WE'RE JUST TRYING TO DISTRACT YOU WHILE OUR FRIENDS DEFEAT YOU!
HEY! UP HERE, YOU BIG DUMMY!

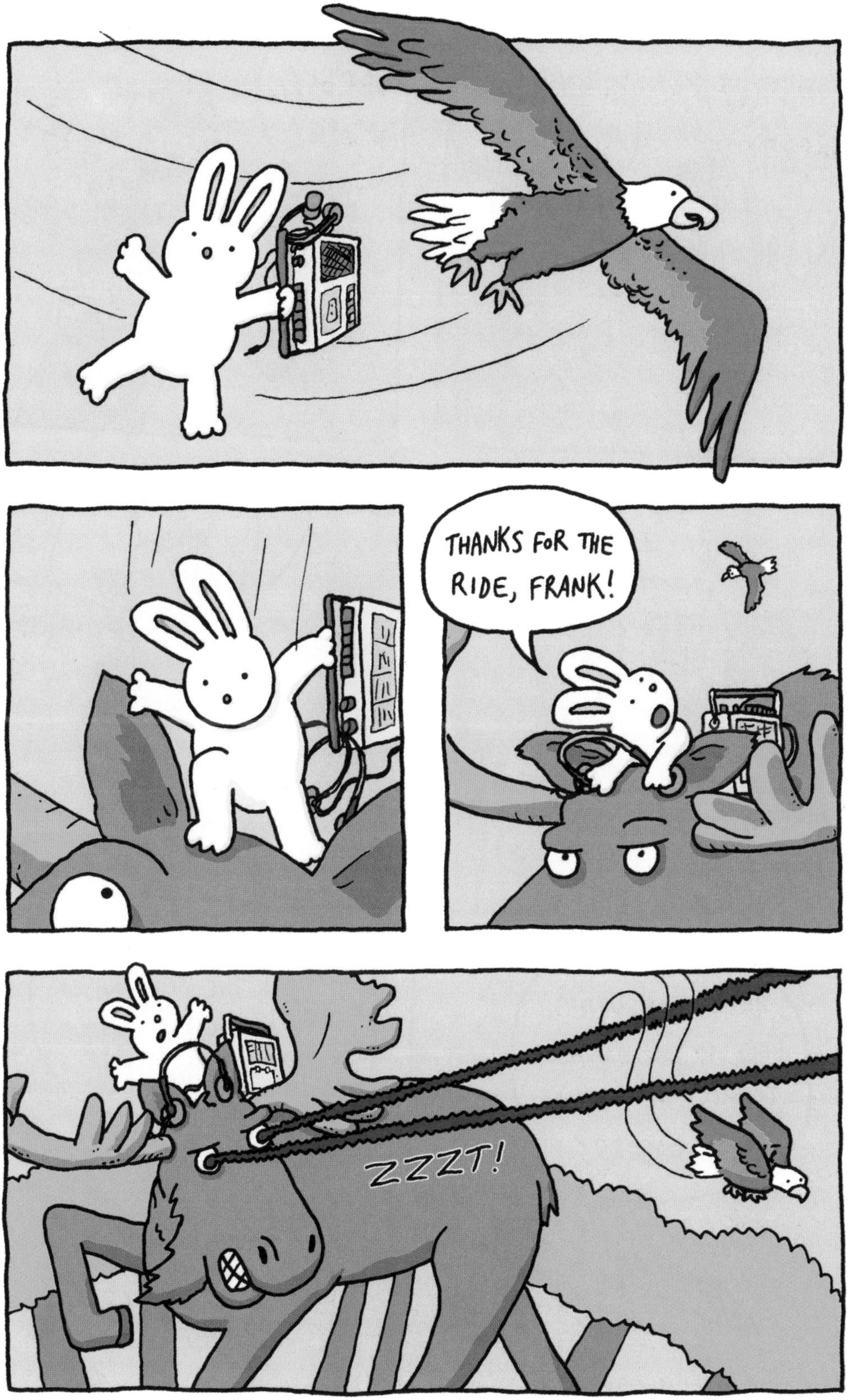
THANKS FOR THE RIDE, FRANK!
ZZZT!

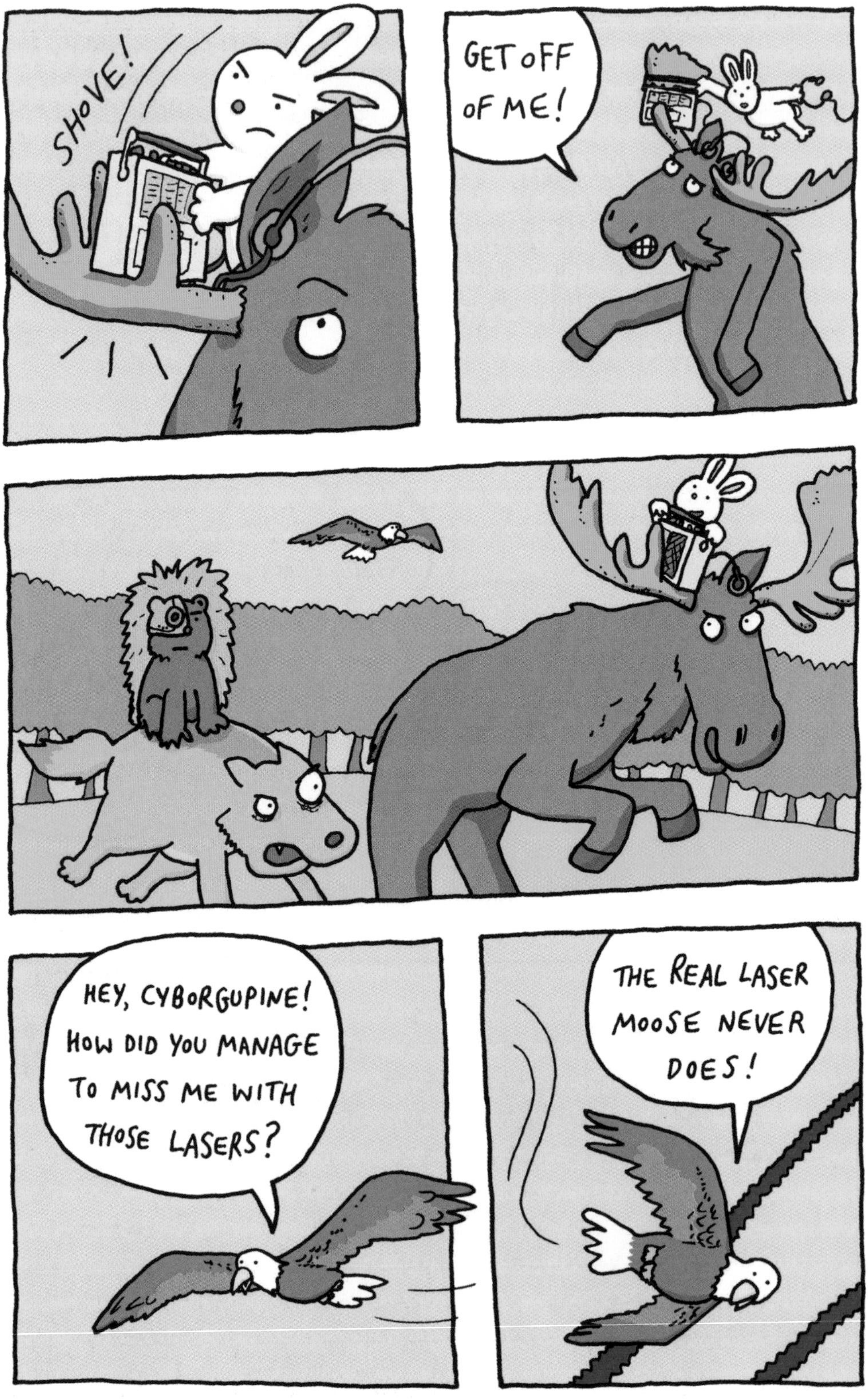
SHOVE!
GET OFF OF ME!
HEY, CYBORGUPINE! HOW DID YOU MANAGE TO MISS ME WITH THOSE LASERS?
THE REAL LASER MOOSE NEVER DOES!

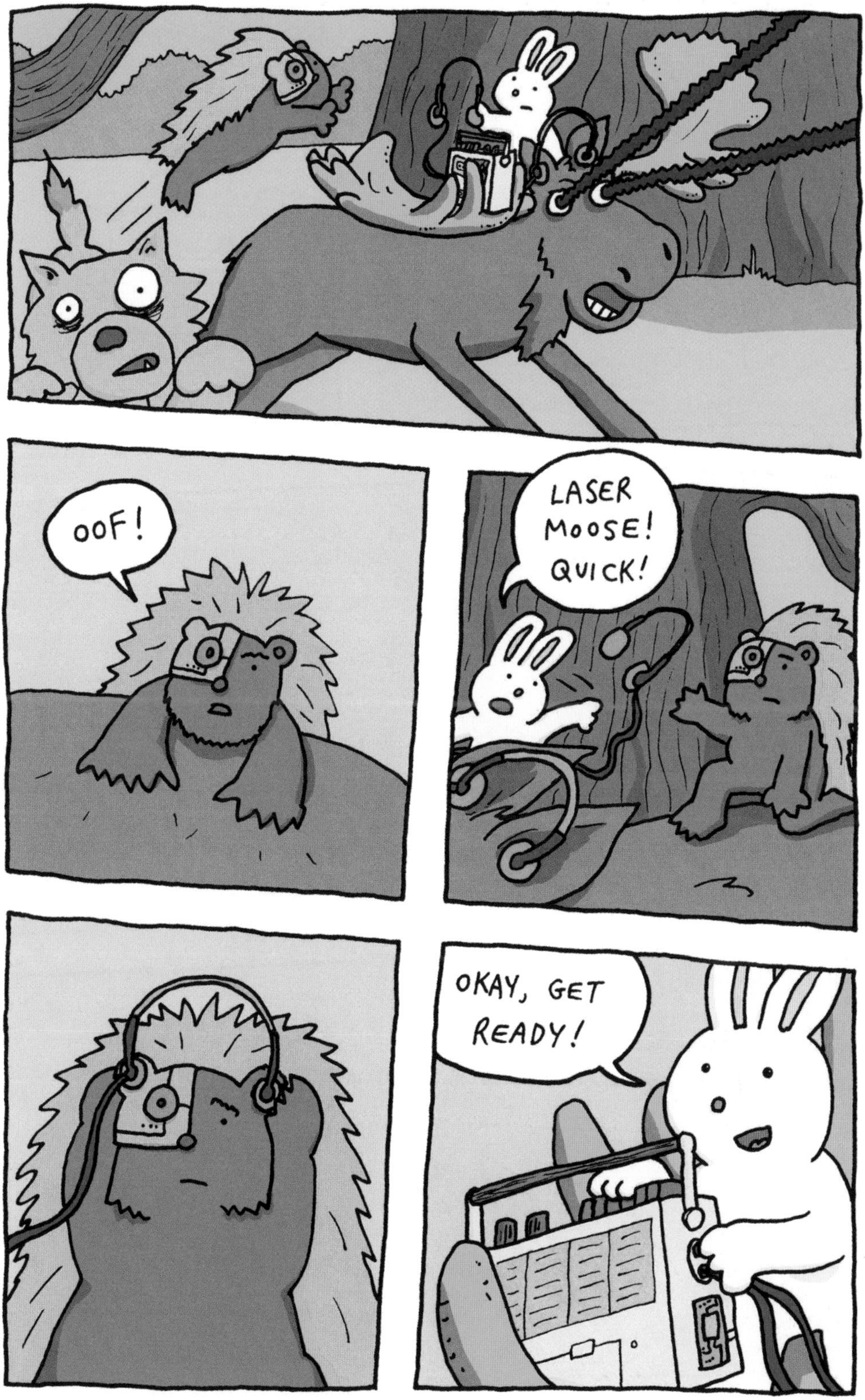
OOF!
LASER MOOSE! QUICK!
OKAY, GET READY!

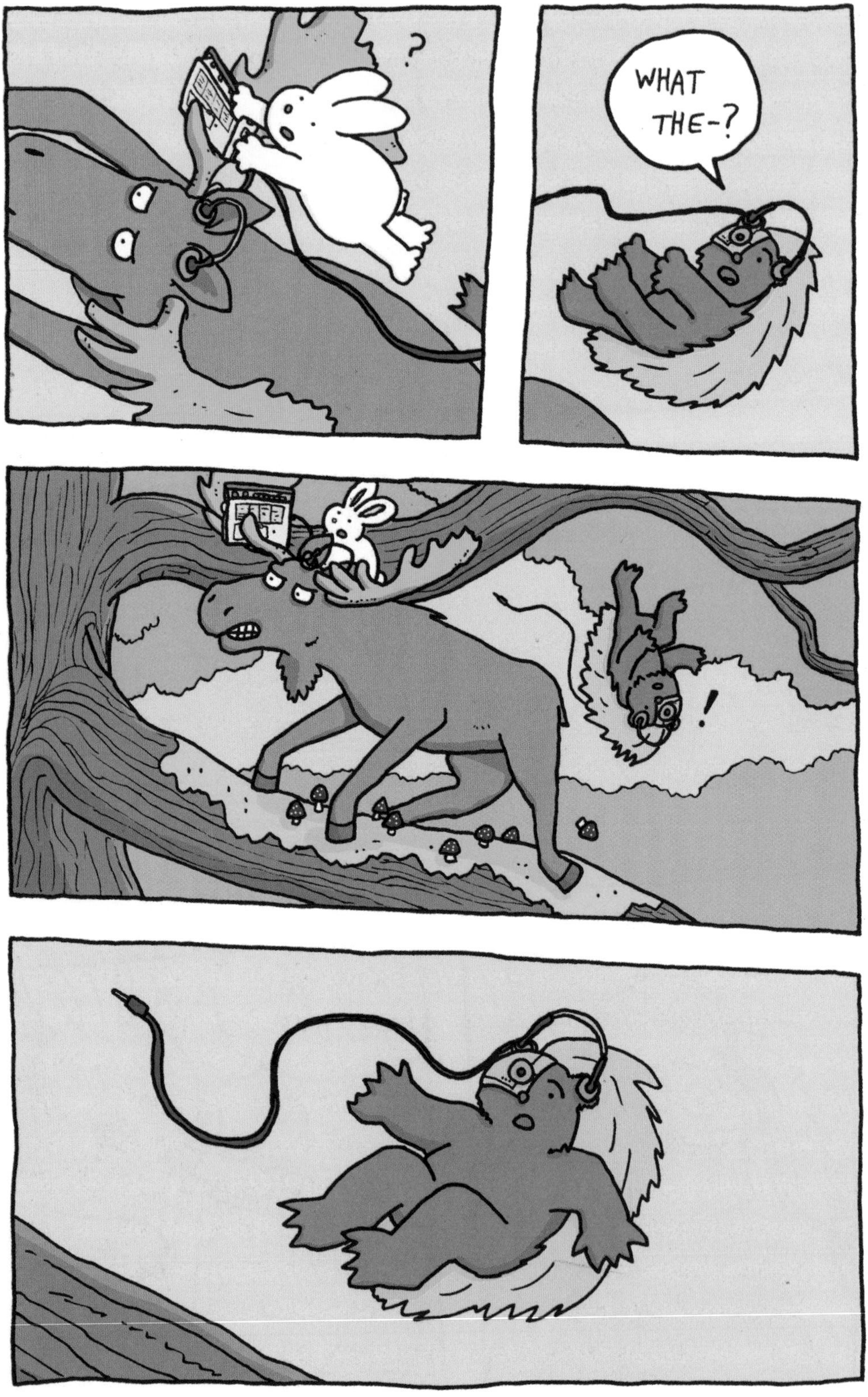
?
WHAT THE-?
!

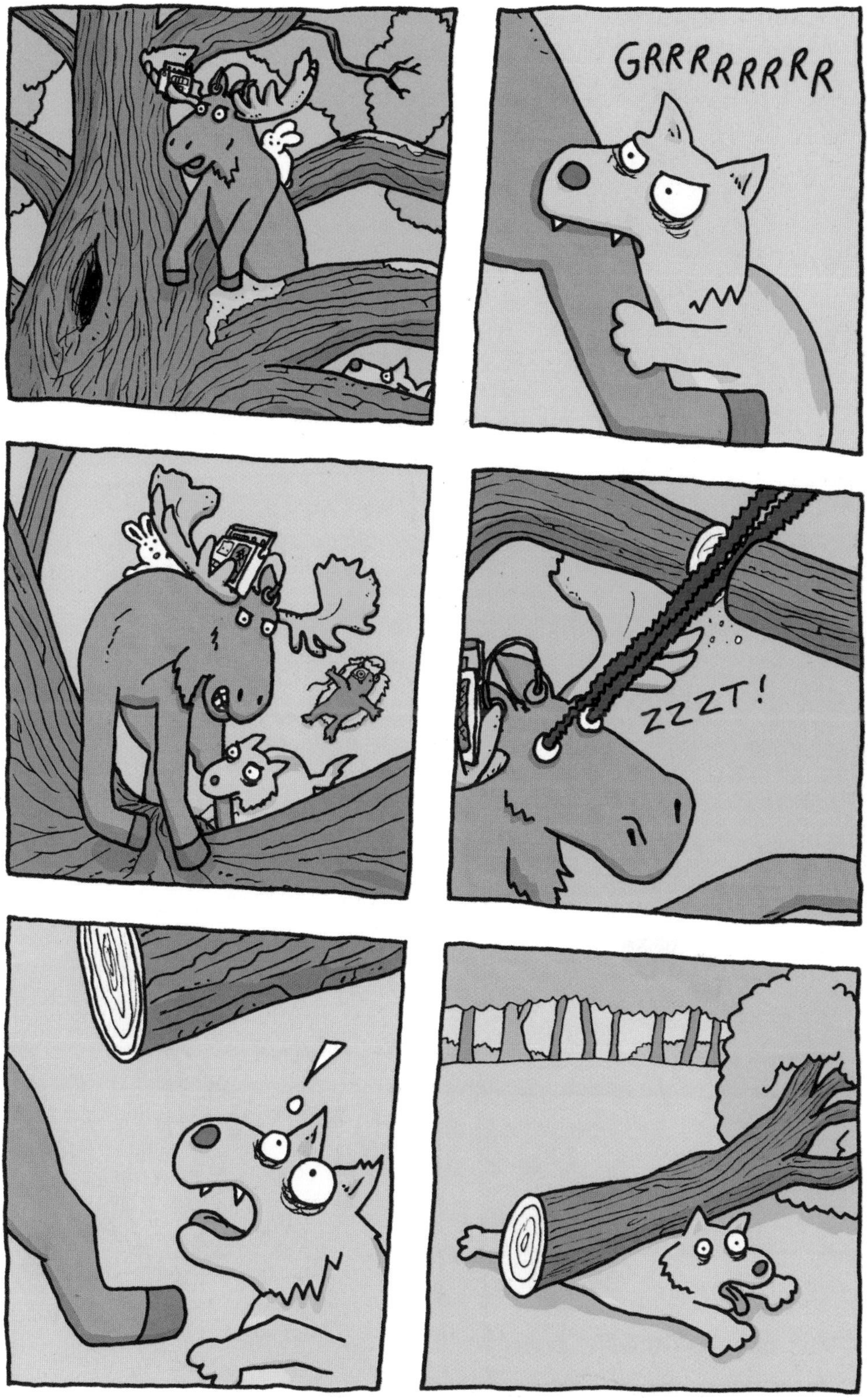
GRRRRRRRR
ZZZT!
!

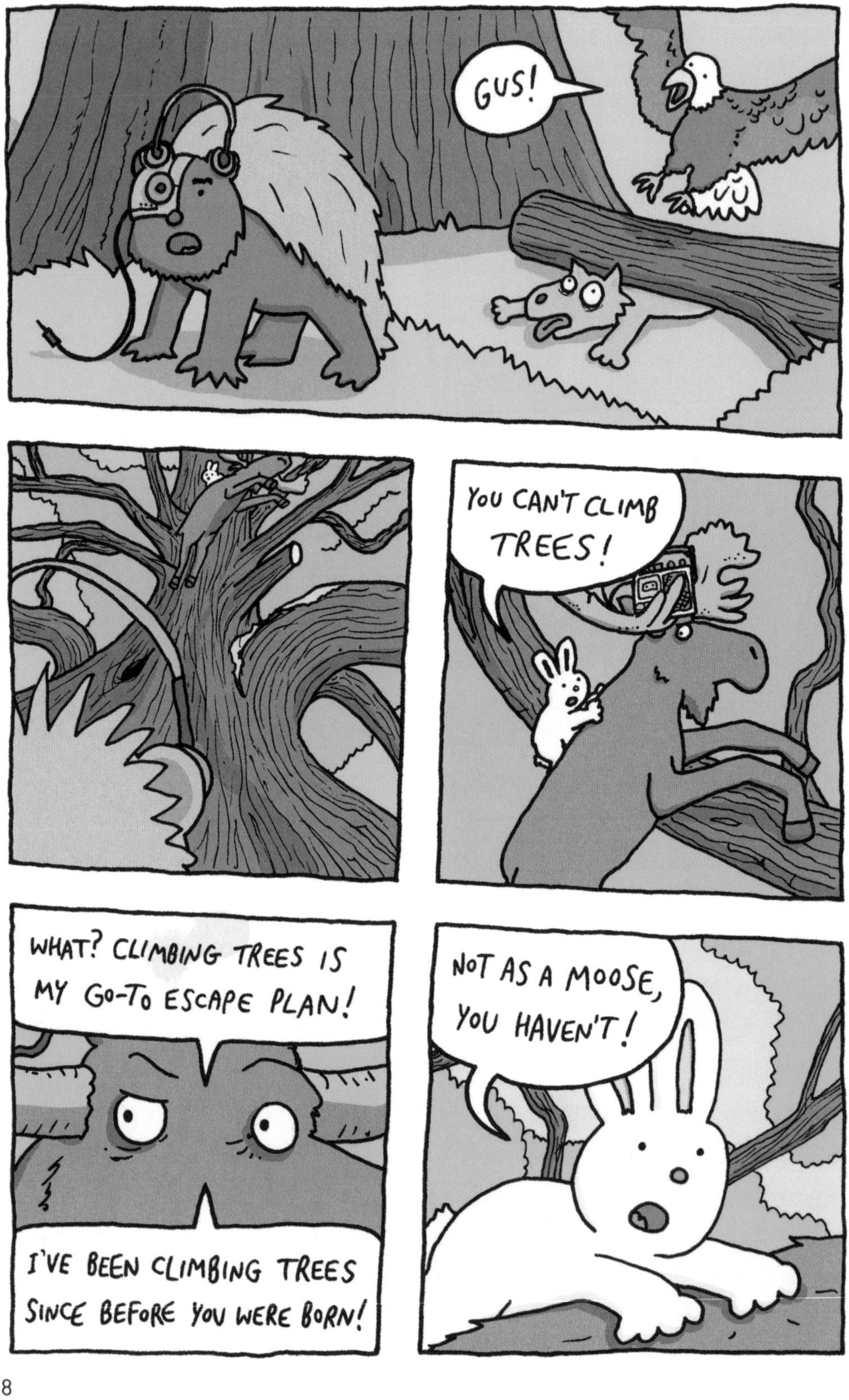
GUS!
YOU CAN'T CLIMB TREES!
WHAT? CLIMBING TREES IS MY GO-TO ESCAPE PLAN!
I'VE BEEN CLIMBING TREES SINCE BEFORE YOU WERE BORN!
NOT AS A MOOSE, YOU HAVEN'T!

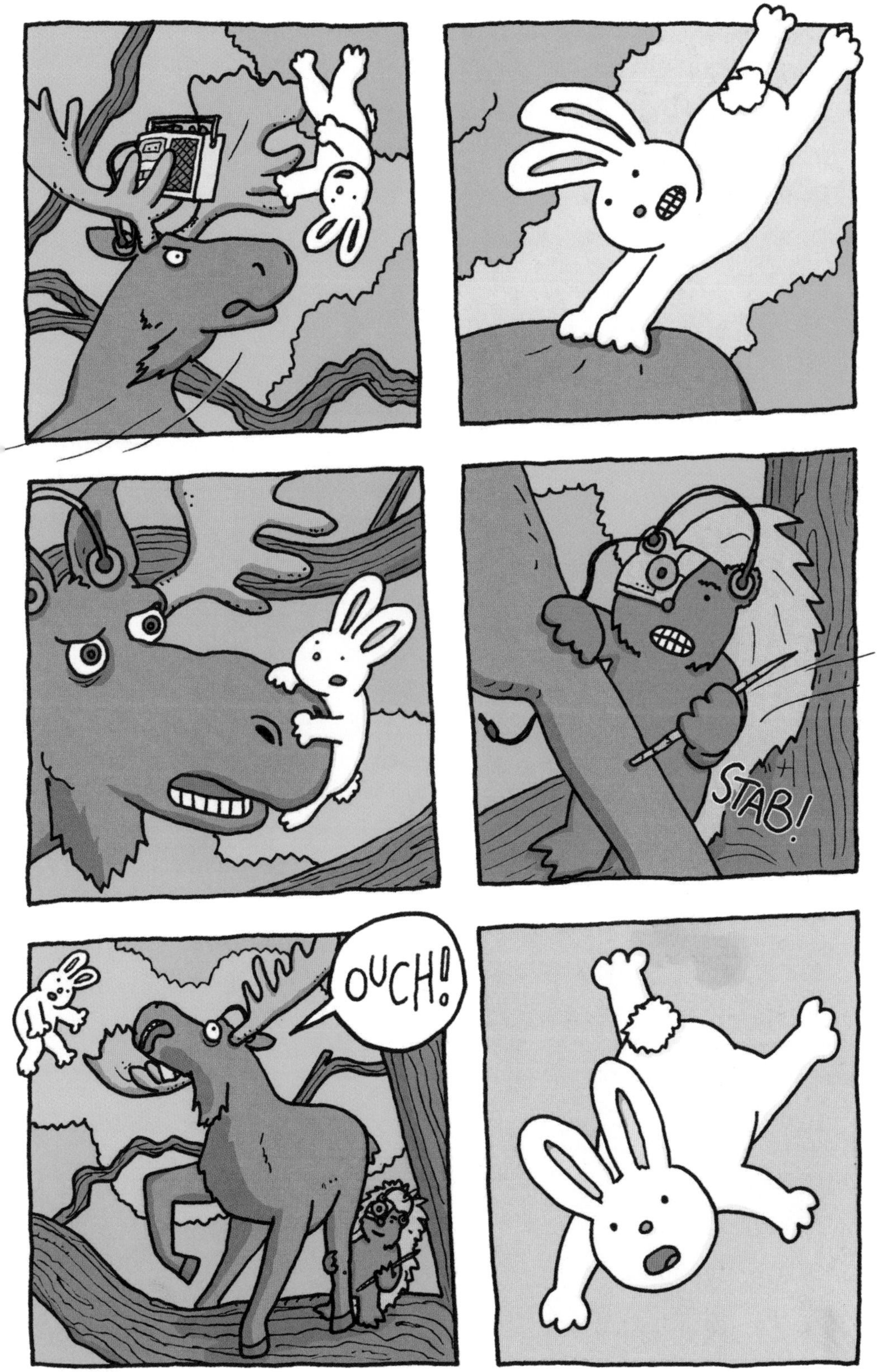
STAB!
OUCH!

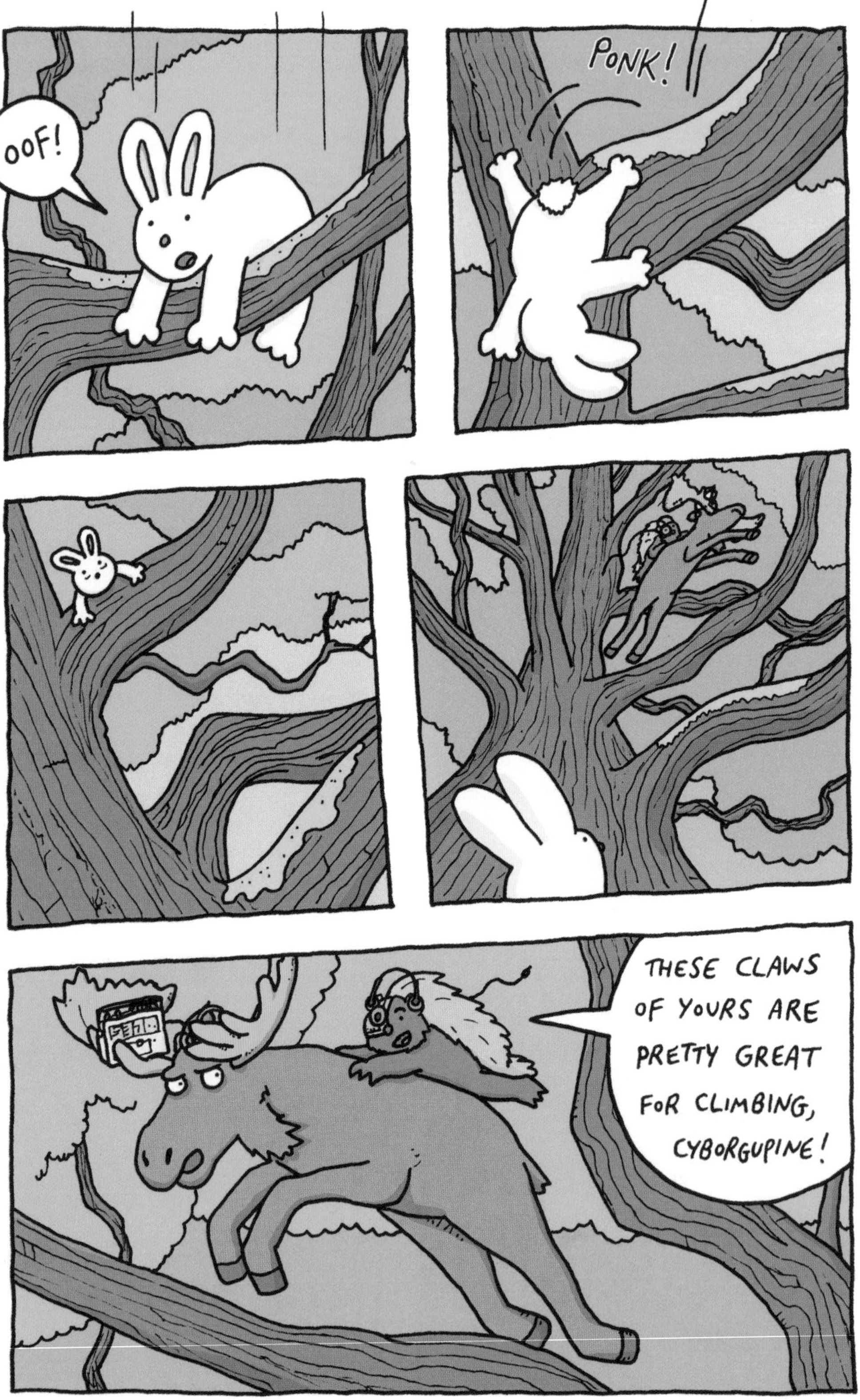
OOF!
PONK!
THESE CLAWS OF YOURS ARE PRETTY GREAT FOR CLIMBING, CYBORGUPINE!

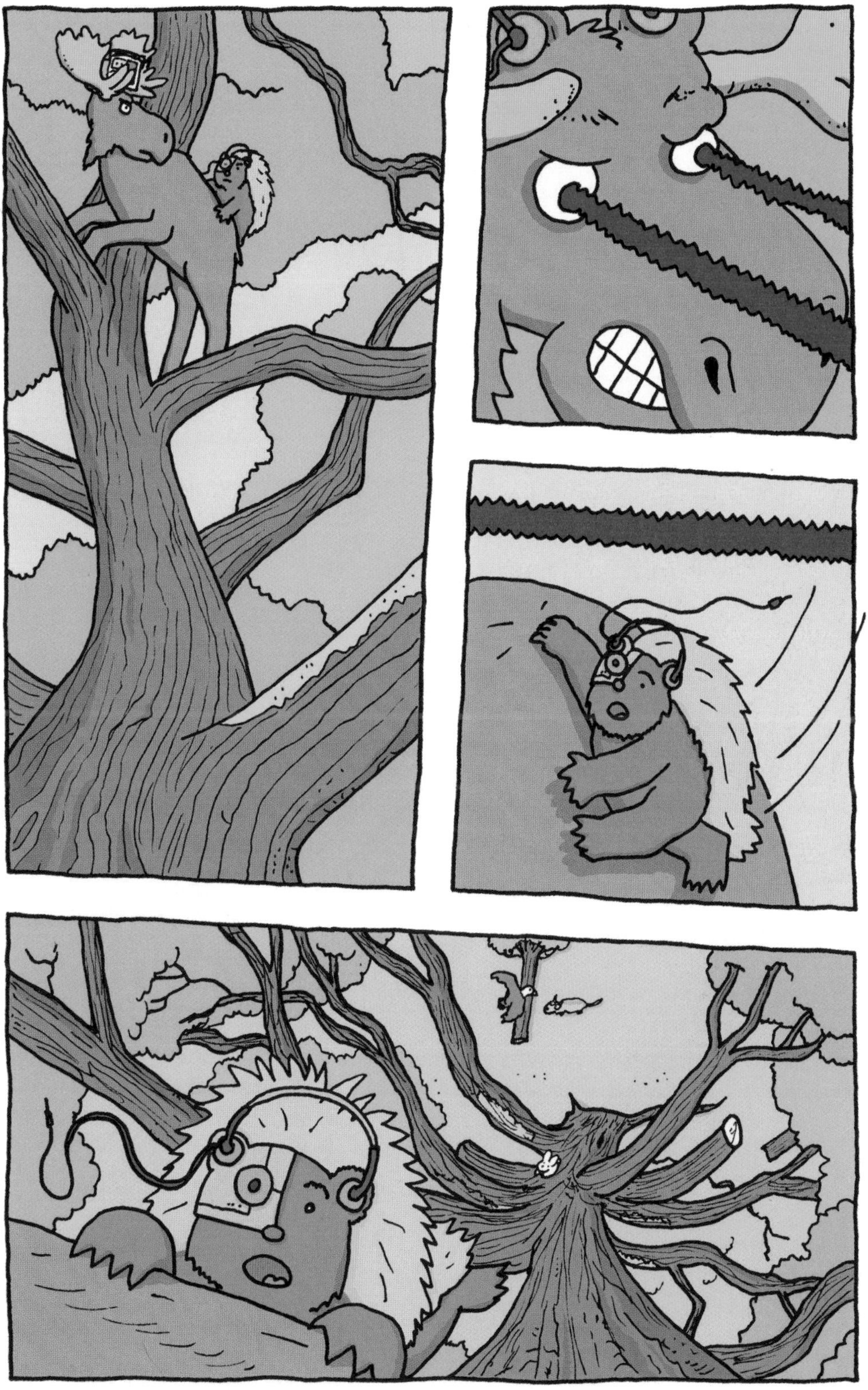

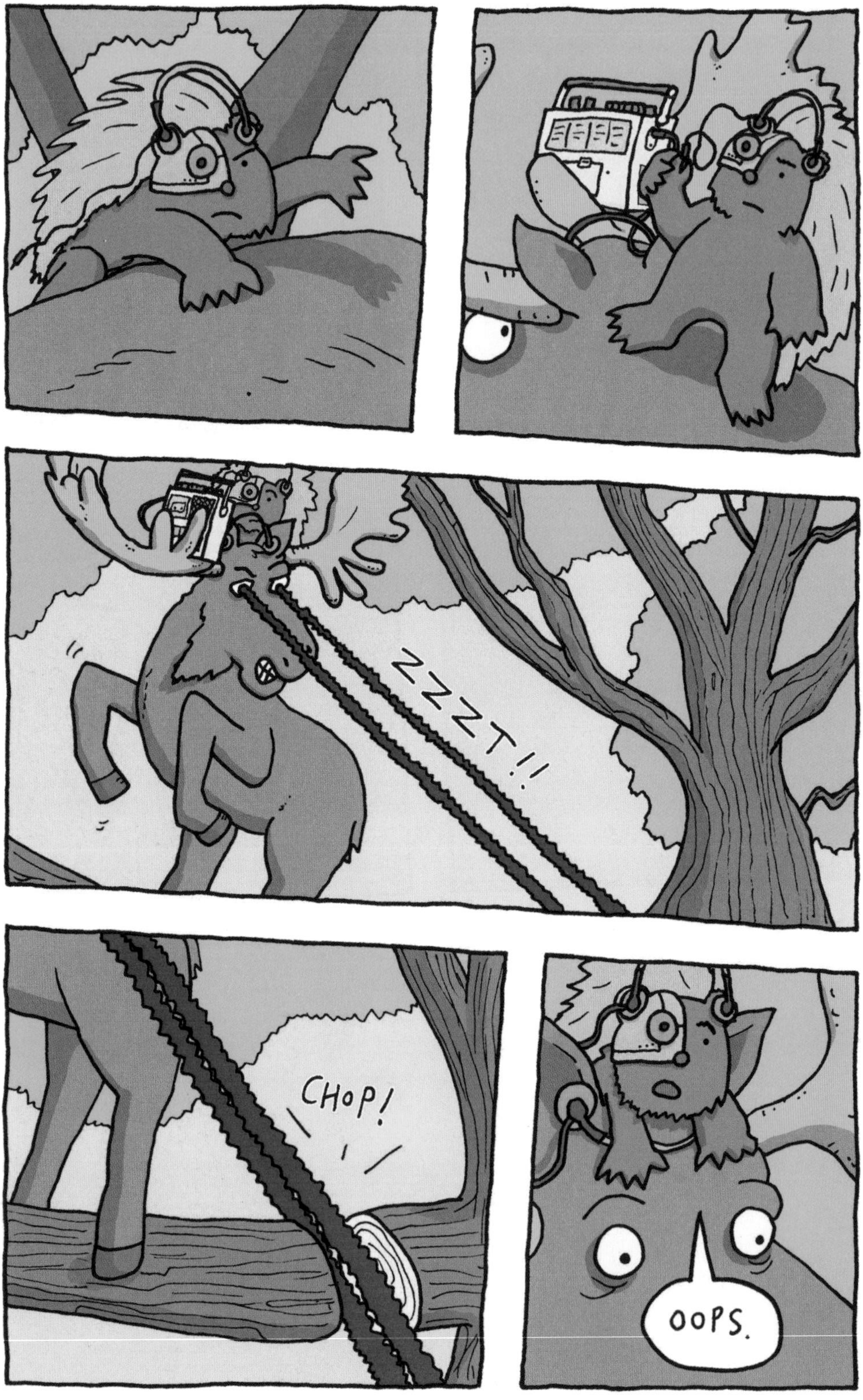
ZZZZT!!
CHOP!
OOPS.

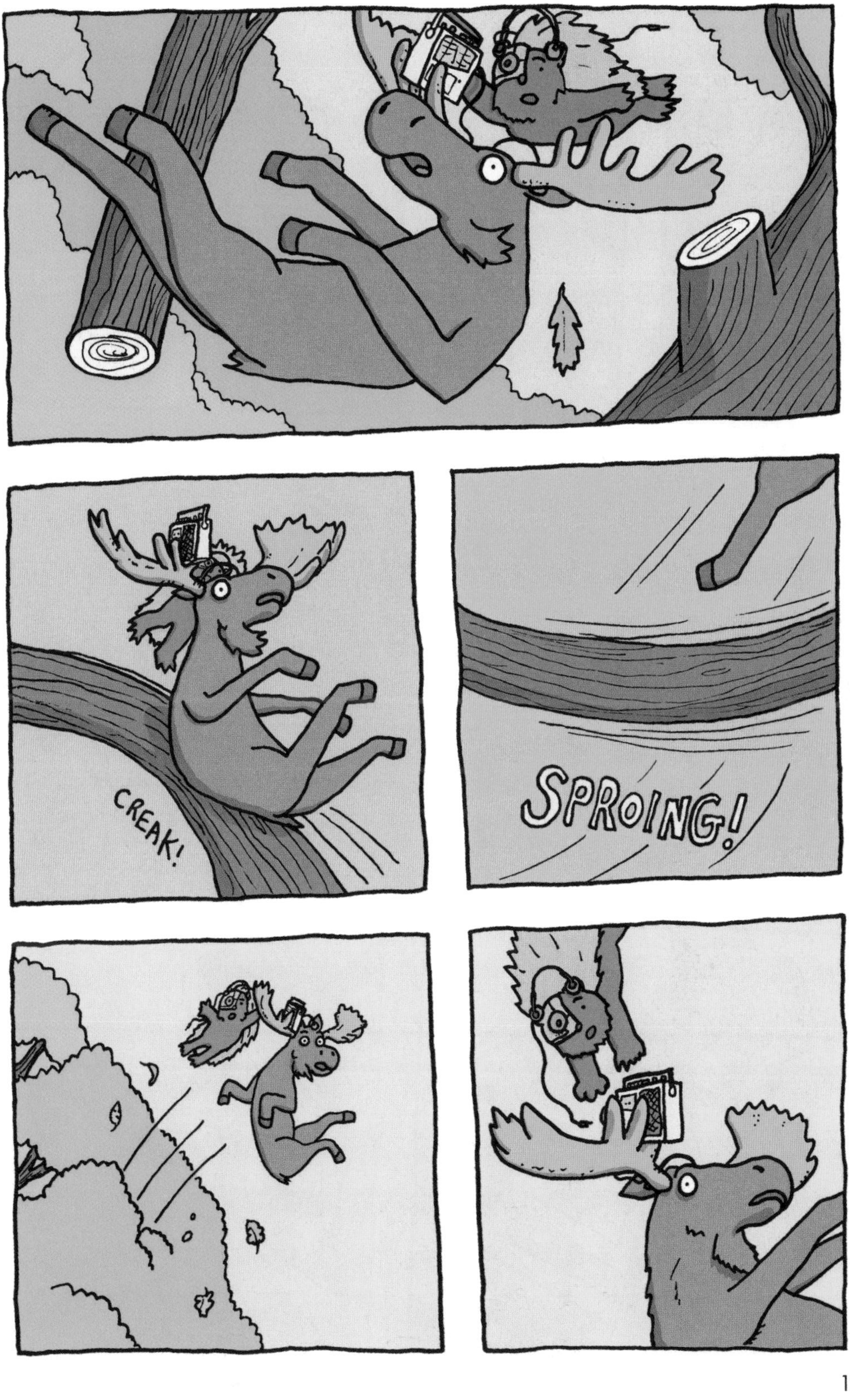
CREAK!
SPROING!

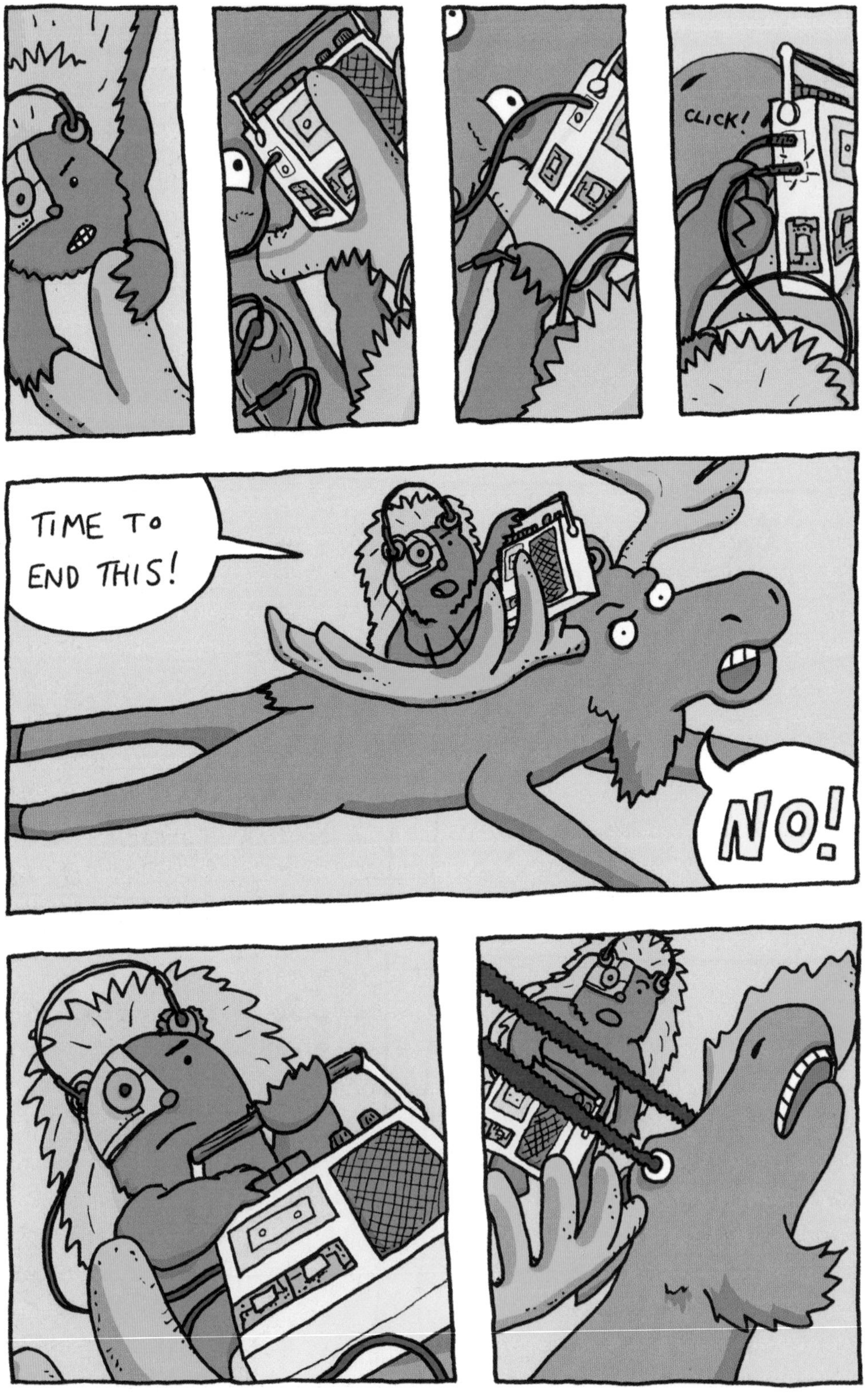
CLICK!
TIME TO END THIS!
NO!

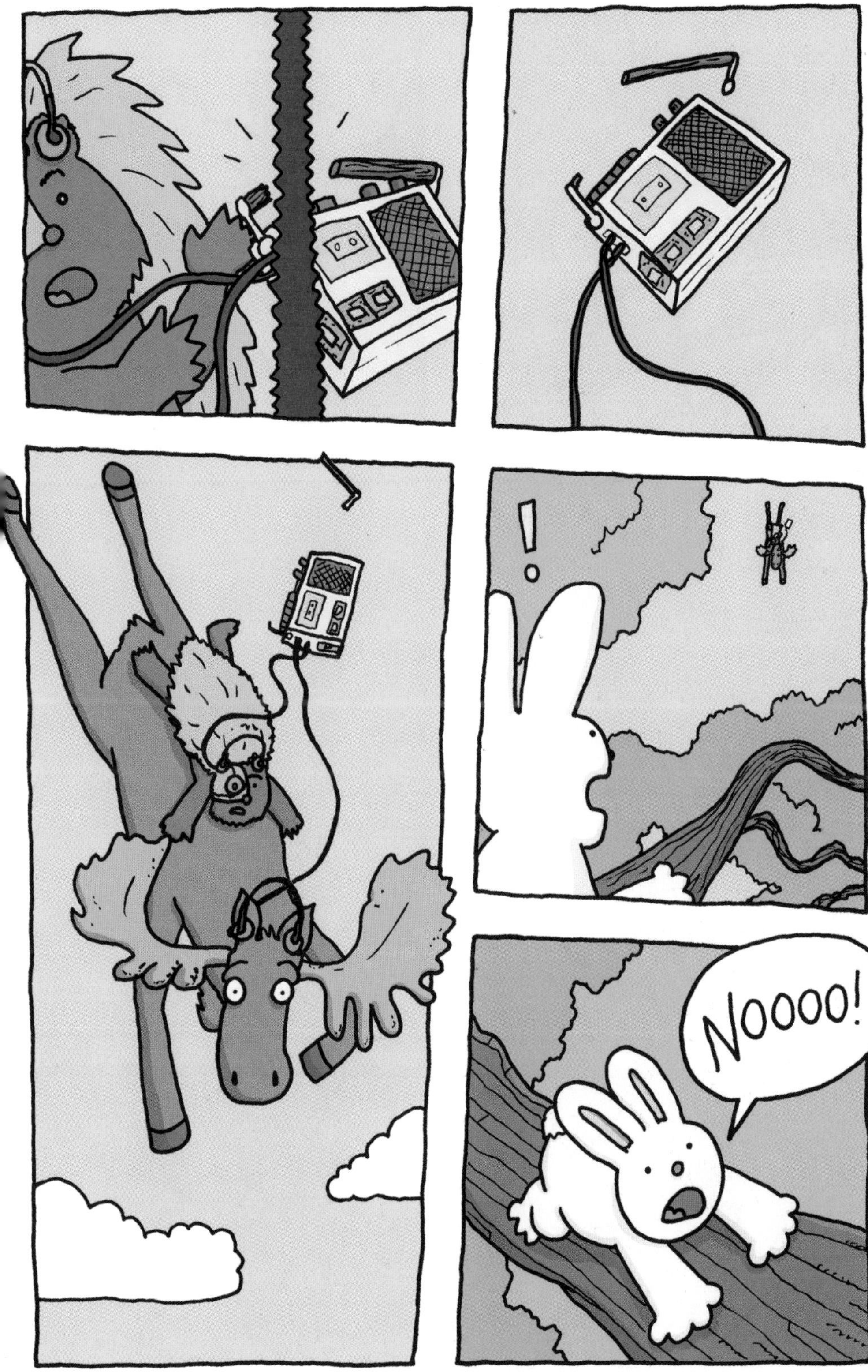
!
NOOOO!

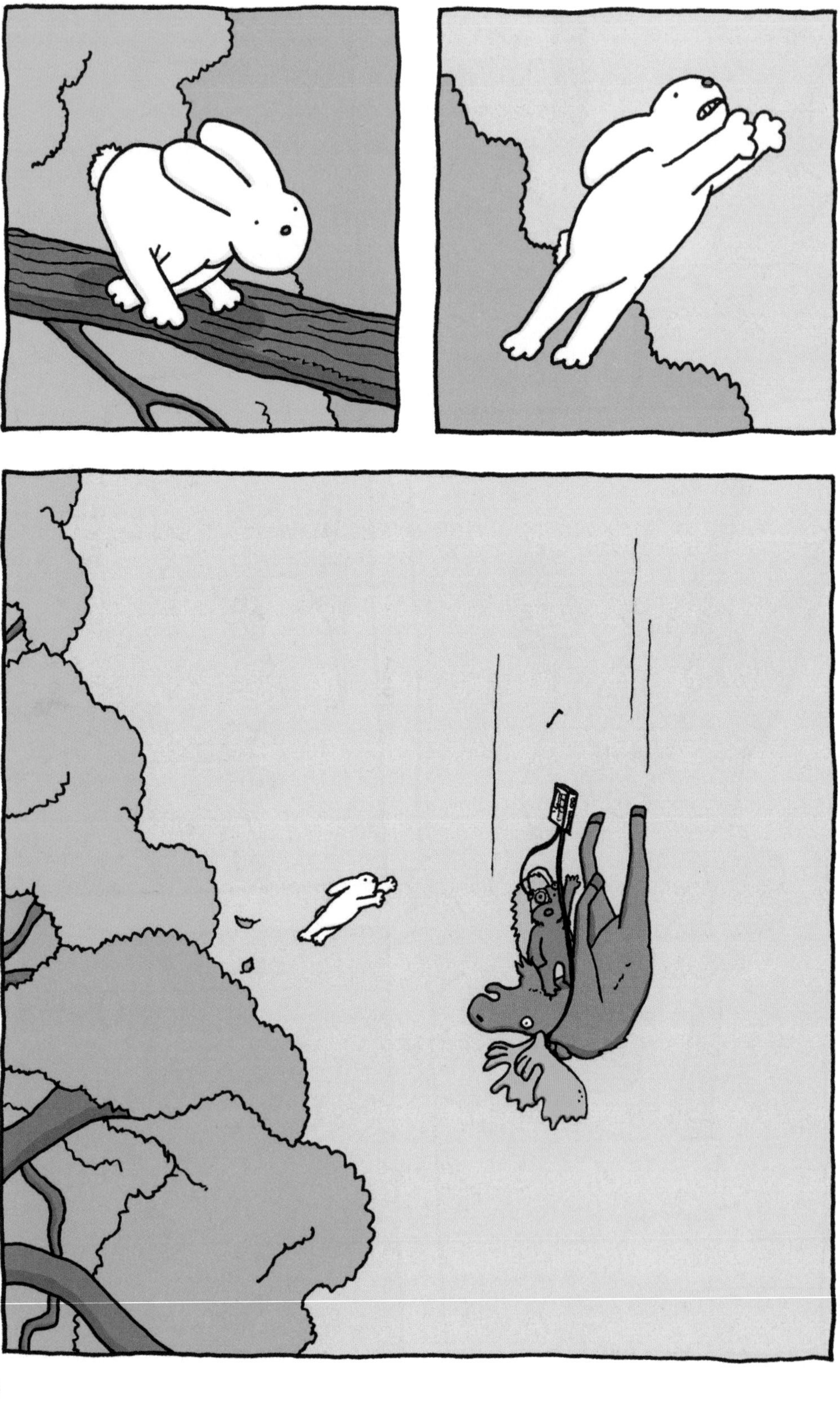

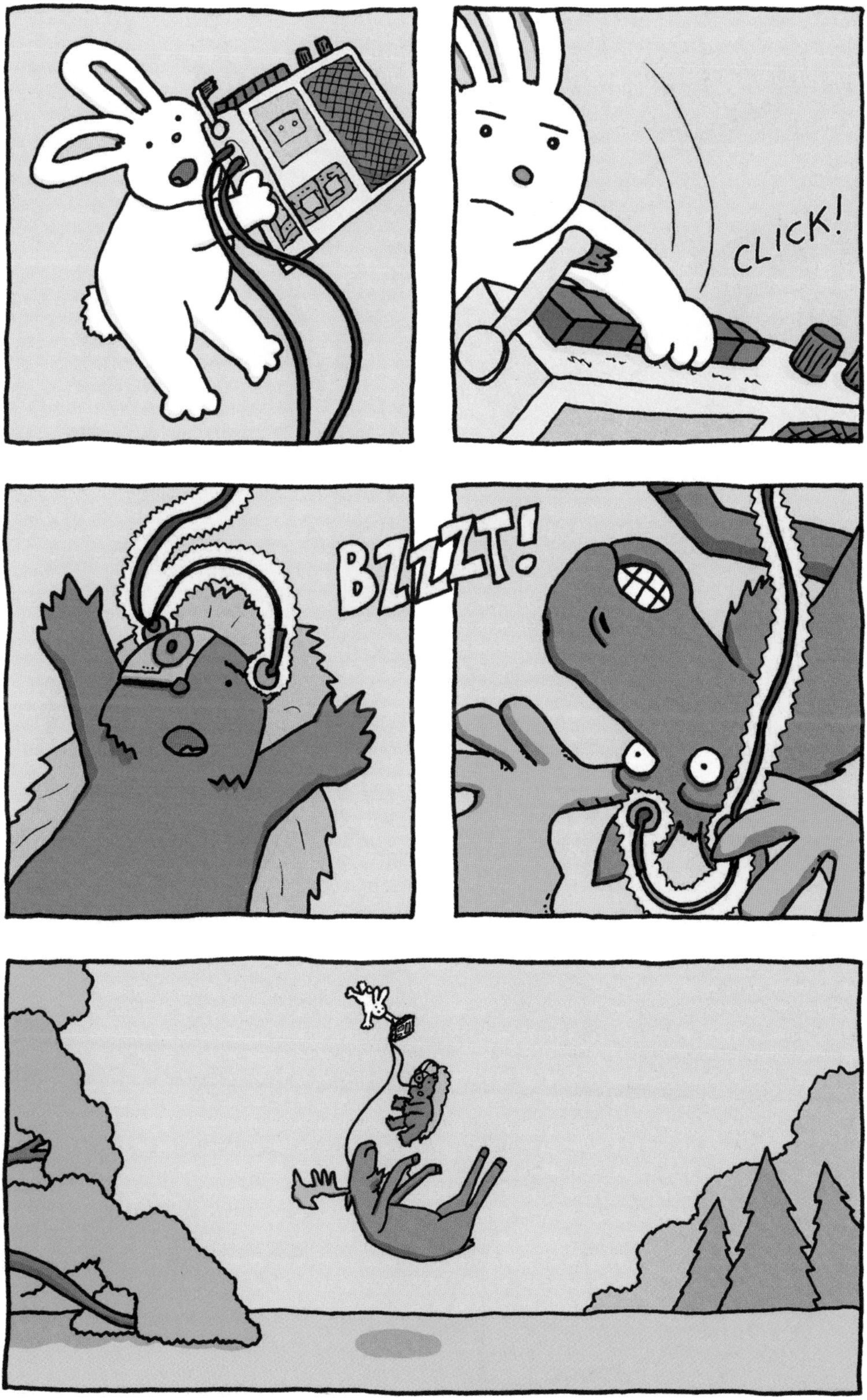
CLICK!
BZZZT!

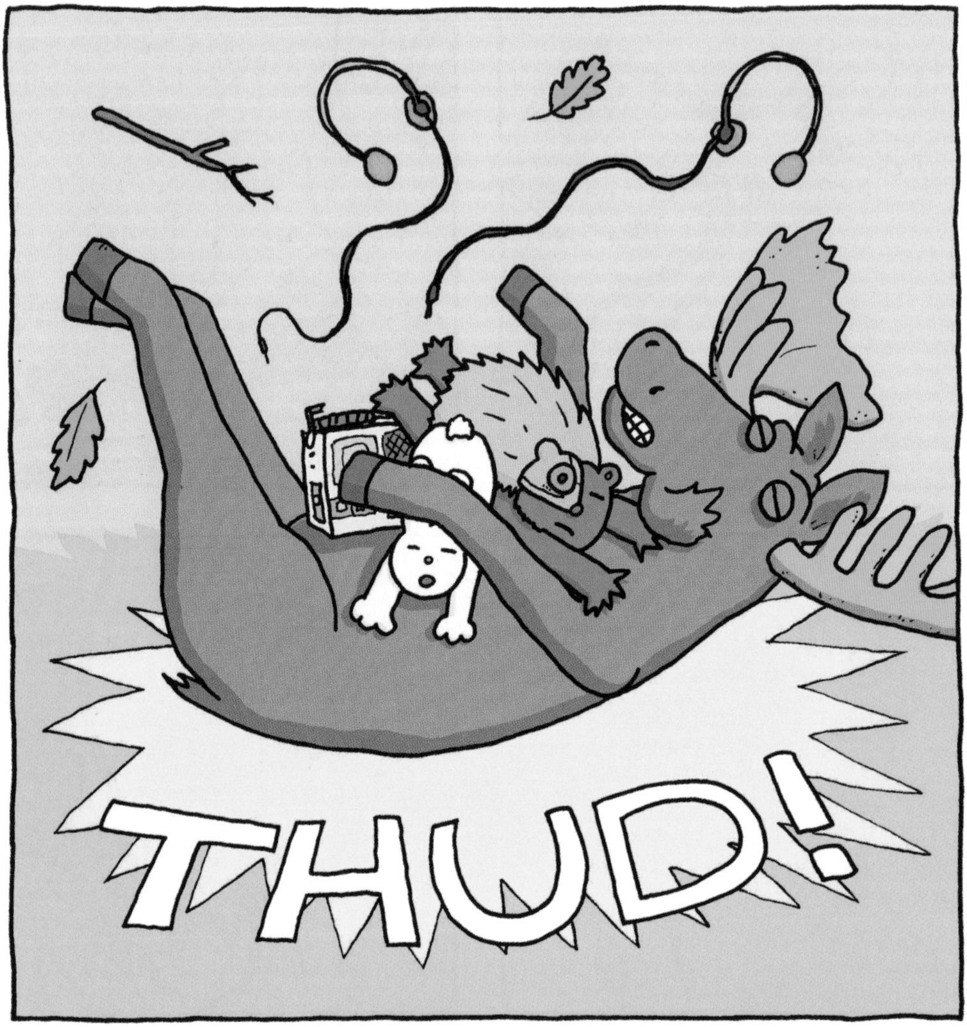
THUD!

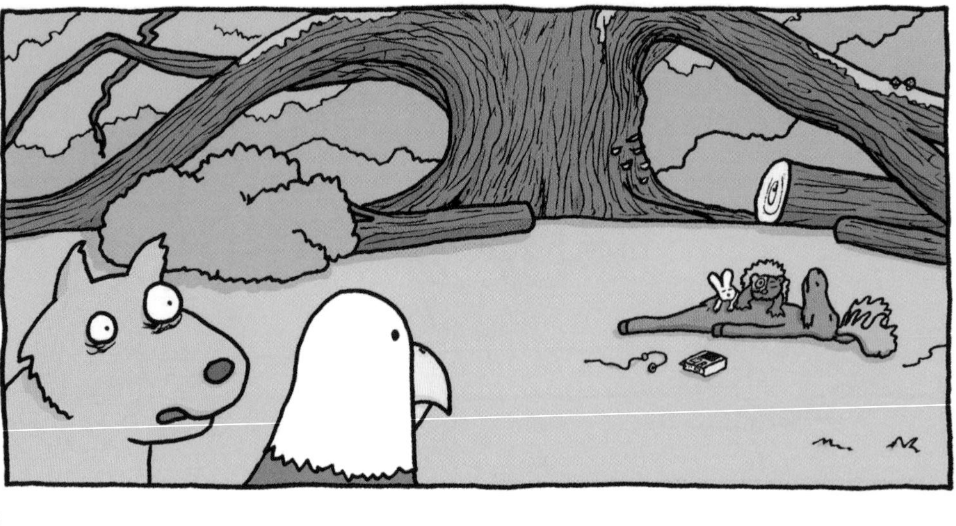

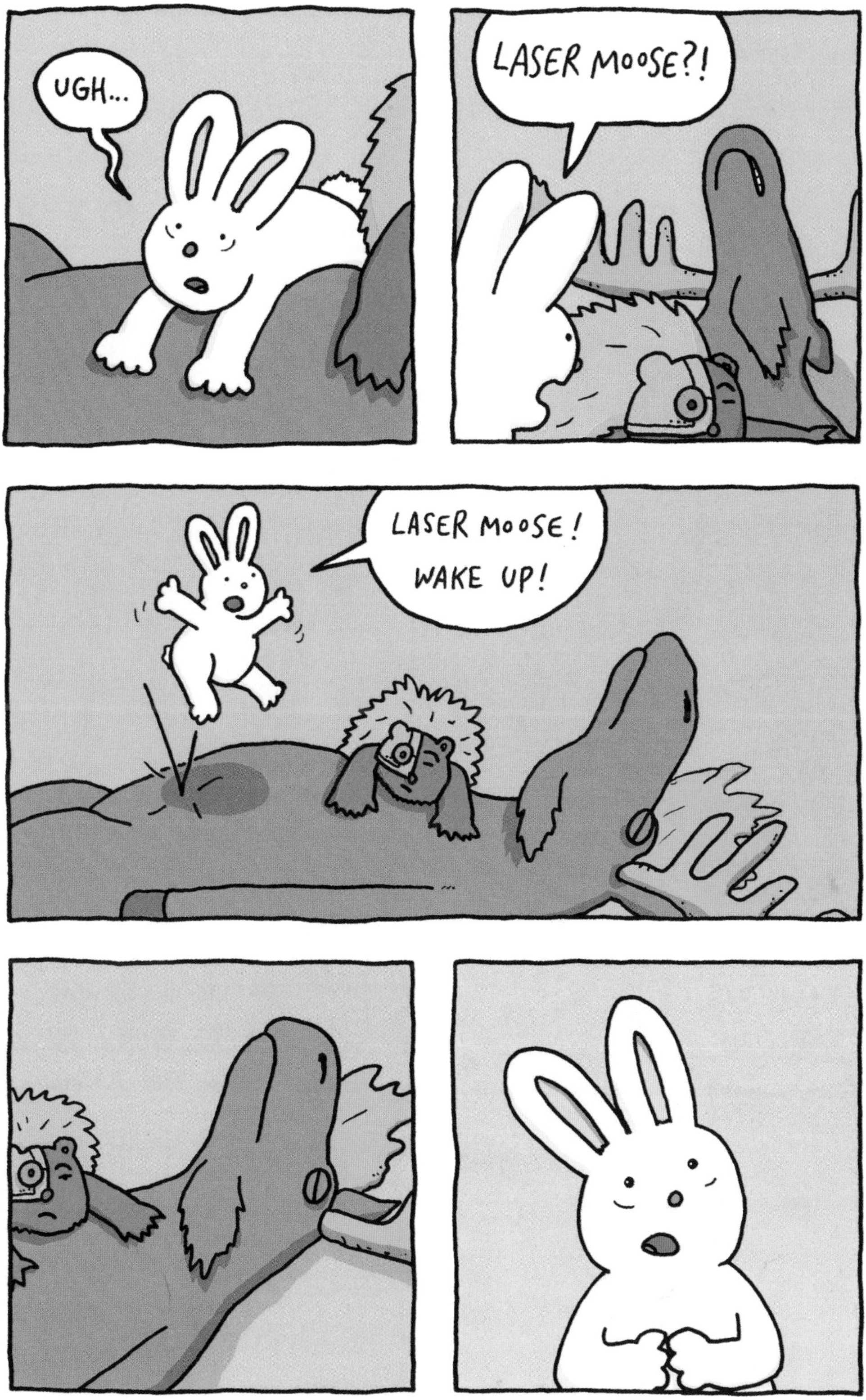
UGH...
LASER MOOSE?!
LASER MOOSE! WAKE UP!

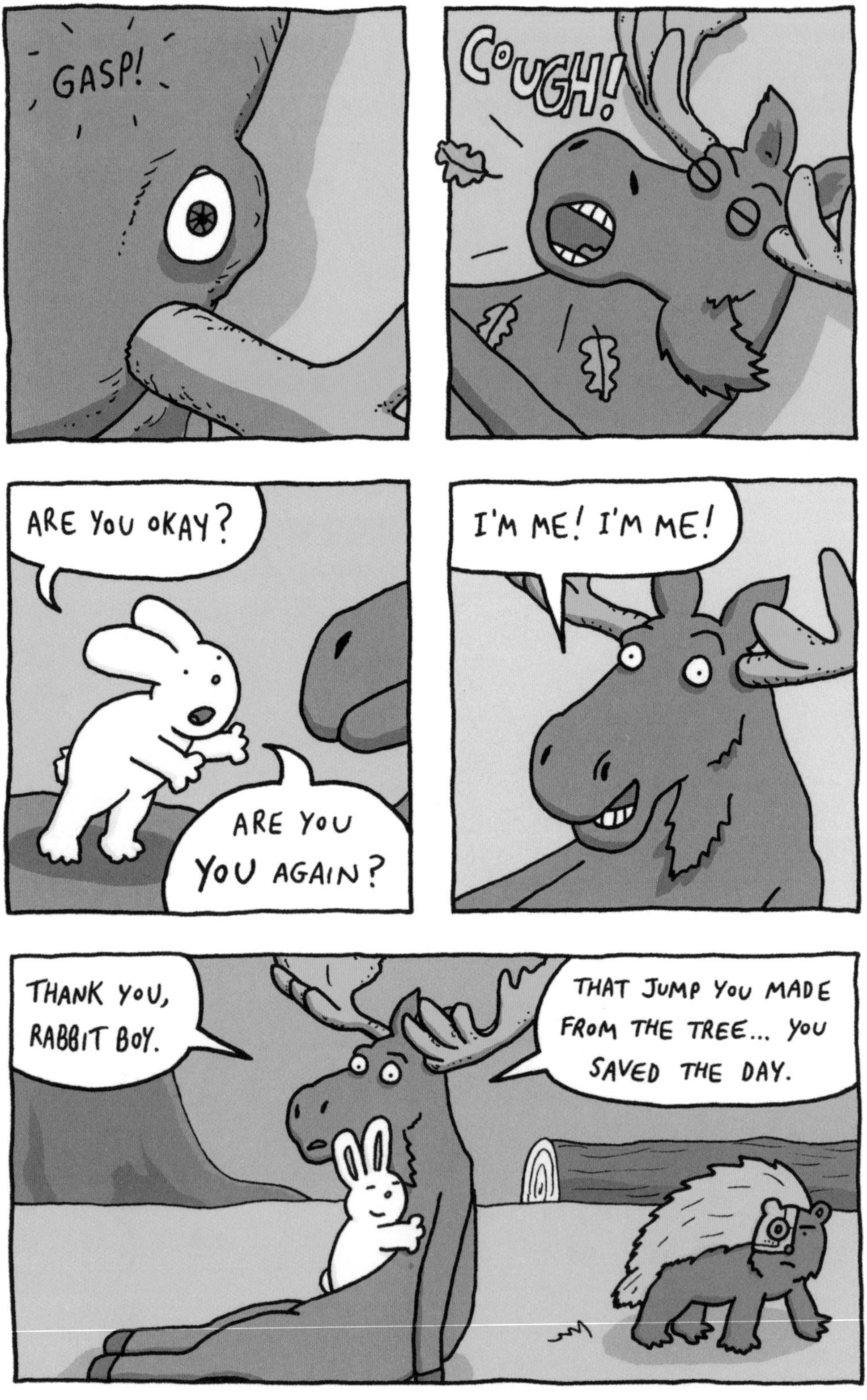
GASP!
COUGH!
ARE YOU OKAY?
ARE YOU
YOU AGAIN?
I'M ME! I'M ME!
THANK YOU,
RABBIT BOY.
THAT JUMP YOU MADE
FROM THE TREE... YOU
SAVED THE DAY.

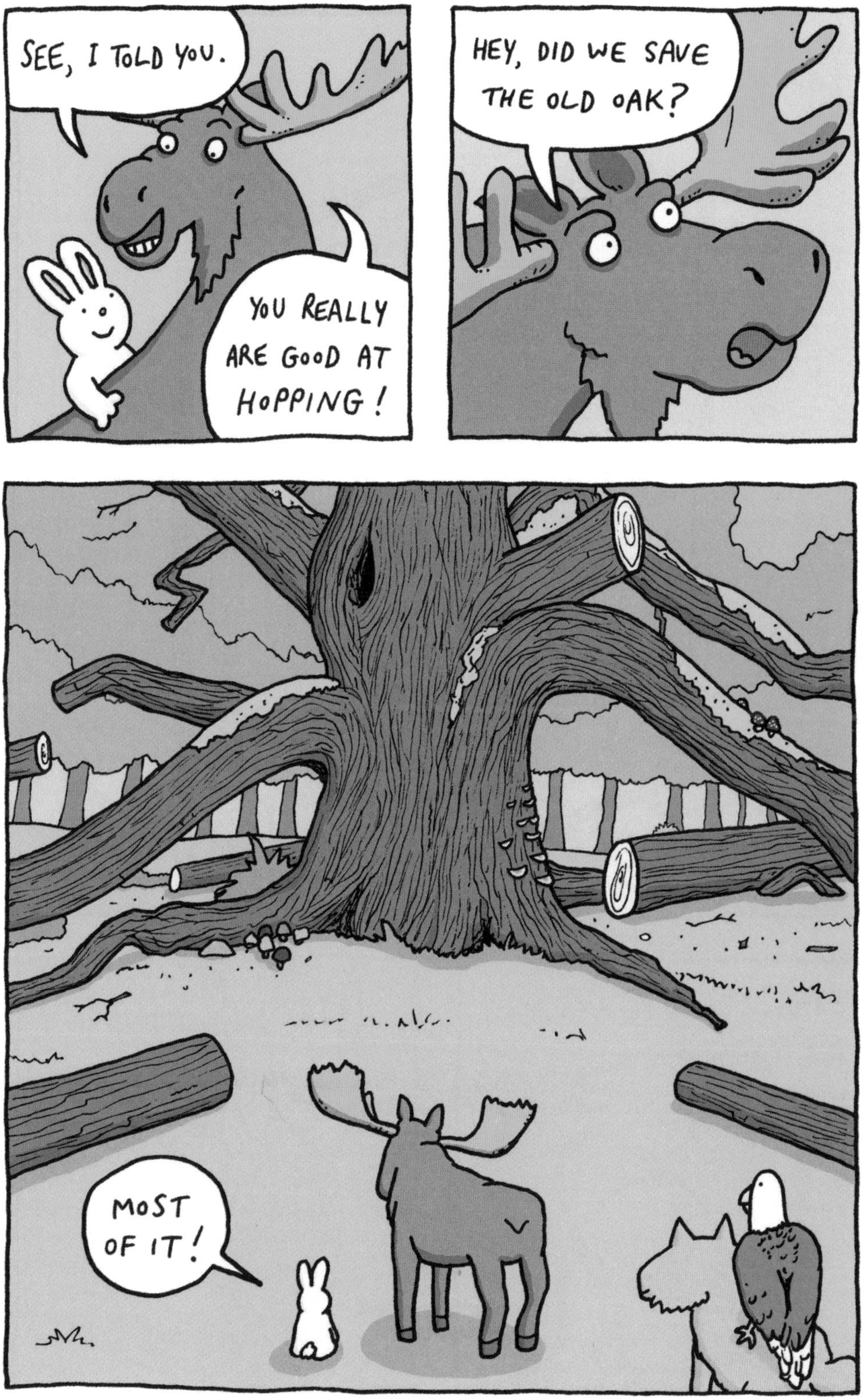
SEE, I TOLD YOU.
YOU REALLY ARE GOOD AT HOPPING!
HEY, DID WE SAVE THE OLD OAK?
MOST OF IT!

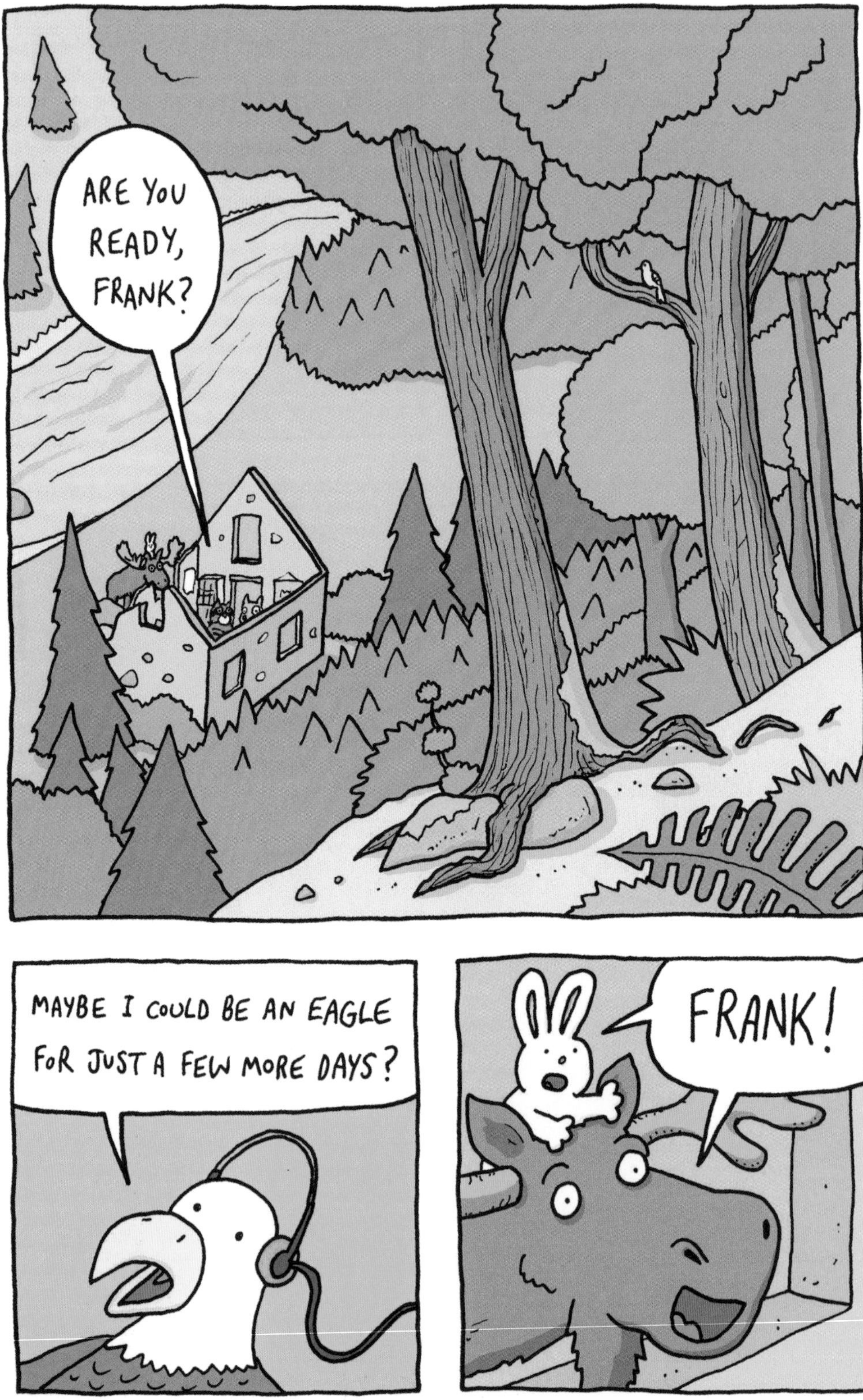
ARE YOU READY, FRANK?
MAYBE I COULD BE AN EAGLE FOR JUST A FEW MORE DAYS?
FRANK!

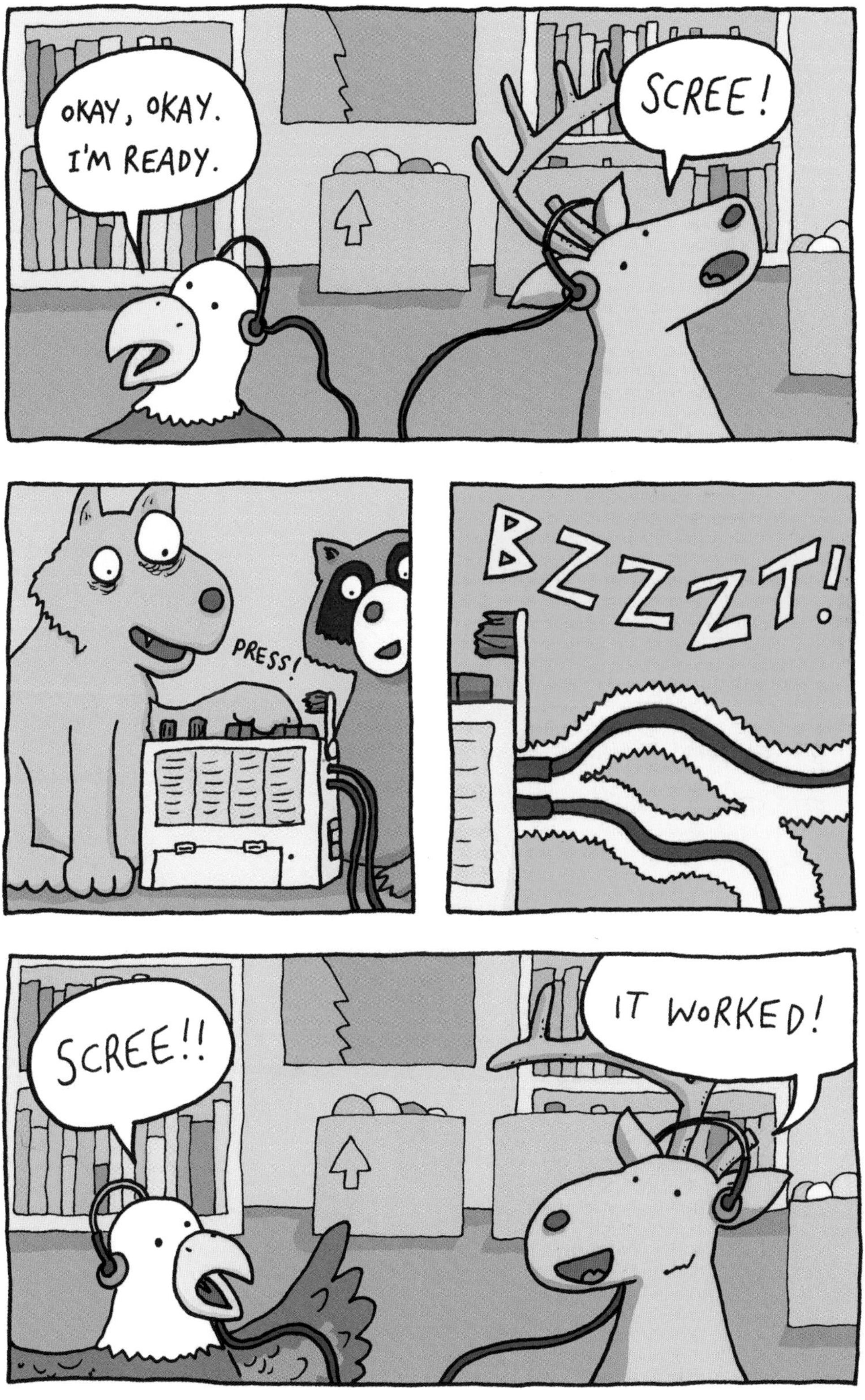
OKAY, OKAY. I'M READY.
SCREE!
PRESS!
BZZZT!
SCREE!!
IT WORKED!

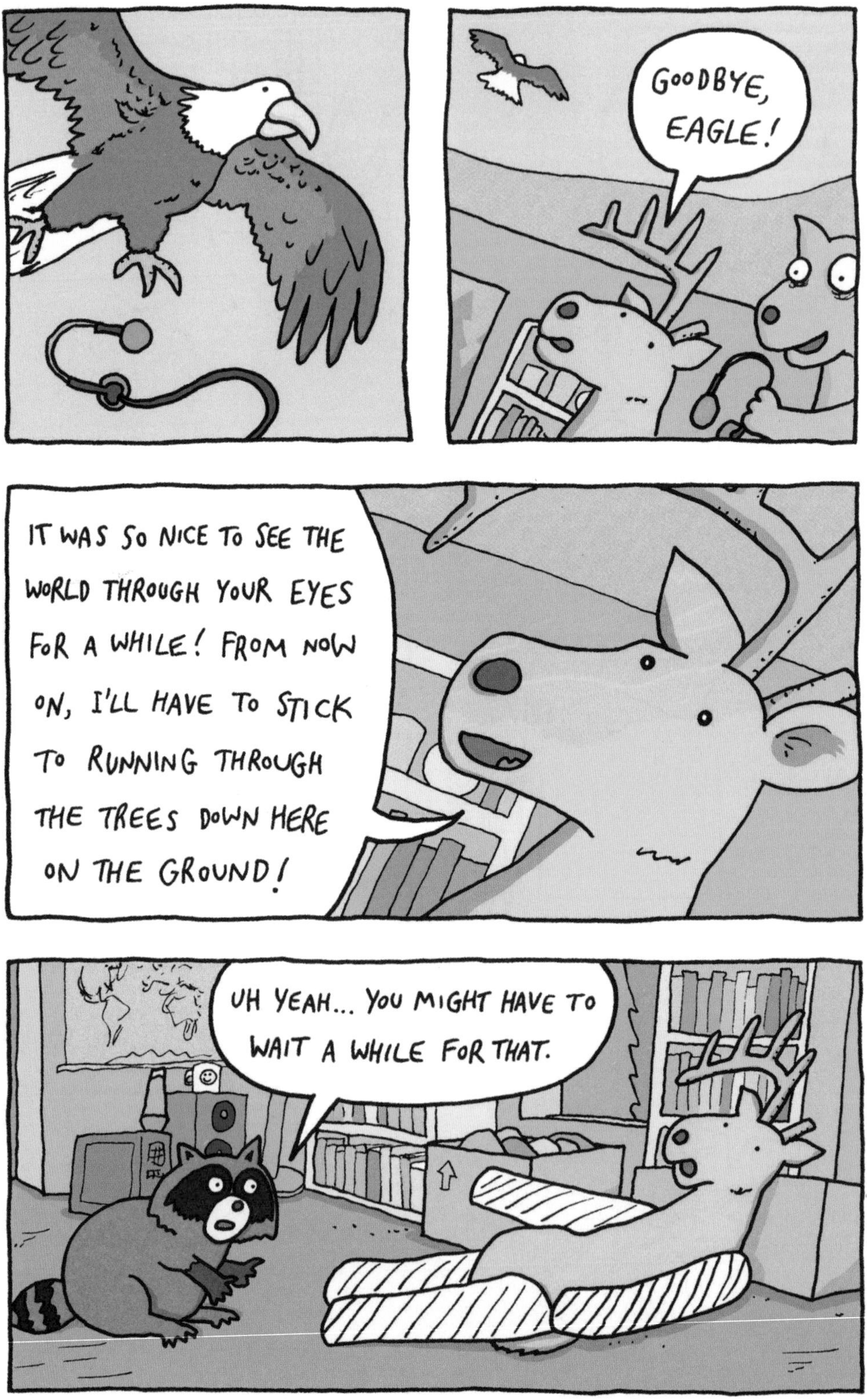
GOODBYE, EAGLE!
IT WAS SO NICE TO SEE THE WORLD THROUGH YOUR EYES FOR A WHILE! FROM NOW ON, I'LL HAVE TO STICK TO RUNNING THROUGH THE TREES DOWN HERE ON THE GROUND!
UH YEAH... YOU MIGHT HAVE TO WAIT A WHILE FOR THAT.

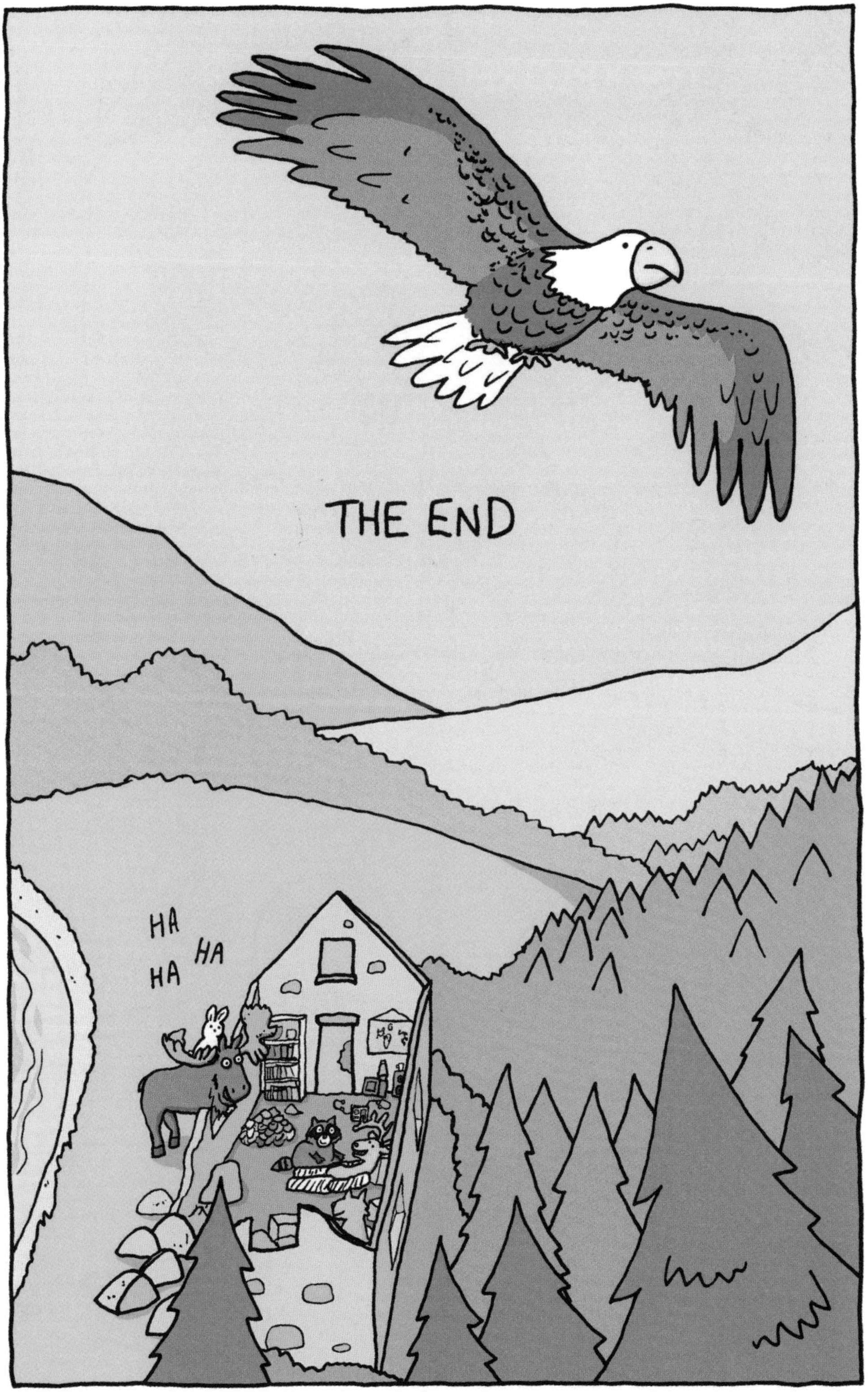
THE END
HA
HA
HA

MORE TO EXPLORE! | Learn About TREE RINGS!

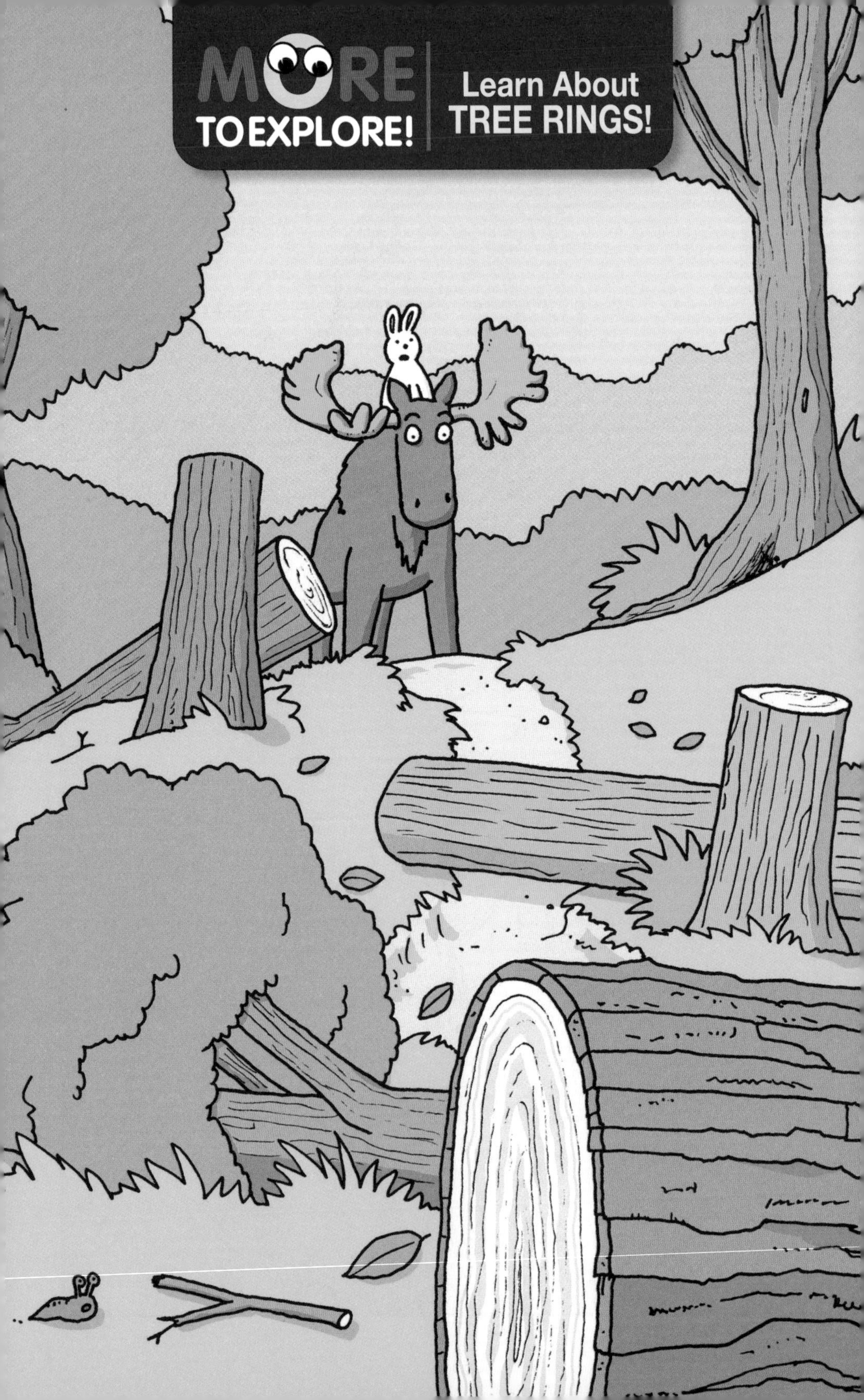

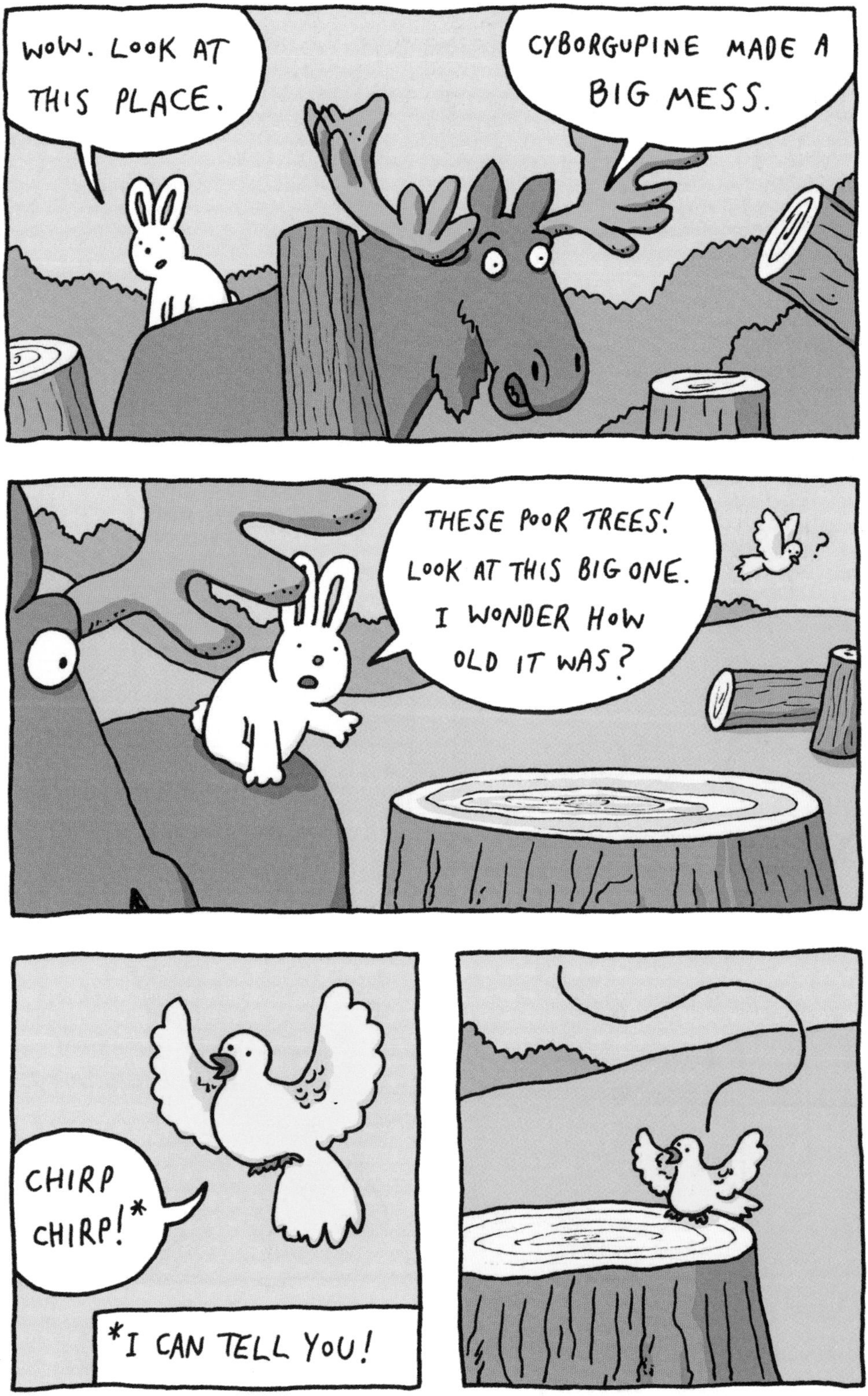
WOW. LOOK AT THIS PLACE.
CYBORGUPINE MADE A BIG MESS.
THESE POOR TREES! LOOK AT THIS BIG ONE. I WONDER HOW OLD IT WAS?
?
CHIRP CHIRP!*
*I CAN TELL YOU!

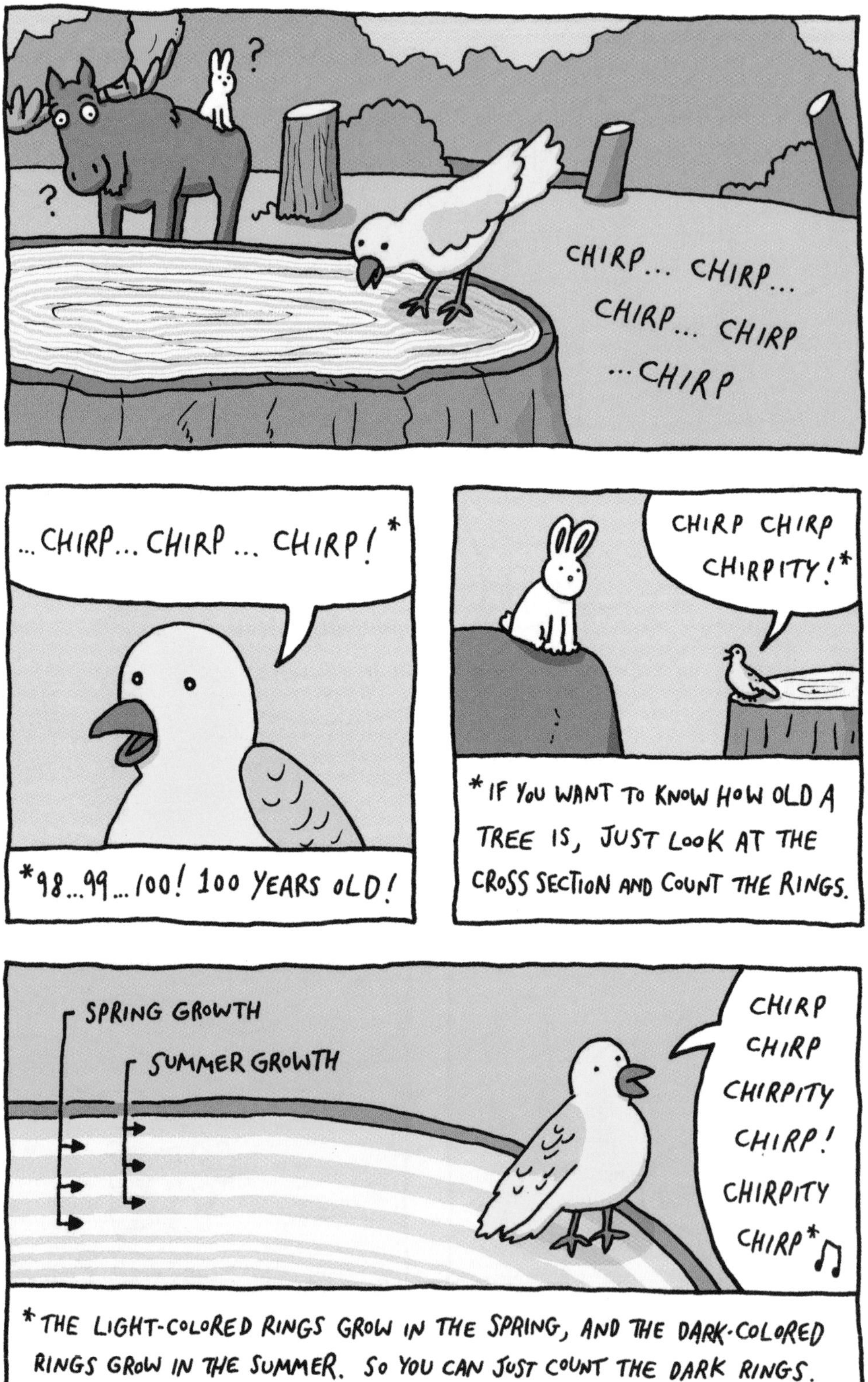
?
?
CHIRP... CHIRP... CHIRP... CHIRP ...CHIRP
...CHIRP... CHIRP ... CHIRP! *
*98...99...100! 100 YEARS OLD!
CHIRP CHIRP CHIRPITY! *
* IF YOU WANT TO KNOW HOW OLD A TREE IS, JUST LOOK AT THE CROSS SECTION AND COUNT THE RINGS.
SPRING GROWTH
SUMMER GROWTH
CHIRP CHIRP CHIRPITY CHIRP! CHIRPITY CHIRP*
* THE LIGHT-COLORED RINGS GROW IN THE SPRING, AND THE DARK-COLORED RINGS GROW IN THE SUMMER. SO YOU CAN JUST COUNT THE DARK RINGS.

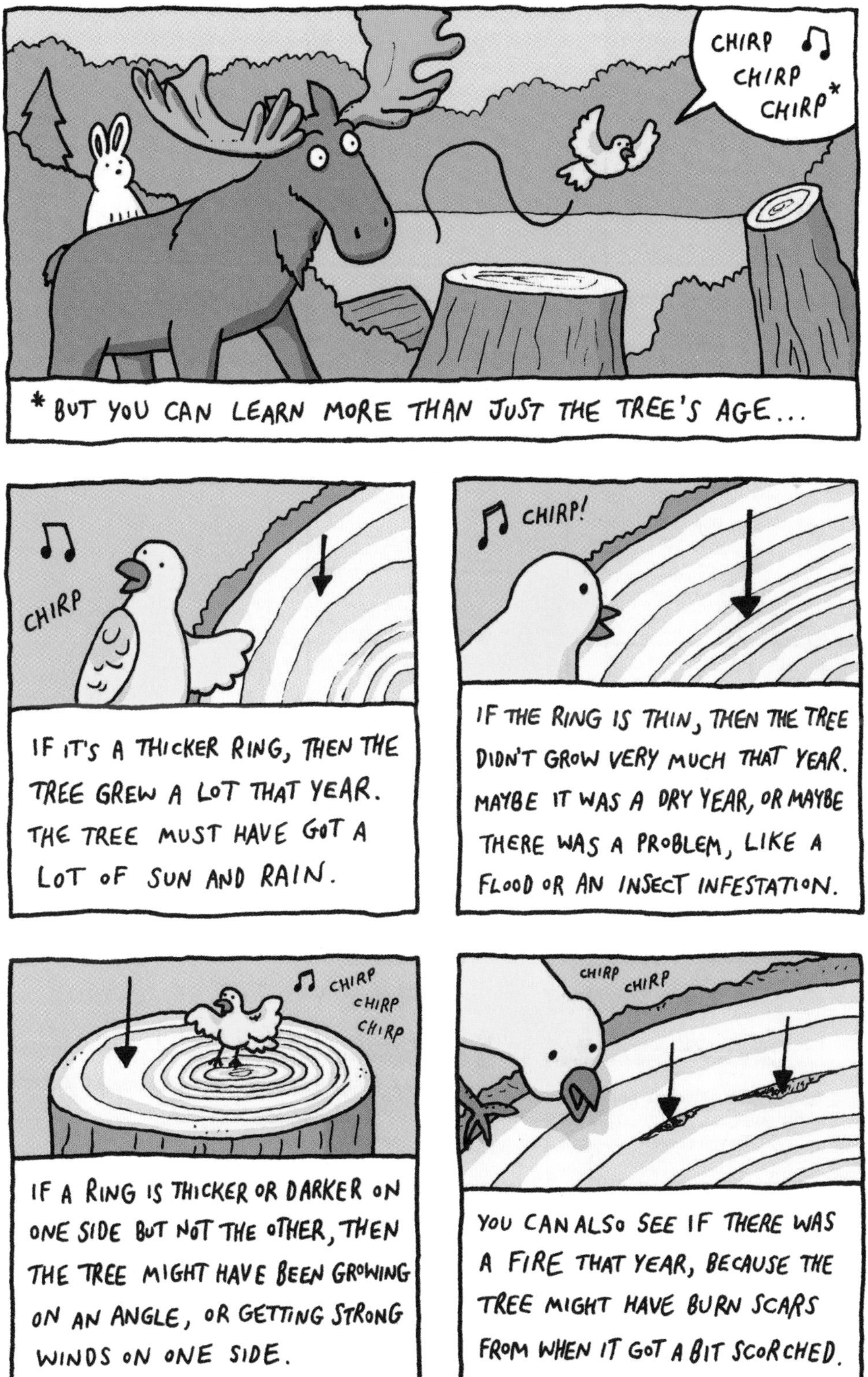
CHIRP ♫ CHIRP CHIRP*
* BUT YOU CAN LEARN MORE THAN JUST THE TREE'S AGE...
♫ CHIRP
IF IT'S A THICKER RING, THEN THE TREE GREW A LOT THAT YEAR. THE TREE MUST HAVE GOT A LOT OF SUN AND RAIN.
♫ CHIRP!
IF THE RING IS THIN, THEN THE TREE DIDN'T GROW VERY MUCH THAT YEAR. MAYBE IT WAS A DRY YEAR, OR MAYBE THERE WAS A PROBLEM, LIKE A FLOOD OR AN INSECT INFESTATION.
♫ CHIRP CHIRP CHIRP
IF A RING IS THICKER OR DARKER ON ONE SIDE BUT NOT THE OTHER, THEN THE TREE MIGHT HAVE BEEN GROWING ON AN ANGLE, OR GETTING STRONG WINDS ON ONE SIDE.
CHIRP CHIRP
YOU CAN ALSO SEE IF THERE WAS A FIRE THAT YEAR, BECAUSE THE TREE MIGHT HAVE BURN SCARS FROM WHEN IT GOT A BIT SCORCHED.

THE STUDY OF TREE RINGS AND THE COOL PATTERNS THAT SHOW UP IN THEM IS CALLED "DENDROCHRONOLOGY." "DENDRO" MEANS "TREE" AND "CHRONOLOGY" MEANS "TIMELINE." TREE TIMELINE!

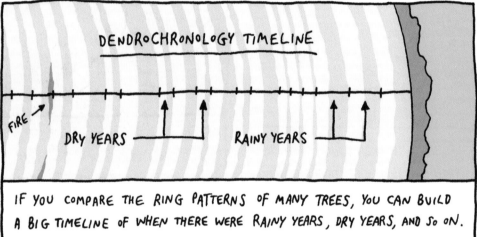

DENDROCHRONOLOGY TIMELINE

FIRE →

DRY YEARS

RAINY YEARS

IF YOU COMPARE THE RING PATTERNS OF MANY TREES, YOU CAN BUILD A BIG TIMELINE OF WHEN THERE WERE RAINY YEARS, DRY YEARS, AND SO ON.

CHIRP CHIRP CHIRP

TO FIND OUT WHEN A TREE WAS ALIVE, YOU CAN COMPARE IT TO THE TIMELINE.

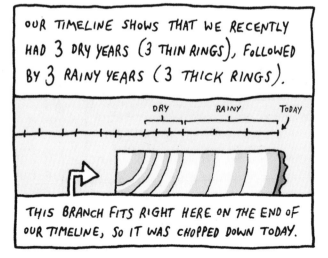

OUR TIMELINE SHOWS THAT WE RECENTLY HAD 3 DRY YEARS (3 THIN RINGS), FOLLOWED BY 3 RAINY YEARS (3 THICK RINGS).

DRY   RAINY   TODAY

THIS BRANCH FITS RIGHT HERE ON THE END OF OUR TIMELINE, SO IT WAS CHOPPED DOWN TODAY.

CHIRP

CHIRP

BUT THIS BRANCH...

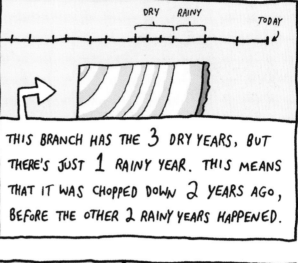

THIS BRANCH HAS THE 3 DRY YEARS, BUT THERE'S JUST 1 RAINY YEAR. THIS MEANS THAT IT WAS CHOPPED DOWN 2 YEARS AGO, BEFORE THE OTHER 2 RAINY YEARS HAPPENED.

MAYBE YOU CHOPPED THIS ONE DOWN, LASER MOOSE!

ANYWAY, YOU CAN COMPARE ANY TREE TO THE DENDROCHRONOLOGY TIMELINE AND FIGURE OUT WHEN IT WAS ALIVE, EVEN IF THAT TREE HAS BEEN TURNED INTO A TABLE OR SOMETHING!

THIS BIRD SURE HAS A LOT TO SAY!

CHIRP

CHIRP!

TOO BAD WE CAN'T UNDERSTAND ANYTHING THEY'RE SAYING!

TRY IT!

CREATE A TREE CROSS SECTION THAT REPRESENTS YOUR OWN LIFE!

START WITH A SMALL CIRCLE TO REPRESENT YOUR FIRST YEAR...

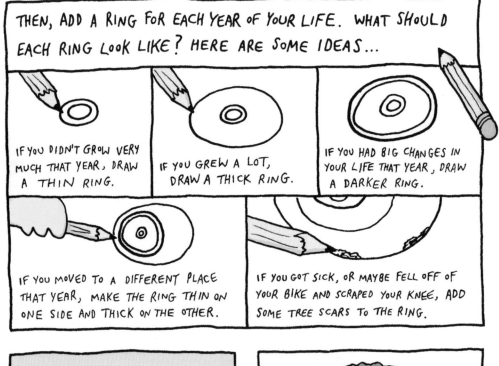

THEN, ADD A RING FOR EACH YEAR OF YOUR LIFE. WHAT SHOULD EACH RING LOOK LIKE? HERE ARE SOME IDEAS...

IF YOU DIDN'T GROW VERY MUCH THAT YEAR, DRAW A THIN RING.

IF YOU GREW A LOT, DRAW A THICK RING.

IF YOU HAD BIG CHANGES IN YOUR LIFE THAT YEAR, DRAW A DARKER RING.

IF YOU MOVED TO A DIFFERENT PLACE THAT YEAR, MAKE THE RING THIN ON ONE SIDE AND THICK ON THE OTHER.

IF YOU GOT SICK, OR MAYBE FELL OFF OF YOUR BIKE AND SCRAPED YOUR KNEE, ADD SOME TREE SCARS TO THE RING.

DRAW EACH RING AROUND THE PREVIOUS RING UNTIL YOU'VE DONE ALL OF THE YEARS OF YOUR LIFE.

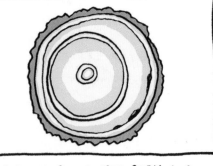

ADD COLOR AND TREE BARK AND YOU'RE DONE! YOU'VE GOT A TREE THAT REPRESENTS YOUR LIFE!

Andrews McMeel Publishing
a division of Andrews McMeel Universal
1130 Walnut Street, Kansas City, Missouri 64106

www.andrewsmcmeel.com
www.lasermooseandrabbitboy.com

21 22 23 24 25 SDB 10 9 8 7 6 5 4 3 2 1

ISBN: 978-1-5248-6475-0

Library of Congress Control Number: 2021936766

Made by:
King Yip (Dongguan) Printing & Packaging Factory Ltd.
Address and location of manufacturer:
Daning Administrative District, Humen Town
Dongguan Guangdong, China 523930
1st Printing—7/5/21

Editor: Kevin Kotur
Art Director/Designer: Julie Barnes
Color Assistance: J.L. Martin
Production Manager: Chuck Harper
Production Editor: Amy Strassner
Demand Planner: Sue Eikos

Look for these books!

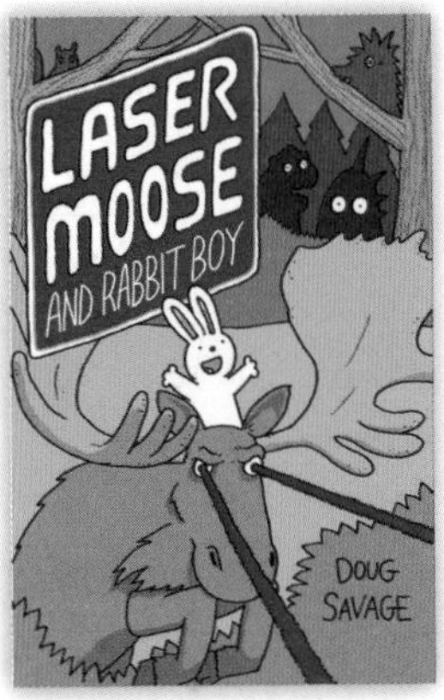
LASER MOOSE
AND RABBIT BOY
DOUG SAVAGE

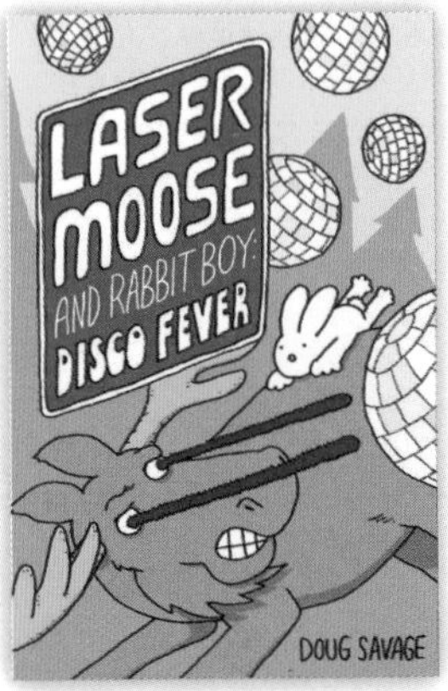
LASER MOOSE
AND RABBIT BOY:
DISCO FEVER
DOUG SAVAGE

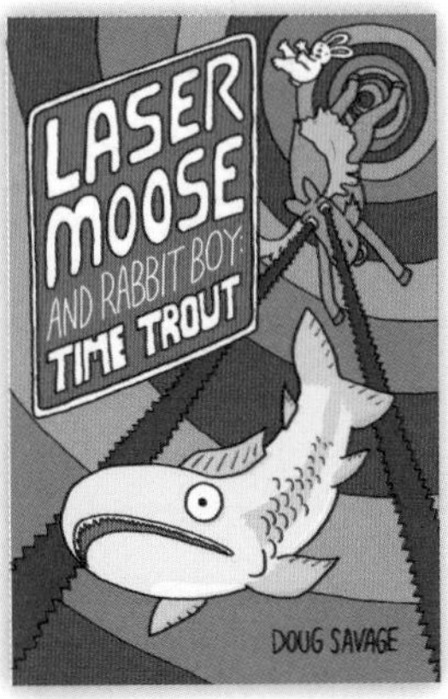
LASER MOOSE
AND RABBIT BOY:
TIME TROUT
DOUG SAVAGE

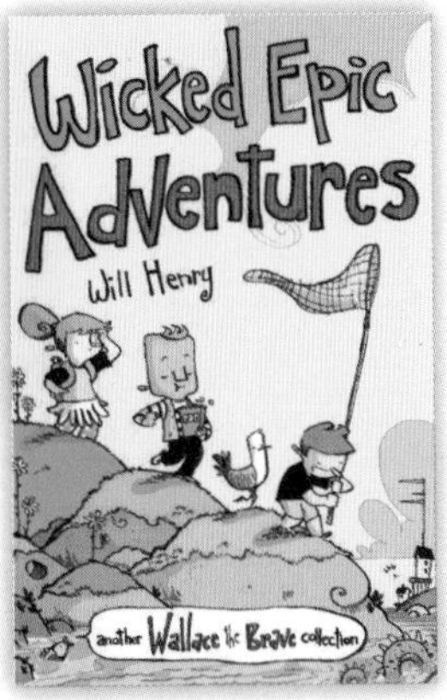
Wicked Epic Adventures
Will Henry
another Wallace the Brave collection

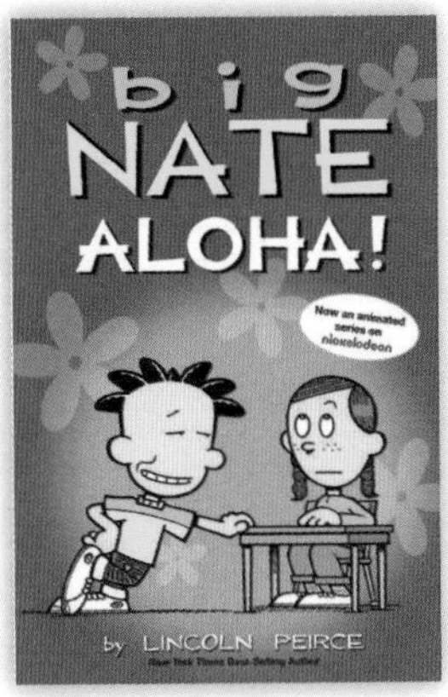
big NATE
ALOHA!
by LINCOLN PEIRCE

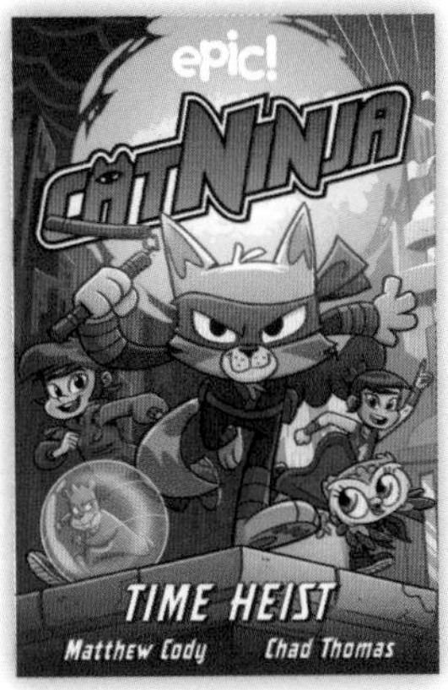
epic!
CATNINJA
TIME HEIST
Matthew Cody
Chad Thomas

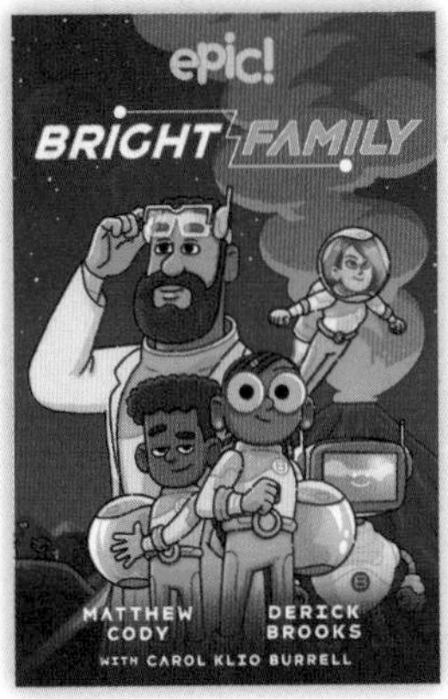
epic!
BRIGHT FAMILY
MATTHEW CODY
DERICK BROOKS
WITH CAROL KLIO BURRELL

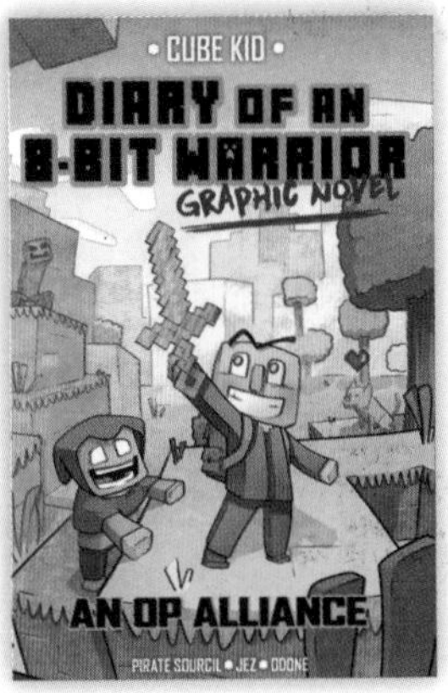
CUBE KID
DIARY OF AN 8-BIT WARRIOR
GRAPHIC NOVEL
AN OP ALLIANCE

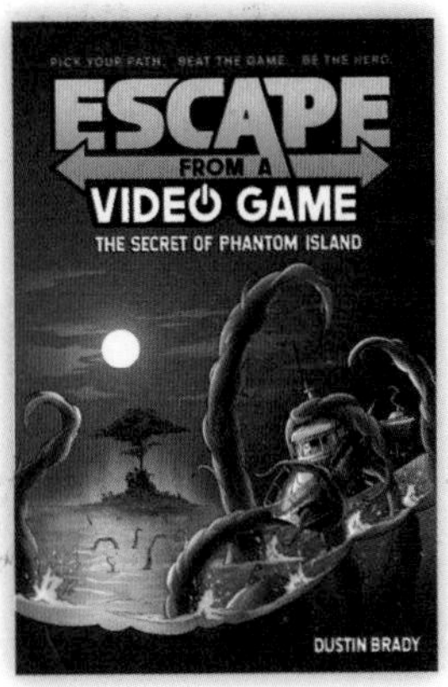
ESCAPE FROM A VIDEO GAME
THE SECRET OF PHANTOM ISLAND
DUSTIN BRADY